THE COPPER PR ⁣⁣ ⁣ D0862519

"A fast-paced and original new voice in heroic fantasy"
Adrian Tchaikovsky, author of the Shadows of the Apt series

"*The Copper Promise* is near-perfect fantasy adventure fun and a breath of fresh air in a genre choking on its own grittiness. Read it and remind yourself what made you fall in love with fantasy books. 10/10"
Starburst Magazine

"There are pirates and magic, demons and disciples, undead soldiers and noble knights. If you're thinking this sounds like a lot of fun, you'd be gods damned right."
Den Patrick, author of The Boy with the Porcelain Blade

"Fresh and exciting, full of wit and wonder and magic and action, *The Copper Promise* is the fantasy novel we've been waiting for."
Adam Christopher, author of Empire State *and* Made to Kill

"*The Copper Promise* is the kind of swords and sorcery fantasy which will make you remember why you became a fan of the genre in the first place, and fall in love with it all over again."
Geek Syndicate

"A killer of a fantasy novel that is indicative of how the classic genre of sword and sorcery is not only still very much alive, but also still the best the genre has to offer."
Jet Black Ink

"Williams' fast-paced narrative never leaves room for a pause and captivates from page one."
Sci-Fi Now

"*The Copper Promise* didn't so much arrive as kick the door in and demand to know why it wasn't already drunk... Pick it up, before it picks your pocket and sells your stuff back to you."
Alasdair Stuart

"You guys need to read this book. Sooner, rather than later."
Booksnobbery

BY THE SAME AUTHOR

The Iron Ghost
The Silver Tide

JEN WILLIAMS

The Copper Promise

ANGRY
ROBOT

ANGRY ROBOT
An imprint of Watkins Media Ltd

Lace Market House,
54-56 High Pavement,
Nottingham,
NG1 1HW
UK

angryrobotbooks.com
twitter.com/angryrobotbooks
Sleeping gods lie

First published in the UK by Headline in 2014
This Angry Robot edition published in the US in 2016

ISBN 978 0 85766 576 8
Ebook ISBN 978 0 85766 577 5

Printed in the United States of America

9 8 7 6 5 4 3 2 1

For Sidney and Phyllis Fulker, with love.

PART ONE

Ghosts of the Citadel

1

All the other cells in the dungeon stank of fear, but not this one. Lord Frith's last surviving son was simply too proud to be afraid. Even now, as Yellow-Eyed Rin laid out his instruments on the blood-stained bench, holding each wicked blade up to the torchlight, the young man kneeling on the stone floor had only anger in his eyes.

The blood of his father is on that bench. His brothers' too, thought Bethan. *And soon his as well, but he'll defy us to the end. Stubborn bastard.*

The dungeons of Blackwood Keep were small and thick with shadows, which meant that Bethan had to stand rather closer to Yellow-Eyed Rin than she would have liked. He was a greasy wart of a man; shiny bulges of flesh poked through his leather tunic, and lank strands of grey hair stuck to his bulbous scalp. The rheumy eyes that gave him his name watered constantly, but not out of any sympathy for his victims. Rin might be foul to look upon, but his ability to summon excruciating pain with a few carefully placed cuts was invaluable to Bethan.

Despite the rough treatment they'd shown him so far, young Aaron Frith was another matter. With the strong jaw and grey eyes of all the Friths, his brown skin and fashionably long dark hair, he was a comely young man. Bethan had an appreciation for beautiful things; she had commanded that the finest paintings in the castle be taken down from the walls and packed into crates for her personal perusal later. It pained her greatly to spoil that warm skin, those pretty eyes. In the initial scuffle Frith had taken a blow to the temple, and now the dried blood was making his hair stick up at strange angles on one side. And Yellow-Eyed Rin would only make things worse, of course. *Such a waste.* Still, they needed him to talk, and soon. If they went another day without answers, then Fane might come up to the Blackwood himself, and no one wanted that.

"Anything more to add, Aaron, before this gets bloody? Or should I call you Lord Frith now? Your father died in here yesterday."

Aaron Frith slumped a little where he knelt, glancing away from her. For a brief moment she felt sorry for him, but the sensation didn't last. The black velvet and silks he'd been wearing when they took the castle were stained and ragged now, but this was a man who'd been born into a privileged life. A silver brooch in the shape of a tree was still pinned to his breast, with tiny chips of sapphire in the branches that could have been leaves or could have been stars. It was fine work; Bethan made a note to make sure that it ended up in her pocket at the close of this messy business.

He looked back up at her and his eyes were dry.

"I have nothing to say to Istrian scum."

Bethan sighed, and looked around the squalid cell. The torches only made the corners darker.

"You want to end your days here, Lord Frith? For the sake of what? Some jewels, some gold? Coin you'll probably never get around to spending?"

Frith said nothing. Bethan felt a stab of impatience.

"We know the vault is hidden somewhere in the forest, Frith. Everyone knows that. We'll find it eventually, but I'd much rather you told me. It's a lot quicker that way."

To her surprise, Frith grinned.

"You think you'll find the location scribbled on a piece of parchment, a footnote in my father's will perhaps? I'm not sure you understand how secrets work."

"*You* tell me, then. You're the last. I may even keep you alive. The Istrian people are fascinated by the aristocracy of their neighbours, and they'll pay good coin to come and gawp at you." She tried to inject a reasonable tone into her voice. "Tell me now, Aaron Frith, and I swear this will go better for you. You've nothing to gain from adopting the stubbornness that killed the rest of your family."

"Tristan was nine years old. He was not stubborn, he was terrified."

Bethan took a step towards the prisoner. She could feel her face growing flushed, much to her annoyance.

"You would end your life here, in the dungeon of your own castle? Hundreds of years of the proud Frith family, and you'll all end up in unmarked graves in your own damn forest."

In answer, Aaron Frith spat on her boot.

"Enough talk," said Rin through a throat full of phlegm. He picked up a vicious blade no longer than Bethan's smallest finger. "Time to see the colour of the young lord's blood. I heard it's black, like their trees, but it's all been red so far. Very disappointing, that."

Bethan shook the spittle off her boot.

"Get started."

Bethan left Rin to his work – there was, in the end, only so much of it she could watch – and spent some time patrolling the castle, checking on her men and their search through old Lord Frith's private documents. The servants had been rounded up in the Great Hall, and Carlson, her second-in-command, had made some attempts to beat the information out of them, but they clearly knew nothing of use.

The question of the vault was a vexing one. The Frith family were famous not only for their wealth, but also for their paranoia. Several generations back the Lord at the time, one Erasmus Frith, had ordered a great vault built out in the middle of the Blackwood. Each day, the men who worked on it were taken to the location blindfolded, with one member of the Frith family on hand at all times to supervise the plans. Hundreds of years later, and all anyone seemed certain of was that it was in the Blackwood somewhere, hidden in that huge and unknowable forest. The Frith family fortune, just waiting for someone to steal it.

A number of hours later Bethan returned to the dungeon. As she approached the cell she listened for the noises men made when they'd reached the end of their endurance, but the stone halls were quiet.

"Please tell me you have some answers, Rin."

The torturer wiped his hands on a bloody cloth, grimacing.

"The boy is just as big an idiot as the rest of them."

Aaron Frith was strapped to the bench, his arms held down by his sides with iron cuffs. Rin had long since removed the expensive velvets and silks, so that he lay shivering in his smallclothes. One side of his face was slick with blood, and one hand was red to the wrist. His chest was livid with burn marks, and Bethan could smell the hot, sweet scent of scorched flesh.

"I've done all the usual. Hot pokers, burning needles under the fingernails – once that didn't work I just ripped 'em off – some cuts here and there. Took one of his ears, and I thought he might give in then, but it doesn't look like he's paying much attention now. You want me to put one of his eyes out?"

Bethan watched the young lord carefully. His eyes were closed, his breathing rapid and shallow. He looked like someone caught in the midst of a deep fever, but she thought he could hear them, all the same.

"Hold off for a moment."

She went over to the bench and took hold of Frith's jaw, turning him to face her. One of his eyes flickered open; the other was caked shut with blood from a deep cut on his cheek.

"Put away your pride, Lord Frith. Tell me where the vault is."

For a moment the look in his one open eye was confused, as though he didn't know where he was. Then he focussed on her and she saw that look sharpen to hate.

"The Blackwood will have your blood, *peasant*."

Bethan took her hand away.

"There is a grave out there in your precious forest, and it isn't for me." She turned back to the torturer. "The mallet, I think. I want his legs broken."

2

"We tread carefully here, master."

Gallo looked up from the map. The guide was running his fingers over the red granite walls, sniffing and frowning as though he'd trodden in something regrettable.

"Really? There's nothing indicated on here." Gallo shook the map at him. "And I'd really prefer it if you didn't call me master, Chednit. I am your employer, not your overlord. We're practically partners!"

Chednit turned his mismatched eyes towards him. One was brown as a nut and narrow with caution; the other was false, a ball of green jade etched with a silver pupil. It swivelled in his eye socket.

"You trust the map?"

"It's all we've got to go on. And it's not as though I bought it from one of those grinning charlatans we saw down in the city – I've no doubt there's a little house somewhere in Krete where a hundred skinny children sit drawing fake maps to the Citadel – *this* was stolen from the ruins of a temple in Relios, snatched from under the noses of the Chattering Men." Gallo paused to let this sink in; he was still proud of that.

"As you say, master."

Gallo cast a look back the way they'd come. He could still see the last of the desert daylight far above, framed in the distant doorway like a window of gold. They had walked cautiously down a steep set of plain stone steps, treading carefully for fear of traps, snakes and scorpions; it was said that the haunted Citadel had a thousand grisly ways to kill you, each more unpleasant than the last. In front of them was a chamber made of grey stone. It was a little colder than he'd been expecting, but there was nothing obviously untoward. On the far side were the entrances to three passageways, each shrouded in darkness.

"What is it you fear?"

The guide screwed up his face and shook his head.

"I fancy I hear things. Every now and then, a rumble, a sigh."

"You do?" Gallo stood very still and listened, but all he could hear was the rush of the wind sighing past the door high above them, and the sound of his own breathing. This far above Krete it wasn't even possible to hear the cacophony of the city, shielded as they were by the solid weight of the ancient stones. He laughed suddenly, and clapped Chednit heartily on the back. The guide winced.

"Look at us! We have barely made headway into the first level of the Citadel and already we are twitching at every noise, as nervous as mice. Let's keep moving." Gallo looked at the map and nodded to the entrance on the far right. "We take this one."

"As you say, master."

In the next chamber they found a narrow stairwell leading downwards. The light from Chednit's torch only illuminated the first few steps before the darkness seemed to eat it up.

"We should light another torch, master."

"I'd rather have my hands free." Gallo patted the scabbard at his hip.

"I do not like this." Chednit frowned at the dark, pushing his leathery old face into a thousand crinkles. The light from the torch reflected on his jade eye, making it glow like a cat's. "We should have waited for your friend to join us. Another sword hand, yes, that would have been most wise. We can still go back, await him in Krete."

Gallo shook his head impatiently.

"I could waste my whole life waiting for Sebastian while the Citadel sits here, all its secrets undiscovered. And besides, we've already given the guards their bribe." There had been a time when his friend would have been the first down the steps into the Citadel, a wild gleam in his eye and his sword drawn, but now he spoke of waiting and, worse, *honour*. It was enough to turn an adventurer's stomach. "Look, if it makes you feel better, my blade shall go first." He drew his sword and gave Chednit his most reassuring smile. "Follow me close. We shall need what light that torch of yours can cast."

They descended the stairs, Gallo in front, Chednit coming along behind, holding the torch high above his head. The passageway was narrow, the steps uneven. Gallo brushed his free hand against the stones and his fingers came away covered in a thin green slime. Ahead there was a darkness as deep and complete as anything he had ever seen; it was like a solid thing, so that he almost feared to go too quickly lest he collide with it. Their footsteps echoed strangely, seeming to fade away and then come back again faster, or slower. A few more steps, and his ears popped.

"A dark place, that is for certain," said Gallo. He wanted to talk, to cover up those uneasy echoes, but his voice sounded strained and weak to his own ears. "Sebastian would not like this at all. He prefers his open skies and his mountains."

"As you say, master." Chednit sounded as though he couldn't give two shakes of a donkey's arse about Sebastian's mountains, and Gallo couldn't blame him. Even so, he could not stop talking.

"Do you know Ynnsmouth, Chednit? Strange place. They worship their mountains as gods, and there are secret shrines that only the Ynnsmouth knights can find. Sebastian promised to take me to one once, even though it is forbidden."

Suddenly Gallo was filled with the certainty that he would never see the mountain shrine – would never, in fact, see daylight again. The thought caught his tongue and held it, filling his chest with an alien tightness. He cleared his throat but said no more, and they walked on in silence.

Ever downwards they went, with no change to the steps or the rough walls beside them. They walked for so long that Gallo began to wonder if this was one of the mythical traps of the Citadel, one so subtle and simple that you could be walking for years before you realised you had grown old and doddery. Gallo was a man who prided himself in the physical condition of his body – when he had stolen the map from the Chattering Men he had outrun them all and barely felt it – but a sweat had broken out on his brow and his legs were starting to ache.

A faint rustling from above stopped Gallo in his tracks. It reminded him of the sound ropes make on the docks when the boats cast off – rough hessian rubbing against splintered wood. He looked up, but Chednit's torch cast only the faintest of glimmers toward the ceiling.

"What is that?" he said, his fear briefly lost in curiosity. "Say, can you see something?"

There was a brief suggestion of movement, followed by a blood-curdling scream from behind him. Gallo turned in time to see Chednit's legs vanishing upwards, his body pulled up into the darkened ceiling. Like most men who sell their sword for money Gallo was as quick as a cat. His arm shot out and grabbed hold of his guide's boot.

"Help me, help me!" squealed Chednit. The torch dropped down onto the steps, smouldering and smoking. Whatever had him was fearsomely strong. Gallo pulled down on Chednit's boot but the force pulling him up only increased, nearly yanking him up with the hapless guide. He tried to drop the sword to grab on with both hands, but his hand would not obey.

"Chednit!"

As quick as that the boot was gone, and Chednit flew up into the dark recesses of the ceiling. Gallo held his sword over his head as, unseen, his guide began to scream, over and over. There was a patter of what felt like warm rain against his upturned face, and something small and round dropped down past his nose, to chink against the stone steps and then bounce away into the dark beyond. He saw it only for a second in the guttering light of Chednit's torch, but he recognised the jade eye with the silver pupil, now lost to the shadows at the bottom of the unending steps.

The whole thing had taken no more than a handful of heartbeats. Gallo picked up the torch and blew it back into life, noticing that it was now sticky with blood. When the light was strong again, he held it up over his head, half fearing to see Chednit's grinning corpse flattened to the ceiling, a hole in his face where his eyes should be... but there was nothing there. He saw more of the same grey stones, the same green mould, and no sign of his guide. Gallo swallowed hard and tightened his grip on his sword.

"The place is cursed," he spat. As the terror passed, he was filled with a black fury. How dare it take his guide from him? To suffer such a loss at the very beginning of the adventure was unthinkable. Sebastian would be insufferable, for a start. "A foul thing, to pick off an unarmed man from above."

"Would you prefer to meet face to face, young warrior?"

The voice was so close behind him Gallo could feel the tickle of warm breath on the back of his neck. He spun, sword out, but what met him on the steps of the Citadel drained all the strength from his arms with one slow smile.

"I thought not," it said, with a note of long-suffering humour. "They never do."

3

"You're a dirty cheat! Everyone knows it! That's what everyone says."

Wydrin drew the last of the cards towards her across the table, snatching a quick glance at whoever might be listening in the crowded tavern. Good rumours, bad rumours; they were all the same to her. Unfortunately, an early summer's evening in the Hands of Fate tavern was a busy time, and no one was paying much attention to an argument over a game of cards. *Not until it gets bloody, anyway*, she thought.

"Have you forgotten the rules again, Sammy?" She smiled up at him, and was pleased to see his face turn a darker shade of pink. "I'll be glad to explain them to you, but the gist of it is, well, you lost. Fair and square. The Copper Cat plays a clean game. Well, clean *card* games, anyway."

"I want my money back." Sam Larken slammed his fist down on the table, causing the small pile of coins to jump. "You'll give it back now, you lying little thief."

Wydrin leaned back in her chair and patted the two daggers at her belt.

"Thief, is it? You want to take that up with my claws here?"

There was a slight hesitation from Sam Larken now, and this, too, pleased Wydrin. It seemed he wasn't a total fool after all.

"I just want what's mine, that's all, or I'll tell everyone—"

Wydrin drew the dagger, too fast for him to follow, and then very slowly flipped one of the cards over with the point. It was the eight of cups.

"You'll tell everyone *what*?"

"Uh..."

A shadow suddenly loomed over them. Wydrin looked up to see a tall, broad-shouldered man with long black hair tied into a braid and an enormous broadsword slung over his back. He was carrying a tankard in each hand, and he gave Wydrin a pained look before turning to Sam.

"I've told you before, Sam. If you still insist on playing cards with her you can't keep complaining you've lost all your money. Rats learn faster than you."

Sam backed away from the table awkwardly, half taking the chair with him. His eyes were glued to the sword.

"Fine, whatever." He shot a poisonous look at Wydrin. "Can't get an honest game in this shit hole of a city."

Wydrin watched him back away into the crowd. She gave him a little wave.

"Really, Sebastian," she said as the big man sat down, carefully placing the tankards away from the cards. "I wasn't even cheating this time. As soon as he gets some decent cards it's written all over his stupid face."

Sebastian shifted in his seat and glanced back towards the door. He was a big man, muscled and powerful, but with a kind face, a long nose and blue eyes, which Wydrin liked to tease him about. No fearsome knight had eyes that pretty, she said.

"It would be helpful if you could avoid starting any fights while we're waiting to meet a potential client."

Wydrin rolled her eyes and took a mouthful of ale. It was warm and tasted of oats. Not bad for Krete.

"What's the matter with you? You look like someone's pissed in your beer."

Sebastian sighed and picked up his tankard.

"This job. I'm not certain it's wise. After what happened we should be all the more cautious."

"This is what you wanted, Sebastian." Wydrin slid her dagger back into its scabbard and lowered her voice. "We can find him this way. Gallo was an idiot, and we're not. We'll be fine." Catching the look on his face she changed her tone. "Besides which, anyone stupid enough to explore the Citadel will be paying through the nose for it. We'll be set for the rest of the year. No more working for tiresome little merchants who want their poxy wagon trains guarded." She sniffed. "I was thinking of getting some new leather armour, too. Red, maybe, to match my hair."

Sebastian laughed at that; her hair was short, scruffy, and carroty.

"I suppose," he said eventually. "We have to go in there after him, and this is as good a way as any. We can't even afford to bribe the guards by ourselves."

"Who is this client, anyway?" asked Wydrin. "I'm curious to know what sort of fool is so eager to go exploring such an infamous death trap." She cleared her throat. "Besides Gallo, of course."

"A lord of some sort." Sebastian took a sip of his ale, and shrugged.

"A lord! Bound to have plenty of coin, then."

Wydrin's eye was caught by a slim figure pushing his way through the crowded tavern. He walked with a stick and had a shock of white hair, but as he got closer she saw that he was startlingly young; no older than her, certainly. He had a livid scar down one cheek, and he was glaring around at the patrons as though they had each done him a personal insult.

Wydrin looked at Sebastian and tipped her head towards the newcomer. Sometimes they would keep an eye out for easy targets, men or women who wouldn't last the night in a city like Krete and might be in need of protection. It was an easy way to make some coin.

Sebastian looked, and then sat up straighter in his chair.

"By Isu, I think that's him."

Wydrin raised her eyebrows.

"I thought you said he was a lord?"

Spotting them, the white-haired man came over, doing his best not to limp too obviously. He wore a heavy black cloak that didn't quite disguise his emaciated frame.

"My lord?"

The man eyed them, an expression of distaste turning his mouth down at the corners.

"You are Sir Sebastian Carverson, the Ynnsmouth Knight? And the... Copper Cat of Crosshaven?"

"We are, my lord." Sebastian gestured to a seat and the man sat.

"I'm the Copper Cat." Wydrin thrust a hand across the table and when he didn't move to take it, picked up her tankard instead. "Although you can just call me Wydrin. The Copper Cat thing, well, it's my meat and gravy but it takes half a bloody day to say it."

"We are told that you have a journey in mind, one that needs a couple of strong sword arms." Sebastian waved at the barkeep for more drinks.

"It is a journey, yes, but not a long one. I need to get inside the Citadel, to explore its lower chambers." The white-haired man rested his stick against the table. "There are stories about the Citadel and what it contains. I assume you have heard them?"

Sebastian nodded.

"Legends, yes, everyone knows them. Even in Ynnsmouth our old women tell tales of the long-dead mages of the Citadel."

Wydrin leaned over the table eagerly.

"I've heard there's an entire hall filled to the ceiling with gold coins and jewels from across Ede, and that they had a sword that sang in the presence of demons and a set of armour that summoned an army of ghosts."

Sebastian glanced at his colleague before turning back to their client.

"I'm afraid tales are all they're likely to be, my lord."

"All rumours contain an element of truth. The Kretian council keeps a guard on the one entrance, but I have already taken care of the bribe. My main concern is the interior of the Citadel itself." The white-haired man took a slow breath. "It is said to be a labyrinth in there."

"That is where we may be able to help you." Sebastian reached into his belt and pulled out a length of parchment covered in inky squares and circles. "My friend had a map to the Citadel, and I have a partial copy. It may get us part of the way at least."

"Where is your friend now?" asked the white-haired man.

Sebastian frowned.

"I don't know. He… went ahead without us."

"Then you must assume him dead?"

Sebastian looked down at his tankard.

"He is not so easy to kill," he said eventually. "He may still be in there, exploring the lower reaches, or else he has made his way back out again under the cover of night, too ashamed by his failure to seek me out. If we get into the Citadel and find him, we can make use of the complete map."

The white-haired man leaned forward to glance at the parchment, and as his hair fell across his brow Wydrin saw that there was a gnarled lump of scar tissue in place of one of his ears. It had been cut off and none too carefully either.

"It is a start." He sat back in his chair and looked at them both. Wydrin didn't like the assessment in that gaze. "Now, if I am to employ you I would ask some questions."

"All you need to know is that we're the best," said Wydrin with a shrug.

The white-haired man raised an eyebrow at her, perhaps suggesting that he was yet to be convinced, before turning to Sebastian.

"Why did you leave the Ynnsmouth knights?"

"Who says I left?" There was a flicker of anger in Sebastian's voice. "I still carry the shield of Isu." He indicated a badge sewn to the shoulder of his cloak. It depicted the outline of a jagged mountain top picked out in silver thread against a red, storm-laden sky. There was a series of letters in an alphabet Wydrin could not read sewn along the bottom, which Sebastian had told her spelt "Isu". "My sword was blessed at the mountain spring of the god-peak."

"Every man I spoke to told me how you were expelled from the order for some unspecified crime. They all knew the truth of this, although none of them knew exactly what it was you had done. I will not go on this journey with a man whose crimes are an unknown factor. I must trust you both to some degree." The white-haired man glanced at Wydrin. "And the last I heard, the Knights of Ynnsmouth do not take up petty mercenary work."

Sebastian pursed his lips, scowling down at his ale as though it had turned to bile. In the silence the barkeep bustled over bringing three fresh tankards. Sebastian waited for him to leave before he spoke again.

"The Order of the Knights of Ynnsmouth, in their wisdom, exiled me. I will not speak of why, but I will tell you that I do not consider what I did to be a crime, and that *you* are certainly in no danger."

Wydrin laughed at that. "Let us just say that his idea of brotherhood was not quite the same as his superiors."

Sebastian shot her a dark look before turning his attention back to their client.

"You are correct, my lord, raiding temples is hardly a knightly pursuit, but a man trained in the way of the sword has to make a living somehow." His lips creased into a faintly bitter smile.

"Actually, I have a question." Wydrin took a gulp of ale and belched none too quietly into her hand. "You intend to come with us on this trip to the bowels of the Citadel?"

"Of course. It is imperative that I come. There are certain items, certain knowledge that I must acquire."

"Exploring the Citadel is likely to be dangerous and exhausting, and that's even if we don't meet with some nasty surprises down in its darkest depths." She turned over a few more cards at random; the ace of wands, the crystal ball, the bear. "We will need to be quick, and strong. And you do not look quick – or strong."

The white-haired man looked down at the table for a moment, every line in his face rigid.

"You do not know me, Wydrin of Crosshaven, otherwise you would not ask such a question. I am Lord Frith of the Blackwood, and the Friths are not so easily put aside." Again there was that look, as though he were holding on to a rage he could barely contain. "I'm stronger than I appear."

Wydrin shrugged.

"Fine. That brings me on to my favourite subject, our fee."

Lord Frith glanced at Sebastian and then back to her.

"I have already spoken of this to your contact. We agreed a fee then. I see no reason to negotiate further."

"Oh I don't know; I enjoy a bit of negotiating myself." Wydrin winked at Frith. "What have we got? Expenses, danger money, a spot of bodyguarding too, I reckon. Let's go over the details once more for fun, shall we?"

There then followed a protracted argument over their fee that cost Lord Frith the promise of a further eight hundred pieces of gold and Sebastian two more rounds of ale. When everything was agreed Wydrin sat back in her chair feeling pleased with herself; an interesting job for a ridiculous amount of coin, and someone new to argue with.

"That's settled then, we'll leave in the morning. Consider our swords at your service. And the copper promise should always be sealed with a toast." Wydrin lifted her tankard. "To sacking the Citadel!"

Sebastian and Frith raised their own drinking vessels reluctantly, and she crashed her tankard into theirs, spilling more than a little over Lord Frith's embroidered cuff.

"We'll have such stories to tell."

4

"Krete is less a city and more an infection," muttered Frith as he hobbled his way through the crowded streets. The Citadel was the pustule in the middle of it, rising from the city's heart to stare blindly across the desert lands beyond; the houses and taverns and markets, the brothels and warehouses and gambling dens that grew beneath its walls, were the signs of its feverish pestilence. Even in the early morning light the day was already too hot, and the sun was a white disc in the pale sky.

"A hideous place." He limped around a market stall selling birds roasted on sticks. They'd left the brightly coloured tail feathers on. "So many people, so little space. And the *stink*."

"Do you think so?" The mercenary called Wydrin walked just ahead. "It doesn't smell half as fishy as Crosshaven. Where I'm from this would be considered an especially fragrant day."

Frith frowned. "I'm sure it would."

He had heard many stories on his long and painful journey from Litvania. The Copper Cat of Crosshaven, they said, was a fearsome swordswoman with flaming red hair, a pair of silvered daggers at her hips and a love of danger almost matched by her love of men and gold. It was said there was no deadlier dagger for hire in all of Crosshaven, and, given the latter's reputation for privateers and scoundrels, that was quite impressive in itself. Her partner, they said, was a cold-eyed killing machine filled with the fury of his icy mountain gods, with as much warmth and mercy as those perilous peaks.

Frith had imagined a tall, curvaceous woman, with hair as red as blood tumbling unbidden to her waist, a pair of green eyes as playful and cruel as a cat's, and armour that perhaps did not leave much to the imagination. In truth the Copper Cat was a young woman of average height with short, carroty hair, freckles across her nose and almost every inch of her covered in boiled leather armour. As he watched, she paused to kick a lump of something unmentionable off one of her boots; it didn't appear to make the boots any more presentable.

The Ynnsmouth Knight at least looked formidable. Even on such a warm day he wore the traditional armour of his order, a mixture of boiled black leather, fine mail and silvered plate, and people seemed naturally to move out of his way, like a river flowing around a rock. Other than his size and the enormous broadsword slung across his back, he gave no further impression of barbarism. His face was long-featured and clean-shaven, his eyes clear and blue.

"Have you seen the Sea-Glass Road before, my lord?" Sebastian asked.

"I have not. I came to Krete from the North, travelling down through Creos." He opened his mouth to say more, and then thought better of it. "It was an uncomfortable ride."

"It is quite a sight. One of the wonders of Ede."

"I am not here to see the sights."

Frith had to imagine it was finer to look upon than the streets of Krete itself. Timbered alehouses crowded to either side, each belching out a hot wind reeking of stale beer and old vomit. Butchers flung their offal directly into the streets, so that a tide of feral dogs moved from one shop to the other, only pausing to fight over the choicest scraps, and whores dangled out of windows, resting their doughy breasts on windowsills and calling down to the men below. Oxen moved slowly through these streets, hauling wagons piled high with produce rushed across the Creos desert from distant Onwai and the island of Crosshaven, whilst traders rushed between them, doing deals on the run. Men and women shouted to each other, children screamed and shrieked, and over it all the baking desert sun beat down, making everything fever-bright and fever-strange.

As they moved closer to the centre of the city the houses grew more ramshackle, the people poorer. The Citadel sat at its heart at the top of a small hill, surrounded by the impoverished and the desperate. Although it had been dormant for centuries, no one liked to live too close if they could possibly help it. On quiet nights, they said, you could hear the ghosts calling.

Frith found it hard to imagine there could ever be a quiet night in this place.

"There, look, my lord." Frith looked where the knight was pointing. Between two warehouses, one of which appeared to have partially burned down recently, he could see a wide strip of startling blue-green, rippled with bright sunlight. It truly was like suddenly coming upon the sea in the middle of the city. At the sight of it he felt his heart quicken, and he forced himself to walk faster. *The path of the gods.*

"Good, let us hurry. I have had more than enough of this pestilent city."

When they reached the edge of it, though, Frith found that he had to pause. The Sea-Glass Road swept up through the city of Krete like a great frozen river, the surface warped and glossy, and it was indeed an arresting sight. The heat shimmered off it in waves, and if you could bare to look for long enough you could follow its path up the hill to where the Citadel crouched, red stone and black shadows under a merciless sun.

Frith reached down and quickly massaged his stiff leg. It was already aching from the walk through the city.

Wydrin appeared at his side, her hands on her hips. She, too, glanced up towards the Haunted Citadel, and nodded as though this were exactly what she was expecting.

"How about it, princeling? Race you to the top?"

Wydrin took the lead. Sebastian and Frith followed behind, the latter taking great care on the slippery surface beneath his feet, the discomfort evident on his face. After a few moments Wydrin paused, letting them catch up with her.

Unfortunately for Frith, the Sea-Glass Road was the only way into the Citadel. The four iron gates set into the red-stone walls had long since been soldered shut to keep out the curious and the greedy, whereas the Sea-Glass Road ran straight up from the Creosis Sea, across the sands and up to the very walls of the Citadel, meeting a wide stretch of broken masonry. It was a curious thing, wide enough for ten of the heaviest carts to roll up it side by side, if the horses could abide walking on the warped, shiny surface. Most of them disliked it as much as Frith. It was sufficiently steep so that even

Wydrin in her tough leather boots was making slow progress. The glass beneath her feet was a deep green, like the sea it was named after, and the early morning sun created shimmering white lakes of light ahead.

"Who would put such an awkward thing here?"

"You mean you do not know?" asked Frith.

"I have told her," said Sebastian, in a weary tone. "But she does not listen."

"Nonsense," she replied, cheerfully. Sebastian was always talking about some old history or another, how was she to know which ones were worth listening too? "You've never mentioned such a road. I swear it on my claws." She patted the sheathed daggers at her waist.

"Here, then, stop and listen."

They paused. The city of Krete pressed in on either side of the Sea-Glass Road, like ports against a river, and here and there someone had tried to set up a business on the rippled surface, but it was hard going. They had passed a couple already, men selling red meat on sticks or cold glasses of spiced milk, but the sellers were all frazzled-looking and exhausted. No one attempted to make a living on the slopes closest to the Citadel: they were too close to the guards, and too close to the ghosts. The road itself stretched far into the distance, passing out of the city and dwindling to a slim green thread. On the horizon was the sapphire-blue band that marked the Creosis Sea.

"It's a long damn thing," she said, covering her eyes with one hand to better see the road. They could still smell smoke from the city below, the occasional whiff of sweet spices from the meat sellers, and a slight hint of salt from the sea.

"It grows no shorter as we stand here," put in Frith. He was wearing a black woollen tunic and a black cloak, with leather boots gone grey with travel. Leaning heavily on his stick, he looked less than comfortable in the heat. Sebastian, however, who had grown up surrounded by books and histories, was getting the look he got when he had a story to tell. He pointed to the beginning of the Sea-Glass Road in the far distance.

"This was all sand too, once, thousands of years ago. But then there was a war between the gods and the mages, one that threatened to wipe out all life on Ede. In desperation, the great mages of that time gathered together all of their most powerful weapons, all of their most mysterious and dangerous artefacts, and built a citadel to protect them. When word reached the gods that such a cache of power was hidden in a human citadel, they raced across the Creosis Sea to get here, churning up the land as they went so that it fused and turned to glass. But it was all a trap. Once inside they could not get back out again, and so the war was ended."

"And all the artefacts remain. All the ancient seals of power," continued Frith. "Yes, it is a fine story."

Wydrin shrugged. The Sea-Glass Road was certainly impressive, an extraordinary natural formation perhaps.

"In Crosshaven we prefer stories about pirates and sea-nymphs, or the salt-spirits and the Graces. Usually, a salt-spirit will turn himself into a human man for the day, and get some fish-wife pregnant. That sort of thing. There's normally a song or two in the middle."

Sebastian sighed.

"Let's keep moving, shall we?"

It was a hard climb, and at the very top they were met with the equally hard faces of the guards. There were four in all, patrolling the broken expanse of outer wall that marked the end of the Sea-Glass Road. The inner walls of the Citadel rose behind them, and above that the fat drum-shaped bulk of the central building itself, all constructed from the same dull, red stones. The place was certainly large, impressive even, but hardly opulent enough to be the prison of gods, Wydrin thought. The first guard approached them, a tall, lean man with a neat grey beard and dark circles under his eyes. He had a spear in his hand but he wasn't pointing it at them. Wydrin thought that could all change fairly quickly. The three other guards watched closely from their positions on the wall; two men of middling age and one younger lad, who was watching them with eyebrows that disappeared beneath his half-helm. Wydrin suspected he'd probably only been in the job for a month at most.

"Lost, are we?" cried Greybeard. There was a suggestion of a smile at the corner of his mouth. "The taverns and whorehouses are back down there a ways."

They drew level with him.

"No doubt you know of the best pillow-houses, Grandfather," said Wydrin, giving him her cheeriest grin. "Tell me, do they grant discounts to the greatly aged?"

Greybeard's little smile faltered somewhat.

"You tell me. Are you feeling generous today, whoreling?"

Sebastian cleared his throat.

"Apologies for my colleague," he said. "We are here on business, actually."

The three other guards were edging closer, intrigued. Wydrin suspected that usually trespassers were quickly chased off with a spear point in the ear for their trouble.

"What business could that be? No one's got business in the Citadel save for the dead, and you all look a little too lively for that." He looked at Frith, and shrugged. "Save for the cripple here, maybe."

The white-haired young man bristled visibly, his eyes narrowing.

"I am Lord Aaron Frith of the Blackwood. I have spoken to the Kretian Council and agreed a – price. You should have been informed of this."

Greybeard leaned on his spear, rubbing his chin. He made a great show of looking off into the distance, searching the edge of the horizon for something known only to him, and then finally shook his head.

"Can't say I have, actually."

Inwardly, Wydrin sighed. She couldn't abide a man who could not summon up a decent falsehood.

Frith stepped forward awkwardly, his stick skittering on the glass.

"I'm telling you, *guard*," he spat the word, "the bribe has been paid. Now stand aside."

The three other guards were now at Greybeard's back. Wydrin caught the eye of the young nervous one and gave him a wink. He looked momentarily terrified, and tore his gaze away.

"Well, maybe a bribe has been paid," said Greybeard slowly. "Maybe it has, maybe to someone who isn't me. Maybe that there is your problem."

"What?"

Sebastian held up his hands, palms out.

"I'm sure we can come to some sort of agreement. We are adventurers, after all, and we may–"

"I am not paying this man a single coin," snapped Frith. "He is a vulture, picking at the carcass of someone else's deal."

"Right, well." Wydrin slid her daggers from their sheaths, letting the early morning light play along their silvery blades. The young guard's eyes nearly popped out of his head, but his two companions only drew their own weapons, two notched short swords. Wydrin grinned at the sight of them. "I said we should do this in the first place, didn't I? Easier just to kill them."

Sebastian sighed. "You did not say that. You said that if we did that—"

"I changed my mind. It's been a slow morning and I am easily bored. You, fresh-meat. Would you like to die first?" She held up one of her daggers, showing it to the youngest guard. "This one is called Frostling, and the other is Ashes."

"That's the Copper Cat," he blurted. "She'll kill us all, and take our bodies back to Crosshaven to feed to the Graces!"

Triumphant, Wydrin turned to smile at Sebastian.

"And you said that rumour wouldn't stick—"

"Enough of this." Frith hobbled forward, coming face to face with the head guard. "I've paid our way, and paid well. Now get out of my path."

Wydrin hefted the weight of her daggers, watching Frith closely. He was standing his ground, his gaze unwavering, and she saw no fear on his face. Greybeard wasn't as impressed with Frith's bluster, however, and he lowered his spearhead to point at the young lord's gut.

"Bloodshed will serve none of us." Sebastian inserted himself between the guard and Frith, and for the first time they seemed to take note of his size, and the shining broadsword slung across his back. "Wydrin, please. Put your claws away for now."

Wydrin rolled her eyes, but did as he bid. In return, Sebastian glowered at Greybeard until he lowered the spear.

"Go on past, then. You won't last till midday. No one comes out of there alive, everyone knows that. All you adventurer types, with your big shiny swords, your plate armour and your empty heads – you all die down in the dust somewhere."

Wydrin walked calmly past the guards, pausing to lay one hand on the shoulder of the youngest. "I'll remember that when I'm reclining on silken pillows in my own marble palace. I shall say, the ugly guard told me I would come to this, and I did not listen." She gave him another wink while the boy gaped at her.

Greybeard spat in the dust by her boot.

"There would have been another man, some weeks back," said Sebastian. "Did you see him come past?"

"I saw him, aye, young idiot. Blond hair and more knives than sense. He hasn't come back, either, and neither will you." When they looked at him blankly, he waved them on with his spear. "Go on, then, go and get yourselves killed. It's no skin off my arse."

5

Round the corner and out of sight of the guards, they walked within the shadow of the inner walls. Here and there were piles of sand, blown up by the desert winds and left stranded. Spindly plants with long needle-like leaves had sprouted colonies where the stonework had started to crumble. Sebastian looked at the walls and thought of his father. *He would have said it was a wonder*, he thought. *What would he say if he knew I was standing here today in front of one of the greatest man-made structures Ede has ever seen?*

His father had spent his whole life working with stone; breaking it, sculpting it, shaping it to his will. Perhaps everything would have been simpler if he'd just gone into the family business as his father had wanted in the first place. *If the mountain hadn't spoken to me, if the Ynnsmouth knights hadn't taken me in...* He felt a stab of mingled bitterness and longing at the thought of home; the grey stones of the squire house and the treacherous training slopes, all dusted with snow. *I live my own life now*, Sebastian reminded himself.

Frith appeared at his side, still scowling after their skirmish with the guards.

"I believe we'll have need of your map soon, for what it's worth," he said, pointing to the walls ahead of them. "I don't want to wander about needlessly."

A huge ornate archway stood in front of them, partially fallen into rubble. As faded as they were it was just possible to see the shapes that had been carved directly into the red stone; heroes with swords, strange animals with more teeth than legs, men who appeared to be half dog, women who appeared to be half fish. Their faces were rubbed smooth and expressionless by the passage of time, as though they couldn't bear to look upon the place they inhabited. Through the archway a series of low walls formed a sort of maze, which led towards the huge drum-shaped building that squatted at the centre of it all. Once there had been small lawns and rockeries between the walls, but now there was only dirt and weeds, with the occasional lonely statue missing a limb or two.

"That looks to be the way," said Wydrin. The desert sun had turned her hair the colour of beaten gold. "Let's get in there, shall we?"

Frith nodded and drew his cloak closer around his shoulders, and despite the heat of the day Sebastian felt a shiver work its way down his spine. There was an ill feeling here, a quiet sense of anticipation, of loneliness, that felt quite out of place so close to the city. He thought of Gallo coming this way, full of excitement for what he was about to find.

They walked through the archway and into the ruined gardens. Frith, still leaning on his stick, chose the path dictated by the low walls, but Wydrin climbed over them, heading in a straight line for the heart of the Citadel. Sebastian followed behind Frith, in truth in no hurry to put a stone ceiling over his head. Out here, at least, he could hear the harsh cries of the gulls overhead, and the fat, lazy hum of desert bees. Passing by an overgrown salt-rose bush he heard the slither and hiss of a snake moving in its lower branches, and caught a brief glance of glittering red scales; a ruby adder.

"There are snakes, Wydrin. Keep an eye out, if you must go traipsing through the undergrowth."

"Ha!" cried Wydrin, drawing one of her daggers. "Cats are faster than snakes."

"Cats don't have venom in their claws."

He caught up with Frith. There was a thin sheen of sweat on the young man's brow already, and his mouth was turned down at the corners with the effort of walking at such a pace. *So angry*, thought Sebastian. *He reminds me of me, a few years ago.* Up close, Sebastian was surprised to see how young Frith looked, despite his brittle, bone-white hair. He'd done his best to hide the extent of what had happened to him, but Sebastian had sharp eyes, and when the winds were gusting out on the Sea-Glass Road he'd seen the terrible hole that had once been Lord Frith's ear. *An angry man indeed.*

Frith caught him staring, and scowled. Wydrin was off in front, hacking at bushes with her daggers.

"What is it?"

"Nothing, my lord. Just contemplating the journey ahead."

"I'll get no m'lords off of that one," he said, nodding towards the Copper Cat.

Sebastian had to smile. "I suspect you won't, no."

"Do you trust her? Is she trustworthy?"

Sebastian looked up to the sky, still a bright, blameless blue. In Ynnsmouth the sky was often that blue, but the air was always fresh. Here, the air smelt like a dung heap left to fester.

"Inside that ratty bag she wears across her back there is a pack of cards," he said quietly. "Eventually she will ask you if you fancy a quick game of Poison Sally. Find an excuse not to play. Don't tell her you don't know the rules, she'll only offer to teach you, and then you'll be truly done for. But outside of card games? No more untrustworthy than your usual sell-sword."

"I am greatly reassured," said Frith sourly. "And how did a knight of Ynnsmouth come to be partners with a card shark?"

Sebastian thought of the chaotic time just after he'd left the Order, and frowned.

"It's a long story, my lord, and quite tedious, I assure you."

Frith shot him a look, but said nothing.

Just ahead of them Wydrin now stood by the great curving bulk of the Inner Keep, rubbing her fingers lightly over the red stones.

"They're cold," she said, a note of wonder in her voice. "Come, touch them."

Sebastian did so, pressing his hand to the wall. It *was* cool, just as though the Citadel did not crouch under the punishing sun every hour of the day, but there was something else too… a vibration? Sebastian frowned, trying to place it, but Frith stepped up next to them and whacked the wall with his stick.

"We are not here to caress the Citadel, we are here to crack it. Where is the nearest entrance?"

Sebastian took his hands away, trying to ignore how the stones had unsettled him. He took the unfinished map from his belt and unfolded it to the light.

"There is a door," he said, tracing the lines with a finger. "There is a door to the right of us. We must keep walking."

They circled the inner keep until they found the entrance. It was difficult to miss; debris from it was strewn across their path, and pieces of the door stuck out jaggedly like a row of broken teeth.

"This is made of ebony," said Frith, looking closely at the remains of the entrance. Sebastian thought to mention that they were not there to caress the doors, but knew that would only encourage Wydrin to say something worse. "It only grows in Litvania."

"Expensive door, then," said Wydrin. "Someone made short work of it, though."

"That would have been Gallo," said Sebastian.

Once the door had stood a good ten feet tall, the wood a foot thick and banded with iron. Now it was a pile of pricey timber and twisted slag. Sebastian was glad to see such a sign of his friend's passage, but it also made him uneasy. There was no doubt now that Gallo had been there, and no doubt he'd entered the Citadel. So where was he?

Beyond the shattered door there was a dusty floor surrounded by deep shadows.

"How?" asked Frith. He ran his gloved hand over a sprouting of splinters.

"There is a certain black powder you can buy in Crosshaven," said Sebastian. "Mixed with a number of other chemicals, it becomes–"

"Explosive, yes." Frith nodded. "I have some knowledge of this. Still, to bring such a quantity of it across the desert... that would be a dangerous task indeed."

Sebastian nodded.

"Gallo liked to take the occasional risk. Likes, I mean."

"Well," Wydrin slapped Frith on the shoulder, nearly sending him face first through the entrance, "shall we get in there? I'm all for standing around discussing the whys and wherefores, but I'd rather save that until we've some idea of what we're dealing with."

Inside, the desert sun became a distant dream. Sebastian wore several layers of clothing; smallclothes, tunic, leather armour, chainmail, and on top of it all a heavy black cloak, but even he felt a cold chill creep down the back of his neck as they stepped over the threshold. Wydrin, who habitually wore a long shirt under her boiled leather bodice, frowned and hugged herself. The room they entered was wide and spacious, and there were three doorways on the far side, each with steps leading down. On the walls there were rough carvings, partly hidden by dust and shadows, but Sebastian could just about make out shapes suggesting animals and people, and an alphabet he couldn't decipher. Motes of dust and sand swirled in the daylight streaming through the door.

"We take the door to the right," he said, trying to sound more certain than he felt. "That should take us into the lowest chamber we can access at this point. These others lead only to the floor beneath this, and if we are going by the stories, the mages kept all their greatest artefacts at the very bottom of the Citadel."

Frith pulled a small glass oil lamp from the bag at his belt and carefully lit it. Warm orange light spilled onto the stone floor.

"The haunted Citadel awaits."

6

They walked. And walked. And walked some more. The steps were wide enough for the three of them to walk abreast, but Frith tended to move in front, setting the pace and lighting the way. Wydrin would pause now and then to scratch a great cross on the wall with the point of her dagger, marking their progress in case they should need to head back that way in a hurry. Sometimes the steps would turn, left then right again, and sometimes they would level out for a while, but always they were heading gradually downwards.

"So, what is it you hope to find at the bottom of these steps, princeling?" asked Wydrin, after they had been walking for around an hour. "I thought that princelings had treasure enough already."

Even in the inconstant light Frith's scowl was impossible to miss.

"Do not call me that. You only need concern yourself with reaching our goal. What I choose to do with what we discover is none of your business."

"Oh, I don't know. I think it could be my business. Everyone knows this place is haunted. Everyone knows that no one makes it out of here alive. We're putting ourselves in considerable danger, for you. I think that sort of makes it my business." Wydrin patted the daggers on her belt. "What is so important that you would pay us to brave the ghosts of the Citadel?"

Frith grunted.

"Ghosts, indeed. It's all nonsense. Stories made up by fools who don't understand what they're dealing with. The mages have left more than their treasures behind, and if there are voices in the walls, it is only evidence of their magic."

Wydrin sniffed.

"That's what you're after, then, is it?"

Frith fell silent.

"I'm sure I don't know either way," said Sebastian. "But if anywhere were to be a home to ghosts, I think it would be this place."

At the bottom of the steps was, finally, a door. As they approached, Sebastian waved a hand at them to stop.

"There is a light," he said, squinting to see. "Through the crack in the door."

Weak, shimmering light moved at its edge. Frith pulled his cloak over the lamp and they could see it even more clearly.

"What is that?" asked Wydrin.

"I do not know," said Sebastian. After a moment's pause, he drew the sword from its scabbard on his back. "But we may not be alone down here."

Let it be Gallo, he thought. *Let it be him.*

They approached the door, Sebastian leading. Wydrin strained her ears, trying to gather any clues about what might be in the next room. Sebastian turned to her and nodded. She returned his nod, and rested one hand on a dagger. Sebastian would enter first. It was difficult to miss him, with his height and broad shoulders, and while any potential attackers were watching the broadsword in his hands, she would slip in behind; small, slim, unthreatening. People would often only notice the daggers she wore when one of them was buried to the hilt in their throats.

Sebastian pushed the door open, stepped through, and uttered a low cry of surprise. Wydrin rushed in behind him, blades in hand, and then stopped dead, staring at what met them. She felt Frith step in close behind her.

"By all the gods… what are they?" said Frith in amazement.

They stood in a room vastly different to any they'd seen before. The walls were of brown marble, and hanging from the high ceiling were soft yellow lamps, casting light over row upon row of strange glass capsules. They were partially sunk into an earthen floor, and each of them contained a small, pale figure, no bigger than a child. The room was long, and there must have been around fifty of the smooth glass tanks. There was a strong chemical smell, reminding Wydrin of the apothecary shop to which her father would sometimes send her on errands.

"Are they dead?" Whatever they were, she did not like it.

Sebastian stepped up to the nearest capsule and knelt, peering closely at the occupant.

"I don't know what they are," he said eventually. "Look at their faces, they look... unfinished, somehow. They all look the same."

Wydrin joined him at the side of the glass. The figure within was so pale he seemed almost translucent, the skin on his smooth cheeks looking thin enough to break and reveal the dark flesh beneath. He had no hair, no eyebrows, no blemishes, and rather than clothing he was wrapped in what appeared to be soft white bandages, from his wrists down to his ankles. Wydrin peered closely. It looked as though there had once been writing on the bandages, but the ink had faded with time to a pale, unreadable yellow. The figure was very still.

Frith tapped on the glass with his stick, and Wydrin winced, suddenly afraid that he would wake it.

"A mystery," he said. "What *are* they? Some remnant of the mages?"

"We are soldiers in an ongoing war."

The voice came from the far side of the room; a figure identical to the creatures in the capsules stood in the doorway. As they watched, he walked rapidly towards them, his soft feet making barely any sound on the dirt floor. Wydrin raised her blades.

"Not so fast, little man."

The creature did not slow, but came on until he stood on the other side of the glass capsule. His eyes were like black pools of almond-shaped ink. Looking down at his brother in the tank, he nodded as though satisfied and looked up at the trio of surprised adventurers.

"Leave now. Seals have been broken. We no longer hold the perimeter."

"What are you?" demanded Frith. "Who are you to tell us to retreat?"

Another of the pale child-men appeared in the far door, and another. They, too, entered the room, walking swiftly without noise.

"I am known as Inkberrow. My brothers, Yarrowfoot and Peaseworth."

"Well, Peasefoot and Yellow-thing, I'd keep back." Wydrin glanced behind her, suddenly convinced there would be more of the pale men sneaking in behind them, but the doorway was dark. "We mean to go through this chamber and out the other side. We'll just let the rest of your family here sleep."

"No, no place for you here," the creature called Yarrowfoot said. His voice was a touch higher than his brother's, but it was the only difference between them. "There is danger, death."

Wydrin laughed.

"I love it when people say things like that. You know that is only meat and bread to adventurers such as ourselves?"

"Wydrin…" said Sebastian, a note of warning in his voice.

"Dust and death," said Inkberrow. "Darkness and evil. The power that waits below is truly awake again for the first time in centuries."

"Power?" said Frith. "What power is this?"

"The one that sleeps," Peaseworth said, shaking his head. "Her agents are moving through the Citadel. If they meet you, you will become hers too."

The three pale men moved forward as one then, as though to physically push them from the chamber. Sebastian raised his sword, resting its point a few inches from Yarrowfoot's throat.

"Tell us what you are, and we *may* leave."

The one called Inkberrow sighed, and Wydrin noticed a small cloud of dust emerge from his mouth.

"We are Culoss. The mages made us to wait forever in the dark, guarding the seals and holding the perimeter. To watch over the gods they imprisoned."

"But the seals are broken, and the perimeter…" The Culoss known as Yarrowfoot shook his head anxiously.

"Are you saying there are *gods* are down there?" Wydrin could not keep the scorn from her voice.

"Only one," said Inkberrow. "She has eaten the others."

Wydrin laughed again.

"They have gone mad, down here in the dark."

"It is the mages we are interested in," said Frith. There was a feverish light to his eyes now. "What is left of their power? Of their artefacts? Can you tell us?"

"There is a lake–" began Peaseworth, but the Culoss called Inkberrow silenced him with a look.

"Enough," he said. "Her agents move. You will leave now."

"Wait," said Sebastian. "I had a friend, he came here before me. Blond hair, ridiculous little beard. There would have been a guide with him…"

"No, no, no," said Yarrowfoot. "No more talk. Leave now. We must protect the Citadel."

"I mean to have the secrets of the mages," said Frith. "You will not turn us aside."

"Then we stand against you."

Inkberrow held his arms out to them, and for a bizarre moment Wydrin thought he wanted to be picked up, like a small child tired of walking, but a pair of vicious-looking blades pushed their way through the palms of his hands, each a full foot long. There was no blood at the separating of his flesh, only a thin stream of dark dust.

"What are you?" cried Wydrin, but then the other two stepped forward with identical weapons shooting from their own hands. And from behind them came the creaking of elderly hinges as the glass cases began to open.

The next few minutes passed in a panicked blur for Wydrin. The Culoss were unnaturally fast, running and jumping at them with the speed of birds in flight. She narrowly avoided one strike from Yarrowfoot by stumbling backwards, but he was immediately replaced by Inkberrow, and then she lost track of which Culoss was which. She brought her claws up in time to stop her throat being opened and pushed back against the Culoss with all her strength. He skidded back across the floor, but it was then she noticed that more of the bandaged men were climbing out of their glass beds, every one of them sprouting long, shining spikes from the palms of their hands, even as they were blinking away their artificial sleep.

"Stop this!" yelled Sebastian as he cut his way through them, his sword a silvery blur in front of him.

Wydrin had time to see a Culoss cut in half by that blade, saw the dust and rags that made up its insides, and then they were on her again, three at once. A slash from a razor-sharp sword caught her across the forearm, but it only sliced open her shirt. *Whatever they are*, she thought, *they attacked us. And I don't even owe them money.*

Kicking one in the legs, she plunged Frostling down through the bandages at the base of his neck as he bent over, grunting with satisfaction as the strange flesh yielded. The Culoss fell to the ground in a boneless heap, but two of his brothers circled her, constantly moving.

"Come on, children of worms," she said cheerfully. The next Culoss lunged at her, bringing his swords together in a double-point, but she stepped away from it so that it only scrapped against her boiled leather armour. While he was within her reach, she brought the pommel of her dagger down hard on the top of his skull which, to her surprise, caved in as though made of plaster. He went to his knees, and she took the opportunity to slit his papery throat.

"What are you made of, spit and paste?" she laughed, but the third Culoss wasn't content to listen to her taunting. He ran at her, eyes like empty holes, and his first blade was only turned away by the thin mail over her leather vest. The second he threw up towards her face, and for a terrible moment Wydrin thought she'd lose her nose, but Sebastian was there, pulling the Culoss off her by the scruff of his neck.

"Bastard thing nearly had my face off," she had time to say before they were rushed by five more. It was around this point that Wydrin thought to wonder how Frith was faring. She saw him some distance away, his white hair the brightest thing in the room. He was leaning awkwardly on the wall, but he had a rapier in his hands and was holding the Culoss at bay, the blade almost moving too quickly for her to follow.

Where did that come from?

There were dead Culoss by his feet, but even from where she stood she could see the exhaustion on his face.

She hacked, and slashed, parried and stabbed, over and over, until her shoulders began to sing from the ache of it. She stole glances at Sebastian occasionally, shouted encouragement or mockery, but his face was closed and still, as it always was during a fight. The Culoss just kept coming, always pushing them back towards the door, stepping over the torn bodies of their brothers and producing their strange blades from within their bodies. Wydrin felt sweat begin to trickle down her back. They were trying to press them back, towards the exit, and they were succeeding. *They might be short and strange-looking, but they are so many, and for every one, two blades.* Wydrin took a breath, preparing to tell Sebastian it was time to run for it, when there was a shuddering crash and the chamber was filled with bright, greenish light. She almost lost her footing, but when she looked up she saw around fifteen freshly dead Culoss, and Frith standing beyond a veil of smoke.

"What the hell was that?"

Wydrin saw hope in Sebastian's eyes and knew he was thinking of Gallo, but as she watched, Frith reached into his cloak with his free hand and produced something small and round. He threw it on the ground nearest a group of the Culoss and there was another bang. This time, Wydrin saw the brief burst of green flame and the curling cloud it produced. Several of the Culoss were thrown back by the initial impact, but those who were caught in the cloud began to writhe and scream, their powdery white skins turning black. The Culoss who were attacking them paused in their efforts, looking back at their brothers in apparent horror.

"What are you doing?" she cried, but Frith, apparently seeing them both for the first time, motioned impatiently for them to take cover. Hurriedly she threw herself into the corner, before Frith hurled another of his grenades right into the midst of the stunned Culoss. This time the explosion was so close it made her ears ring, and she cringed away from the poisonous cloud.

The Culoss that were left turned and fled then, back through the far door where Yarrowfoot and Inkberrow had first appeared. Wydrin slid down the wall, exhausted. Frith came over to them, his slim sword thick with black dust and tattered pieces of bandages. She watched him retrieve his stick from the floor, and slide the blade back into its hiding place. The Copper Cat of Crosshaven began to laugh.

"So why did you employ us at all, princeling?"

7

They had left the chamber of the Culoss, moving slowly, wary of another attack. Now they walked through a series of low-ceilinged rooms, many of which contained empty glass tanks. Frith saw several that seemed to hold Culoss who had not lived long enough to protect their precious Citadel; they were mouldering piles of bandages, dust, and short, rusted blades. Why those ones had not survived he couldn't say, but there had certainly been enough of them to cause trouble. He watched carefully, searching every shadow for a hidden assailant, until his head began to ache.

Every part of Frith ached. His right arm and shoulder were especially tender; it had been a very long time since he'd swung a sword in defence of his own life, and the sell-sword woman seemed amused that he could fight at all.

"Your clothes are torn," he said.

Wydrin looked down at her forearm and seemed surprised to see her shirt had been shredded by the Culoss blades.

"Huh. They did all that, and never managed to cut me. Useless."

With a sharp tug she pulled the remains of her sleeve away from the rest of her shirt, revealing a tattoo that curled all the way to the top of her shoulder.

"Sharks?" asked Frith when finally the pattern was revealed. There were three of them depicted in slim black lines, twisting sinuously around her arm.

"The Graces," replied Wydrin, holding her arm out. "The Three Graces of Crosshaven."

"Your gods are fish?"

"Not gods, as such, more... priestesses. The sea is the only god we

44

worship. If you come back to Crosshaven with me, I will show you."

To his own horror, Frith felt his cheeks grow slightly warm. "Why would I want to go to that pirate's den?"

"You don't want to, believe me," said Sebastian. "Anyone outside of Crosshaven tends to find the rites of the Graces somewhat grisly. Or anyone with any sense, anyway."

Rather than looking offended, Wydrin laughed.

"It makes for a good day out," she said. "Besides, our princeling here has a stronger stomach than you give him credit for, Sebastian. There were bits of those dwarves all over that chamber by the end of it."

"Yes," agreed Sebastian. He gave her an appraising look. "You realise your other sleeve is torn too, on the back?" She twisted round to look, and swore. "That shirt is ruined." He turned back to Frith as the Copper Cat began to tug her shirt out from under her leather bodice. "What were those spheres you were throwing? And what was in them?"

Frith hurriedly averted his eyes from Wydrin, who was now pulling the remnants of the ruined material over her head, and in doing so revealing more cleavage than he thought was seemly in a sword for hire. He took one of the remaining acid grenades from within his cloak and passed it to the knight.

"Handle it carefully. You have to throw them quite violently for the chemical process to begin, but it is always best to assume they are dangerous. There is the initial explosion, of course, which is enough to cause a reasonable amount of damage, and then the acidic cloud that spreads afterwards, certainly the more unpleasant way to die. Fortunately, it disperses quickly, or we'd all have boiled lungs by now."

"Where did you get these from?"

Sebastian was turning the ball over in his hand. They were small, innocuous-looking things, round and greenish, with a slightly greasy texture. If you made enough of them, your fingers started to turn green. Frith's father, who had spent much of his time studying chemicals and their uses, always had faintly green fingertips despite every effort with a scrubbing brush. His study, Frith remembered, always carried the slightly caustic whiff of his experiments. All gone now, of course.

"I have some education in the alchemical arts."

"Very bloody handy," said Wydrin. She'd removed her shirt, and now her arms were bare save for the leather vanbraces and copper bracelets at her wrists. "As was that hidden sword. Our princeling has many secrets, it seems."

Frith clutched his stick, ignoring the steady ache in his shoulder. "And they are still none of your concern."

They continued on through the next series of chambers, occasionally pausing to consult what they could of Sebastian's map. They were sloping gradually downwards still, and the further down they went, the warmer it grew. Frith's heavy black cloak was stifling, seeming to push down on his back with every step, but he would not take it off. To do that would reveal his thin, wasted body, and even if his companions already knew he was weak, he was not ready for them to see the full extent of the damage.

Wydrin took his arm suddenly, startling him and banishing his dreams of revenge.

"You were miles away then. Care to tell us what you were thinking, with your handsome face so tense?"

Frith shook her off awkwardly.

"A man's thoughts are his own."

Wydrin sighed.

"And curiosity killed the cat."

She walked off ahead, pausing to scratch another cross on the wall before moving on, eager to see what was through the next door. The queer golden lights of the Culoss chamber had continued beyond it, so that they no longer needed the oil lamp.

"You fascinate her, I think," said Sebastian in a low voice. "She has a weakness for mysterious men."

Frith pulled his cloak closer around him.

"I have no reason to reveal my business to her."

"I don't know about that," Sebastian's tone was light. "We're down here with you, aren't we? Fighting side by side. Would it be so terrible to let us in on your plans?"

"You know all you need to know," said Frith.

The big knight was quiet for a few moments. When he spoke again his tone was one of mild speculation.

"If the tales of what is hidden here are even partially true, it would be a significant find. The remnants of magic here could still be powerful. A man could do a lot with such power."

Frith frowned, not looking at the knight.

"You are perceptive, and free with your words. Is that why your Copper Cat likes you?"

Sebastian chuckled.

"If only Wydrin listened to half of what I said. I told you, she likes mysteries, not explanations."

"You two are not... lovers, then?"

This time Sebastian guffawed, his surprised laughter echoing off the flat stones. Frith turned to him, raising an eyebrow. Seeing the look, Sebastian reined in his laughter, and shook his head in apology.

"I'm sorry, my lord. Wydrin is a good friend, that is all. But I do not... I do not believe I am her type, as it were."

Frith took a deep breath.

"Whereabouts are we?" he said. "What does the map tell you?"

Sebastian held the sheet of parchment up to the light. After a few moments, he frowned.

"We've gone off course, actually. That's what comes of letting Wydrin go ahead, I suppose. We'll have to turn back, take another turning." He cupped his hands round his mouth and called his companion. "Wydrin! We have to go back a bit!"

They heard her light footsteps on the floor before she came through the door.

"Got us lost already, Sebastian?"

"Come on."

As they turned to retrace their steps, the floor beneath them rumbled, nearly throwing Frith off his feet.

"What is that?" cried Wydrin.

The low grinding below continued, growing in volume until dust and debris on the ground began to jump with the vibrations.

"The door," said Sebastian, "Quick!"

But before they could reach it an iron portcullis swept down, its sharp points hitting the floor with a crash. The way back was cut off.

Frith and Sebastian tried desperately to pull the portcullis up, but its bars were solid and heavy, despite their age.

"But the Culoss wanted us to leave," said Sebastian. "Why would they cut off our retreat?"

"Maybe they're not the only ones in the Citadel," said Wydrin. Her usually cheerful face was troubled. "They did say they were fighting a war, and it didn't sound as though they were winning."

Frith nodded reluctantly.

"We must carry on, then," he said. Their progress was slow, much too slow. "Is there a way we can turn around later, according to what we have of the map?"

Sebastian looked at it again, and shrugged.

"In all honesty, if we keep heading in this direction this piece of parchment becomes more useful as lantern fuel. I just didn't get enough time to copy it this far."

Frith shook his head.

"It matters not. It seems there is only one way we can go now."

And so they did, now wary that each entrance might contain another portcullis. The passages were growing narrower, the walls danker and lined with moss and mould. There was an old, dark smell, that spoke of centuries of neglect, and the deeper they went the more Frith fancied he could feel the weight of the stones above pressing down on them. Every now and then they heard a faint but unmistakeable rumble, and a vibration would pass through the stones and up through their feet.

"Is it following us, do you think?" said Wydrin after a while. She had paused to take a drink from the skin at her belt. When she passed it to Frith, he was surprised to find it filled with a sour red wine.

"Is what following us?"

"The noise, that movement. Whatever you want to call it." She slapped the wall to her left. "It's like something very large is moving alongside us, watching what we're up to."

"That's preposterous," said Frith, his voice slightly unsteady. He looked at the walls, and wondered what would happen if something powerful decided to push them down on their defenceless group.

"The sooner we get out of these passageways, the happier I'll be," said Sebastian. He was looking distinctly less comfortable the further down they went. There was sweat on his forehead now, and his mouth was tense at the corners, almost as though he were concentrating very hard on not being sick. "It's all too narrow. If we get caught here there's no room to fight."

To Sebastian's obvious relief they eventually came to an entrance that led down to a widening set of stone steps. The room beyond was larger than any they'd been in for hours, its floor covered in big square flagstones. On the far side was another set of steps leading to a tall wooden door, and the yellow lamps hanging from the ceiling revealed a pair of carvings in the dark grained wood: a nude woman emerging from a great lake, water running from her cupped hands, and on the other side, a naked man doing the same. Wydrin hooted with amusement.

"Filthy buggers!" She walked down the steps onto the square flagstones. "Someone has put a lot of work into that. I've never seen one of those where they've actually managed to get the shape–"

"The mages were said to be great artisans," said Frith, hurriedly.

"Artisans with an eye for a decent pair of–"

Without warning, Wydrin pitched forward violently. Sebastian made to grab her, but he also lurched to one side. Frith opened his mouth to shout to them when the flagstone beneath his feet dropped several inches, causing him to fall heavily onto the stone floor. He cracked his elbow badly, but worse than that was the sickening sense of movement; the stones beneath were rising and falling as though they were being disturbed by something below.

"Careful!" shouted Sebastian. "Something's pushing up through the stones."

They were all in the centre of the room, too far from either set of steps for immediate safety. Frith climbed awkwardly to his feet, leaning on his walking stick. Now he could see it. A glowing green substance was pushing up through the joins between the stones, pushing them apart like a great eldritch sea. The flagstone he had his weight on tilted to one side and his boot was briefly doused in the substance. There was a hissing sound, and the scent of boiling leather.

"Don't touch it," he said, his voice hoarse with panic. "It burns."

Wydrin was swearing loudly and attempting to hop from one flagstone to another, but many were already sinking beneath the green lava, leaving her fewer and fewer places to step. Sebastian was faring even worse, his size and the weight of his sword keeping him off balance. The edge of his cloak was already smoking from contact with the liquid.

Frith jumped awkwardly from one stone to the next, each step sending a stab of pain up his weak leg. His limbs felt numb from the previous sword fight and he had nothing to lean his stick against. Cold sweat ran down the back of his neck.

"There's something else here!" Wydrin was closest to the far side, but she had stopped in front of a wide trench of the treacherous green goo and seemed unable to go further. "Something under the slime!"

"What?"

As Frith watched, the surface of the poisonous pool began to seethe, and a long shape disturbed the surface. It was sinuous and thick with muscle, and barbs bristled from its slimy skin. From all around them came a loud chittering sound that made all the hairs on the back of Frith's neck stand up. Wydrin drew her daggers and balanced herself as best she could, but the shape under the green surged towards her, revealing a long tapering tentacle with sharp, teeth-lined mouths on the underside. It swept at her feet, trying to knock her into the slime, but she jumped over it and brought both daggers down on its fleshy hide. The chittering turned briefly into squealing and it retreated rapidly beneath the surface. Wydrin only avoided following it when Sebastian took hold of her waist and pulled her back. Her daggers came out of the creature with a sickening pop, and a jet of bright blue fluid spurted over her leather bodice.

"Quick! While it is injured!" cried Frith, struggling to catch up with them, but the creature was already stirring in half a dozen places, other tentacles rising up out of the slime like cobras.

Frith took one of the acid bombs from the bag inside his cloak and threw it at a flagstone near the creature, but it sunk harmlessly into the green. He drew his sword instead, trying to ignore how his boots were smoking and the flagstones were gradually sinking. A tentacle struck at him, clinging to his cloak with a hideous sucking noise, and another wrapped around his left leg. He struck down at it with the point of his rapier, jabbing with all the strength he could muster, and smiled grimly at the blue blood that leaked out of it. The tentacle around his ankle withdrew, but the one on his cloak was now tangled in it, dragging him out towards the acid. He turned and slashed, slicing through the thick material but completely missing the monster. Behind him, Wydrin was releasing a continual stream of curse words and Sebastian was shouting commands, and all the time there was the endless clacking and squealing of the huge thing beneath them.

A tentacle crashed onto the stone between his feet. Frith fell to his knees and cried out in pain as the green substance burned into his legs. For a brief second he was back in the dank little dungeon cell, and Yellow-Eyed Rin was leaning over him with a hot poker.

He lashed out with the rapier again, this time cutting the tentacle clean in half with one stroke. He scrambled up and away from it, very nearly stepping right back into the green slime, but the chamber was suddenly full of yellow light. For an instant everything was black and white. One of the tentacles flailed past him, a burning arrow jutting up from its barbed flesh. There was a whoosh, another blaze of light, and the creature was squealing in agony. The green acid below began to seethe ever more violently. He had to crouch to keep from going straight in it.

"Make for the edge, friends!" came a voice from behind him. "It doesn't much like the touch of my hot fingers."

Frith turned to see a man standing on the far steps with a bow in his hands, cocked and ready with a fiery arrow. He was short and slim, with wavy blond hair and a small pointed beard. The man took aim and fired once more, the arrow finding another length of tentacle and biting deep. The creature began to withdraw, pulling its arms below the surface. Ahead of Frith, Sebastian and Wydrin were clambering awkwardly to the far steps, hopping from one broken flagstone to the next. They were both shouting excitedly, although Frith could not understand why. He hobbled over as best he could and almost made it to the edge before losing his balance. He pin-wheeled backwards, waving his arms desperately for balance but then Wydrin was there, dragging him with her onto the steps. His boots splashed through some of the green acid but he did not fall.

"That was close," said Wydrin. Frith looked at her sharply, sure she was mocking him again, but rather than her usual crooked smile she looked pale, her hair hanging in her eyes. On the steps in front of them, Sebastian was marching up to the blond man, who had slung his bow onto his back.

"Sebastian!" he cried. "You're looking well."

"And so are you, Gallo." The big knight looked confused for a few seconds, before breaking into a huge grin. "Where the bloody hell have you been?"

He swept the smaller man up into a bone-crushing hug.

"It's good to see you, Gallo," said Wydrin. She waved to the smaller man as Sebastian put him back down. "You always did have a fine sense of timing. Been having fun?"

Gallo grinned.

"But of course. Let's find a friendlier chamber. This could take a while."

Gallo and Sebastian stood together, laughing and clapping each other on the back, exchanging exclamations of surprise and cries of "Well, you took your time!" and "Fancy seeing you here!". Wydrin had found a pile of rocks and was perched on its edge, using the point of her dagger to scrape the last of the green ooze from her clothes. Frith crouched beside her, watching the two men.

"That is definitely him?" he asked Wydrin in a low voice.

Wydrin glanced up and shrugged.

"It is. I'd know that smug little beard anywhere."

Frith frowned. Finding Sebastian's partner here, in the depths of the Citadel, was disconcerting. A corpse would have been easier to deal with.

"Is he trustworthy?"

Wydrin slid her blade back into its scabbard and laughed.

"Gallo? Of course not. He's a scoundrel." She paused. "I've always liked him."

"And yet Sir Sebastian seems to be an honourable man."

"Well, you know they say opposites attract." She grinned up at him in an unnerving fashion. When he scowled at her she stretched her arms above her head until the bones in her shoulders popped. "You know where I first met Sebastian? In the middle of a street brawl." The two men were still talking animatedly, taking little notice of their companions. Even so, she lowered her voice. "When those pompous bastards threw him out of the Order he was heartbroken. And grieving." A shadow passed over her face. "He'd goaded a bunch of Crosshaven scum into a fight – five on one it was, the idiot, and he was keeping them off with his bare hands. Didn't even draw his sword. I happened to be passing and, well, I didn't like the odds so I joined in. When they'd gone, skittering back up the street like rats, I realised that the giant knight with all the hair was stone-cold drunk."

"Sir Sebastian?"

"He was a mess, full of rage and grief at what they'd done to him. We became friends, and he started helping me out on some jobs."

She looked up at her friend, her gaze considering. "He wanted to be the worst of us, you see. The most feared, the most ruthless sell-sword." Wydrin smiled faintly. "He certainly had the skills for it – I'd never seen anyone fight like him, but that wasn't really Seb." She grinned in the dark. "Oh, he was wild for a while and we got into some right scrapes, but in the end –" She paused, searching for the right words. "In the end he became a steadying hand on the rudder. Sebastian's a good man, and he can't ever escape that."

"And Gallo?"

"And Gallo," the blond man stepped forward, sketching them an elaborate bow, "is here to be your guide to the depths of the Citadel."

"It's a good thing you turned up when you did." Sebastian appeared at his shoulder. "The architecture in this place is distinctly unfriendly."

Frith stood up.

"You have explored this place? You have the map?"

"My dear man, when you have come to know this place as well as I do, you have no need for maps."

8

Sebastian felt as though a dark cloud had been lifted from his heart.

The whole thing had been Gallo's idea; break into the famous Citadel of Creos and carry off the loot. Simple enough, but no other adventurer had ever managed it – and that of course, was the point. A story to tell in the taverns that no one else could rival, and, Gallo insisted, they would have more offers of work than they knew what to do with.

Sebastian had been reluctant. For one thing, no one was paying them to do it. Usually they raided a tomb or a temple because some half-sane crackpot was after the sacred gem of something or other, but even your biggest crackpots steered well clear of the Citadel. And secondly, they were shorthanded; Wydrin was away visiting with her brother Jarath, and not expected back for weeks. He insisted they wait: to gather information, find a patron, give Wydrin a chance to join them. Anything rather than take on the Citadel underprepared.

And Gallo's patience, what little of it there was in the first place, had run out.

"If you had come when I asked you to, none of this would have happened," said Gallo. "I couldn't stand all that waiting and planning, Seb, you knew that. There were adventures to be had, places to be explored! Secrets to be uncovered. And, let me tell you, I have found a few."

Wydrin and Frith were following on behind, both looking a little frazzled, but Frith looked up at the mention of secrets.

"What is it you have found, exactly? I have paid your companions a great deal of money to explore this place, and if you have access…"

"All in good time, my white-haired friend!" Gallo called back over his shoulder. Lowering his voice, he leaned in to Sebastian. "Where did you find that one? He speaks like his tongue is made of silver but he looks like a mongrel's favourite pissing post."

Sebastian suppressed a chuckle.

"He is the Lord of the Blackwood, heir to Blackwood Keep. Fallen on hard times recently."

Gallo nodded sagely. He turned to Wydrin and Frith and gave them his most charming smile.

"You are tired, and hungry, and no doubt smelling quite terrible by now. I will take you to a place where we can rest for a while and eat. Then we can talk about what I have found here."

But that wasn't enough for Frith.

"How is it you are still here? You have been here weeks, by my reckoning, yet you look none the worse for it."

Gallo waved a hand at him dismissively.

"I shall get to that. Here, down these steps and then there will be time for questions."

They trooped down a winding staircase, so narrow that Sebastian's shoulders brushed the stones on either side, until they came to a tall, thin set of doors. Gallo pushed them open and threw his arms out to his sides in a gesture of welcome.

"I present to you, the banqueting hall of the mages! Come, sit and eat."

They stepped into the room beyond. Wydrin swore softly under her breath. Sebastian shook his head as if to clear it.

It was a long room of dark grey marble, with a huge table running the length of it, and a hundred chairs set for dinner. On the walls were great stained-glass windows that shimmered in a thousand different colours, casting a rainbow of lights onto the stone floor. There was no possible way daylight could reach them down here, and yet they shone as if a bright summer's day waited just outside. More extraordinary still was the contents of the table itself: it heaved with food.

"How is this possible?" asked Frith.

"Who cares?" cried Wydrin. "I'm half starved."

"A feast," said Sebastian as he approached the table. "Food fit for a king. For the mountain gods themselves."

There were whole roast pigs with apples in their mouths, their skins crisp and glistening with fat. There were silver platters full of rich red meats, and wooden bowls full of potatoes, carrots and parsnips, steam rising off them gently as if freshly cooked. Tureens of huge, rainbow-scaled fish with their heads still on nestled next to smaller bowls filled with the tiny salted shoaling fish of the Yellow Sea, and the famous blue lobsters of Crosshaven. There were red apples stuffed with spiced raisins; fat golden pastries filled with cream and dusted with sugar; huge loaves of crusty bread pierced with toasted seeds, and whole hams, pink and juicy. And all around were tankards, flagons, bottles and barrels of beer, ale, wine, mead, brandy and Tocar, the fiery drink native to Pathania.

Wydrin took a seat and began tearing into a loaf of bread with her hands, while Frith approached more cautiously. He picked up a goblet of wine and sniffed it.

"Magic?"

"You could say that." Gallo walked the length of the table, plucking an apple from a silver tureen and polishing it against his sleeve. "Go on, eat. It's not poisoned." He took a bite out of the apple and chewed with apparent relish. The crunch sounded very loud in the empty hall.

Sebastian realised how hungry he was. How long since they had eaten? He and Wydrin had grabbed a hurried breakfast of eggs and blood sausage at the Boiled Dog, but that had been so early the sun had barely been poking its shining brow above the horizon.

"It must be late by now," he said. "We've probably missed more than one meal."

With a lurch, Sebastian realised he had no idea what the time was, or even how long they had been inside the Citadel. Time was strange here, down in the dark between these secret walls, as though it were draining away down hidden cracks, pooling in unknown crevices. The thought made him uneasy, so he picked up a flagon of mead and took a long, deep swallow. It tasted of summer days, bright and unending.

"The mead is good, anyway," he said. Frith looked less than convinced, picking up a slice of ham and turning it over in his fingers, but Wydrin was already dragging the plate of blue lobster towards her, a silver fork held in one fist as if to harpoon it.

They sat and ate for a time, the drinking and chewing and swallowing filling up the need for conversation, until they could consume no more. Sebastian took a last gulp of the glorious mead and, setting down the tankard, mouthed the traditional prayer of thanks to Isu. Looking up, he saw Gallo staring at him, the ghost of a smile on his lips.

"You still do that, then," he said, pointing to the badge of Isu on Sebastian's cloak. "Still praying to your chilly mountain gods."

Sebastian rubbed the crumbs from his fingers, suppressing a sigh. He and Gallo had never agreed on the subject of Sebastian's faith.

"Enough of my little quirks, Gallo." Sebastian cleared his throat. "You've yet to explain how you're here, what you've found, or how you've existed in the Citadel all this time. I'm sure you have some stories you're dying to tell us."

"We need to know what you've found," put in Frith, leaning over his plate. The Lord of the Blackwood had eaten slowly and carefully, cutting up each piece of meat and using all the correct cutlery. "Have you seen a chamber, somewhere far beneath the central structure of the Citadel, containing a pool or a lake?"

Gallo nodded hurriedly.

"Yes, I have seen evidence of such. But let me tell it from the beginning, my friends. I understand I have a lot to explain."

Wydrin belched into her hand and waved at Sebastian to pass another bottle of the rich red wine.

"You talk, we'll drink," she said cheerily.

And so he did. Gallo told them of arriving in Krete, drunk on adventure and desperate to explore the Citadel, how he had paid off the Kretian Council with the money he and Sebastian had collected and hired a guide with what remained. Sebastian felt a flicker of annoyance at that, as Gallo passed over his betrayal as though it were a small thing. He told them how they had entered the Citadel with the aid of his explosives, and how he had lost his guide.

"How did you manage that?" asked Wydrin.

"There was a terrible creature hidden in the ceiling." For the first time a shadow passed over Gallo's face. "It reached down with inhuman arms and pulled poor Chednit up into the shadows. I didn't see what happened to him but I heard the screaming, and I saw the blood."

Sebastian stiffened, horrified to seehis friend in such pain.

"I'm sorry, Gallo."

Gallo nodded mournfully, staring down at his plate.

"Chednit was a good sort. Brave, even if it was braveness for the sake of coin."

"Nothing wrong with that," said Wydrin.

"He told me we should wait for you, Sebastian. He wanted another sword arm in that dark place. Perhaps he was right."

"What happened then?" The light from the lamps cast Frith's scarred face into sharp relief. There was a hunger in his eyes that Sebastian did not like.

"I wandered, lost." Gallo did not raise his eyes from the table. "For the longest time. My supplies ran low, my water ran out, but I couldn't bring myself to turn back, not after... not after what happened to Chednit. Not after taking my good friend's money. It was dark, but I eventually found places that were lit, like this one. I soon discovered that the map made no real sense, and so I moved listlessly from room to room, searching for something, anything, to make this adventure worthwhile. Eventually, just as I thought I would die of thirst, I found it."

"What about those strange little men in bandages? Very pale, dusty, sleep in glass tanks?" Wydrin broke in, holding up her goblet and swishing the wine around for emphasis.

"What?"

"We were attacked by a group of these beings," said Sebastian. "They tried to force us from the Citadel, and told us they were fighting a war. They called themselves Culoss, I believe."

Gallo smiled, although it looked false.

"The Citadel is full of wonders, but these I have not seen."

"Let him continue," demanded Frith.

"I lost track of time. I could have been wandering for days, weeks even. Just when I thought I would die down here and never feel the sweet kiss of sunlight on my face again, I found a room containing a number of huge, clay jars, each nearly as tall as a man and all sealed with a blue wax. It took a great deal of work to get the lid off the first jar, and by that time I was very weak, but when eventually I broke the seal I found a cache of wonders."

"Like what?" asked Frith.

"Treasures beyond counting, and enough gold to get even *your* blood flowing more quickly, your lordship." Gallo grinned, although the humour was lost on Frith's stony expression. "And secrets, more of them than I could count. There were maps to enchanted rooms such as this one, where the mages would come to eat their fill every day and never have to lift a finger for fetching or cooking. It saved me from certain starvation."

"What of the treasure?" said Wydrin. Her green eyes were wide, and Sebastian fancied he could almost see golden flecks glimmering there, reflections of a thousand gold coins. "Where is it all?"

"Too much to carry, my Copper Cat," Gallo said, "but I did keep this bow for myself." He indicated the fine longbow that had saved them. "And this was too special to leave behind." He drew a dagger from the belt at his waist and held it up to the light. It was an exquisite thing; the grip was covered in fine red leather and traced with golden wire, while blue sapphires and fire-bright rubies glittered on the narrow crossguard. Even the blade was enamelled gold and etched with strange runes, but for all its finery it was fearsomely sharp. Gallo laid it against a side of beef and the flesh parted as though the dagger were white-hot.

Wydrin was entranced.

"It is beautiful." Sebastian could see her imagining how it would look hanging at her waist, perhaps in place of one of her own claws. "And there are more like this?"

"Swords and daggers beyond counting, as well as crowns, coronets, necklaces and rings set with gems as big as your thumb, a thousand–"

"What of these maps?" asked Frith abruptly. "Did they show the location of a great lake?"

Gallo frowned again. There was something in that frown that looked a little forced to Sebastian and that made him uneasy.

"No, my white-haired friend, but there were other rooms with other jars, not far from here."

"Can you take us there?" said Frith.

"Hold on a moment, what about the treasure Gallo has already located?" said Wydrin. "I say we go and gather as much as we can now, before the Culoss come back."

"It might be useful to catalogue what is here," said Sebastian. "We can add to the map, share our information."

To his surprise, Gallo shook his head and stood up.

"Why go over old ground, when there is so much more to explore? Now that you are all here with me, this will be three times as enjoyable." Gallo flashed that grin of his again, and Sebastian couldn't help returning it.

"All right, but I'm not leaving this room without taking something to eat on the way." Wydrin unrolled a small sack from a loop on her belt and began filling it with bread rolls and honeyed pastries. "Sebastian, how do you feel about carrying a few bottles of that wine?"

9

The jars were every bit as impressive as Gallo had described. Frith, ignoring the dull ache in his leg, hobbled over to one and placed his gloved fingers against it. The jar was only a head shorter than himself, and wide enough in circumference for him to have climbed inside it and sat quite comfortably, had he been able to perform such a feat with a crippled leg. It was made of red clay, covered with an intricate pattern of swirls and circles. The longer Frith looked at them the more he thought that they had a meaning beyond decoration, but if they did, he doubted even a lifetime of staring would reveal it. The lid was sealed over with blue wax, smooth and somehow unpleasant to the touch, even through the leather of his gloves. He circled the jar, looking for clues as to what might be within.

"Have you seen these books?" said Sebastian. The big knight was standing by the wall, looking up at the library arrayed there, his face alight with wonder. And in truth, it was an extraordinary sight. The room they were in was small, but the ceiling was very high, and each wall was lined with bookshelves right up to the very top. They were clearly ancient, their spines crooked, and a good few of them were encrusted with mould. The books were of all shapes and sizes; a true treasure-trove of knowledge. Even the library at Blackwood Keep was not as well stocked, and Frith's father had spent years gathering his collection from all over Ede. At the thought of his father and his cosy, cared-for library, a shadow passed over his heart. No doubt the books were all gone by now, sold on to collectors across Litvania and beyond.

"They are strange, though," said Wydrin, who had joined Sebastian by the bookshelves. "Look, how would you reach those ones at the top? There are no ladders. And here –" she tried to pull one of the volumes from the shelf, disrupting a small civilisation of dust, but a thin metal chain had been poked through the spine, preventing it from being removed. She gave it a tug, only to discover that the chain passed through all of the books on that shelf, holding them all in place. "What is the point of a library if you can't read the books?"

"It hardly matters," said Gallo. He was pacing around the room, staring at the jars. "Are you not anxious to see what other secrets are held in these jars? They are not easy to open, I promise you, so best get to it."

Frith saw Wydrin raise her eyebrows.

"You can make a start, Gallo," she said. "Nothing's stopping you."

Gallo laughed, and held up his hands with the palms facing up.

"And deprive you of the discovery? I wouldn't dream of it."

Frith looked up at the rows and rows of books, and dismissed them. It would take an age to look through them all, even if they could get the volumes down from the shelves. The jars were a faster prospect, and if Gallo was correct, they could well contain the information he needed.

"He's right," he said, pulling a dagger from his belt. "Start removing the wax."

Wydrin gave him a poisonous look, but came over all the same.

It took them a good while to get into the first jar, just as Gallo warned; the wax was thick and ancient, dried so hard it was almost stone. Wydrin suggested just pushing the jar over so that it smashed against the flagstones, but Gallo spoke up against that quickly, and Frith agreed. They had no way of knowing what was inside, and they could be destroying something delicate with their impatience to get at it. Frith was thinking of the maps that could be in there, so frail and thin by now that a careless fingertip could cause them to crumble into dust, taking the location of the mages' secrets with them.

Eventually, Wydrin managed to get a large chunk of the wax off by pushing the edge of Frostling under an overhanging lip and wiggling it about, and after that it was easier. Beneath was a fabric seal covered with the same odd writing they had seen here and there all over the Citadel. Wydrin pushed the tip of her blade through it and tore it open with a loud ripping noise. A puff of dust made them all cough, and it was followed by a terrible stench.

Wydrin pressed the back of her hand to her nose, frowning.

"It smells like something died in there."

Gallo paced impatiently around them.

"Come along then, have a look. It's bound to smell a bit off. Thousands of years have passed."

Frith reached up and pulled the fabric back, looking eagerly down into the depths of the jar, so long hidden, but it was too dark to see anything clearly. The glinting of gold or jewels was conspicuously absent.

"It looks empty." He was unable to keep the frustration out of his voice.

"Here." Sebastian picked the jar up in both arms and tipped it forward. It was heavy, but it was barely a strain for the big knight. After a moment a pile of what looked like red and brown rags fell out onto the stone floor, and the smell of corruption and rotten meat increased tenfold. Sebastian grimaced as he set the jar down.

"If this was treasure once, it is no longer."

Wydrin bent to the rags and poked them with Frostling.

"I don't know what this is," she said after a moment. "But I don't think it was ever treasure, Sebastian."

Frith knelt next to her and removed his leather glove. He saw her glance at the ruined tips of his fingers, but he ignored the curious look and touched the pile of stinking matter. He felt no rough weave as he would expect to feel from a piece of cloth. It was tough and irregular, like leather, or dried meat. There was lots of it, enough to fill his arms if he tried to carry it away, although the gods only knew why anyone would want to do that. He stood, angry at this further distraction.

"This was a body once, or part of a body."

Wydrin took her blade away hurriedly.

"Why would the mages store a dead body in a jar?" asked Sebastian.

"It hardly matters," said Gallo. The three of them turned to look at him. The young blond man was agitated, pacing back and forth. There was a thin layer of sweat on his brow, despite the relative cool of the chamber. "Open the other jars, and quickly now. If there's nothing here we should move on. Quickly."

"Perhaps first we–"

"No!" His interruption was almost a shout, and Sebastian actually took a step back.

"Open the jars." And then he seemed to remember himself. The flashy smile made another appearance. "Please."

They did as he asked – more quickly now that they knew the method to get them open – but each contained only the same as the first. When they opened the fourth and final jar, there was a great rumble from beneath their feet, so violent that the dried remains jumped and shivered on the flagstones. Gallo was breathing hard and staring down at the ground as if he expected it to rise up and swallow him. Sweat was running down his cheeks.

"What was that?" said Wydrin. The chains that held the books together were trembling, and then one by one they snapped, throwing up little puffs of metallic dust. The rumbling died away, but as Frith opened his mouth to answer, the door on the far side of the chamber flew open and a Culoss came charging in, his mouth open wide with shock. He was followed by three more.

"You have broken the seals!" cried the first. "The final seals! She is stirring!"

"What are you talking about?" Wydrin had drawn both her daggers. "Have you come back for another dance, worm-men?"

Gallo was laughing.

"I am glad you find this amusing," snapped Frith. "But these creatures nearly killed us last time we met."

"Oh no," said Gallo. "The Culoss wouldn't do that. Would you?" he said, addressing them directly. He laughed again. "Spilt blood is far too dangerous in this place. Which reminds me." Moving faster than Frith would have believed possible, Gallo stepped up next to Sebastian and, drawing the wicked golden dagger from his belt, thrust the blade at his friend's neck. The enamelled brooch that held Sebastian's cloak turned the weapon from its killing thrust but the blade still sunk into the knight's breast. Blood, startlingly bright after so long in the dusty halls of the Citadel, poured forth in a red gush, spattering the floor and the clay jar in front of Sebastian. Frith saw the big knight's eyes go wide with shock and pain, and then he fell to his knees. His hands went to the hilt now sticking from the thick muscle below his breastbone.

Wydrin screamed wordlessly and turned on Gallo, her daggers a deadly blur, but the blond man danced out of reach. He was still laughing, and there was a manic and terrible light in his eyes.

Meanwhile, the Culoss were gathered around Sebastian on the floor.

"What have you done?" demanded Frith. The rumbling from below was back, only now it was falling and rising, falling and rising. Like a heartbeat.

"She rises," said Gallo. "She rises, and she's bringing an army with her."

Wydrin flew forward again, fury in her eyes, and this time Frostling found purchase on Gallo's arm, tearing into the flesh there, but he hardly seemed to feel it. Instead he turned and ran for the door.

Wydrin made to go after him, but Sebastian called her name from the floor. Already his voice was weak.

"Leave him," he said. The Culoss stood shoulder to shoulder, whispering frantically with each other.

"Why did he do that? Why?" Wydrin looked lost, her face very pale under the lamp light. Frith knelt by Sebastian, trying not to show the dismay on his face. The Culoss had torn a piece from the big knight's cloak and were pressing the fabric against the wound in his chest, but the front of his tunic was already soaked with blood, and it was rapidly pooling on the floor. Sebastian tried to lift himself up, but the pain was too great.

"Try not to move," said Frith.

"You," Wydrin grabbed hold of one of the Culoss and shook him fiercely, "you will tell me why he did that. What is going on here?"

For a moment it looked like the Culoss wasn't going to answer, but he exchanged a look with the others, and sighed.

"He was an agent of Y'Ruen, the last of the gods. Our prisoner."

"He wasn't," said Sebastian. His voice was little more than a ragged whisper. "He was my – friend. He wasn't an agent of anyone."

"Sebastian, don't talk," said Wydrin. She released the Culoss and put her hand on her friend's arm. "You'll only make it bleed more."

"Take the knife out," said one of the Culoss, the one who had been first through the door.

"No," said Frith. "If you remove the blade, he will bleed to death all the quicker. Tear the cloak into more strips, and then we will press the fabric to the wound. Pressure should help stem the flow." He took a deep, steadying breath. "But I want you to tell us the rest of it. Now."

They shifted the big knight round to reach him better. Sebastian grunted with the pain, but did not scream. Frith had to admire that; he had done plenty of screaming, down in the dungeons.

"Your friend with the golden hair. He was not an agent of Y'Ruen when he came here, no, no," said the Culoss as they tore Sebastian's cloak into long strips. Frith held a wad of the fabric to the wound. "He wandered the Citadel, and she takes her agents where she can find them. It does not cost her much to take a mind."

"I don't understand," said Wydrin. "What is this Y'Ruen?"

"She is the last god. She wants to be free." The Culoss wrung his hands together as he spoke. "For thousands of years Y'Ruen has been pushing at the boundaries, weakening the seals. Extending her influence. She is so close now. If this man dies–"

"You are telling us that this Y'Ruen is a god, or something equating that, and it is somewhere beneath us?" Frith could not keep the incredulity out of his voice. "If that was the case, *if the stories are true*, then where are the mages? Immortal, powerful beings sworn to keep the rebel gods trapped for ever?"

"They could not live for ever, although they tried." The Culoss shook his head slowly. "In the end, their lake no longer worked. They began to grow old and weak, as all men. That is why they made us. To keep watch after they were gone, but now–"

"But now you have broken the last four seals!" The Culoss busily tearing Sebastian's cloak into strips glared at them all. "The great final spell that is written in these books," he gestured at the mouldy library. "It is now useless."

"Why couldn't Gallo break the seals?" asked Wydrin. "He said he'd already broken into other jars..."

"Lies," snapped another of the Culoss. "She cannot touch the sacred seals, no, and neither can her agents. He needed you to do it."

"When the last of this man's life-blood falls onto the stones of the Citadel, Y'Ruen's prison will finally be broken," added the first Culoss.

"Then help us get him out of here," said Wydrin. "You know the way back better than us. If we hurry–"

"He will be dead before you see daylight."

They pulled Sebastian forward so that they could tie the bandages round his chest. The knight protested weakly.

"I'm stronger than I look. I can make it. I can."

"No time," said the first Culoss. He wiped his bloody fingers on his own dusty bandages. "There is only the lake now. Pray that it has lost none of its properties."

"The lake?" said Frith, sharply. "You know where it is?"

The Culoss nodded irritably.

"What lake? What are you talking about?" Wydrin pushed Sebastian's long black hair back from his face. There was blood on his lips.

Frith stood up.

"I'm talking about the whole reason I came here."

10

His weight was heavy on her shoulders, and the stench of his blood thick in her nostrils. Every now and then she would gag, but Wydrin was determined not to vomit. She had seen many men bleed out, of course she had. More often than not she had been the cause of it too, but the blood of a friend was different from the blood of an enemy.

Sebastian groaned. He wanted to lie down, he said, just for a quick rest. Once he was rested, he told them, he would feel much better and they would move more quickly.

"Here, hold this," she told him, pressing a bundle of fabric into the hand not resting against her shoulder. "Press it against your wound. You need to keep the pressure up."

He did as he was told, although sluggishly.

"How much further?" demanded Frith. Two of the Culoss were helping Wydrin carry Sebastian while the other two walked in front, leading them down passageway after passageway. The flagstones and bricks of the room with the jars had disappeared some time ago, to be replaced with tunnels carved straight out of the living rock. The echoes were strange here, and twice Wydrin had been convinced that something was following them. Their way was lit by strange gatherings of luminescent moss that had colonised the ceiling, giving everything a yellowed, watery hue.

"Not far now," said the lead Culoss. He'd told them that his name was Marshum. "How is the knight?"

Wydrin glanced up at Sebastian's face. He was staring down at the hilt of the dagger sticking out of his chest as though he didn't quite know what it was. His face was parchment white, and there were ominous dark circles under his eyes.

"How do you think he's doing? He's bleeding like a stuck pig!"

"He must not die," warned Marshum. "His life-blood must not be shed on these stones."

"I'm not that keen on the idea myself," said Sebastian, but so weakly only Wydrin could hear it.

They walked on. Wydrin, more than a head shorter than Sebastian, was soon sweating, her hair plastered to her forehead. *So heavy*, she thought. *I should tell him to leave the sword behind, but he'll need that. If I let him lose it I'll never hear the last of it.* Besides, she dare not stop, not even for a moment. If she did she wasn't sure she could get him up again, and then if what the Culoss said was true, they would all die down here. Instead, she concentrated on the ragged sound of Sebastian's breathing and the steady tap, tap, tap of Frith's walking stick; it apparently took a lot to tire the Lord of the Blackwood.

It was just as Wydrin could no longer feel her feet and her shoulders were screaming with agony, that the Culoss in front gave a small cry of triumph. They stumbled out of the tunnels and onto a set of wide stone steps. At first Wydrin wanted to kick them; what were they so excited about? More steps to shuffle down, so what? But then she heard Frith exclaim too, a hoarse bark of something that was almost laughter. Wydrin lifted her weary head, and for a brief second she forgot about the ache in her back and the blood soaking into her clothes.

They stood at the entrance of an enormous cavern, the biggest space she had ever seen. The ceiling was lost in darkness, the craggy walls to either side partially obscured by a rolling mist. And spreading out below them was the Mages' Lake.

"This is it!" cried Frith. "I knew I would find it."

"The Culoss found it," pointed out Wydrin, although in truth she barely knew what she was saying. She couldn't take her eyes off the lake. It was the bright blue of the Creosis Sea, shimmering under the hottest summer's day – no, brighter than that. It was lit from within with its own strange light, so that the surface fractured and glimmered like diamonds. After a few seconds she had to look away; the lake drew her eyes and seemed to feast on them, something that frightened her badly.

"Why is it moving?" she asked through numb lips. "Shouldn't it be still?"

"The magic contained within is as lively as ever," said Marshum. "Which is all to the good. Quickly now, we must get the knight into the water."

They began to shuffle down the steps, but Frith held up a hand.

"I will go first," he said. There was a hunger in his voice. "To test it. After all, we don't know how it might have changed over the last thousand years."

"Oh no," cried Marshum. "The power is limited. Only one can bathe in its magic, only one every ten years. The Mages made it so."

"Why would they do that?" The look on Frith's face was a dangerous one. Instinctively, Wydrin put a hand on the pommel of her dagger.

"To ensure that no single mage became more powerful than the others. The effects of the lake are – extreme, addictive. It would be much too tempting to go back again and again, growing younger and more powerful with each exposure. The mages made it so that once one of them had taken of its gifts, they would all have to wait another ten years before they could do it again."

"That cannot be!"

"It doesn't matter," Wydrin dragged Sebastian down another step, and another. The blue waters of the lake were lapping at the bottom of the steps, kissing them with jewelled lips. "Just give me a bloody hand, will you?"

The Culoss rushed to her aid, but Frith just stood very still. His grey eyes were wide. The light from the lake made them look full of tears.

"Help us, Frith!"

Beneath their feet the rumbling had returned, and it was growing stronger. Sebastian's eyes were closed now, and Wydrin feared she could no longer hear his breathing. *I can't hear it over my own, that's all*, she told herself. *There's still time.*

They were ten feet away from the waters when she saw Frith reach within his cloak. She knew what he was doing before she even saw the greasy green ball in his hand.

"No!" she screamed, but it was too late. Frith threw the bomb just in front of them and the explosion threw them all back. Wydrin fell awkwardly against the steps and whacked her arm so hard she lost all feeling in it, while Sebastian rolled away from her. Of the Culoss, only two remained; the others were a confusion of dust and torn bandages.

She lifted her head just in time to see Frith walk into the shimmering waters.

11

The bejewelled waters of the lake swept hungrily over Frith's boots, rising up over his ankles to his shins. His first confused impression was that it was hot, the temperature scalding him through the worn leather of his trousers – it was like a bath freshly drawn, too warm to be comfortable. The lights grew more lively, swarming around him like something alive, a shoal of hungry fish perhaps. He reached down and put his hands under the water – distantly he could hear Wydrin cursing him, but it was very far away – and his fingers tingled uncomfortably. Pulling off his gloves he could see that the tips of his fingers, scarred and wrinkled where Yellow-Eyed Rin had torn his fingernails off with pincers, were smoothing over. There was an odd pressure, and then a thin ellipsis of a hard material began to push through the flesh. His nails were growing back.

"Yes!" he cried. "It is working. I will be whole again…"

There was a tremendous crash from behind him, just as though the sky were caving in, and he heard Wydrin's yelling take on a note of panic, but nothing could tear his gaze from the rippling waters. He thought he could hear voices now, whispering from further out in the lake.

"Who are you?" Frith took a few steps forward. The poorly healed bones in his leg began to throb, and he stumbled. "What do you want?"

"What do *you* want?" echoed the whispering voices.

"Your power, your strength," he answered. The water was up to his waist now, rushing to run phantom fingers over every scar and fractured bone. He thought of Sebastian's pale face and his blood-soaked tunic, but almost immediately the image was replaced with another; his younger brother Tristan, his small body beaten and broken. There was no turning back now.

"Then take it," answered the mages as one.

There was a deafening crackle and Frith was filled with an excruciating pain. He fell to his knees in the lake so that the water came up to his chin, filling his mouth, but still he screamed. A thousand hot pokers seared his skin, a thousand knives gouged his flesh. Every bone felt as though they had shattered and the shards were burrowing their way out of his body.

"Are you strong enough, Aaron Frith, Lord of the Blackwood? You are no mage." The voices were full of mockery, he realised, somewhere underneath the pain. "The lake will destroy you."

Frith, unable to move or even to think beyond the agony, pitched forward and felt the shimmering waters close over his head. The last thing he heard before the water plugged his ears was a hundred newly opened throats, screaming for victory.

12

Wydrin pulled Sebastian upright, wincing at the sharp pain in her arm, but the big knight only slumped back down onto the steps, his eyes rolling up to the whites.

"Is he...? He hasn't...?"

"We will know soon," said Marshum. Around them the rumble was now a continuous roar. Dust and debris, shaken loose by the commotion, was floating down from the ceiling to cover them in a thin grey blanket. Stones and rocks jumped loose from the steps, so that dark holes appeared all around them.

"This god," shouted Wydrin. "What is it, exactly?"

"A terrible being," said Marshum. "A creature of unspeakable evil. She lives only to feast and destroy, and only ruin brings pleasure to her heart."

"Yes, but what *is it*? I would feel a lot better if I had some idea of what was about to climb up through the floor at me."

"Oh, it won't be her," said the second Culoss. The blast from Frith's bomb had torn away some of the bandages from his left side, leaving him limping and ragged. "She will send her army up first."

"Her army?" Wydrin looked down at the nearest hole. There was movement there, down in the dark. "These mages can't have been very wise, to have interred an army down there with her."

"They did not," snapped Marshum. "She has been breeding them."

At that moment, the first of the soldiers arrived. A slim arm, green as a spring apple, appeared over the nearest hole. The hands were long and sharp, ending in curving black claws. The hand scrabbled for purchase and the rest of the creature climbed into view. It was human in shape and aspect, even beautiful in a way, tall and lithe, with a long elegant face and large, almond-shaped eyes that were entirely yellow save for a slim black slit running down the centre. *Snake's eyes*, thought Wydrin, her stomach turning over. There were luminescent scales on the creature's arms, forehead and shoulders, and long silvery white hair flowed down its back. The armour it wore looked almost a living thing itself; huge golden scales twisted and curved to fit the sharp angles of the creature, and where that was too cumbersome a fine shimmering mail covered the body, so delicate it looked like silver cloth. The soldier smiled, revealing white, pointed teeth.

Behind the beautiful soldier, more were appearing every second, every one as silvered and perfect as the last. And each carried a long thin sword made of blue crystal. As they swung their weapons, the air filled with a sonorous whine.

"They're all… It's an army of women."

"Not women," said Marshum. "Not close to human, no."

Wydrin stumbled away from them, pulling Sebastian with her down towards the edge of the lake. The scaled soldiers watched closely, their finely angled faces breaking into a hundred identical smiles. There were more coming through the door now, edging down the steps. Their bare feet were eerily quiet on the stone.

Pushing Sebastian's limp body behind her, Wydrin drew both her daggers and carefully kissed their hilts. Watching the warriors approach, she noticed that some of them weren't quite as finished as the others – a few were missing their armour, some their fine white hair – but when their feet touched the crimson trail left by Sebastian's wound, golden scales would push from their bodies as though they were made of dough, and long claws sprouted from the ends of their fingers.

Wydrin took a deep breath, and looked inside herself for a calm place, a place to stand. She remembered her father, black-bearded and booming, taking her out in the little cog *Haven's Champion* for a quick jaunt across the Stony Sea.

"Find a quiet place inside you, my little kit," he had said. "Place your feet against the deck and listen to the sea. She'll tell you all you need to know."

"He was full of bilge, my father, but he was right about that," she said in a low voice. Marshum and the ragged Culoss looked up at her in confusion, but she shook her head. "Never mind. Are you ready?"

"It is hopeless," stammered Marshum. "The army has risen. She will be close behind."

The scaled warriors edged closer, with looks of almost polite curiosity on their beautiful faces. Wydrin shrugged.

"That may well be, but I'm not dying down here without taking a few of these bitches with me."

The Culoss exchanged a look, and then produced their blades from the palms of their hands in one fluid movement. Wydrin grinned.

"That's the spirit."

As if sensing their intent, the closest scaled warrior stepped up and swung her blue crystal sword at Wydrin, but the Copper Cat evaded it easily, bringing her own daggers around to clash against the blade. The steel striking against the crystal made a strange, high-pitched whine and the scaled warrior took a step back, her teeth bared.

"Not heard the ring of steel before, huh?"

Wydrin reached in under her guard and Frostling pricked at the pale skin. Blood as deep and green as emeralds bubbled up at the warrior's waist, and Wydrin stepped away before she could retaliate.

"They bleed," she told the Culoss. "They can be killed." She showed them the green blood on her dagger, but when she looked up, the warrior she had cut was laughing. The light from the lake glittered off her pointy teeth.

"These ones fight," she said. Her voice was warm and slightly husky, a voice dipped in honey and rolled in smoke. "Mother will enjoy that."

"What are you supposed to be, anyway?" called Wydrin. "Your armour is gaudier than a tart's jewellery box."

"I am the Two Hundred and Eighty-First. We carry your death on our blades, and we are many."

As one, the scaled warriors advanced, blue crystal blades flashing. Wydrin and the Culoss found themselves with their backs to the lake, and there was nothing to it but to fight. *It could be worse*, thought Wydrin. *This is a death worthy of a hundred stories.*

Grinning, she became a blur of arms and steel as she threw off one attack after another, slicing green flesh where she could and watching for the spatter of green blood on the stones. Steel clashed against crystal until the strange ringing became a sort of music, echoing in the cavernous room. The Culoss were as swift and deadly as they had been back in their hibernation chamber, and they carved limbs from the scaled warriors as though they were slicing through saplings in a wood, but all the time more snake-eyed women were climbing through the holes in the steps.

A blue flash skimmed past Wydrin's stomach and she staggered backwards into the lake to avoid disembowelment. The glittering waters splashed harmlessly against her ankles, and she had a moment to wonder whether they were truly as magical as the Culoss claimed, but then the next scaled woman was upon her, all pointed teeth and streaming white hair. Wydrin pushed her blow aside and thrust Frostling up at her face; the warrior looked rather less beautiful with a pair of ruined eyes, and she fell head first into the water.

"Good thing this place isn't healing any more," she shouted to Marshum and the ragged Culoss, "or the bastards would never stay down!" She turned back to face the next opponent only for her vision to explode in a confusion of black stars. Dimly she felt the warm rush of blood across her face, and suddenly it was difficult to tell which way was up and which was down.

Wydrin swore bitterly and blindly held her daggers up in front of her.

Within the waters of the lake, Lord Frith burned.

A thousand tiny demons with teeth made of fire nibbled at every inch of his skin. He was curled up in a ball, trying to keep his limbs close, trying to force the pain away, but it was impossible. Distantly he could hear the mages laughing as he suffered.

Why? he demanded, with the tiny part of his mind the pain had not consumed. *You have no need of the power any longer, why?*

Because you are no mage, they answered. *You are not strong enough, little man. You presume to greatness, and for that you will suffer.*

Suffer? He remembered his father's face the last time he'd seen it, contorted with fear and rage as the doors crashed down. He remembered the dungeon, the small room that smelt of blood and shit, the podgy but deft fingers of Yellow-Eyed Rin. The knives that had danced across his skin, the glowing red metal that had caressed his flesh, over and over and over again. He thought of the fat man's watery yellow eyes, looking down at his suffering with pleasure. With satisfaction. With greed.

A wave of rage overcame him then, and with wonder he realised it was hotter than the pain. More real than the pain. He sought it, caught it within his breast and nurtured it.

They are enjoying this, he told himself. *They are watching me writhe and weep and it feeds them.* The fury became a white-hot heat, and the pain became a bellows. *I have faced this before, and it didn't end me then, either.*

Instead of fighting the pain, he welcomed it. Every nerve ending in his body lit up and sang. So much pain that he thought his mind might come away from its tethers entirely and leave him gibbering in the centre of the lake, but no, he was still there. He was stronger than it.

With a grunt, he rose shaking from the waters. Inside his head he heard the gasps of the mages. Their confusion and terror was as sweet as the taste of a fine wine in the back of his throat.

How can you do this? they screamed. *You are no mage!*

He blinked the water from his eyes and looked down at his hands. The fingernails had all grown back, his leg no longer stabbed with pain when he leaned his weight on it, and when he pressed a hand to the side of his head… a wonder! His ear, as good as new. But it was more than that – there was a sense of coiled energy within his chest, a churning of light and sound that he could almost see. All the hair on his arms was standing on end, his skin rigid with goosebumps. And the pain was gone. All of it. He began to laugh, until he saw the scene around him.

Sebastian lay at the edge of the lake, his face turned towards the distant door, while Wydrin stood over his body. The two Culoss were there too, their blades flashing away as they fought off the strangest-looking army Frith had ever seen. Hundreds of women in golden armour were pressing through the doors with icy-blue swords clutched in their hands. Their skin was as green as jade, and their faces seemingly finely carved from that rare stone. He grasped for his sword, only to find he'd lost it in the waters of the lake.

"Wydrin! We need to retreat!"

Wydrin turned her head at the sound of his voice, a spasm of anger briefly replacing the fear on her face.

"You!" she cried. "You dirty, low, cowardly–"

The Culoss were whirling like spinning tops, keeping the terrible warriors at bay, and Wydrin had done her fair share of fighting, too, judging by the thick green fluid encrusting her daggers, but she'd also taken a blow to the head, and one side of her face was slick with blood. The warriors appeared to be unending, but they seemed strangely reluctant to come near the blue lake despite the fact that it would take mere seconds to outflank the small group.

"Get behind me," he shouted as he splashed up to them. "Get into the lake, there's nothing in there to harm us now."

Wydrin staggered back, deflecting a series of blows from one of the soldiers almost instinctively. Her arms were trembling with the effort now.

"Why should I do anything you say?"

"Just do it!"

She must have seen something in his face then, a hint of what he intended to do, because instead of arguing further she put her daggers back in their sheaths and took hold of Sebastian, dragging him deeper into the water but taking care to keep his head above it. At the sight of the knight, his tunic soaked in blood, Frith felt his stomach turn over. Marshum and the ragged Culoss followed suit, looking up at Frith with wide dark eyes.

"What have you done?" asked Marshum.

Frith shook his head, unable to explain. The warriors advanced up to the edge of the lake and stopped.

"Come and fight," called one of the warriors at the front. She bared long pointed teeth at Frith, running a dark green tongue over them suggestively. "We like the taste of your blood, little warm things."

"Not bloody likely," shouted Wydrin back. "How about you behave like good little snakes and slither back underground?"

The warrior laughed, and reached behind her to pull a slim golden bow from her back. Amongst the scaled golden armour the bows had been well camouflaged, and as Frith watched the whole front line began to draw them, notching short, barbed arrows.

"Well, we're dead," said Wydrin.

"No," said Frith. There was something growing within him, an extension of the light and power that had been with him since he'd been submerged under the lake. He felt it building, like a kettle of stew left on the stove too long, or water surging up from a well during flood season. He held out his hands in front of him and let the sensation over take him. "They are."

There was a tremendous flash of light and a great wave of blue fire rolled out from the palms of his hands, surging towards the crowd of green warriors. Some of them dropped their bows, others turned to run, but found only hundreds of their sisters in their way. The fire was on them in an instant and the great cavern filled with screams as their flesh melted away from their bones, and their heads lit up like torches.

Frith laughed. The palms of his hands were itching.

"How did you do that?" asked Wydrin, her voice shrill with astonishment, and Frith tried to tell her, but she could not hear it over the screaming of the warriors. Those still alive were now retreating for the far door, swords held over their heads. And there was another sound. A deep and ominous rumble from beneath their feet.

"She is stirring," said Marshum. "She is not completely free yet, I do not know…"

Frith knelt by Sebastian and took hold of the big knight's face between his fingers. He was as white as paper and the skin around his eyes was bruised a deep purple, but he could feel the slither of life still there, a tiny hot thread amongst all that cold.

"He's still alive, but barely."

"Then we need to get out of here." Wydrin looked back towards the far doors, but the snake warriors were still crowded there, watching them with yellow eyes. *They will gain their courage again soon enough,* thought Frith, *and then what?* Now that the adrenaline was fading, his legs felt weak and his head was spinning. Could he keep up the fireballs long enough to fight to the surface? Long enough for Sebastian not to lose his grip on life on the way out? He thought not.

Instead he searched the new knowledge he'd wrestled from the mages. It was strange, he did not feel as though he'd learned anything new, but he could remember things about the Citadel, things he hadn't known before. And he thought there was a way out, after all.

"I'm going to bring the ceiling down," he told them.

"*What?*" The portion of Wydrin's face that was not covered in blood was milk white. "Did that little soak in the lake soften your brain?"

"Just watch, and be ready to run."

The simmering ball of light and noise had already begun to grow again in his belly. Frith looked up at the ceiling and tried to see it clearly. The smoke from the fire and the height of the cavern made that difficult, but he knew it was there, and the mages knew its weaknesses. He reached out with his mind and he could *feel* the cracks up there, rents and fissures torn by the passage of time. For thousands of years the cavern had supported the weight of the Citadel, for thousands of years it had been strong, solid. And now it was time for it to come down.

Light leapt up out of his hands before he even knew what he was doing, and this time it looked like forked lightning, brilliant and white. It travelled up to the distant ceiling and licked along the surface. For a few seconds they could all see it – black rock and weathered stalactites lit up in harsh blacks and whites – and then it was gone. Wydrin was letting fly a long series of colourful curses. Frith took a deep breath. He needed to concentrate. *Let's see what I can do.*

Heat streamed out of Frith's fingers towards the ceiling. His heart raced inside his chest so fast that he could hardly breathe, and for a brief second he could feel the broken surface of the ceiling under his fingertips. The fissure was a dark, secret place; he could sense the emptiness behind the rock, the places where the stone was weak. All it took was a little pressure…

Wydrin closed her eyes against the blinding light, but they were soon forced open again when a series of small explosions turned the lake into a frenzy of waves. There was an ear-splitting crash and suddenly it was as though they were being lifted towards the ceiling on a surge of water. It was only when the scaled warriors began to shriek that she realised it was the ceiling coming down towards them.

She flung herself over Sebastian's body, painfully aware that such last-minute heroics were pointless, and then it all went black.

It was the sun that woke her. It was a gentle, warm hand on her head, and for a few moments she imagined she was back on the deck of the *Haven's Champion*, sailing on a hot day. She even fancied she could taste the salt…

Wydrin opened her eyes to blue sky and rubble. The Citadel, having stood for thousands of years, was now a mountain of broken masonry and shattered red brick. Pulling herself to her feet she saw that they had been thrown down onto the Sea-Glass Road. Frith was there, standing and looking down at his hands like he'd never seen them before, and Sebastian was lying a few feet away. Of the Culoss there was no sign. They were all covered in a thick layer of dust.

"What on earth did you do?"

Frith looked up at her. The long twisting scar from his face was gone, and he was standing straight and true, but his hair was still bone white.

He looked like he was trying to formulate an answer, but then Wydrin noticed something behind him, in the ruins of the Citadel. Red against red.

She ran back up the Sea-Glass Road, weaving through the debris and ignoring the throbbing in her head. Amongst the broken stones of the Citadel were four equally broken bodies, dressed in brown leather armour. A shattered spear still poked from the hand of one of them.

"The guards," she said. Her stomach turned over slowly. "They're all dead, just look at them. Didn't the Culoss say...?"

A tremendous roar from below caused the words to die in her throat. The ground around them began to shake, and a series of huge cracks ran down the Sea-Glass Road like the lightning that had brought down the Citadel.

"She's coming," said Frith. "We have to get out of here."

"What is *she*?" cried Wydrin. The rubble began to churn, throwing pieces of rock and stone down at them as something huge began to push its way up from below. There was another roar, turning Wydrin's blood cold. It was the roar of something that ate creatures her size as an appetiser. And she couldn't drag her eyes away from it.

An enormous reptilian head pushed through the ruin of the Citadel. It was covered in shining scales, each as deep a blue as the ocean. Its huge yellow eyes were full of fire, and when it opened its mouth a belch of greasy flame shot forth. Y'Ruen pulled herself free of the rubble and flapped a pair of leathery wings, each as big as the sails on Wydrin's father's largest boat.

"A dragon," said Wydrin weakly. She could feel all the strength draining from her legs, despite her brain's frantic instructions to *run*.

"A dragon, a god, what does it matter?" Frith was next to her, and as Y'Ruen turned her huge fiery eyes upon them he slipped an arm around her waist and pulled her close to him. She had a second to notice that already he had hold of Sebastian by his cloak before the desert sky began to distort and twist.

"What are you doing?!"

"Taking us away. Now hold on."

Before they vanished from the Sea-Glass Road, Wydrin twisted her head for one last look at the monster they had unleashed. Distantly she could hear screaming as the city of Krete awoke to its long-neglected guest.

Y'Ruen roared, blue scales winking in the sun, and the city began to burn.

PART TWO

Children of the Fog

13

The Thirty-Third walked down the cobbled road, her bare feet silent against the stones. Across the way she could just make out the slim shape of her brood sister, the Ninety-Seventh, crouched over something twitching on the floor. It was making noises, and she could feel her sister's pleasure as a warm space in her mind. The Thirty-Third smiled, tasting smoke on her tongue.

They had no names, the brood army, but the Thirty-Third knew where she had been spawned, and when. She had grown in the cold and dark over many long years, nestled closely to her sisters, tasting their minds all around her until she knew each of them without needing to look at their faces. There were those who were before her, and those who were after, and that was all. And Mother, of course.

A small shape came careening out of an open doorway, skidding to a halt in front of her. Its eyes were wide with panic, and immediately the Thirty-Third was in pursuit. There was no need to think; the creature was small and warm and terrified, a thing of prey. It made the mistake of turning and running back into the darkened household, and the Thirty-Third followed.

The family had gathered in the parlour, and were now huddled together around the remains of the dining table. The Thirty-Third could see the vestiges of relief on the mother's face, relief at the return of her son who had so foolishly run away. The Thirty-Third watched as the tatters of this emotion were replaced with flat terror. It was fascinating, really. The mother gathered her son into her arms, pressing him to her skirts.

"Hello," said the Thirty-Third. It was interesting to speak. Each word was a new flavour.

"Get out." The father was a skinny man with a shining bald spot poking through the wisps of brown hair on his head. He was crooked from a lifetime of pushing carts and she could see from the glassy look in his eyes that he'd never needed to be brave before, but now here he was, doing it anyway. She grinned. "Get out and leave us alone," he said again.

The Thirty-Third drew her sword. It was made of blue crystal, and it hummed as it slid against the golden scabbard. The family shuddered as one at the noise; they'd all heard that sound in the last few hours, and already knew what it meant. The Thirty-Third knelt and placed it on the floor in front of her feet.

"I am only here to talk," she said, in what she hoped was a friendly tone. The boy whined, and twisted his fists into his mother's apron. "It is a new thing, this… talking. I wish to ask you questions, hear your answers, and then you can go, yes?"

The man and woman exchanged a look. There was hope in that look, a tiny candlelight you could never quite put out. It was one of the things she was learning about them.

"We can go?" asked the woman.

"Yes. Tell me, what is the boy's name?" She pointed to the child with one delicately clawed finger.

"Ben, his name is Ben." Now that they'd grasped the idea, they were eager to run with it. The man nodded and even smiled, just as though all his neighbours weren't dead and the city burning. "Our lad, he's just had his ninth birthday."

"Really?" The Thirty-Third felt genuine delight at that. It was similar to the feeling of satisfaction that came when something previously unbroken snapped under her foot. "So have I! Well, my first. My first birthday."

"That's nice," said the woman. Her voice was tight.

"And you live here, in this city." The Thirty-Third gestured around at the four walls of the small room. "What does that mean, to live in the city?"

The tentative smile on the man's face froze, becoming a mask of something else. He didn't understand the question, she could see that, and he knew that failing to answer would be dangerous.

"I don't – what do you mean?"

She took a step towards them, and as one they shuffled back. She smiled a little wider.

"You build things, make things, and then put them all together in one place, and then eat and sleep and rut and die next to each other. Why is that?"

"It's – this is Krete. There have been people here for thousands of years, it's a place of great civilisation. There was the Citadel..." he cast around for something else but found nothing.

"Yes, there was," agreed the Thirty-Third. "I am done. You may go." She gestured to the doorway behind her.

"We can leave?" asked the woman. She had not once taken her eyes from the green-skinned soldier during the conversation. "You'll just let us go?"

"By all means," said the Thirty-Third, and then felt pleased with herself. She was picking up their phrases already. Or had that come from somewhere inside? "The boy first, please. Send him out the front and follow on behind. If you are quick and do not draw attention to yourselves, my sisters may not catch you."

"And you won't hurt us?" asked the woman, but already she was pushing the boy beyond the table, her hands on his shoulders. "No tricks?"

"No tricks," agreed the Thirty-Third, affably enough. "My sword is on the floor."

The child, Ben, shuffled forward a few steps at a time. He glanced at the empty doorway, to the tall soldier with the pointed teeth, and then back to the doorway.

"Go, Ben," said the father, with forced cheeriness. "We'll see you outside."

"Do as your father says, Ben," said the Thirty-Third in a solemn voice, but as he passed close to her she reached out with her clawed hands as if to caress his cheek and tore out his throat instead. The hot blood soaked her arm to the elbow, and she felt that warm sensation of satisfaction again. She turned to the parents just as the mother started screaming.

The sword only sped up the process, after all.

Outside, the streets were bright with fire. The Thirty-Third, now full and indolent as a snake, stood and looked into the billowing smoke. She was thinking about the questions she had asked, and some of the things she'd said.

"By all means," she murmured to herself. The words were both strange and not strange. There was someone else with her, in her blood, something that was not her mother. She knew it as well as she knew the faces of her brood sisters.

"We carry you with us, Father," she said to the bloodstained cobbles. "Can you feel it?"

Lost in a nightmare of blood and fire and pain, Sebastian heard the voice that called him father – and felt his heart stop.

14

Wydrin forced her eyes open and stared up into a purple sky framed with black branches.

Enormous trees loomed to either side, with gnarled trunks and branches filled with slick, dark green leaves. Bulbous populations of fungi crouched within the roots, like pale, watchful children, and wind moved mournfully through the treetops. Normally Wydrin disliked asking obvious questions, but on this occasion she felt she could hardly avoid it.

"Where am I?"

There was no answer.

Krete had the aroma of a slop bucket left in the sun but the air here was fresh and clean. There was soil beneath her, dark and moist. She ran her fingers through it, taking in the smell of mud and trees, the deep earthy scent of an old place long guarded by nature. The dusty ruins of Krete had been replaced by a silent forest, and the dark skies above were mercifully empty of dragons.

She sat up, and all the aches and pains came flooding back. There was a sharp throbbing in her arm that was probably a fracture, and the top of her head was sore where one of those green bitches had surprised her. She looked down and was surprised to see that she was bloody all over. A few more memories clicked into place.

"Sebastian!"

She scrambled to her feet. They were near a narrow ditch, fringed with ferns and squat bushes. A wave of dizziness caused her to stagger, and she spotted Frith lying off to one side, his white hair in disarray and his clothes still damp from the lake. He was rubbing his eyes with trembling hands. Sebastian lay on his front, some distance from the pair of them. He wasn't moving.

She ran to his side and pulled him round to face her. The violence of their journey had removed the dagger, but his body felt boneless, and too heavy.

"Wake up!" She shook him by the shoulders. "We're out of there now. We're out of the Citadel!"

"That will not help him."

Frith appeared at her shoulder. There was a smudge of dirt on his cheek. Wydrin narrowed her eyes and punched him hard in the face. Frith went flying backwards into the mud.

"You!" She dropped Sebastian and went after Frith, her fists tingling. "You let him die!"

"Wait." There was blood running from his lip. He held up a hand to ward her off. "I know how to help him."

Wydrin pulled Frostling from its scabbard. "Your lies won't save that pretty throat of yours now, princeling."

"The mages, there must be a healing spell, don't you see?" Frith got to his feet warily, watching the blade. "Let me try, at least. If I cannot do it, then you can still cut my throat."

Wydrin paused, anger giving way to hope. Sebastian would have advised caution, would have told her to calm down and give the princeling a chance. Stupid Sebastian. Reluctantly, she sheathed the dagger.

"Go on, then," she said, trying not to let the fear show in her voice. "But I hope your mage's tricks are effective, for your sake."

Frith went to Sebastian's side without looking at her, and took the big knight's head between his hands.

"See if you can open his eyes," he said in a low voice.

Wydrin did as he instructed, although her stomach turned over anew when she pulled Sebastian's eyelids up and saw the lifeless gaze they shielded. His blue eyes looked black in what little light there was.

"Good," said Frith. He undid the straps that held Sebastian's chainmail in place and pulled back the fleece beneath until the wound was revealed. The cut was small but deep, the skin there saturated with blood. Pressing his fingers against the wound, Frith bent his head as if in prayer.

"What are you saying?" asked Wydrin.

He spared her an angry glance.

"I'm not saying anything, fool. Be quiet and let me think."

Wydrin briefly considered punching him again, but decided to let him do his work. After a few moments, during which it seemed to Wydrin that the forest grew unnaturally quiet, a soft rose light grew from the spaces between Frith's fingers. It crawled over Sebastian's bare chest like honey, and Wydrin saw the edges of the wound begin to close up.

"It's working," she said, but Frith paid her no attention. He was sweating now, she saw, long strands of his thin white hair sticking to his forehead with it, and he was trembling all over. The pink light grew under his hands until it was so bright Wydrin could barely look at it.

"It's difficult to control..." he said, although Wydrin didn't think he was talking to her. "I don't remember. It's different."

After a few minutes the light began to throb rhythmically, and his eyes widened in surprise.

"There!" he gasped. Lifting his hands up from the wound the skin was smooth again. Sebastian jerked violently and started coughing, while Frith looked down at his hands in wonder.

His eyes met Wydrin's, and the smallest of smiles touched his lips.

"I could feel it rising up inside me, like a vast tide. Like the lake." His voice became distant, as though he were walking away from her down a long tunnel. "I think..." And with that his eyes rolled up into his head and he fell backwards into the mud for a second time. After a few moments Sebastian sat up, rubbing his head. He looked down at his blood-soaked clothes, and then to the prone form next to him.

"What happened to Lord Frith?" he asked, his voice little more than a croak.

Wydrin sighed.

"The princeling is so overcome with joy at your recovery he has, in fact, passed out at your feet." She paused, and punched Sebastian lightly on the arm. "It is good to see you up and about, though. Want to help me figure out where we are?"

15

"You've done what?"

They were sitting around a small fire, huddling close to the flames. It had taken a while to get it going, with Wydrin cursing the damp forest in a colourful manner for many minutes, until, finally, a few weak flames had shown against the all-too green branches they had gathered together. Sebastian had helped as best he could, despite Wydrin's insistence that he sit still and gather his strength. In truth, he felt as well as he ever had. The terrible burning pain he had been dimly aware of since Gallo had stabbed him had completely gone, and even the aches and pains he might have expected to feel after the fight with the Culoss were not there.

"Where else would you propose we go?" said Frith. Now he was awake he appeared to be in a foul mood. Sebastian suspected he was embarrassed by his fainting fit. "Returning to Litvania was my goal all along."

"So you threw us back into the middle of this gods-forsaken wood? Wouldn't your big cosy castle have been a little more useful?" Wydrin snorted and poked at the fire with a stick. Frith glowered at her.

"This is not an exact science. I don't know if you recall, but we were rather in danger of being eaten by an enormous dragon at the time."

"Yes, about that," said Sebastian. "What do you propose we do about it?"

He watched Frith and Wydrin exchange a look, their bickering temporarily forgotten.

"Do?" asked Frith. "What do you mean?"

Sebastian looked up at the sky. It was full dark now, and the stars were largely obscured by clouds, but here and there he could see a pinprick of light. They made him think of eyes, watching them.

"We unleashed a *monster*." He met Frith's gaze, and then Wydrin's, who was watching him carefully. "Worse than that, an entire army of monsters. It's our *fault*. We have to go back and stop it. What do you suppose happened to Krete after we left? To the people that live there?"

"I'm sure I don't know," said Frith. There was a new chill to his voice and Sebastian realised he would get little help in that direction. "The City Guard will deal with it, I expect. Either way, my concerns lie here, in this forest. My castle is still in the hands of the People's Republic of Istria, and now that I have the means" – he held up his hands as if they might explode at any moment – "I intend to take it back. What you two do is of no concern to me. Go back to Creos, if you wish, and enjoy slaying your dragon."

"He's got a point, Seb," said Wydrin. "We are… what, a thousand leagues from Creos now? More than that, probably. What can we do? Besides," she turned back to Frith and kicked his boot, "the princeling here still owes us money. As far as I'm concerned, the job is done."

Frith scowled.

"Once I have my castle back you will have your coin, wench."

Sebastian bit down a protest, turning a hot chestnut over in his fingers. They had told him what had happened while he'd been unconscious, sharing the details of the lake under the Citadel and the last desperate stand of Wydrin and the Culoss against the scaled warriors (at which point Wydrin had shared her opinion on Frith's actions in long and withering detail), and they had told him of the dragon that crawled out of the ruins of the Citadel afterwards; even Frith had seemed awed by it, shaking his head slowly as he described the creature's eyes of boiling yellow fire. What Sebastian couldn't tell them was how *he knew all this already*. He'd felt the movement of the scaled soldiers in his own blood, felt the rise of the creature called Y'Ruen into the sunlight for the first time in millennia. If he closed his eyes for more than a few seconds he could almost see them; the shining crystal of their swords streaked with blood, the skies over Creos a baleful orange as everything burned. Y'Ruen had to be stopped, but Wydrin was right. *How?*

She and Frith were arguing again. He dragged his attention back to the fire with effort.

"… how you expect to do that, anyway?"

"You have seen what I am capable of," spat Frith. "I destroyed the Citadel."

"I'm assuming that's not what you want to do with your castle?" replied Wydrin, grinning wickedly. "Be a bit of a wasted effort, really."

"I don't need to discuss my plans with the likes of you."

"Besides, are you really sure it's worth it?" Wydrin gestured to the black trees rising around them like sentinels. A bitter cold had come with the night and now tendrils of mist were swirling around the trunks, like cautious ghosts come to inspect the visitors.

"And what do you mean by that?"

"Well, you know –" Wydrin shrugged, and picked at the blood drying in her hair. "It's a bit, you know. Lots of trees, which is nice, if you like trees. Big, solid-looking trees. But that's about it. If I were you, I'd write it off as a loss and go and find something more interesting to do. Crosshaven is always looking for enterprising men with money in their pockets and a talent for destruction."

Frith glared at her. He stood up abruptly, his white hair falling over his forehead and obscuring the outrage in his eyes.

"I'm going for a walk." And with that he stalked off between the trees, his shoulders as narrow as a knife blade.

Wydrin caught Sebastian's eye, a look of polite astonishment on her face that soon disintegrated into laughter. Despite himself, Sebastian joined her.

"You've done it now."

"Oh, well, it's the least he deserves." The mirth faded and her face became serious again. "He really would have left you to die, Seb. Me as well, although I'm not saying I couldn't have fought my way through those pointy-toothed devils."

"Perhaps he had a plan all along," said Sebastian, although he didn't really believe that. "And I suspect that split lip of his is your doing?"

Wydrin tipped her head to one side.

"Like I said, it's the least he deserves."

"Either way, he shouldn't be out in that by himself." Sebastian nodded towards the trees where he had vanished. The dark had closed over the young lord like a curtain. "The Blackwood isn't the friendliest of forests. Wolves, bears. There will be all sorts of predators out here."

"Aye, I'll go after him." Wydrin stood up, and when she saw the look of surprise on Sebastian's face she shrugged. "He still owes us money, remember? I'm not having him eaten by a wolf before he gets to that castle of his."

"Wydrin," Sebastian smiled; it felt strange on his face, but not unwelcome, "your taste in men is perpetually disastrous."

"No worse than yours."

She made a face at him and sauntered off into the trees.

Frith was stalking about some distance from the fire, just beyond its soft circle of light. His white hair shone under the moonlight like a beacon. From his stiff-legged stride and hunched shoulders, Wydrin could tell he was sulking. She'd seen her own brother in that pose often enough.

"Watch where you're going, princeling!" she called after him. "Sebastian says there are animals in this forest that would consider even your scrawny hide a tasty meal."

Frith glowered at her as she approached.

"What do you want?"

"Just to make sure you're not thinking of doing anything stupid. You still owe us quite a bit of coin, you know."

"You'll get your money, sell-sword." He spat the word.

Once her eyes were adjusted to the gloom she could see the sharp angles of his face bathed in the glow of the distant fire. He really is quite comely, she thought, despite the hair.

"They have taken everything from me," said Frith suddenly. He wasn't looking at her; instead he was staring off into the dark as though his enemies were hiding between the trees. "My family, my home. Everything we'd ever owned, it's all gone. They dragged me out of the dungeon once, you know, and took me up into the courtyard. The Lady Bethan insisted that I be washed, as I was stinking up *her* castle." He snorted. "They threw buckets of water over me while there was still ice on the ground, and as I lay there shivering in the dirt I saw that they'd hung our servants from the walls. Every one of them. Their faces were all purple. Men and women who'd known me since I was born..." His voice trailed off.

Frith hadn't told them much about what had driven him from his home, but it wasn't difficult to work out that it hadn't been pleasant. As Sebastian pointed out to her between pints of ale, as long as they got paid, it didn't matter that Lord Frith wanted to keep the details to himself. But Wydrin was curious by nature, and tactless by choice.

"Why did they do it?"

Frith glared at her for a few seconds before he answered.

"Why do thieves do anything? To take what isn't theirs, to ruin the lives of others." He gestured around at the crowded darkness. "The Friths have always been part of the Blackwood. It's been our home for as long as anyone can remember. They used to say that if you cut a Frith they would bleed as much sap as blood. We have always been here."

"Was it an old enemy?"

Frith shook his head.

"There were rumours that a group of mercenaries had crossed the border from Istria, and perhaps if my father had taken more notice…" Frith shook his head, as if completing the sentence was futile. "My brother Tristan was nine years old. I don't even know what they did with his body."

Wydrin found she didn't know what to say. She also found that she was feeling a little guilty for punching Frith in the mouth, and she didn't like that at all.

"Listen," she said, scratching the back of her head. Her hair felt caked with dirt. "You saved Sebastian. It was your fault that he was in that state in the first place and you would have left us both for dead, and it was only lucky that the lake worked at all and –" she took a deep breath – "what I mean to say is, thank you. For saving Sebastian. You brought him back and I'm grateful for that."

Frith cleared his throat.

"I didn't mean to cause either of you injury."

"How did you do it? Useful thing to know how to do."

Frith shook his head, looking out into the dark.

"I'm not sure I could tell you, even if you were capable of understanding. The knowledge is there inside my head, but it's like it's written in a language I cannot decipher. Sometimes, like when I brought down the ceiling in the Citadel, or I healed the knight, the power that is simmering inside me seems to boil up and take over."

"And you brought us here from Krete."

"A useful power, but a dangerous one. My control over where we arrive is shaky at best, if you recall. It seems to be summoned by desperation, or fear. I'm not sure I could even do it again." He frowned. "If you really want to know, I did intend to land us somewhere within the grounds of the castle. The kitchens, in fact, but this –" he gestured around at the trees pressing in on all sides – "Blackwood trees, soldier pines, red oaks… we could be anywhere. Not to mention I am unsure what the violence of our passage has done to the place we've left behind."

Wydrin shrugged.

"With a bit of luck, it will have killed the rest of those pointy-toothed bitches. I took quite a beating from them, I don't mind telling you, and I'm a tough old feline."

"Where are you injured? Perhaps I can help." Frith stepped up close to her.

"Nothing too drastic. Don't you worry your silvery head about it, princeling. I've had worse."

"I can help though." He took hold of her arm, and she gasped.

"There?"

"I think I took a good knock to it when I fell on the steps. Probably bruised a bone or something. Not that I'm going to keep on about it but that *was* your fault. And I cut my head."

"Of course," he murmured. "I saw the blood." Keeping one hand on her arm, he placed the fingers of his other hand on one side of her face, and then gently pushed them back into her hair. His eyes were unfocussed, and his face was very close to hers.

"What are you doing?" Being this close to him made her uneasy. His hands felt warm against her cold skin.

"Be quiet," he said. A flicker of annoyance passed over his face. "The power is rising. Do not disrupt it."

"There really is no need. A glass or two of mead and I'll be right as–"

"Wydrin." His tone brooked no argument. "Be quiet."

She did as he bid, quietly making a note to get her own back later. His hands were more than warm now, they were hot, and her skin was beginning to tingle where he touched her. It was not an entirely unpleasant experience. A soft pink glow began to grow between them.

"I think it's working," said Frith, a hint of wonder in his voice.

"I can feel it." Wydrin couldn't help grinning, and he returned the smile. "It's like slipping into a bath that's slightly too hot, and it makes you kind of sleepy..."

A low rumbling growl from behind them dried up the words in her throat. Looking over Frith's shoulder she could see a pair of huge green eyes emerging from the gloom, just above a slavering set of pointed teeth. The creature that lumbered towards them out of the dark was a walking nightmare; it resembled a bear, but it was taller, with longer, thinner limbs and short grey hair on its musty pelt. The head was elongated, apparently to make room for the row upon row of jagged teeth set in its jaw, while its luminous eyes seemed to swivel in their sockets. It came for them on its back legs, seven and a half feet of muscle and teeth.

Wydrin broke away from Frith's embrace and slid both daggers from her belt in one smooth movement. Frith looked momentarily dazed, but when the animal roared again, a furious rattle in the back of its throat, the pink glow around his hands vanished abruptly and he turned to face it.

"A Blackwood bear," he said as he retreated. "Very dangerous."

"Tell me something I don't know, princeling!"

The creature dropped to all fours and roared again, peeling blackened lips back from teeth shiny with slaver. The back of its throat was very pink, and Wydrin found she could hardly drag her eyes from it. As she watched, it lowered its head and dragged its paws through the dirt, leaving ragged lines on the forest floor.

"Get behind me," said Frith.

"Get behind you? I'm the one with the daggers!"

"I can stop it."

"And you know how to do that, do you?"

But before he could answer the bear was charging. Wydrin dived out the way and ran for the nearest tree, but Frith only sidestepped, holding his hands up as if they were powerful weapons.

"What are you doing? Run!"

The bear came to a stop some feet away before shaking its long narrow head and sniffing the air noisily. The oddly blind-looking eyes swivelled round to find them again, and soon it was shifting around for a second strike, saliva dripping from its jaws. Frith watched it warily, circling constantly to prove a harder target. Wydrin paused at the foot of the tree, torn between running for safety and seeing the source of her future riches get ripped into tiny pieces.

"I can do this," cried Frith, but there was no light of any kind emitting from his hands now; no rosy glow, no forked lightening. For a moment the animal paused, as though it were confused by its prey's failure to retreat. "I just need to… remember."

"It's going to eat you!"

The bear rose up on its back legs again, roaring as it threw itself towards Frith. Swearing bitterly, Wydrin ran at its back and jumped, hooking both daggers into the creature's meaty shoulders. It bellowed, so loudly that Wydrin thought she would fall off from the force of that alone, and hot blood soaked her forearms. She pulled one dagger free and tried to bring it down once more into the animal's thick neck while digging her knees into its back, but it took the opportunity to shake her off, and the next thing she knew she was face down in a clump of thistles.

She turned over onto her back only to see the creature looming above her. Beyond its head she could see the cool indifference of that evening's stars, and the black branches of the trees stretching towards them, forever out of reach. The bear roared again, blasting her with its foul breath.

"*Urgh*. You smell as bad as you look."

Wydrin instinctively grabbed for her daggers only to discover she had neither; one, presumably, was still stuck in the creature's back, and she'd lost the other when she'd been thrown to the ground. She just had time to curse Frith and his reliance on magic before the bear lunged at her, teeth bared. Suddenly, however, it sprouted three feet of silvery steel from its neck. Wydrin saw the puzzlement in its eyes before it fell over sideways, revealing Sebastian on the other end of his sword. He placed a booted foot on the animal's head and drew it free again, the blade slick with blood.

"As I think I mentioned before, this isn't the friendliest of forests," he said.

16

The roof of the building had caved in, opening it to the night sky. The rows and rows of wooden shelves were on fire, as were their contents, but fire held little threat for the Thirty-Third. She walked sedately down the burning aisles while ash and flakes of paper flew up towards the hole in the roof, carried on the waves of heated air. They spiralled past her like errant fireflies, although she wasn't sure why she thought that. Certainly she couldn't remember ever seeing a firefly herself. Clouds of black smoke were making it hard to see, and the smell was scratching at the back of her throat. It would be uncomfortable to stay here much longer.

"Sister." A lithe figure stepped from the smoke to her left. It was the Ninety-Seventh, her green skin smudged with ashes. "Do you know what this building was?"

The Thirty-Third looked around, taking in the brick walls, the shelves with their rows and rows of squarish, leather covered-items. Some of the shelves reached halfway to the roof. She picked one of the items off a shelf that was only smouldering and turned it over in her hands until the word came to her.

"These are books," she said.

"Yes." The Ninety-Seventh came towards her. She had handfuls of blackened paper in her fists. "And this was a *library*." She said the word very carefully, as if not entirely sure how it sounded. "Isn't it curious that we know?"

"Is it?" The Thirty-Third shifted her weight. It was hot, and she was growing bored.

"I think so, yes. Do you remember knowing the words before? When we were below the rocks?"

"How would I know? We have never seen these *books*."

"But we know what they are." The Ninety-Seventh looked down at the paper in her hands. The heat was now intense enough for it to have burst into flames again, so she threw it onto the floor and snatched the book from her brood sister's hands. "Here, look at this." She opened it to a random page, revealing lines and lines of small black shapes. She held it up in front of the Thirty-Third's face. "Look at it!"

The Thirty-Third ran her eyes down the page, and to her surprise, images came to her mind that weren't there before. A green meadow with a swollen stream at its heart, still choked with pieces of ice from a recent snowstorm. She shook her head abruptly.

"What was that?"

"Words. Books. Library. Words!" The Ninety-Seventh shook the book at her. Her delicate features were twisted in confusion. "We can speak and we can read. These are the words in our heads written down." She turned to another page and read randomly, *"in the spring the ice-melt will be gone and the salmon will return."*

"So what?" said the Thirty-Third. She felt uneasy.

"This is new. Beneath the ground we knew none of this. We slept, we ate, we waited. We listened to the sound of our mother's voice. There were no words in our heads."

For a moment the Ninety-Seventh's lips trembled, and the Thirty-Third took hold of her arm firmly. She could feel her sister's confusion, and for the first time in her short life she was afraid.

"It doesn't matter," she said, forcing her voice to be steady. "We should leave now."

As if summoning it, there was a huge roar from outside, and the walls of the building shook, sending an avalanche of dust into the fires. The library would not be standing much longer.

"Mother is calling us," said the Ninety-Seventh. Her eyes caught her sister's and the Thirty-Third knew they were both thinking of the same thing. Of the *other* one. Where was he now?

The Thirty-Third and the Ninety-Seventh of the brood army left at a pace, heading for the cool evening air beyond the smouldering doorway. The Ninety-Seventh still clutched the book to her chest.

17

Sebastian stood alone in a field of blood. In the distance he could see the jagged blue mountains of home, the sacred god-peaks of Isu, Ryn, Ynn, and Isri. He could feel them watching him, particularly Isu, to whom his sword had been sworn, but they were so very far away. For a moment he felt the longing he hid from himself in the waking hours; to be back with his sworn brothers, the weight of the mountain's voice forever in his heart.

He looked down and was surprised to find he was wearing the clothes he had worn on his first pilgrimage to Isu. A thick cloak of blue wool covered his shoulders, and his surcoat was embroidered with the symbols of a novice. The closed fist, the hawk in flight, a ring of stones – each constituted a hard-won lesson. There was a pain in his chest, sharp and insistent. Had he been wounded?

A roar dragged his eyes back up to the horizon, and his nostrils filled with the stench of burning flesh. A great shadow was coming, passing over the god-peaks and covering them in a deep darkness, as though they were little more than hills in the sand. It rushed on towards him, bringing a tide of smothering fear. Sebastian shrank back, fumbling to draw his sword from its scabbard with fingers suddenly numb, but the shadow passed on and over him before he could strike. The roar sounded again, so loud that Sebastian dropped to his knees.

"What are you?" he cried, and a thousand voices answered.

"We are ruin. We are your children."

He woke with a start, the pain in his chest fading swiftly, although the images from the dream did not. Wydrin stood over him with one boot resting on his leg and her hands on her hips. There was a strong

102

scent of cooking eggs in the air.

"If you want any breakfast, you want to move fast," she said. "Three days in this miserable forest have given me quite the appetite." She gave his leg another shove for good measure, and went back to the fire. Frith was bent over the battered iron pan with a fork and an expression of intense concentration on his face.

Sebastian sat up, wondering if his colleague had spotted the way his hands were trembling. She didn't normally miss such things, but then Wydrin before breakfast was somewhat unpredictable. In truth, he had rarely felt less like eating.

"Where did we get eggs from?"

"Our woodsman here found a nest," said Wydrin, gesturing to Frith. "Weird little blue-green eggs; I wouldn't touch them, but he reckons they'll taste fine once they're all scrambled up."

"And that is not all I found," said Frith, looking up from the pan. "There is a small town less than an hour's walk from here."

Despite the dread lining his stomach, Sebastian was glad to hear that. Since their sudden arrival in the midst of the Blackwood they had been walking, trying to find one of the numerous small villages Frith insisted populated the region. The problem was that Frith only had the vaguest idea where they'd arrived, and so far the place had been conspicuously free of landmarks. By the second day, Wydrin had taken to exclaiming wonder at each new copse of trees or pile of stones, until Sebastian was certain she and Frith would come to blows again. It didn't help that twice now Frith's magic had burst into life of its own accord, setting fire to a bush on one occasion, and later lighting up the young lord like a beacon and scaring scores of birds from the surrounding trees. He said there was nothing he could do to control it, and the apparently random nature of the mage's power seemed to have put Frith in a volatile mood, particularly when Wydrin insisted on referring to it as "the princeling's little problem".

"Is it a place you know?" Sebastian seated himself by the fire, glad of its scant warmth, and Wydrin pressed a clay cup filled with tea into his hands.

"If it is the town I believe it to be, then yes, I visited it once or twice in the company of my father. Pinehold. There was a tower, an inn, the usual collection of peasants." He shrugged. "We should be able to find horses there and gather supplies."

"Those eggs are starting to burn," put in Wydrin. Frith took the pan off the fire and wedged it in the dirt between them.

"I will announce myself to the jarl in charge, and commandeer what we need. We may even be able to take a small force of men to Blackwood Keep, although I doubt I shall require them."

"Is that wise?" said Sebastian. He took a spoonful of the eggs. They were salty and slightly blackened on the bottom, but despite his lack of appetite the taste of hot food was glorious. "Forgive me, my lord, but you have no way of knowing the situation in Pinehold. It could be occupied by the Republic's forces."

"He's right," said Wydrin. She shovelled a portion of eggs into her mouth and spoke round them. "Best have a look at the situation first before you go in there all lit up like a lighthouse."

Frith frowned into his breakfast, obviously unhappy with this plan, but Sebastian could see that he understood the necessity of it too. What made a man so relentlessly self-reliant? It clearly pained him to take the advice of anyone. Sebastian looked up to see Wydrin wiping her mouth on the back of her hand. *I suppose we are hardly the wisest of advisors.*

"I do not understand it," said Frith. "When we were in the Citadel the power surged through me, and all I needed to do was think, and it obeyed. I could hear the mages too, the whispers of their lost knowledge were like echoes in my head." He shook his head and scraped the last of the eggs from the pan. "Now that is gone, and the power works only when it wishes to." His hand tightened on the pan until his knuckles turned white. "Why? How can it be? Did I travel so far for nothing?"

"Perhaps the remnants of the mages were an influence," said Sebastian in a quiet voice. "We know so little about them after all – their history, their methods." *We were like children poking at a viper's nest*, he thought. *What can we know about what we've unleashed?*

"No," said Frith to no one in particular. He threw the fork into the pan with a clatter. "I took the power from them, and I shall bend it to my will. It's just a… period of adjustment, that's all." He looked up at them both, his dark brows knitted together in a determined expression. "Do not take too long over breakfast."

18

Pinehold was much as he remembered it.

There had been a time when Frith's father had developed a sudden and keen interest in all the small towns and villages dotted throughout the Blackwood. He had travelled to each of them, sometimes with one or all of his sons, and always with a small retinue of household servants.

Frith remembered his father on those trips as clearly as if it were yesterday; sitting atop his grey horse in the weak spring sunshine, a small smile beneath his neat brown beard. All Lord Frith's smiles were small things.

Their visit to Pinehold had been marked by a sudden spring snow. Frith, in his early teens then, had clung to the neck of his horse and complained bitterly about the cold. His father, as usual, had ignored him. As they emerged from the treeline to the wide clearing that marked the edge of Pinehold, he'd gestured at the town wall with one gloved hand.

"An ancient place, Aaron," he'd said. "One of the oldest."

"It certainly looks likely to fall down any moment," Frith had replied sourly.

"Not at all, boy." His father's eyes had narrowed. "The men and women who built these places knew what they were doing."

And perhaps he'd been right. The town wall, built of solid chunks of dull grey stone, was still standing much as it had been. The tops weren't brushed with snow, but that was the only difference Frith could spot. The southern gate looked as strong as it had done ten years ago, although it stood wide open today. They could see the tops of the roofs from where they stood, and there was a thin haze of smoke from numerous wood fires hanging over the town. At the furthest edge of Pinehold a slim shape poked towards the sky, stark against the black of the trees. Wydrin pointed at it.

"What's that?"

"The Queen's Tower." Frith blinked as more memories came back. "It was where the old jarl lived."

"Not a bad place to make your home."

Frith nodded. The tower was constructed of pale milk-stone, a material not found locally and very expensive to transport. At regular intervals there were wide windows, and even a balcony, although they couldn't see that from where they were.

"It was built for Queen Alynn of the Blackwood, back when they had kings and queens. The people loved her so they paid for many such monuments." Frith paused, remembering. "My father used to tell me stories of Good Queen Alynn, about how she rid the forest of bandits and fought for her people. He was very keen on history. I think those stories were his favourites..." He cleared his throat and turned to look at the pair of sell-swords. "I am not certain this is the best course of action."

"Of course it is," said Wydrin immediately. "You can't go in there, not without knowing who might be there to greet us. And even with the white hair someone could recognise you. And Sebastian here, well," she gestured at the knight's imposing frame, and the broadsword slung over his back, "I'm the least conspicuous of the three of us. People very rarely notice me until it's too late." She smirked, but when she caught Frith's expression her face grew serious again. "I'll go in there and have a look around, that's all. Give me some money."

"What? I've already given you money."

"Which is now mine. I need coin for the furtherment of our mission, which will be coming out of your pocket."

"What for?"

In answer Wydrin gestured at her bare arms, and Sebastian's torn and bloody cloak.

"We need some new clothes, and you need a good hooded cloak so that we can cover you up, pretend you're a leper or something." Frith didn't move, so she held her hands up, palms out. "Do you honestly think I'm going to scarper now? I'll go in there, buy some supplies, find out if the town is crawling with enemies, and then I'll come straight back. I swear it on my claws."

Frith sighed and passed her a coin purse from his belt.

"Do not squander it. My funds are not inexhaustible."

She smiled, pocketing the purse, and headed off towards the town. He and Sebastian watched as she left the trees and strode along the path to the distant gate, growing smaller all the while. Frith cleared his throat, suddenly filled with unease.

"She does not seem built for stealth."

A ghost of a smile moved over Sebastian's face.

"Then you have never seen her sneaking out the back way when it's time for the bar bill to be paid. Don't worry, Wydrin can be sensible sometimes. She'll get what she needs in there and be back before we have a chance to enjoy the silence."

Wydrin headed straight for the tavern. A number of years exploring strange towns had given her an instinct for locating the best drinking hole. A quick pint, she reasoned, just for refreshment purposes. Refreshment, and possible information gathering. The princeling could hardly begrudge her that.

The guards on the gate had watched her closely as she entered, but she had squared her shoulders and walked past them just as if she'd been there a thousand times before, and they hadn't said a word. Although she had been careful not to make eye contact, she had taken note of their uniforms; decent mail and boiled black leather. They all had a strange symbol painted onto their round, wooden shields – a red oval, with two black holes in the upper half. It vaguely resembled a very simple face, or perhaps a mask, covered in blood. Was that the sigil of the People's Republic of Istria? She couldn't be sure, but she didn't believe so. Sebastian would have known in a second.

She saw more of these guards as she headed deeper in, and these ones had the look of battle-born men about them, carrying swords that looked well cared for. Wydrin was careful to appear deeply uninterested in them.

The town of Pinehold itself was rather gloomy, thanks to the smoky rock its stones were hewn from and the dark timbers of the Blackwood. Here and there huge oak trees grew, spreading their branches in a protective gesture over the town below. Someone had hung strings of blue and white bunting between the branches to cheer the place up a bit, but recent rains had soaked the fabric through and they clung to the bark like bedraggled lovers. The people didn't do anything to dispel Wydrin's disquiet either. She saw men and women with baskets of bread, mothers with children hanging on their skirts, all going about their daily business, but it was impossible to miss the haunted expressions on their faces. *It's almost normal*, thought Wydrin, *very almost completely normal apart from the way they look at the guards, and the way they look at the tower.*

The pale edifice stood at the far end of the town, its lower half hidden by wagons full of mouldering hay. A black flag was flying from the top, embroidered with the same red mask face she'd seen on the guards. The windows she could see were wide and generous but dark, and she could not see inside. The townsfolk kept glancing fearfully up at the tower, as if they didn't dare to look away for long. *They have the look of a dog that has been beaten too often, and now lives in constant fear of its master's hand*, thought Wydrin.

The tavern, when she found it, was called the Alynn's Pride, and she stepped through the door gratefully, glad to be off the street. Inside it was so dark that she had to blink for a few seconds to get her bearings; chairs, tables, a bar that had seen better days, made all the grubbier by the dirty light managing to force its way through the thick leaded windows. Wydrin dragged a boot through the sawdust on the floor. It was reasonably clean, and the air smelt more of ale than of vomit. Even more encouraging, there didn't appear to be any bloodstains on the tables. Wydrin relaxed a little. She had a long and varied history with taverns, and knew the dangerous ones on sight.

There were a handful of townspeople inside, sipping foamy ale with their heads down. A few looked up as she entered the bar, and Wydrin saw one or two glance towards the daggers on her belt. She ignored them and stepped up to the counter, placing her hands flat on the top and beaming at the serving woman.

"Mead, please."

For a few moments the woman looked as though she wasn't going to move, let alone fetch Wydrin her mead.

"And who might you be?" she said eventually.

"A traveller from the Stoney Sea," said Wydrin, readily enough. There was no use in lying, Wydrin knew she could not disguise the salt of Crosshaven in her voice. "Just making my way through. And you are?"

The woman frowned.

"Mead, was it?"

She bustled off, apparently no longer interested in an exchange of information. She returned with a slightly warped glass filled with a warm golden liquid; it was the brightest thing in the place. Wydrin fished a few coins from the purse on her belt and put them on the counter.

"Thank you kindly. So what's the news from Pinehold?"

A strange parade of emotions flickered across the woman's face then; Wydrin saw shock, and anger, and lastly fear. The woman glanced around the tavern, as though she were looking for someone.

"Just drink your mead and get out," she spat before walking stiffly up the other end of the bar to refill another glass.

Charming place.

Wydrin took a sip. It tasted like it might have seen some honey once. Or possibly a few dead bees.

Glancing down the bar she noticed two men nursing full tankards. Neither looked to be fighting men, and yet they both wore bloody bandages. One held his drink awkwardly, apparently missing two fingers on his left hand, and the other leaned heavily on the bar, his head half covered in bloody rags.

Wydrin looked away hurriedly. There was trouble here, and not the useful sort that ended in a large bag of coins...

"Have you travelled far, child?" came a voice in Wydrin's ear. It was close and soft, and very precise. "You appear to have rolled down a hill of thistles."

Wydrin turned to find a tall, older woman standing next to her. She forced down the initial surge of alarm with effort; very few people could sneak up on her so successfully, even in a tavern. The woman who had moved so silently was as thin and hard as a poker. Painfully sharp cheekbones pushed at warm olive skin, and she wore dark blue robes over worn riding leathers. The most striking aspect of her appearance were the tattoos; writing in a strange alphabet covered both her cheeks from her eyes downwards, and her arms and hands were covered in the same text. A Regnisse of Relios, then, otherwise known as a fire-priestess. Wydrin knew without having to look that the woman's back would be covered in more of the holy writing, as well as other areas best not mentioned to a holy person. *Oh, that's all I need,* she thought. *A priest.*

"It's been a long time since I was a child, sister."

"And I am not your sister."

Wydrin caught the older woman's eye, and there passed a moment that flickered between mutual dislike and mutual amusement. Relios was the tempestuous land beyond the deserts of Creos. Her father had said it was a place of angry gods and sharp people. The land itself would shake apart regularly, leading to huge fissures in the ground and whole cities lost in a few moments of violence. The Regnisse Accordance were made up of two groups of priests: those who studied history and ancient languages, and dedicated their lives to the spread of knowledge, and those who usually stayed within Relios and watched the trembling earth for signs from their gods. To Wydrin it sounded rather like looking up at the clouds and searching for the shape of a bunny rabbit or a castle, or listening to the sound of waves crashing against your hull and hearing voices. She'd pointed this out to a fire-priest in a tavern in Pathania once and still had a small scar on her left forearm as a memento of the occasion. Holy people they might be, but they still knew how to handle their blades.

"Can I buy you a drink, Regnisse?" said Wydrin, deciding to err on the side of caution.

The fire-priestess glanced at the glass of mead.

"You didn't answer my question."

Wydrin took another sip, playing for time.

"I have travelled a long way, yes." She gestured at her ragged appearance. "I tangled with one of your bears on the way here. Nasty great brute."

"A Blackwood bear?" The Regnisse raised one thin eyebrow. "If you had truly fought one of those, you would be dead." She glanced round at the other customers, her lips pressed together into an expression Wydrin couldn't quite read. "And I wouldn't talk about that here, if I were you. Not a good subject for general discussion, shall we say."

Wydrin's small amount of patience for priests was suddenly exhausted.

"Listen, I'm just here for a quick drink before I pick up some supplies and move on, so I could really do without all the cryptic warnings and veiled threats."

The priestess sighed.

"Yes, I can see that all warnings and threats will have to be loud and possibly written down in large simple letters, if there is to be any hope of your understanding them." She leaned in close and lowered her voice. "My name is Dreyda, and I am telling you, young woman, that this is a bad place for strangers at the moment. A bad place for everyone. They let you in the gate, yes? Just walked in straight past them, yes? You will find it significantly more difficult to walk back out again, child. You can come in, but you can't go back out again. Those are Fane's orders."

"Who's Fane?"

Dreyda looked pained, and gestured at Wydrin to keep her voice down.

"You have seen the guards, yes? With the painted face on their shields?"

Wydrin nodded.

"Fane commands them, and these days the people of Pinehold live in fear."

"Why?"

"Because he's killing them."

19

"She should be back by now."

Frith paced back and forth, trying to keep his eyes on his boots. If he looked up he was drawn back to the town and the tower, and he was sick of looking at the damn place. Instead he forced himself to enjoy the newly fluid movement of his leg, the shattered bones within now completely healed. The limp was gone, his ear had grown back, and the scar had vanished from his face. It was a joyous thing. A miracle.

"It really is quite intolerable!" he snapped. "How long can it take one person to fetch supplies? Must we wait out here all day doing nothing?"

Sebastian, crouched against the wide trunk of an oak tree, grunted in response. And that was the other irritation; the big knight, usually so calm and accommodating, now appeared distracted, even moody. Frith was regretting hiring either of them.

The afternoon was drawing on, and the light filtering down through the trees was growing dimmer all the time. Familiar bird calls filled the air, making him think of his boyhood hunting in the woods around the castle, and such memories only made him more anxious to move. He stopped pacing and put his hands on his hips, facing the walled town.

"I think we should go in there," he said. "She clearly cannot be trusted to do this, so we must do it ourselves." He kicked Sebastian's booted foot. "Get up, Sebastian. Let's go."

Sebastian lumbered to his feet wearing a conciliatory expression.

"Give her a little more time, my lord. We have no idea what the situation is, nor how many people might recognise you. It would be wise to–" Before he could finish Sebastian staggered, swaying on his feet. Frith frowned.

"Are you well?"

"I don't – I don't feel..." The tall man had gone almost as pale as when Gallo had stabbed him, and his eyes looked glassy and unfocussed. Frith didn't like it.

"You are ill," he said. "I told you not to let her cook that rabbit. I'm surprised we're not all emptying our bowels into a ditch somewhere."

A rush of blood came from Sebastian's nose, soaking his mouth and chin and running down his neck. The knight pressed his fingers to his face and the blood ran between his fingers.

"They're burning everything," he said, quite clearly. "Killing it and cutting it and I can feel the blood moving." Sebastian dropped to his knees, muttering.

"What is wrong with you? Get up."

Frith bent down and slung an arm round the knight's shoulders in an attempt to drag him to his feet again, although his hopes of achieving that were rather slim. Sebastian was a big man, and if he wanted to sit down Frith would be unable to stop him.

"Come on now, I didn't heal you just for you to go bleeding all over the place again."

He heaved, feeling Sebastian's battered armour digging into his side, when a nearby shadow peeled away from the trees and approached them, sword in hand.

"You don't want to be doing any bleeding round here," the stranger said.

Frith whirled, his hand reaching for the rapier that was now lost beneath the Citadel.

"Stay back!"

The newcomer looked at him, his expression unreadable. He was a rangy, gaunt man, as tall as Sebastian but with narrow shoulders and long wiry arms that suggested a kind of contained strength. He wore a ragged mixture of leather and wool, and there was a huge fur pelt slung over his back. There was, Frith couldn't help noticing, a lot of dried blood on his fingers, and the short sword he carried looked well-used.

The man looked from Frith to Sebastian, who was now sitting with his legs out in front of him and his head tipped back to stem the flow of blood from his nose.

"No blood," he said again, nodding at Sebastian. "Not if you know what's good for you."

"What are you talking about?"

"Course, it would be a mercy to those poor fellas if you was to distract them for a bit. Would that be a mercy, though? Or would that be prolonging it, like? I reckon another night in those cages could be worse, you know, than getting all torn to bits, but what would I know? I don't and I don't want to, and who would? No one, that's who."

Frith blinked a few times. Despite his vaguely aggressive appearance, the man seemed more intent on talking than killing.

"Who are you?" he said, as clearly as possible. "And what do you mean?"

The stranger frowned at him as though he were unused to other people asking questions, and then nodded at Sebastian.

"You want to put something cold on that. That would be the safest thing. You want to know who I am, do you? My name is Rognor, although how that helps you I'm sure I don't know. Best bury those bloody rags, son, and bury 'em somewhere you won't be returning to."

Sebastian's nose bleed appeared to have stopped, although his face was still white.

"Why?" His voice was muffled and thick.

"The bears, of course." Rognor gestured behind him, as though the entire forest were bristling with bears. "They'll be down here at dusk, looking for what they've put out fresh, and maybe they'll fancy some proper sport rather than taking whichever poor bastard has been put in the cages. If I were a bear, would I want to chase and hunt? I think I would."

Frith and Sebastian exchanged a glance.

"Cages?"

Rognor walked round with them, keeping to the treeline. He nodded at the black-clothed guards on the wall surrounding Pinehold. They had clearly spotted the small group skirting along the trees, but were doing nothing besides watching their progress.

"They won't come down here now, you see, too close to feeding time. I come up here as the sun goes down and I tries to clear away what I can, and as long as I don't try to free the poor buggers or scare the bears off they leaves me be. Once or twice I've moved away enough of the mess so that the animals have left them alone for the night, but does that help? Another night in those cages, I tell you, I wouldn't want it."

"But why?" asked Sebastian. He still felt lightheaded and his nose was throbbing faintly. Concentrating on the tall man in the furs was difficult. Inside his head he could still smell the smoke as the city burned. "Who would do such a thing?"

"A leader of men, or the biggest monster amongst a horde of demons." Rognor twisted his lips and spat into the bushes. "I live out in the Blackwood, don't go in the town much, see? So I wasn't here when the guards and the red faces came. Once they came, the townsfolk weren't let back out again. I've heard the guards talking, though, when they don't know I'm there. You think any of them ever walked through a forest with a mind to be quiet? Have they, buggery. His name's Fane, is what I heard. Come up from down south."

Frith stopped suddenly.

"Fane? Fane is here?"

"You know him, do ya?" Rognor turned a speculative eye on Frith, raising one bushy brown eyebrow. "He's a demon worshipper, is what I've heard."

But Frith was already turning towards the town wall, a look of alarming fury on his face. Sebastian reached out and snatched at his arm, holding him back.

"Where do you think you're going," he hissed, before adding, in a milder tone of voice, "my lord?"

"Fane is in there." Frith's grey eyes were shining fever bright. "The man who ordered the execution of my family, who took my castle, who had me tortured…" He wrenched his sleeve from Sebastian's grip so violently the fabric ripped down the seam. "I will go in there now, and I will separate his head from his body." He pointed at the wall, where the guards were starting to take more of an interest.

"'Ere, what's that you're talking about?" Rognor was peering closely at Frith's face.

"Nothing, just – nothing." Sebastian fixed Frith with what he hoped was his most reasonable expression. "Think, my lord. Think. We must know everything we can first. The size of his forces, his reasons for being here—"

At that moment a terrible scream wrought the air. It went on for some time, and then degenerated into noisy sobbing.

"Damn the gods, they're early," said Rognor.

And with that he set off at a run. Frith and Sebastian had little choice but to follow him, although Sebastian soon came to wish they hadn't. Around the corner from where they had stood, five large metal cages were set close to the town wall. They were tall and narrow, too thin for a man to sit down or even crouch in. Two of the cages were still occupied with living people; a fat man and an old woman, both naked and both gripping the bars of the cage in terror. The cages were hanging on chains from a makeshift gallows that stuck out from the wall, and as the man screamed (it *was* the man screaming, Sebastian noted as his stomach turned over, although his voice had lost all gender in his terror) his cage rocked wildly back and forth. And the noise was only attracting the bear all the more.

It was, Sebastian guessed, a good foot taller than the bear that had attacked them in the forest, and certainly bulkier. It had the same long narrow head and shining eyes, and its black claws were already streaked with gore. The other three cages contained bodies in various stages of decomposition, all with terrible wounds.

Rognor blew air through his teeth, frowning.

"Bloody creatures are learning to come at the same time each day, whether they can smell it or not." His weathered face twisted into a grimace.

"Why are they doing this?" said Frith. His earlier expression of fury had fled, and been replaced with one of extreme distaste. "For what end?"

"For information, they says." Rognor nodded towards the guards. "The Friths had a great treasure, they says, but no one knows where they hid it. Fane intends to find out, and he's got a whole team of torturers in that tower there. The man is dead keen on torture, that's what they say."

"The Friths?" said Frith. He looked like he'd been struck in the stomach.

"Whatever it is, I am stopping it now," said Sebastian. He drew the sword from the scabbard on his back and revelled in the sound of its escape. He'd been idle too long. Perhaps he couldn't stop the slaughter happening in a distant city on another continent but that didn't mean he would stand by while other innocents were killed.

"You can't!" Rognor slapped the big knight on the shoulder. "Do you not think I'd have done that if I could? Look." He pointed to the guards again, and this time Sebastian saw the longbows. "They'll shoot, don't think they won't. And they're good shots, too."

"I still have to try."

He turned away from them and ran at the approaching bear. For a few seconds it was too intent on the blood-smeared cages to take notice, until Sebastian shouted in its direction. It was important to get its attention away from the prisoners.

"Hoy! You ugly creature! Dinner's been cancelled."

The luminous eyes swivelled towards him then, and the creature growled, revealing long yellow teeth. Distantly Sebastian could hear shouting from the wall. The animal turned and lowered its head, bellowing.

Sebastian hefted the weight of his broadsword in his hands, and ran towards it, slightly to its right. The animal shifted that way, expecting the attack, so Sebastian turned swiftly to the left and swung low at the bear's shoulder. At that moment an arrow thudded into the ground next to his foot, the red fletching feathers bright against the soil, and he stumbled, turning the blow so that it only scraped against the bear's flank. The animal roared and flung one huge, razor-clawed paw in his direction, but for all his size Sebastian had always been quick on his feet, and he moved out of its path just in time. Another arrow struck the steel plate on his arm at an angle, ricocheting off and undoubtedly leaving a bruise, and then another took the bear in the leg. The animal, already bleeding from where Sebastian had struck it, tossed its head in pain and fury and backed away. It cast one last look at the shivering humans in the cages and disappeared back into the forest. Sebastian watched it go before looking back at the guards on the wall. They all had their bows trained on him. The next voice that spoke was coming from behind him.

"You'll die for that, you big bastard."

There stood a group of about ten guards, all dressed in black leathers and with a red mask sigil on their shields. Rognor and Frith were in front of them, the guards holding short swords to their throats. The guard who had spoken was a squat, powerfully built man with ruddy marks on his face from some pox he'd suffered in the past. He grinned at Sebastian, revealing rather more gums than teeth.

"We'll kill your pretty little friend here first though."

"No, wait." Sebastian sheathed his sword and held up his hands. "We have information for you."

"Shut up, Sebastian," said Frith. The burly guard laughed.

"What sort of information is that, then?"

Sebastian took a deep breath. "The location of the Frith vault."

Frith swore loudly, the first time Sebastian could recall him doing so. He didn't look at him, and kept his eyes on the guard instead.

"You tell me, then, and maybe I'll let you go."

Sebastian shook his head. He was very aware of the people in the cages behind him; the fat man, the old woman. He could feel their eyes on his back.

"I want to speak to Fane. He's the only person I'll be telling anything to."

The guard frowned.

"You're not in any position to be bargaining, my son."

"Maybe not, but how many of your men do you think I can kill before you kill me? Enough to make them hesitate before they come over here, I'll bet. Take me to Fane. I'm sure he'll be anxious to hear what I have to say."

The guard looked angry then, and for a moment Sebastian thought he'd pushed it too far, until he turned and gestured at a few of his men. Within moments he was forced next to Frith, swords and crossbows at his back as they were marched round to the gate.

"You are an idiot," hissed Frith as their jailors conversed with the guards on the wall. "Even worse than her. I should have left you both in Creos."

"You *will* tell them, Frith," Sebastian spat the words. "There are innocent people dying, and for what? Your bloody inheritance."

The gates opened, revealing the dismal town beyond. Frith leaned in close. His eyes were the colour of storm clouds.

"I don't *know* where the vault is, you damned fool. You've doomed us all."

20

Wydrin walked out of the tavern with the woman Dreyda at her back.

"He will be in the market at this time of day, if you wish to get a look at him. He likes to parade himself and his personal guard when the town square is at its busiest, so people cannot forget that he is here." She laughed. It was a small, bitter sound. "At night he retires to the tower, for his *entertainment.*"

"I would like to see him," said Wydrin, as casually as she could. "And I have a few supplies to pick up." The evening was drawing in now, the grey clouds above soaking up the dark like a sponge in a pool of ink. The sky that she could see was violet.

"Then I shall walk with you there. Come on."

The tall priestess took her arm, and they walked up the street at a steady pace.

"Do not make eye contact, if you can help it," said Dreyda of the guards. "Pinehold has been like a slow-cooked pot for weeks now, and some of them are just looking for ways to draw the steam off. And believe me, you do not want to be on the receiving end of that."

"Why are you helping me?" said Wydrin. The Regnisse's grip was quite firm.

"I had a vision," said Dreyda in a matter-of-fact tone. "I dreamed of Renethena, the goddess of scrying and fortune. She showed me the words in a surge of boiling lava, and I knew that I would meet a woman with red hair and a trio of sea monsters on her arm, and she would be the saviour of a town caught in the vice grip of—"

"Oh, piss off."

"Not going to work on you?" Dreyda caught her eye and gave

her a very ungodly smirk. "It normally goes down so well with the young men I meet. Never mind. I just happen to think you look like a woman who has seen plenty of trouble in the past, and might be up to handling some more. The people here, my child, they have had all the courage shaken from them, and now they cringe their way around their own homes for fear of being fed to the bears. For fear of Fane."

They had reached the marketplace. It was still lively enough, with wagons and stalls crowded with people doing their last bit of shopping before heading back for the evening. There was a noticeable lack of produce; half the groceries on display looked rather elderly, and there was a great deal of questionable meat for sale. People were still buying it though.

They reached the centre of the square, where a tall, graceful statue stood on a raised stone platform. It depicted a young woman with a long bow at her side, and she was staring off to the tower beyond. Three men sprawled around its base, watching the market.

"The one in the middle. That's Fane," said Dreyda, although she needn't have bothered. It was clear who he was.

The man screamed violence. Like the tower, the eyes were drawn to him again and again, as they are drawn to a house fire roaring out of control, or the red tendrils of infection from a diseased wound. He was a tall, powerfully built man with brown hair oiled back from his forehead, and his jaw was square and dark with stubble. Wydrin supposed he was handsome, if you could look past the malevolent gleam in his eyes. And the scars. The scars were something else.

"What happened to him?" she asked Dreyda without turning round.

"No one seems very clear on that point," said the fire-priestess. "The prevailing rumour is that he did that to himself, or paid someone very skilled with a knife to do it. You see the significance of the red faces on the shields now?"

The broad planes of Fane's otherwise unmarked face were scored with red, squarish patches, where thick sections of skin had apparently been removed and then the flesh underneath allowed to scar. There was a piece missing from both cheeks, running from just below each eye down to the line of his jaw, a smaller section on his chin, and a horizontal rectangle of scarring on the right side of his forehead. It gave his face an odd, patchwork appearance, as though someone were sewing him together from pieces of old skin and they hadn't quite finished yet. The sections of raw flesh didn't appear to cause him any discomfort. As Wydrin watched he turned to trade a joke with the men sharing the space on the platform, and he laughed and grinned just as though he wasn't missing pieces of his face. He wore black boiled leather armour, turning grey at the elbows and knees from use, and there was a sword at his hip, although that was nothing special; it was the sword of a soldier, sharp and well maintained. In one hand he held a battered half-helm.

"And what about those two?" said Wydrin, indicating the men either side of Fane. They looked a lot younger than their employer, no older than sixteen or seventeen. One of them was leaning on the statue in an overtly relaxed posture. "What are they supposed to be?"

For a moment, Dreyda didn't answer, and when Wydrin turned to look at her the older woman pursed her lips, as though she didn't like to speak the words.

"What is it?"

"Ungodly things, is what they are," she said shortly. "Abominations. The Children of the Fog, he calls them."

The two young men were certainly nearly as strange as their lord. Clearly brothers, or more accurately, twins, both were tall, as lean as alley cats, and both had long blond hair the colour of honeyed milk. Their armour was light, made from pieces of fine red leather, save for a single gauntlet each, which appeared to be made of a dull black metal. *How sweet*, thought Wydrin, *brothers with matching gloves*. They were so nearly identical that the only way Wydrin could tell them apart was by the weapons they carried; one had a pair of straight-bladed swords, and the other had a curled whip hanging from his waist.

"Why does he call them that?" asked Wydrin. All three men looked like trouble.

"They do magics," said Dreyda in a tone of voice that suggested said magics were low and filthy things. "And they smile while they kill, like cats."

"Hey," said Wydrin, absently. "Cats aren't cruel, it's just their nature."

"Cruelty is *their* nature," said the Regnisse. Lowering her voice, she took hold of Wydrin's arm again. "Do not stare too long. Come, you said there were supplies you needed."

Wydrin made to go with the fire-priestess, but a commotion at the edge of the market caught her eye. A number of the black-clad guards were pushing their way through the evening's crowd, escorting a very familiar pair of figures at their centre.

"Oh, for the love of all the gods!" cried Wydrin.

The guards marched Sebastian and Frith and a third man Wydrin didn't recognise up to the statue, while Fane looked on in lively interest. Around them the people of Pinehold murmured uneasily. Wydrin caught the eye of a young man standing near a fruit and vegetable stall, and he raised his eyebrows at her, as if waiting for her to act. He had untidy brown hair and a finely featured face she was sure she should remember, but she didn't recognise him. She frowned at him, and shook off Dreyda's hand.

"What are you doing?" hissed the priestess.

"I have to know what's going on there," said Wydrin, and she slipped to the front of the gathering crowd.

Frith stared at the man who had ruined his life, and found he didn't know what to say.

They had spoiled everything. When he made his attack on Fane he intended it to be brisk and devastating. He had pictured himself arriving, perhaps at his very own castle, to find Fane relaxed and undefended, secure in the knowledge that he had taken the Blackwood, and then Frith would tear him apart with the elemental forces he now had at his command. Everything he'd inflicted on his family, Fane would suffer tenfold. Instead of that, he had been forced into a confrontation with the man at sword point, in rags, and with little understanding of how the elemental forces he'd taken from the mages worked, let alone how he could best use them against this man. The simmering power he'd felt inside the Citadel was a quiet whisper in his head, and he did not know how to rouse it to a shout. If only Sebastian had kept his mouth shut.

But Fane appeared to have no interest in them. Instead he gestured at Rognor, a broad grin on his face.

"My friend! You have had enough of skulking around outside the walls of our town, then? I am so pleased you have decided to join us after all." He had a warm, affable voice, the sort of voice that might ask if you needed help carrying that pile of firewood.

Rognor frowned deeply, his long face furrowed with anger.

"I'll not converse with monsters, I won't," he said. "You can ask me whatever you want and I won't take no notice. I have nothing to say to the likes of you."

Fane shook his head gently, a faint smile on his face.

"What did you hope to achieve, my good man?"

"Just mercy," said Rognor. "Something a monster like you wouldn't know nothing of."

"Those people, out in the cages, are blessed." Fane raised his voice so that everyone gathered in the market place could hear. "They are offerings to Bezcavar." He paused and lifted his half-helm to his face. He kissed the battered metal fondly. "They needn't have been, but they would not give up what they knew and Bezcavar is always hungry. His belly rumbles and we all must heed it." He touched his fingers to his scarred face.

"Ya demon worshippin' scum," said Rognor. Sebastian muttered a few words at him, trying to get the tall man to calm down, but he either didn't hear or didn't care. "The lowest, a monster, that's what you are and no mistake," Rognor continued. "Can't be telling me any different or no one else here, no–"

Fane waved a hand at one of his lieutenants.

"Enri, Bezcavar hungers. Make an offering of this idiot."

Sebastian stepped forward.

"No, wait–"

Moving with unsettling speed and grace, the slim blond man to the right of Fane grabbed his whip, shook it out, and flicked it. There was a crack, painfully sharp in the evening air, and suddenly Rognor was on his knees, a length of barbed leather wrapped round his throat. His fingers scrabbled desperately at the coils, trying to find purchase. The man called Enri laughed and tugged sharply on his end of the whip. Rognor fell to the ground, making strangled choking noises. Blood ran from his torn throat as his face began to turn purple.

"Stop it!" cried Sebastian. The big knight was straining at his captors, a look of utter horror on his face.

"Bezcavar requires an offering," said Fane in a mild tone of voice. "But you are right, the night draws in and I have other business. Enri? Stop it."

The blond man pouted.

"But I have only just—"

"Enri."

The blond man sighed, and placing one foot on Rognor's shoulder, heaved on the whip so that it tightened violently on the tall man's neck. There was a moment of pressure, then his throat seemed to burst apart in a torrent of blood.

Frith winced, stepping away as Rognor slumped onto the dirt. The man called Enri took a moment to retrieve the whip, before tying it back onto his belt, still dripping blood. The people at the market place had fallen utterly silent, and Frith thought it likely they had seen many such "offerings".

"What else have you brought me then, Bruger?" asked Fane. His eyes crawled over Sebastian, disregarding Frith entirely. "These two do not look like the peasants of Pinehold that I have come to know and love."

The strange identical-looking men standing next to him laughed softly.

"The big one reckons he knows where the vault is, m'lord," said the burly guard, whose name was Bruger. "Caught 'em both outside the gate, antagonising the bears."

Fane raised his eyebrows. The raw red flesh on his forehead stretched and wrinkled.

"We can't have that. The bears here are not to be trifled with, isn't that right, Roki?" The slim blond man to his right tipped his head, the briefest impression of a nod. "Roki and Enri are rather fond of the bears in this forest. In Istria we have bears, but they are smaller, rather more docile. They only present a danger to the fish in our rivers. So what is this about the vault?" Fane didn't pause to let him answer but moved on to another line of questioning. "You're a knight, aren't you? I recognise the badge. One of those mad mountain cults."

Casting his voice as low as he could, Frith leaned close to Sebastian.

"You name me now and you shall wish I'd left you to die at the Citadel."

Sebastian didn't even look at him.

"My lord, I do not know the location of the vault, but I know who does. I only ask that you release the man and woman held in the cages outside the town walls."

The good humour on Fane's face seemed to disappear. He took the black helm in both his hands and turned it over in his fingers.

"Demands? When held at sword point? I thought the Ynnsmouth knights were known for their wisdom."

Sebastian took a step forward.

"The man standing next to me is Lord Aaron Frith, the last living heir of the Blackwood."

There was a flurry of noise from the slowly gathering crowd; gasps, murmurs and questions. Frith thought he heard swearing from someone who sounded suspiciously like Wydrin, although he could not see her.

"Can it be?" Fane moved slowly from the statue, coming towards them both. Now his eyes were trained on Frith, and the man moved like a cat hunting something small and warm-blooded. "The Friths all died, running from my men like cowards. I cannot tell you the number of arrows we pulled from their backs…"

"YOU LIE!" All of a sudden the hot fury thundered back into life, and the guards were straining to hold Frith back. "You murdered my father and my brothers. You tortured them to death!"

Fane paused, and a slow grin slid across his face like blood seeping into a bandage.

"It *is* you," he said, and suddenly all the warm, friendly tones were back, just as though he were greeting an old friend. "Bethan said you nearly died in the dungeons but some peasants with delusions of bravery smuggled you out. She assured me that you would have died from exposure in the heavy snows, but here you are – yes, take away that white hair and old Lord Frith lives again. You know, I was most displeased that I didn't get to Blackwood Keep in time to meet you. How utterly perfect this is."

"I will kill you," said Frith, no longer shouting. The anger had closed his throat and left him unable raise his voice. The hot feeling of it prickled all over his skin. "That is a promise. I will kill you and tear you to pieces and when I am done I will leave your remains in the forest for the rats to eat."

"Roki, Enri, take our young lord here to the Queen's Tower. I'm sure Yellow-Eyed Rin is anxious for a reunion." He turned back and winked at Frith. "He has so many new tricks to show you. Guards, kill the big one and don't be making off with his sword. I like the look of it."

Several things happened in the space of a few seconds. The

prickling heat swarming over Frith's skin increased in intensity and seemed to combine with the cold churning in his stomach. All at once, an eldritch-green fire flickered into life along his hands and arms. There was a pause, a moment of kindling, and then he was consumed with the emerald fire. The guards holding his arms leapt back, shouting, and there were answering shouts in the crowd.

"Don't let him go," bellowed Fane, "It's just some conjuror's illusion," but it wasn't, Frith realised with a sudden fierce joy. The fire leapt from his body and streamed in several directions at once, and what it touched exploded with hot, yellow flame. The guards who had been closest to him were now screaming, their faces melting and their clothes on fire.

Sebastian stumbled away from him, too surprised to reach for his own sword, while the guards who weren't on fire came to carry out Lord Fane's wishes. There was a flash of silver amongst the crowd and Wydrin flew out from the front row, her first dagger ripping through one man's throat as though it were a bushel of hay at harvest time, and her second clashing with a short sword, driving the blow away from the big knight.

"I will kill you!" Frith shouted again. The guards were falling away, some of them desperately trying to beat the flames out with their hands. Fane had retreated to the statue again and all that stood between Frith and his revenge were the two men with long hair and identical faces. He would burn them too. *Burn everything and everyone.*

21

The people were screaming.

Sebastian moved as though he were in a dream. His body fell into the old patterns, the routines he'd spent years learning; they were a part of him now, so entrenched he barely had to think. He parried a blow there, took out a man's ankle in one low stroke, felt the bones there shatter, and caught another guard under the chin with the back swing. There was blood, and screaming, and the scent of scorched flesh. It was here, and it was real.

She is not here, he told himself firmly, but a cold hand seized his heart and panic started to build. *She is* not *here*.

The swarming guards were falling back now, parting to let some newcomers through. The two men from the dais came forward, drawing their weapons. Sebastian pushed his rising fear aside and tried to concentrate on these two, because these two were clearly very different from the poorly trained men that had fallen to his sword so easily. One had drawn a pair of exotic-looking swords – long straight blades with edges that looked sharp enough to slice bone – and the other carried the bullwhip that killed Rognor, still red with his blood.

"Pair of posers," muttered Wydrin next to him.

As he watched, the dull grey metal of their gauntlets began to glow with a soft, orange light, tracing shapes that had previously been invisible. Sebastian blinked a few times, sure it must be a trick of the light, but the glow only intensified. It grew so bright that they were difficult to look at, and then through squinting eyes Sebastian saw the twins double, so that there were four blond men approaching. He shook his head, absolutely convinced for a bare second that his vision had failed him, but when he looked again they were still there; four men where there had been two, a pair with swords, and a pair with whips.

"What is this now?"

Sebastian glanced at Wydrin, whose face was rigid with shock, and then the men were on them.

Wydrin had perhaps a handful of seconds to process what had happened before she found herself dodging a shining blade as it whistled past her ear. She moved, smooth as silk, light as foam, and brought Frostling up and round to bury it in the blond man's head, but her dagger passed straight through him and out the other side just as though he were made of mist. He grinned at her, his teeth very neat and white next to his pink lips.

"I am Roki, little girl. I shall enjoy playing with you."

Wydrin glanced over to Sebastian to see his own sword passing through another of the blond men. *The Children of the Fog*, Dreyda had called them.

"They're not really there!" she called to Sebastian and Frith. "They're just made of vapour. Ignore them and go for the big man!"

The words were barely out of her mouth before the blond man called Enri flicked the bullwhip at Frith, the end of the lash catching the young lord across the top of his forehead. In an instant the green flames that surrounded him winked out of existence and he was thrown to the floor, a bloody gash staining his white hair crimson.

"Forget I said that!"

She jumped back to avoid another strike from Roki's blades only for the end of the whip to grab her arm in a viper's embrace. Even through her leather armour she could feel the burning points of metal digging into her skin. Ashes dropped from her fingers and she could do nothing but watch with horror as the dagger skittered across the cobbles away from her. There was a sharp tug and she was off her feet and on her knees, being dragged towards the grinning form of Enri. Sebastian came at him, the long sword flying in a deadly silver arc, but Roki moved in front and met the giant blade with two of his own. Another tug, and Wydrin could see blood seeping up through the torn leather.

"Some more of that green fire wouldn't go amiss, princeling!" Wydrin pressed the edge of her remaining dagger against the whip and was dismayed to find it barely made a mark on it.

"Bezcavar enjoys your suffering!" called Fane from his space between the stalls. He was wearing his black helm now and that was glowing too, with the same strange markings as those adorning the gauntlets of Enri and Roki, but there was still only one of him. *What does it do?* Wydrin sensed this was an important question if they wished to survive the next few moments. Fane hadn't even drawn a weapon.

She turned back to see Frith picking himself up from the floor, his face a sheet of blood, and Sebastian working hard to keep back the three identical men, the muscles in his neck and shoulders bunched like grapefruits. As she watched, his sword passed harmlessly through the body of one of the Rokis, only to meet the solidity of the sword with a discordant crash.

"Bring them in, that's it," Fane was bellowing now. Distantly Wydrin could hear shouts from the crowd, but whether it was encouragement or mockery she couldn't tell. "Keep the girl alive too and we'll have some entertainment tonight."

Ignoring the agony in her arm, Wydrin pulled back on the whip and forced herself to her feet. She raised Frostling, preparing an over-arm throw she hoped would find Fane in his thick chest and split his rotten heart, when suddenly the young man from the crowd with the untidy hair was in front of her. He winked.

"What are you...?"

He produced a strange knife from an inner pocket; it was clear and sparkled as if made of crystal. The young man pressed it against the whip and it snapped almost instantly. Wydrin staggered back and he caught hold of her hand.

"We must run now," he said. He had an accent she couldn't place. "If you and your friends wish to live, keep with me."

"Sounds good," said Wydrin.

She snatched Ashes up from the cobblestones and shouted at her companions; Frith and Sebastian followed readily enough, but so did the four identical men, whooping and howling as they came. The crowd parted for them and the young man led them deep into it, amongst the stalls and boxes, turning wildly here and there. All the time he kept Wydrin's hand in a vice-like grip, which normally would have annoyed her, but she was afraid that if she pulled free she would lose him instantly in the swarms of townspeople. There was a clatter of wood against wood and she realised the guards on the walls were loosing their longbows, and only the shelter of the stalls protected them.

"Where are we going?"

"Keep close, little cat! Run where I run!"

They passed a cart filled with a towering heap full of mouldering pumpkins. There was a shout, and suddenly the pumpkins were tumbling from the cart onto the ground, directly into the path of the pursuing guards. Wydrin glanced over her shoulder just in time to see Dreyda back there behind the cart, her long thin face pinched in triumph, and the young man tugged her another way, moving towards the back of the market. The rolling root vegetables gained them a few seconds, enough to get out of sight of the Children of the Fog.

"Who are you?" said Wydrin, between gasps.

"My name is Crowleo." He did not turn to look back at her, instead dragging her towards a ramshackle stone building across from the main bustle of the market. A pile of old leaves had collected in the doorway and the small windows were broken. "Are your friends still with us?"

"We are," said Frith. His hair was stuck to his forehead with blood. Sebastian looked sickly and distracted. "What is going on?"

He gave a brief bow, and swung open the door.

"No time to talk. Inside now."

"How do we know this isn't a trap?" asked Frith, but he followed them in just the same. Inside they could just make out an altar surrounded by broken wooden benches, and there was a slight smell of incense, like an exotic ghost.

"A disused temple?" said Wydrin.

"No time, no time."

From outside came the sound of men shouting, obviously trying to decide in which direction they had run. Wydrin thought they'd figure it out in less than a handful of heartbeats, and she could see no doorways out of the temple.

"Listen, friend, if you've led us into a dead-end..." She patted the dagger on her belt threateningly, but Crowleo was ignoring her. He walked up the centre aisle with his eyes on the floor, and then dropped to his knees in front of the stone altar. There was a mouldy rug on the floor which he picked up gingerly and moved to one side.

Beneath it were flat grey flagstones. As she watched, he took a slim object from an inner pocket and pushed it against a small gap in the floor. There was an audible click and the flagstones swung away into the darkness below.

"What was that?" said Wydrin. Crowleo held up the object for her. It was a narrow rectangle about as long as the palm of his hand, apparently made of pink glass. Now the voices outside were very loud.

"A secret key for a secret door," he said, smiling slightly. "Now, down here, if you please, or we'll all be flayed alive. If we're lucky."

The three of them followed him down into the dark. There was a short drop and a strong smell of earth and leaf mould. Crowleo reached up behind them and did something with the glass key that made the flagstones swing back into place, and they were standing together in the pitch-black.

"So, I don't suppose anyone thought to bring a torch with them?" asked Sebastian.

"Funny you should say that…" There was a flicker in the dark, and Crowleo's face was lit with a warm, sunny glow. He held a glass globe in his hand, and inside it was a hot ball of yellow light.

"Oh, what is this now?" said Wydrin, starting to get a little annoyed. This Crowleo character was a little bit too confident for her liking; she liked to be the confident one.

"It is a remembrance of light, that is all." Crowleo looked up at them all. The light made him look older. "You have questions."

"I certainly do," snapped Frith, "Where do you think you've taken us? And what do you know about Fane?"

"And who is this Bezcavar bastard?" added Wydrin.

"We will walk and talk," said Crowleo, and with that he set off ahead, his ball of light revealing mould-encrusted stone walls to either side. They were in a tunnel. As he walked he spoke softly. "You are the young Lord Frith, returned to us, it seems, from a shallow grave. My mistress saw your arrival here in one of her glasses, and knowing you would meet with difficulties sent me to retrieve you."

"How could she possibly know that?" said Frith. "We arrived here entirely at random. No one could have known we were coming."

"My mistress makes the finest of glasses," said Crowleo smoothly, just as though Frith hadn't spoken. "And like the glass, all will become clear. Do you see?" He turned and winked at Wydrin. "It is a joke. Now, this tunnel will take us out under the walls of Pinehold and some way into the forest, and from there I shall take you to see my mistress."

"And who is she?" asked Sebastian.

"An old friend of the family. One who knows how to keep secrets."

22

After a long walk in the dim light of his globe, Crowleo led them to a set of rough steps cut directly into the earth, and they emerged blinking into the middle of the forest. Amazingly, there was still some light in the sky. *Time is strange when you are fighting or fleeing,* thought Sebastian. *You think you have struggled through hours, when it has been mere minutes.*

"How far are we from Pinehold?" asked Frith.

"Far enough."

"And if Fane's men pursue us outside of the town?"

"The tunnel under the old temple is one of the many secrets my mistress keeps, and they will not find it. Now, we must walk north, and swiftly. The night is coming on and I do not wish to meet anything hungrier than me under these trees. The Secret Keeper is waiting."

"The Secret Keeper?" Wydrin smirked.

"As I said, all will become clear."

Crowleo had a delicate face, with tanned skin and dark brown hair that fell in a centre parting, framing his jaw. The faintest dusting of stubble across his chin made him appear younger rather than older. Looking at him somehow made Sebastian think of Gallo, and that caused a brief constriction of grief in his chest. Crowleo caught his eye and gave him a look, as though he knew what he was thinking. Sebastian turned away. "We'd best get going, in that case."

The Secret Keeper's home was not especially secret, it seemed to Wydrin. They had not walked for too long a time before they came to a place where the ground beneath them grew rockier and

133

steeper, following a path that only Crowleo could see. The trees became scarcer, until they emerged on an outcrop of earth and rock, thrusting out over an unbroken sea of dark trees. On the cliff's edge sat one of the oddest houses she'd ever seen, undoubtedly visible from the sweep of the Blackwood below, if you happened to be above the treeline.

The normal concept of a house – squarish, orderly, symmetrical – had apparently been lost on the architect. It was more a meandering collection of rooms, piled next to and on top of each other with little thought as to how you might get from one to the other, and every single one had a window. Small ones, round ones, large ones, square ones; the peculiar house glittered with them in the last of the evening's light. It was built largely from wood, and ivy had grown over portions of the walls, giving the place a queer, organic look. At the very front of this confusion was a large drum-shaped bunker, built from old grey stone. This was the only part of the structure that had holes rather than glass windows, and it was from those that they could see a fierce light glowing. Every now and then a thick cloud of black smoke would emerge, and they could clearly hear a female voice muttering and cursing.

"I like it," Wydrin said as they stood outside. "Understated. Subtle."

"My mistress has eccentric tastes," said Crowleo evenly. "Her work has made her so. She sees things differently, you could say."

"So much glass," said Sebastian, impressed. "That must be expensive."

Crowleo shrugged.

"Perks of the profession."

He led them over to the stone room, and waved a hand at them to keep back. He leaned in the doorway and spoke softly. An elderly female voice answered. They couldn't make out the words, but the voice was rough and full of impatience. Crowleo reappeared, that half-smile back on his lips. Wydrin thought his gaze lingered on Sebastian, but then there was a lot of Sebastian to see.

"You are to wait inside. My mistress is just finishing up some work."

"Where is she? It is quite urgent that I talk to her." Frith glanced at the door to the stone room. Patterns of red and yellow light spilled out onto the ground.

"She will be with us shortly. Believe me, it is not worth disturbing her while she is working. I shall never hear the last of it."

Crowleo led them to the nearest door in the wooden portion of the house. Inside they found themselves in a large but crowded workroom. There were benches everywhere, covered with all sorts of odds and ends, the purpose of which Wydrin could only guess at. There were glass jars filled with all manner of substances, delicate vials containing brightly coloured liquids, and a huge pestle and mortar covered in something black and crusted.

"Come in." Crowleo began moving some of the debris from one of the lower benches with a deftness that suggested he did this quite often. "Have a seat. There are more comfortable rooms, yes, but she'll be finished soon and she's always happier in here than anywhere else."

Wydrin perched on the bench, trying to take it all in. Sebastian looked uncomfortable, no doubt concerned that his bulk or his sword might break something. Frith stood with his arms crossed over his chest.

Crowleo cleared his throat.

"Can I get you a drink?"

Wydrin looked around at the bottles and jars full of viscous liquid. "Is that safe?"

Crowleo laughed, and his cheeks turned a little pink. *He is uncommonly pretty when he blushes*, thought Wydrin. She glanced up at Sebastian to see if he'd noticed, but the big knight was backing slowly away from the table, not paying attention.

"I have some blackberry wine here somewhere. Don't worry, it is entirely not poisonous. Holley is very partial to it." He opened a small cupboard and began pushing bottles aside.

"Holley?"

"The Secret Keeper. That is her name."

Crowleo fetched four glasses and a tall bottle filled with a dark purple liquid over to the bench, when the door was flung open and the Secret Keeper came in.

"Is that the good wine, Crow? Only the best for our Lord of the Blackwood."

She was a well-built woman in her late fifties, with black hair just turning to grey in little flurries at her temples, and a tanned face with deep lines at the corners of the mouth and eyes which spoke of a lifetime of hard work. She wore a grey shirt under a thick leather apron streaked with soot.

Crowleo poured a glass of the wine and passed it to his mistress, who took a sip, and shrugged.

"It'll do, I suppose. Now, what do you want?"

Frith stood up straight, bristling at the direct question.

"Your... assistant here escorted us from Pinehold. He seems to know who we are. He even claimed that you knew in advance that we were coming."

"And who are you, exactly?"

Frith frowned, obviously confused.

"I am Lord Aaron Frith, of course."

Wydrin took a glass from Crowleo and drank down the blackberry wine in one gulp. It was good stuff, ripe with the taste of long summer days and meadow grass.

"And how do I know you are Aaron Frith, then?" said Holley. "From what the people are saying, the Frith family were butchered and buried under the black soil, right down to poor little Tristan."

Frith's face contracted with impatience.

"This person said you knew who I was. That you sent him to us! Can you not see?"

"Aye, I see well enough," Holley waved a hand at Frith dismissively. "Don't get yourself all worked up. You have your father's look, right down to that piggish impatient expression he used to get when I was late with a project."

"You knew my father?"

"Your mother's nose, though," continued Holley. "Aye, I'd know who you are even if I hadn't seen you in the glass. What happened to you, boy?"

Frith sipped at his wine, as if to sweeten the taste of his words.

"The castle was taken by Istrian thugs, as you must know, and once they'd tortured and murdered my family they got down to the business of torturing me." He paused, and put down the glass. His fingers were trembling ever so slightly. "Luckily a group of loyal fighters smuggled me out of the dungeon, although almost all of them died in the attempt. I made my way to Creos, as best I could..." His words trailed off. "What happened then does not matter. What is important is that I have returned, and I have debts to repay." He glared up at Holley. "Is that enough for you?"

Holley sniffed, and emptied her glass.

"A bad business, that's for certain. If I'd seen it in the glass... but there's no point in dwelling on that now. And who are these two? Not Blackwood men, if I'm any judge."

"I am Sebastian Carverson, a knight of Ynnsmouth, and this is my colleague, Wydrin of Crosshaven." Sebastian bowed slightly, narrowly avoiding knocking a row of glasses off the bench with his sword. Wydrin suppressed a smile. "We are currently employed by Lord Frith."

"*Hmph*. Interesting company you're keeping," Holley said to Frith. "I've seen more trustworthy-looking mercenaries ransacking bodies on a battlefield."

"Hey," said Wydrin. She liked this woman. "I am deeply insulted." Holley stood up abruptly.

"It's the vault, isn't it? The greedy, murderous bastards. I can give you the location of the vault. It is yours by right, after all."

"You know where it is?" said Sebastian and Frith together. There was a pause, and they glared at each other. Sebastian rounded on Holley.

"There are people dying in Pinehold, tortured or torn apart by bears, and you sit out here and let it happen? If you know where it is and you know what they want..." There was a tinkling of glass as Sebastian's shoulder brushed a shelf loaded with delicate instruments.

Holley held up hands thick with calluses.

"It's not as simple as that. Put your knightly indignation away, you fool. I hold the information, but only a person of the Frith blood can access it. Besides which, I made certain promises..."

"I don't understand," said Frith. Some of the anger had left his face, to be replaced with confusion. "The secret was kept strictly between my father and my oldest brother. I was only to be told when I, when... No one outside the family was to know. It was our deepest secret."

Holley turned to Crowleo, her eyebrows raised.

"You told them who I was, yes? Particularly the part involving secrets and keeping them?"

Crowleo dipped his head once, smiling faintly.

"Right, good, can't expect everyone to be swift on the uptake I suppose." She gestured at a door on the far side of the room. "Follow me, Lord Frith and associated untrustworthies. I think this will be easier if I show you."

23

Holley led them from the workshop. They walked down a short corridor where the ceiling was so low Sebastian had to bow his head, and they entered another room crowded with books and instruments. A big window to their left, filled with warped, greenish glass, looked out onto the rocky grounds outside. Wydrin looked from it back to Holley and was surprised to see that in this light her hair looked darker, the white hairs at her temple invisible. She even appeared to have fewer wrinkles at the corners of her eyes.

They passed quickly through a further two rooms, these ones much more like those of a normal house. Wydrin saw sofas and chairs, a sink covered in cups and old saucepans, the sort of general chaos found in a home occupied by two busy people. Finally, they came to a room with an ornately carved wooden door. Crowleo threw it open, and Wydrin felt her breath catch in her throat. It was a room filled with light.

Windows stretched from one side to the other, looking out over the cliff's edge to the dark forest below. The last ruddy light of sunset was smeared across the clouds in the distance, filling the room with a deep orange glow. And the items in the room caught that light and twisted it into strange shapes.

"What are they all?"

Beneath the window was a long table, and upon it were hundreds of delicate glass objects, every one different, and every one beautiful. There were globes of all sizes and every colour of the rainbow, strange cubes that sent geometric reflections streaming out in front of them, filigrees of glass clumped together in spirals like exotic, fragile plants, as well as figures of men, women and animals, all created from shining crystal.

"They are the secret holders," said a woman who sounded like Holley, but when Wydrin turned towards the voice there was a much younger woman standing there. She cast about in confusion.

"Where did the Secret Keeper go?" asked Sebastian.

"I am right here." The young woman had jet-black hair, clear unlined skin and looked to be no older than thirty. "Here." She picked up one of the glass globes from the table and passed it to Wydrin almost carelessly. "Look into that, girl, and tell me what you see."

Frowning, Wydrin did as she was bid. The globe was smaller than many on the table, only slightly bigger than a pomegranate, and there was a slightly orange cast to the glass. Peering at it closely, Wydrin turned it around in her hands to catch the light. She could see her own face reflected in it, the confines of the room and... something else.

"I see a landscape," she said, a touch reluctantly. "There's a forest in the distance, and rocky ground. There's a pile of stones, like a temple or a—"

"A cairn," finished the woman. "What you are seeing is what was here before I built this house. The glass holds the secret of this land's past."

"Let me see," demanded Frith. Wydrin passed him the globe, still not quite able to believe it.

"I make magical glass," continued Holley. "I can make it so that through the glass you can see the past, or things that you would keep secret from others. I can even make glass through which it is possible to see the future, although that is incredibly bloody fiddly and you're never really sure which bit of the future you're looking at, so it's not as useful as you might imagine. It's all about bending light, you see. Bending it to show you what you want."

"Right," said Wydrin. "But that still doesn't explain why you've dropped a few decades on our short walk through your house."

"The windows," said Crowleo. He walked up to the panes and pressed his fingers against the glass. There was more than a hint of pride in his voice. "My mistress made these windows so as to cast a certain light. In this light, she is a young woman at the beginning of her career."

"And in the stone room, where there are no windows, you are

your real age," said Wydrin, remembering the elderly voice they'd heard while outside. "Clever."

"Of course. I need all my wisdom and skill whilst I work the glass. These days young Crowleo helps me with the heavier stuff, but inside these rooms I can be whatever age I wish."

"Extraordinary," said Sebastian. He was keeping back by the door, far from the delicate objects. "Truly, a wonder."

"Indeed," said Frith. "I assume, then, that my father entrusted the secret of the vault within one of your objects?" His voice was tight, and Wydrin guessed he wasn't especially pleased by this turn of events.

Holley nodded to Crowleo. The apprentice pulled a pair of brown velvet gloves from a pocket and slipped them on. Reaching to the back of the table he plucked an odd, spiky confection of glass and passed it to Frith. At first Wydrin thought it was in the shape of some kind of elaborate shell, but when he held it up to the light she saw that it was actually a number of clear glass leaves, splayed out in a fan. There was a hint of green to the glass that made her think of the clear water of the Graces' pools, or the Sea-Glass road itself.

"Can I see?" she asked, but Holley shook her head.

"Fierce magic I made for this one. Only those of the Frith blood can hold it with bare hands. If young Aaron Frith here wasn't who he claimed to be, he'd be writhing on the floor by now, blood foaming on his lips."

Frith shot her a dangerous look.

"Good thing that I am, then. How does this work? I can't see anything."

"Look deeper into the glass," urged Crowleo. "Relax your eyes and let it come to you."

Frowning slightly, Frith held the spread of glass leaves up in front of him. The last of the day's light filled it, and soft green reflections played across his face like marsh ghosts. He narrowed his eyes, his lips pursed.

"I still can't – wait, there is something."

"What do you see?" asked Sebastian.

"I see this place, again. I can see the edge of the cliff, but now there is a bridge leading from it. There is no such thing."

"That you can see," agreed Holley. "What else is there?"

"If I follow the bridge, it stretches far across the forest. Here and there it weaves in and out of the treetops, and finally it comes to another cliff, but instead of reaching up to the edge it leads straight into the rock, where there is a dark cave."

"And there you have your vault," said Holley. "It's a long, cold walk, so I suggest you get yourselves moving."

"But the bridge – it was here in my father's time, I assume, but it must have long since fallen into disrepair and collapsed into the forest below. We saw no bridge on our approach."

"You're a fussy one, aren't you?" Holley's face creased up with distaste, and for a moment it was possible to see the older woman who had originally greeted them. "Come outside," she said, waving them all back towards the door. "I'll show you your damn bridge."

Outside the sun had sunk below the horizon, and the sky was shading towards the deep indigo of dusk. Holley had grown progressively older again as they walked through the house and now, outside the influence of her magical windows, she was a stooped old lady with white hair down to her shoulders. Her eyes were as bright and lively as ever, though.

"There, out there, look." She took them to the cliff's edge and pointed to a distant lump of land that burst forth from the black trees like a mottled whale breaching the surface of the sea. "That's where you're heading, all the way across there. Do you see it?"

"I see it, Secret Keeper, but what I do not see is the bridge," said Frith.

"Look through the glass again, impatient Lord Frith," said Holley. "And tell me what you see."

Frith held it up to his eyes, and Wydrin saw them widen in surprise. He took the glass away, looked at the cliff's edge, then back again. He repeated this process twice before he spoke again.

"I see a secret way," he said. "There is a bridge there, but I can only see it when I look through the glass."

"Let me look," said Wydrin.

"It will do you no good," said Holley. "Only those of Frith blood can hold the glass, and they alone can see the secret. You are not of the blood, I assume? And you have not borne children of the Frith line?" She smirked slightly as she spoke.

Wydrin snorted.

"Certainly not."

Frith still held the glass, peering out across the cliff. When eventually he lowered it, his face was set into grim lines.

"It looks very lonely, and very dark," he said, almost as if he'd forgotten they were there. He glanced at them. "But no time like the present." And he started to march towards the edge of the cliff.

"Not so fast, princeling," called Wydrin.

Frith turned back, impatience in every line of his body.

"What is it?"

"Look out there. It's dark now. The people at Pinehold…" Wydrin pursed her lips. Frith and Sebastian had described the remains left outside the town walls on their walk to the Secret Keeper's house. "Those people are long dead."

Sebastian rounded on her angrily.

"We have to go back for them, Wydrin! Once we know the exact location of the vault we can trade the information for their lives."

"We will do no such thing," started Frith hotly. Wydrin held her hands up for peace. She tried to use the same tone of voice Sebastian used on her when it was close to chucking out time and he wanted to go home. "We can't help those people now, Seb. If we're going back to Pinehold–" There was another noise from Frith, but she waved him down. "If we're going back to help, and yes, I do think we should, Sebastian, stop looking at me like that, if we're going back, then we have to go back fighting fit. We need to rest, eat some decent food, and sleep in some decent beds." She jabbed a finger at the cliff's edge. "And I'm not crossing any invisible bridges in the bloody dark. That's if the Secret Keeper wouldn't mind putting us up for the night?"

Holley shrugged.

"We've got plenty of rooms."

Frith sighed heavily, and took a moment to glare at both her and Sebastian. The big knight still looked reluctant, but in the end he shrugged. Lord Frith crossed his arms across his chest.

"An early start, then."

24

"He was a prickly man, your father. Difficult, even. I dare say the staff up at Blackwood Keep dragged his name through the mud more than once, when he was safely out of earshot."

Holley pulled a battered clay pipe from an inner pocket and began to fill it from a leather pouch on the table. She and Frith were alone in a cosy living room filled with over-stuffed chairs and elderly bookcases. In here she looked to be in her mid-sixties, a woman just starting to slow down.

"Distant, but interested. That's how I would have described him."

"That does sound familiar," said Frith dryly. Holley shrugged, and sucked on the pipe, releasing a soft cloud of smoke that smelt of cabbages.

"I knew your family well, boy. Did you know that?"

Frith shook his head.

"I knew your grandfather, and his father before him. I counted your father as a friend, truth be told."

"Have you always kept the secret of the vault, then?"

"Aye. The location of the vault changes, every few generations or so. A new place, and a new glass to keep the secret in, just in case the worst should happen." She took another long drag on the pipe. "In your case, I suppose it did."

Frith ignored this.

"You knew about the bridge, then? You must have, if my father came out here to visit the vault."

"Your father trusted me."

"More than his own son, it seems."

"Look." Holley jabbed the end of the pipe at Frith. "Your father was a decent man. Do you truly think he kept this from you for cruelty's sake?"

There were a few moments of silence between them. The fire in the grate spat and smoked, while all around the house creaked and sighed and settled its wooden bones for the night.

"Why?" asked Frith eventually. He felt tired, possibly more tired than he'd ever felt in his life. "Why all this secrecy? Scores of other old families have similar hoards and they do not insist on such conspiracies."

"And you know what's in there, do you? Been in the vault, have you?" She smiled crookedly.

"You know I have not."

"Whatever it is, your ancestors thought it worth protecting."

"*Do* you know? Do you have any idea?"

Holley shook her head.

"The day your father came to show Leon, your brother, I think it was the happiest I'd ever seen him. He was excited to be sharing the family secret, and, well," she gestured at the room, taking in the enchanted windows, "it's not just any secret, after all."

Frith swallowed hard.

"Not excited enough to share it with all his sons, apparently."

Holley waved a hand at his objection as though swatting away a small fly.

"Oh, you were young, and no doubt he felt he had all the time in the world. It was safer to keep the numbers that knew about it low."

"He was probably right to do so." There was a cold hand at Frith's throat as he thought back to his last months inside Blackwood Keep. His father and brother had known, and kept the secret while under the ministrations of Yellow-Eyed Rin. All day and all night he'd listened to them, the noises they made as they died. Would he have been able to keep the secret? Uphold the family honour? He wasn't certain. Not certain at all.

Some of what he felt must have shown on his face, as the Secret Keeper leaned forward with a stern look.

"There was nowt you could do, boy. You hear me?"

"I didn't tell them," said Frith, his voice small even to his own ears. "I didn't tell them I didn't know because I thought they would just open my throat and have done with it."

Holley nodded.

"It was the right course of action."

"If I'd known the secret I could have saved them. Nothing is worth this, nothing is worth being the one left behind..." He bit down the rest of those words. "But instead they died, and for what?" Frith thumped his fist against the arm of the chair. After a moment he closed his eyes, attempting to hold back the surge of anger. "What could possibly be so important?"

Holley leaned back in her chair, sighing as her old bones popped.

"That, I imagine, you will find out tomorrow."

It was getting late, and the apprentice showed no signs of retiring. Instead, he refilled their glasses with red wine, and pushed forward a plate of cheese and oatcakes.

Wydrin had gone to bed more than an hour ago, complaining of a stiffness in her shoulders and a need for a good twelve hours' sleep, while Frith had retired after a long talk with the Secret Keeper. To Sebastian's surprise, the old woman had not gone to bed at all, but had gone back out to the stone workroom, to potter around, as she put it.

"She doesn't sleep much these days," explained Crowleo. They were in a comfortable room on one of the upper floors. Sebastian suspected it was Crowleo's own study; there was an old but carefully polished desk, a merrily burning fireplace, and a few items of discarded clothing. Young men who were studying rarely remembered to tidy away inconsequential things like clothes, in Sebastian's experience. He'd had similar habits, after all.

"My father was the same," admitted Sebastian. "In his later years he would go to bed last and be up before all of us."

Crowleo smiled.

"She says she can feel the end coming, and she has so much work to do yet. No time for sleep. Was your father a Ynnsmouth knight too?"

"No. He was a stonemason. Not everyone feels the mountains calling."

"But you did?"

Sebastian had to smile at the apprentice's enthusiasm. In the warm glow from the fire his eyes glittered, their gaze always resting on Sebastian's face.

"When I was twelve years old, I had a dream from which I woke covered in sweat."

Crowleo raised his eyebrows. Sebastian cleared his throat and continued.

"I dreamed I walked alone on a mountain path, snow under my bare feet. I came to a great wall of stone that blocked my way, but suddenly it cracked down the middle like an egg, and I could walk through into the space beyond." He paused. The wine was fine and smoky in the back of his throat. "In the dark, the mountain spoke to me. When I told my mother about the dream, she took me to the Order and I was inducted before my thirteenth birthday."

"A tender age."

Sebastian shrugged. "It was a good life for a boy from a poor family. The Order fed me, clothed me and taught me my letters, until I was old enough to swear my sword in front of the god-peak. My mother was very happy." For a moment he remembered the look on her face the last time he'd seen her, and he turned away from that memory quickly.

"I grew up with tales of the Ynnsmouth knights," said Crowleo. "An ancient order. Proud and steadfast."

"Oh yes," said Sebastian, not quite able to keep the bitterness from his voice, "they were certainly full of pride."

Even so, he could not turn from those memories completely. Growing up under the shadow of the god-peaks he'd always felt like he was doing the right thing. He was made to be a knight. That's what it meant when the mountain itself spoke to you.

"How old were you when you came to be an apprentice to the Secret Keeper?"

"Fifteen. My parents died when I was young." Crowleo cleared his throat, glancing at the window. During the day it would have a spectacular view of the forest, but it was full dark now and night filled the glass like ink in a bottle. "My aunt looked after me for a while, but she was old and stuck in her ways. I do not think she liked me very much." Crowleo laughed, although Sebastian thought it sounded a little strained. "I did have a great interest in making things, so as soon as it was seemly she dropped me off here with all my belongings in a bag and a word not to come back too soon. Holley seemed completely unsurprised by my arrival. Perhaps she saw it in one of her glasses. She has never said."

"She does extraordinary work."

Crowleo nodded rapidly.

"Holley says there are two types of magic in the world – that of the mages, and that of Ede itself, a magic that comes from the soil and air. This place, where she built this house, is teeming with magic." He paused, rubbing some cheese crumbs from his fingers. "She can do things with the glass that I can barely comprehend, even after years of working with her, but I am learning. I am starting to see how the light refracts, how it can be separated and combined –" He paused, and then laughed at his own enthusiasm. Sebastian smiled. "I know techniques and secrets that other men and women would kill to get their hands on. It is just a little lonely. A little quiet."

"What, when you get visitors like us?" Sebastian took a gulp of his wine, enjoying the way it made his head spin. "People like us must drop in all the time. Lost lords, mouthy sell-swords."

"Handsome knights?" added Crowleo with a raised eyebrow. They both laughed this time.

"From my experience, you don't learn the value of a quiet life until you lose it," said Sebastian. He suddenly felt rather tired, and older than his years. A long day and too much wine, he told himself. He made a point of yawning, and finished the last of his drink in one gulp. "I think it's time I got some sleep. Lord Frith will be up with the crack of dawn, no doubt, and that one has little sympathy for weary heads."

He stood up with Crowleo watching him closely. The young man's eyes looked almost amber in the firelight.

"There is still wine left, Sebastian. It is bad luck to go to bed on an unfinished bottle."

"You sound like Wydrin now," he said, and forced a smile. "Another time, perhaps."

Despite his protests about needing some rest, Sebastian did not sleep well that night. The small room Holley had given him was warm and comfortable enough, even if the bed was perhaps a little short, but he tossed and turned, at times pulling the blankets up under his chin, and then throwing them off altogether. When he did sleep, his dreams were dark and bloody, and the voices of the dragon's daughters whispered to him as the mountains once had, although with each fitful waking he could remember none of their words.

"She is getting closer," he muttered the third time he awoke with the smell of blood and cinders in his nose. "Closer all the time."

He sat up and looked out the crooked window as the first blush of dawn crept over the tops of distant trees. After a minute or two he realised his nose was bleeding.

25

In this town they were fighting back.

It was late at night, but already many buildings were on fire, and the Thirty-Third had no difficulty following the movements of the people below from the second-storey window where she crouched. Behind her were the remains of the three men who had been hiding in the building. Their blood soaked unnoticed into the floorboards while the Ninety-Seventh rifled through the wooden desk, scattering paper onto the floor.

Word of the brood army's advance was moving faster than they were, and this small town, with its neglected stone wall and half-hearted ditches, had gathered a force together to meet them, men and women in boiled leather and plate. They were different to most of the humans they'd met so far – the fear was still in their eyes, but it was held behind a shield of something else. The Thirty-Third couldn't quite name that shield, but it made her think of their father.

"Why do they do it?" she said aloud. "They must see that it is hopeless."

The Ninety-Seventh glanced up, her fists filled with paper.

"It is that or run and hide."

"Which would you choose?"

As the Thirty-Third watched, a group of men and women on the cobbled streets below brought their shields up and charged forward, trying to gain a few feet on the brood army facing them. There was a chorus of ragged shouts and screams as the crystal blades of her sisters glittered under the firelight, stabbing and piercing. Across the street the buildings were already burning, forcing the humans onto a narrow path.

"Run and hide?" snorted the Ninety-Seventh. She had found pieces of paper full of neat black handwriting, and her eyes were bright with hunger. "Who do *we* have to run and hide from?"

There was a deafening roar from outside and a blast of carrion stench. The Thirty-Third leaned out of the window and looked up just in time to see Y'Ruen come hurtling down from a star-studded sky and crash heavily into the burning buildings opposite. Flaming debris flew everywhere, killing half the humans outright, while Y'Ruen writhed in the destruction. Amongst the fire her scales were black and gold.

"Perhaps sometimes all you have left is the fight," said the Thirty-Third. To her surprise, the surviving humans were regrouping and heading towards the dragon. Several had long-shafted spears which they aimed towards Y'Ruen's belly. They charged, and their tiny human cries were just about audible over the roar of the fire and the dragon.

"See?" she said, gesturing at the fight. The Ninety-Seventh took no notice – she had found a pot of ink and was daubing things that almost looked like words across the paper. "Why do that? They will die now, certainly."

"They will die either way," replied the Ninety-Seventh, unconcerned.

Y'Ruen, body curling like a snake to face her attackers, could have killed all of them with one strike of her tail; instead, her great head shot forward and snapped one of the men between her jaws. His scream the Thirty-Third heard quite clearly.

"Mother is playing with them," she noted. She turned briefly to look at the bodies on the floor. She and the Ninety-Seventh had torn their throats out in short order, save for the fat one who had tried to hide under the desk. The Ninety-Seventh had poked him all over with her sword until he came out, and by then he was half-dead. They'd left him to bleed slowly. Playing with the humans no longer seemed as satisfying as it had once been.

Outside, the group of men and women had broken, and now some of them were trying to run, but Y'Ruen slid her tail around to block their escape. Claws full of reflected fire stabbed at them with playful precision; one man was undone from his throat to his belly, while a woman who'd almost made it into a side street had her legs cut from under her. Y'Ruen bent her head, almost delicately, and the woman was gone.

The word "nightmare" occurred to the Thirty-Third although she wasn't entirely sure what it meant.

The Ninety-Seventh joined her at the window. Her hands were black to the wrists.

"Look, there are more of them coming. They do not give up."

Even as their comrades were reduced to blood and gristle, more of the humans were marching up the street, bellowing, swords held high.

Y'Ruen turned towards them and both the brood sisters felt the wave of simple pleasure emanating from the dragon. It was like stepping from the shade into bright sunshine on a hot day.

"They don't give up because sometimes the fight is all you have left," said the Thirty-Third grimly. Her sister turned away from the window, not quite daring to meet her eyes. Her expression was guarded.

"That's what *he* would say," she whispered.

In the street below, Y'Ruen was spewing fire over the small human resistance, cooking them inside their armour. The smell of burning flesh wafted in through the window. The Thirty-Third thought of his eyes, cold and blue, and the memory of a mountain she had never seen.

"Our *father* would say that."

26

Wydrin was determined to drive him mad. Frith came to this conclusion on the second hour after they were supposed to have left for the hidden bridge. First, she rose later than everyone else, stretching and groaning and padding into Holley's kitchen like a scruffy alley cat. She insisted on a hot bath, causing Crowleo to run off to heat up more water, and afterwards sat at the kitchen table eating plateful after plateful of ham and eggs, steam rising from her sodden hair. And when finally she had dressed, teasing her hair into a configuration that pleased her, scraped the mud from her boots and oiled her knives, it had still taken a fair amount of cajoling from Sebastian and outright threats from Frith to get her outside into the morning air.

And now she stood, surveying the world as if it were waiting patiently for her approval.

"Are we ready?" asked Frith. "Finally?"

"Almost," she said, scratching her head and shaking the last of the water from her ears. "There is one last thing. A request, actually, for the Secret Keeper."

Holley raised a pair of wispy white eyebrows. Outside the house with its distorting windows she looked to be over ninety. She leaned on a walking stick, although Crowleo was always close at hand.

"What is it you wish, girl?" asked Holley.

"Whatever it is, let it be quick," said Frith. "It will be midday by the time we take our leave."

Wydrin ignored him.

"You say that you can manipulate glass so that it shows you what you want."

"In a sense, yes." Holley shrugged her bony shoulders. "With certain restrictions, of course."

"I was wondering if you could make something for me," she said, her head tipped slightly to one side. "A special favour, I suppose, but when our princeling here pays us I will be good for the gold."

"What is it you would like to see through the glass?"

Wydrin smiled, the slow smile of a woman with a secret.

"The truth. Just the truth."

Holley rubbed a finger over her chin and nodded, apparently pleased with the challenge.

"Come into my workroom for a moment," she said, "And I'll make some measurements."

And so they waited, Frith pacing back and forth. Crowleo had prepared small packs for them all – new cloaks, a parcel of bread and cheese, fresh waterskins – and these he passed out with a mildly wistful look, as though he wished to go with them. He even gave Frith the small lighted globe he'd used in the tunnel under Pinehold, for which he gave a quick, muttered thanks.

Eventually the Copper Cat emerged. She and the Secret Keeper shook hands, and she rejoined the group.

"Are you quite finished?" asked Frith. He knew it was only asking for more barbed comments, but he couldn't help himself. "Would you like to dawdle for another hour or so? Perhaps you feel it is time for another bath, or is there some food left in the kitchen that you haven't consumed?"

Wydrin gave him a sunny smile.

"No, that's quite all right. I think it's time to go, don't you?"

Biting down his answer, Frith said his goodbyes and, holding up the chunk of glass, advanced upon the cliff's edge.

The bridge was still there, much to his relief. There was an archway over the entrance, and as he stepped up to it he saw that the symbol of the Frith family had been carved deeply into each wooden pillar; a pair of Blackwood trees, branches spreading out to either side. Looking at that, out here in the middle of nowhere, made his throat feel tight. His father had stood here, who knew how many times, with this same viewing glass, and had walked across this extraordinary bridge so often that no doubt it had become commonplace.

Why did he never tell me about it? To see signs of his family's

existence when he was the only one left still alive was... He decided
not to think about it any longer. Turning back to look at Wydrin and
Sebastian, he saw that they were both watching him closely.

"Well, what are you gawping at? Let's get a move on. I'm sure
you'll be wanting to collect your money and be off."

"After you, princeling." Wydrin gestured at the cliff. "There's no
way I'm walking off the edge of this first. Remember, we can't see
the bloody thing."

"You do not actually have to accompany me, you know."

"What? Let you go wandering off down an invisible bridge by
yourself?" said Wydrin. "You'll either get yourself killed or decide
you don't feel like paying us after all."

Frith sighed. He suspected she was more interested in seeing the
inside of the vault than his safety.

"Very well."

Holding the glass up in front of him, he stepped onto the bridge.
Beneath his feet there was only empty air, according to his own
eyes, but he could feel the firm wooden surface below his feet. The
construction of the bridge was strange, to say the least: there were
no sides, but the floor, made of smoothly joined dark wooden slats,
curved up slightly towards the edge, so that you might have some
small warning before you wandered straight off the side and fell to
your death. Below he could see the rocky side of the cliff, and the
dark canopy of trees. There didn't appear to be anything supporting
the bridge at all. His stomach tried to climb up through his throat.

"I wouldn't advise looking down," he said, dragging his eyes back
up to the piece of crystal held carefully in his hands. "And keep
close behind me. Tread only where I tread." Wydrin and Sebastian
followed behind him, neither looking especially pleased.

"Hoy!" shouted Holley from behind them. "Whatever you do,
Lord Frith, don't you drop that there glass! You think the journey
across is bad enough now; just wait till you have to do it blind. I
don't have another."

Muttering, Frith walked on. The bridge snaked off to the east
first of all, taking a very circuitous route to the distant outcrop of
rock that was their destination. The day was overcast, and there
were darker clouds edging in from the distant border of Pathania,
promising rain. A storm while they were on this bridge would not be
a pleasant prospect. He walked a little faster.

27

Wydrin was sweating. It was a chilly morning, and above the trees there was an icy wind that tugged at her hair and slipped down the back of her neck, freezing the sweat that was breaking out across her shoulders.

Her eyes were telling her they were cheating certain death, her eyes were telling her to brace for the fall, all the time, but she could feel the bridge under her feet, and it felt solid enough. *Concentrate on what you're feeling*, she told herself, *the smooth texture of the wood, the sound your boots make on the slats*, but that was easier said than done.

She glanced quickly at Sebastian just ahead of her. The big knight was turning slightly green. Seeing him hanging there in mid-air made her dizzy, and she laughed nervously.

"I'm glad you're enjoying yourself," he said.

"Oh yes. Best time I've had since we won all that wine, do you remember? I'd never seen so much vomit."

Sebastian grimaced.

"Can we talk about that another time?"

Frith was still in front, the viewing glass held out in front of him stiffly. The wind ruffled his white hair.

"How are you doing, princeling? Anything we should know about this bridge we can't bloody see? Fine trick that, by the way. Not that I'm suggesting your family were a bunch of overprotective lunatics or anything, but most people are happy enough with a few big locks and a guard dog."

"It is not so far," he said, in what he probably thought passed for a patient tone of voice. "Concentrate on walking, not complaining."

155

"Can't you use some magic to make the bridge visible? That would be useful."

"And reveal the path to the vault? Don't be ridiculous." He paused, then said, "There's a sharp turn to the left just here. Keep close behind me."

They continued that way for a good hour, inching slowly across the invisible bridge as it turned this way and that, gradually moving closer to the distant outcrop of rock. Strained sunlight shone off the stone, turning it into a white beacon amongst the dark foliage of the trees, and the sounds of the forest drifted up to them; bird song, the wind tugging ceaselessly at branches just below their feet, and every now and then the crash and thump of larger animals moving through the forest.

Once they heard voices, and Frith motioned them to stop. The three of them stood still and silent, apparently suspended in mid-air as a pair of hunters walked by underneath, completely unaware of the people above them. Wydrin peered down between her boots, for the time being too curious to avoid looking at the drop, and she thought she saw a brief movement of something that could have been a hat, or a pair of shoulders, glimpsed through the filter of the leaves. A snatch of their conversation drifted up through the trees and then they were gone, deeper into the woods. After a few seconds, Frith moved them on.

Eventually the erratic bridge began to straighten out, and the three adventurers stood in front of the mound of stone that housed the Frith family vault. The invisible path led directly into a fissure in the rock. As they got closer, they could see it was actually a sizeable cave, tall enough even for Sebastian to walk in without having to stoop. The stone to either side of the cave was sheer with very few handholds, meaning it would be extremely difficult for anyone to reach from the ground, assuming they knew there was anything to find. The rock was a foreboding, lonely place, and there were no lights in the space in front of them. It reminded her of the Citadel.

"We should go in," she said, reluctantly. "I suppose."

"Yes," said Frith, although he hardly sounded certain. He slipped the viewing glass into a pocket and removed the glass Crowleo had given him. The globe burst into sunny light, revealing the craggy cave entrance. At the far end was what looked like a wall of thick blue ice, completely covering the back of the cave.

"That doesn't look very promising," she said.

Frith marched up to the barrier and laid his hand against it.

"It's glass," he said. "It's not cold at all."

He was right. It was so thick that they could see nothing of what lay beyond; the light from the globe hit it and bounced back, twisted into a cold rainbow of colours.

"Can you see a keyhole?" asked Wydrin.

"What good would that do?" snapped Frith. "When we don't have a key?"

"Blood is the key," said Sebastian. His voice sounded far away. Wydrin turned to look at him and saw that he was swaying on his feet slightly. Against the black of his cloak his face was almost milk white, and she thought it had little to do with the walk across the invisible bridge.

"Sebastian, you look terrible. Are you feeling all right?"

He waved away her question.

"Late night, too much wine, nearly died the other day, remember? I'm fine. Blood is the key, Holley practically told us so. Only a Frith can hold the secret glass, and I'm willing to bet that only a Frith can open the vault."

Frith took a short dagger from his belt, rolled up his sleeve and laid the blade against his forearm. Wydrin watched his face closely; he didn't flinch as the skin split and the blood welled up. Once there was a sufficient amount he smeared it across the thick wall of glass.

For a few seconds, nothing happened at all. They could hear the wind blowing past the cave entrance, carrying the cries of birds and the green scent of the deep forest.

Then there was a shudder so violent that Wydrin stumbled, falling into Sebastian behind her, and the wall of apparently solid glass melted away like the ice it resembled. Beyond it was a large, round room with softly glowing lights in the ceiling. The walls were panelled with warm brown wood, and there were thick embroidered carpets on the floor, giving the impression of an expensive study. Heavy wooden chests were stacked everywhere, with bulging hessian sacks strewn between them. There were paintings on the walls too, all sombre portraits. An odd chemical stink hung in the air.

It wasn't quite as Wydrin had imagined. She had expected dust and cobwebs, and, more importantly, piles and piles of gold coins and jewelled crowns and suchlike. Instead, it was all rather reserved and, well, organised. She walked over to the nearest chest and prised open the lid with one of her daggers. It was full of musty old documents, so she let the lid fall back with a thud.

"Very cosy," she said, and turned back to look at Sebastian and Frith. The young lord was standing in front of one of the portraits. His face was very still.

"That was my father," he said. The painting depicted a middle-aged man with nut-brown skin, dark hair swept back from his forehead, and a long, regal nose. Cool grey eyes stared out of the picture, wise and solemn. Frith nodded to the portrait next to it. "And that was my grandfather, and his father next to him. They must all be here." He swallowed, and Wydrin clearly heard the catch in his throat. "We had portraits like these in the castle, but they seem to have one of everyone here, too." There was a space on the wall next to old Lord Frith's painting, where presumably his sons' portraits would have hung. She could see Frith's face in his father's portrait, and like an echo, she could trace it back through all the paintings of his ancestors. What must it be like, she wondered, to have that much history behind you and to see it all scrubbed away?

Knowing it would do no good at all but needing to do it anyway, she rested a hand on his shoulder briefly.

"I'm sorry," she said.

Frith looked away from the wall, saying nothing.

They searched the vault, and eventually Wydrin did find the gold she was after, in several ornate chests at the very back of the room. Sebastian watched her run her fingers through the coins with a wan smile on his face. Frith was sorting through piles and piles of documents and maps, most of which looked fragile and yellow under the strong lights. The room smelled of dust and old paper, the accumulated scent of forgotten things, with a sharper tang underneath which Sebastian didn't recognise.

"There are coins here from all across Ede," said Wydrin. "And there're an awful lot I don't recognise. Your family has been hoarding for a long time."

"The Friths are as old as the Blackwood," replied Frith in a distracted voice.

"It's good to know we won't be beggaring you by collecting our fee," said Wydrin dryly. She wandered over to one of the hessian sacks and pulled it open. A strong scent of bile and rotten eggs filled the stone room.

"*Urgh*. Whatever this was, I think it's gone off."

Frith glanced at the sacks, and nodded with recognition.

"My father was a skilled alchemist. It seems he kept some of his most valuable and dangerous ingredients out here, where they cannot cause trouble." He gave Wydrin an appraising look. "Best wash your hands as soon as you're able."

Sebastian walked around the room, running his eyes over the crates and chests and sacks without really seeing any of it. He felt too warm, though when he placed his hand against the wall, it was cool under his fingers. It was difficult to think, to concentrate. The question was, of course, what were they going to do next? Frith had recovered at least part of his family's legacy, although what that was worth when his lands were still under the control of murderers and bandits, Sebastian wasn't sure. The young lord still had to take back his castle and have his revenge, whatever form that would take. He and Wydrin could leave now, he supposed. Take what they were owed, the copper promise fulfilled, and head off across Litvania to the distant coast. Take a boat from there over the Stoney Sea to Crosshaven, find another job and another willing employer, since that was what his life had become...

But that wasn't all, was it? What of Pinehold? And what of the dragon's daughters? He could feel them now, a hot stone deep within his chest, like a fever brewing.

He crouched next to Frith. The young lord had spread several yellowing maps on the ground in front of him and was peering at each closely.

"What now, my lord?" asked Sebastian eventually. Frith did not look up. "I know that you have the means to pay us, and you are a step closer to regaining your lands. It may be that it is time for us to part ways." He took a deep breath. "But by the code of the Ynnsmouth knights, I cannot, in all good conscience, leave this land while there are innocents being killed and tortured in the name of tyranny and demon worship. I must return, and I hope that—"

Frith held up one of the maps.

"Does this look like a river to you? There's no key on this drawing, I think it is unfinished." Frith sat back on his haunches, frowning. "All the secrecy, all the conspiracies. By all accounts there should be some sort of huge revelation here, some reason that the vault has been so closely guarded. Yet all I see are maps, documents, and bags of gold. Nothing worth dying over, surely."

"What?" Sebastian glanced at the map, and scowled. "Are you even listening to me?"

"The people, yes, the torture. You know, I believe this is my father's own hand. Where did he get this?"

"Frith," Sebastian stood up abruptly. The fire in his chest was making it hard to think. "How can you sit there talking about the jottings of dead men, when your own people are being massacred? To keep your secrets!"

Frith finally looked up, his eyebrows raised at the volume of Sebastian's voice.

"These are maps," he said, gesturing to the parchments. "Not just of Litvania and her towns and villages, but of the lands beneath." He shook his head wonderingly. "The tunnel that Crowleo showed us is but one of many. Pinehold is riddled with them."

Wydrin appeared at Sebastian's elbow.

"Why?"

"I don't know, but they appear to be ancient. There are maps of the tunnels, all over my lands. It looks as though my father was investigating them."

"What does that have to do with anything?" said Sebastian. His head was pounding now, and he thought he could smell smoke again.

"I have a plan," said Frith, regarding them with his serious grey eyes. "A plan that, if it succeeds, will release Pinehold and destroy Fane and his pet monsters."

28

They were on the border of Relios now. The Thirty-Third knew this because the Ninety-Seventh had found a picture in the book she'd taken from the library, and the picture showed the lands they were crossing. After a moment or two of staring at it, she'd remembered it was called a map.

The village they were at now was apparently too small to be shown on the map, so it had no name. She sat on a low scrubby hill outside it and watched for people escaping. That was her job today; some of her sisters were inside the village, running through the streets and breaking into houses, chasing down the humans inside and killing them. She could hear the screams, and, every now and then, laughter. Her sisters were enjoying themselves.

It was a hot day and the sun had warmed her golden armour until a human wouldn't have been able to touch it without getting burnt. She shifted on the ground, comfortable, content, but alert. The idea of a cat occurred to her, but she wasn't entirely sure what that was.

"Let me see it."

The Thirty-Third looked sharply to her left to see two of her brood sisters approaching. One was the Ninety-Seventh, walking stiffly with her arms at her side, and the other was the Twelfth. The Twelfth was slightly larger than her sister, a little broader across the shoulders. She was following the Ninety-Seventh closely, her yellow eyes half shut against the sun.

"It's mine," replied the Ninety-Seventh. "You can't see it."

The Thirty-Third stood up as they approached.

"What is it?"

The Ninety-Seventh looked up. The book she'd taken from the

library was tied to her back with twine, next to the sword. It couldn't have been comfortable – their armour and swords were as much a part of them as their green skin, grown alongside them in the birthing pits – but the Thirty-Third had seen her carrying it around everywhere, even in the midst of slaughter, and then leafing through the pages late into the night when it was too dark to see.

"She has this book," said the Twelfth. "And she won't let me look at it."

"It's mine," said the Ninety-Seventh. She crossed her arms over her chest. "She can get her own book."

The Thirty-Third frowned. In the brood army, all were the same, and they shared everything. No one had anything the other did not, because they were all the same. But were they? *I am the Thirty-Third,* she thought. *I am not the Ninety-Seventh, or the Fortieth, or the Hundred and Eighth. I stand apart from them, with different words in my head.* She squeezed her eyes shut briefly to try and block some of this out.

"We are all the same," she said, although she was no longer quite sure she believed it. "What does it matter who holds the book?"

The Ninety-Seventh stuck her lower lip out.

"I got this one myself. It's mine."

"I only want to look at the words," said the Twelfth. Her broad face was creased with the same confusion the Thirty-Third felt.

"There will be other books in the village," said the Thirty-Third, suddenly certain of this fact. "Or other things with words on, at least. We should go in there and look for them."

The Ninety-Seventh looked back to the village. One of the small buildings was on fire already.

"But Mother said to stay here," she said, her voice a whisper. "Not to go in the village."

And why was that? It wasn't as though Y'Ruen usually worried about survivors. They caught them all eventually.

"It won't hurt to look," she said. "Then we can all–"

A sudden furtive movement caught her eye; two humans running from the outskirts of the village. At first they made for the low hills, before they caught sight of the brood sisters standing on the thin grass. They turned and ran to the east.

"Humans," she said, and the three brood sisters moved as one, all thought of books and words and disobeying Mother's orders immediately forgotten. The Thirty-Third shot down the hill, drawing the long crystal blade as she did, hearing the soft, sonorous sighs as her sisters did the same. The humans were young, male and female, both fit but neither fast enough to outrun the brood sisters, and soon the Thirty-Third was on the heels of the young woman. She'd pulled her skirts up to her knees to run faster, and the Thirty-Third could hear the high-pitched keening noises humans sometimes made when they were frightened. She lashed out with a clawed hand, dragging it across the young woman's back until she stumbled and fell. At the sound of her distress the man stopped, perhaps to help her back to her feet, but the Ninety-Seventh took his head off with one powerful blow from her sword. It shot into the air and fell to the dirt some feet away.

The woman screamed for a long time. The Thirty-Third found she tired of it sooner than usual, and when she looked into her sisters' faces she saw the same fatigue reflected there. Instead of playing with the creature for a few hours as they usually might, she pushed her sword into the woman's mouth, silencing her for ever.

"Let's search her," said the Twelfth eagerly. "She might have words on her."

"That is silly," said the Ninety-Seventh. Her voice was tight and sour. "She is not a book."

The Thirty-Third licked the blood from her fingers and went through the woman's clothes. In the long skirts there were a number of pockets, and she emptied the contents out onto the grass; three buttons carved from bone, a fabric packet full of seeds, a small knife, blunt and well-used, and a lock of blond hair, tied with a red ribbon. She held this last item out to her sisters.

"What is that?" asked the Twelfth.

The Thirty-Third placed it under her nose and sniffed. It smelt of milk and vomit.

"It belonged to a human infant," she said. An item precious enough to keep in your skirts next to you at all times, but where was the infant now? She remembered the family she'd spoken to in Krete, and how the desperation to save their boy had been pouring out of them like sweat. She couldn't imagine that this woman with her buttons and seeds could have left the child. Unless the child couldn't be saved any more.

She turned the lock of hair over in her fingers. It was very soft.

"Mother is coming now," said the Ninety-Seventh, pointing up into the sky. A great black shape as familiar to the Thirty-Third as her own hands drifted in front of the sun. Y'Ruen had come to destroy what was left of the village.

As the fire began to rain down, the three of them walked away, retreating back to the low hills.

29

It was laughter that told Crowleo they were coming.

He was in one of the topmost rooms, sorting through his mistress's papers when he heard it; high and girlish, and somehow cruel. He crossed to the window and saw a group of men emerging from the treeline beyond the rocky ground. One of them was tall with dark hair, and although it was difficult to make out his features at this distance, Crowleo knew his face would be scarred and raw. The men who walked with him were slim and blond haired, and as he watched they doubled from two, to four, to six. The Children of the Fog were laughing.

Still holding armfuls of the old woman's designs, he flew down the stairs and nearly collided with Holley, who was coming up them. In here she looked to be in her mid-thirties, the first laughter lines creasing her eyes.

"Woah there, boy, you can still break these bones you know."

"They're coming!" gasped Crowleo, shaking the papers at her. "He's looking for them! And you know they won't go away without answers..."

To his irritation, the old woman nodded slowly.

"I know, lad, I know. Listen to me now, close like." She produced a contraption of leather and glass from her apron and pressed it into Crowleo's hands. He glanced down at it briefly to see a smudged inscription on the fabric: *For The Copper Cat. Truth, for what good it'll do you.* "Take that, and go out the back way. Don't stop to take anything else, just go. I want you to go down the Sheer Steps, and wait there. You understand me, boy?"

Crowleo nodded numbly. The Sheer Steps were a series of rough handholds cut directly into the cliff behind the Secret Keeper's house. Halfway down was a ledge, hidden by stubby little trees that grew out of the craggy rock.

"But what...?"

"I'll just have a chat with them, that's all. Now go, or you'll feel the back of my hand. And keep what you've got there safe."

Crowleo went, although he only made it as far as the backyard. He could hear them coming up to the front of the house, chatting and laughing as though they were on their way to market. Despite Holley's instructions, he found he wanted to get a closer look at them so he edged over to the wall at the side and peeked cautiously around the corner. There had to be ten Children of the Fog now, ten grinning, chuckling ghouls with blond hair and sharp smiles. Why were there so many? What was Fane expecting to find?

"Come out, old woman!" bellowed Fane. He was grinning, and Crowleo could see the raw parts of his flesh twisting and stretching. "I've heard so much about you. Had any interesting house guests lately?"

Crowleo couldn't see her from where he stood, but he heard Holley's voice. She sounded unreasonably relaxed, just as though there were no murderous thieves outside her house.

"What's it to ya?"

"A girl, red hair, bit scrawny for my liking but with a reasonable pair of tits, a big man from the mountains, and another one, a skinny streak of piss with white hair and a grudge. Sound familiar?"

Amazingly, Holley laughed.

"I'm sure I've no idea what you're talking about."

Fane nodded, as if he expected nothing less.

"Your boy was recognised, old woman. People saw him fleeing with my prisoners."

"My boy?" Holley shrugged. "My boy has been working non-stop for the last three days, he's had no time for dallying at Pinehold. What's the matter? You killed everyone in the town and now you're looking for fresh peasants to torture, is that it?"

"Roki, bring her to me."

Crowleo tensed, took a few steps towards them, and stopped. What could he do? He was one man, and unarmed. His heart thudded sickly in his chest and he bunched his hands into fists, crumpling his mistress's papers. One of the blond men came forward;

he disappeared from sight for a few moments, then reappeared dragging Holley towards Fane. Beyond the enchanted light of the windows, she was ancient once more, and it was clear she could do little to resist.

"I'll ask you again," said Fane, pleasantly. He pulled a knife from his belt as he spoke. Crowleo saw it glint in the late afternoon light. "These people. The man calling himself Frith. Where are they now? Have you seen them? Are they hiding in this house of yours?"

"By the gods, but you're ugly," said Holley in a conversational tone of voice. "Is that why you keep cutting bits of your face off?"

Crowleo saw the twitch of rage that twisted Fane's face from where he stood. He swore softly under his breath.

"Let me show you," said Fane. He put on the battered half-helm, and it began to glow as Roki and Enri's armour glowed. He held up the knife, and the approaching storm light ran along its surface in a flash. "I make this offering to Bezcavar, he who hungers for suffering, and he who gives us power." He brought the knife down, but rather than attacking the old woman, he cut into his own arm. Blood welled up, painfully bright against his skin. Fane grinned, stretching the scars on his face. "Only for Bezcavar will my blood be spilt."

Hidden behind the house, Crowleo shivered. The temperature was dropping unnaturally fast, although whether that was just the storm approaching, he couldn't have said. He knew he was frightened, possibly more frightened than he'd ever been, even when he'd watched both his parents sicken and die in the plagues. He'd thought the Children of the Fog were terrifying, but there was something else here now, something worse. His skin was crawling.

"Filthy demon-worshipper!" Holley tried to pull away then, to fight. Three more of the Children of the Fog came forward to hold her still.

The anger left Fane's face. Now he looked exalted. He reached out and grabbed Holley by her apron, yanking her off her feet and thrusting her into the air. The Secret Keeper was an old woman and no doubt a lot lighter than she'd been in her youth, but the ease with which Fane dragged her off the ground was still unnerving.

"You will be my next sacrifice, old girl."

Still holding Holley over his head, Fane marched towards the edge of the cliff. Crowleo shuffled backwards rapidly, taking cover behind a pile of firewood. He watched from behind split timbers as Fane walked to the very edge, a few feet away from the first of the Sheer Steps.

"Forgive me, Bezcavar, for these old bones I offer you now," he said. "I promise you fresh blood next time."

And with that he threw Holley off the cliff.

30

By the time they left the vault the storm had broken, and it took Frith a few moments to realise that the darkness hanging over the Secret Keeper's house in the far distance was not just the remnants of heavy clouds moving over it.

"Smoke," he said, and then repeated himself, raising his voice over the roar of the wind. Sebastian, who was carrying several large sacks over one shoulder, lifted his face to the far cliff edge, and frowned, a worried crease appearing in the centre of his forehead.

"One of us should have stayed behind," said Wydrin. She had taken the gold they were owed, carefully wrapping the coins in strips of cloth so that she wouldn't clink when she moved. "I doubt that's an accident."

"Can you see anyone there?" asked Frith, knowing that Wydrin had sharper eyes than he had.

"No one," said Wydrin. From her tone it was clear she wasn't sure if this was a good or a bad sign. Frith moved to the edge of the bridge. There was a new sword at his belt, a thicker blade than his old rapier, but just as flexible and deadly. His hand gripped at the pommel convulsively.

"We must hurry," said Sebastian. "We may still be able to help them."

They headed out into the rain, Frith leading once more with the viewing glass held out in front of him. He soon found it was harder going back; the wind pushed at them like a belligerent child, as if its dearest wish were to see them plummet to the rain-whipped trees below, and he kept having to pause and use the inside of his cloak to wipe the glass clear of moisture. Behind them, the thunder gave voice to rumbling protests and the air smelt sharply of salt.

By the time they finally reached the cliff's edge the rain had moved on elsewhere. Instead of the fresh air normally found in the wake of a storm there was the sour stink of sodden ashes.

"The bastards," said Wydrin. She paced angrily, like a cat in a cage. "I'll have their guts for this."

The Secret Keeper's house was not completely destroyed – the storm had stopped the flames before they brought the entire place down – but the front of it was ruined and black, and every window was smashed to pieces, the sills thick with soot. The grass around the house glittered, the scattered remains were all that was left of the magical glass artefacts it had housed for so many years. Tools and equipment had been dragged out of the stone workroom and those that could be broken were strewn across the grass.

"They had very little patience," came a voice from behind them. Frith turned, his hand back on the pommel of his sword, and saw Crowleo walking towards them. The young apprentice was soaking wet from head to foot. He joined them by the house, not quite looking any of them in the eye. "I have found her difficult in the past, yes. Cantankerous, obstinate. The rights of an old woman, she used to say, were to be cantankerous and obstinate."

"Crowleo," Sebastian put a hand on his shoulder. "Are you all right? What happened here?"

"It is obvious what happened," said Frith. "Fane and his men came here seeking me."

"She's dead, you know," said Crowleo lightly. His eyes were wet. "Holley wouldn't tell them where you were, because she was an obstinate, blind old fool who –" He blinked rapidly. "She is dead, and everything is destroyed save for some small pieces I managed to salvage. And this." He untied a contraption of leather from his belt and offered it to Wydrin. "I believe it is what you asked for. She wanted you to have it, I think."

Wydrin took the object and briefly held it up to her face. Two discs of blue glass covered her eyes.

"I... thank you." She began to root around in her coin purse, but Crowleo waved a hand at her tiredly.

"She won't be spending the coin now, and I don't have the stomach for it."

"What happened to her, Crowleo?" asked Sebastian.

"Fane threw her off the cliff," he said, and there was the tiniest tremor in his voice. "He cut himself first, and said that Holley's death was an offering to Bezcavar."

Wydrin made a small noise of disgust.

"Bezcavar," said Frith, the corners of his mouth turning down. "I am beginning to think I have seen the name. In my father's library. A demon cult out of Eastern Relios. Demon worship might explain the abilities of Fane's henchmen."

"And then they burned the house and smashed everything inside," continued Crowleo. "They left. I was hiding –"

For a moment Frith thought the young man was going to faint, but Sebastian kept a steadying hand on his shoulder.

"She told me to hide, and what could I do?" Crowleo shrugged. "There was just me, and you were far away."

They were all quiet for a moment. The wind, still playful in the wake of the storm, moved through the grass, doing little to dissipate the stink of ashes.

"We should have been here," said Sebastian. "There is so much we should have done."

"They will pay." Wydrin patted her daggers again, as if reassuring them. "I will spill blood for this."

There was no hope of retrieving Holley's body – the forest at the bottom of the cliff was thick and wild, and busy with scavenging animals – so instead they built a cairn in her memory. Wydrin found some lumps of old molten glass in the stone workroom, and placed those amongst the stones too, so that it would glitter with the sunrise and sunset. Crowleo seemed pleased with that, and even offered her a watery smile.

When they were done it was full dark, and they huddled around a fire, still trying to get warm from the soaking they'd taken earlier in the day.

"I will go far away," said Crowleo. Wydrin had been sharing a flask of rum with the boy and he looked a little calmer now. "Take what I know of the Secret Keeper's teachings and start again somewhere else."

"Nonsense," said Frith abruptly. "You will do no such thing."

He saw Sebastian glare at him and ignored it.

"Why would I stay here?" said Crowleo. He didn't sound angry, only perplexed. "There is nothing for me here."

"We need you to get back into Pinehold," said Frith. "And we will need your help once we are in there, too."

"Back to Pinehold?" Now Crowleo looked alarmed.

"Exactly," said Frith, nodding grimly. "I will need to use some of the equipment in your mistress's workshop, assuming it is still serviceable." He cleared his throat and looked at each of them in turn, wondering if they would trust him this far. "And I intend to see that monster suffer, as your mistress suffered, as my family suffered." He picked up a handful of dirt, thick with ashes. "It is time Fane answered to his own demons."

31

The Thirty-Third sat on the floor with the Ninety-Seventh, a pile of books between them. Somewhere in the room beyond, the Twelfth was rummaging through shelves and making the occasional sound of delight.

This was a town called Moritos. It had large brick buildings and a big market square, and to the north of a wide river there were lots of grand houses, with smooth white bricks and little gardens full of fruit trees. Outside the brood army were putting the populace to the sword, but the Thirty-Third, the Ninety-Seventh and the Twelfth had made their way to the big houses, knowing somehow that if they wanted words, this would be the place to find them. An hour or so ago a group of their sisters had come to the doorway, wishing to break things and start fires, but the Ninety-Seventh had sent them away, claiming this area as their own. The Thirty-Third had seen the confusion on their faces and felt uneasy. Sooner or later someone would notice.

"Here, look." The Ninety-Seventh pushed an open book into her lap, a claw pressed against a picture of a man in armour. The Thirty-Third scanned the page; it appeared to be an account of a war that took place many hundreds of years ago, across the Yellow Sea. "This is what *he* is, isn't it?"

She didn't need to ask who.

"Our father is a knight," she said, and paused at the odd tightening in her throat. What was that feeling, exactly? "He carries a sword, like we do, and wears armour."

"Sometimes I think I hear his voice," said the Ninety-Seventh. She traced her claw around the picture. "Not like how we hear *her*, thunder in the blood and *here*," she touched her head, "but quieter."

She touched a hand to her heart.

"I hear him too."

The Twelfth strode back into the room with an armful of books. She was grinning.

"Some of the words are beautiful," she said. She tried to open one book and dropped half the others on the floor. "Look, look. See here? This one." She spread the pages for her sisters. "*Ephemeral.*"

"What does that mean?" asked the Thirty-Third, but already her mind was filling with images and feelings, none of them quite solid or certain.

"There are others, see. Woebegone, ennui, daffodil, crocus!"

"They are lovely," agreed the Ninety-Seventh.

"I want to keep these words with me," said the Twelfth. She tried to gather up all the books and dropped them again.

"Tear out the pages?" suggested the Ninety-Seventh. The Thirty-Third frowned. Somehow she felt their father wouldn't approve of that.

"No," said the Twelfth, who apparently felt the same. "I will make them my name. You will call me Crocus from now on."

"Crocus?"

"Yes!" exclaimed the Ninety-Seventh. "We don't even have names, do we? Not truly. The Ninety-Seventh, the Thirty-Third... these are positions, they don't mean anything. Especially not now we are out of the birthing pits."

"I want to be Ephemeral," said the Thirty-Third. Again there was that tight feeling in her throat. It was important, suddenly, to claim that word for herself, with all the soft images and feelings it provoked.

"That is a good name," said the Twelfth, now Crocus, clearly pleased she had been the one to come up with the idea. "Ephemeral, my sister."

"Oh!" cried the Ninety-Seventh. She gathered all the books to her in a panic and began to leaf through them frantically. "However will I choose?"

"They must be our secret names, though," said the Thirty-Third. She caught hold of her sister's hand and squeezed it, before glancing up at the newly named Crocus. "We must not tell anyone."

"No," agreed Crocus. "They will be our secret words, for us alone."

The sisters chose their names while the town of Moritos burned, and a dark shadow moved restlessly above the clouds.

32

Dreyda touched the taper to the curls of paper in the fire-font, and watched as they spat and hissed into warm, orange life. The scent of spices, fruity and dry on the back of her tongue, briefly filled the room and she thought of her temple back home. There, she would have a hundred fire-fonts, and they would be kept blazing at all times, so that the sick and weary would be kept warm, and see the words that were painted on every spare surface. In here, the outbuilding she'd convinced the blacksmith to rent to her, she could only afford two fire-fonts. Most of the space was needed for sickbeds, and the small bags of powder she'd brought all the way from Relios were feeling lighter all the time. She had to be sparing.

A low moan distracted her from the sudden bout of homesickness, and she went to one of the beds. The man lying there was running a high fever and had managed to throw his blankets off again. The end of one arm ended in a bloody stump bound in insufficient bandages, and the red threads of infection were curling their way up past his elbow and were well on their way to his shoulder. She would need to make a decision soon, she knew that. What was an arm, if traded for a life? But the man was delirious, and all her attempts to get him to understand had failed. Dreyda pressed a damp rag to his forehead and murmured soothing words.

There were nine people in her makeshift surgery now, and she expected more to arrive tomorrow. Not all were victims of Yellow-Eyed Rin's knives or Fane's own strange enthusiasms; some were simply malnourished or ill with common diseases that should have been treatable, but they had long since run out of those medicines. If Fane's men would just let her out to roam in the Blackwood she could collect some of the supplies they needed...

A timid hand touched her bare arm.

"Regnisse? There is another one here to see you."

Dreyda turned to see one of the young women who occasionally helped her to tend the sick. Alice's own brother had suffered in the Tower, his armflayed from the elbow to ends of his fingers; tricky work, but Yellow-Eyed Rin apparently had a great deal of patience. The girl had come in with him to help out, and stayed to tend the others too.

"Show them in."

A figure wearing a thick hooded cloak stepped out of the shadows. Dreyda couldn't see the face under the hood, but it was clear what the problem was. She pointed at the great bulge pushing at the robes.

"You're with child, girl?"

Dreyda had become very familiar with the people of Pinehold in a relatively short space of time – it was all a part of spreading the words to those yet to be enlightened – but she knew of no one who was so heavily pregnant.

The figure pushed back her hood and grinned at Dreyda.

"You must help me, Sister," said Wydrin, patting the bump with apparent affection. "You won't believe the amount of trouble I'm in."

"What are you talking about?" hissed Dreyda.

They had retired to a space at the back of the makeshift hospital. It reeked of old vegetable smells; potatoes, turnips, carrots. The young woman looked less bedraggled than when Dreyda had last seen her; at some point recently she had washed the dried blood from her hair and pulled on a new shirt under her leather bodice. There was an air of energy about her too.

"You're not listening," said Wydrin lightly. "There are tunnels under this town, and I need you to help me locate the entrances. Then we're going to take these bags," she pointed at the pair of sacks that had made up the bump under her robe. They both smelled faintly of chemicals. "And use the stuff inside to leave a trail. I don't understand how it works myself, but I've seen the bombs that Frith made before and they were certainly effective. The first place we need to find is–"

"Enough!" Dreyda held her hands up for quiet. She glanced at the words etched in ink across her knuckles. *Peace. Faith. Kindness,* in the old language. "You have questions to answer first, child. Your friend with the white hair, who is he? *What* is he? He burst into flames in the middle of the market and killed seven men, and ran away unharmed."

"I wouldn't call him a friend as such, more a nuisance. A pretty nuisance, maybe, but–"

"Wydrin!"

The Copper Cat sighed.

"He is the lord of this land, just like Sebastian said. The great big idiot. Big pair of idiots, if you ask me." She scratched the back of her head. "Look, Lord Frith employed us to help him search the Citadel in Creos."

"The mages' Citadel?"

"That's the one. We thought he was after gold and silver, like any normal person would be, but he found a magical lake, and now –" She paused, clearly wondering if she should be telling the priestess any of this. "Now he carries the power of the mages within him."

Dreyda snatched up the young woman's arm. Distantly she was aware that she was squeezing hard enough to leave a bruise.

"That is not possible, child. You lie."

Wydrin shook her off with a scowl.

"And how else do you imagine he produced those flames? He's done other things, too. Healed my fractured arm, for one, although he seems to do little else of use."

"But the power of the mages –" Dreyda's mouth was dry. Inside her chest her heart was thrumming like a wasp in a jar. "They all died, so long ago." She saw Wydrin's quizzical look and her voice became sharp with impatience. "Don't you understand, child? My order have studied the words of the mages for hundreds of years. These words!" She pulled up her sleeve and brandished her arm at Wydrin. It was laced with blue ink, as intricate as the patterns on a butterfly's wing. "We have only the words. The power is long gone! And now you're telling me it's back?"

"What I'm telling you," said Wydrin, "is that we have a way of killing the rabid dogs that are infesting this town. You said to me that I looked like the sort of person who has seen trouble, and doesn't mind dealing some in return. Well, here I am, ready to cause some mayhem. Are you going to help me? I know that you want Fane and his scum gone."

In the room beyond the door, someone cried out in pain. Dreyda heard Alice's soft voice murmur in response, and the cries turned to quiet sobs. The fire-priestess took a slow, deep breath, remembering the words of peace and calm. There would be time enough later. For now she must do the duty of a Regnisse.

"I will help you," she said. "But you must promise me that I can speak with this Lord Frith, when all else is done."

Wydrin grinned and nodded, apparently pleased to be promising something on Frith's behalf.

"Oh, absolutely. Just don't blame me if he's tight-lipped. Our princeling is hardly free and easy with his secrets, believe me."

Dreyda pursed her lips. That would have to do.

"Very well. What is it you have here?"

"First of all, a map." Wydrin pulled a roll of parchment from within her robe and spread it on top of a crate. The oil lamps in the storeroom cast only a dirty, buttery light, so that Dreyda had to peer closely to see the faded black and green lines. She recognised it immediately: the square of the market in the centre, the long road that ran from the south gate to the Queen's Tower at the north of the town, and the buildings to either side. Some of it was not accurate, leading her to believe that it was a very old map, but most of the heavier stone buildings were there. And in green ink there was another set of lines apparently drawn over the map of the town. "Pinehold," said Wydrin. "And in green you can see the tunnels that run beneath."

"Who built them?"

"How should I know? Frith says his father was trying to find out, because there are similar tunnels under lots of places in Litvania. That's not important. Where do Fane's men bunk?"

Dreyda pointed to a large building on the western side of the market square.

"Those are the barracks. And the rest are in the Queen's Tower, along with that unspeakable little toad, Rin."

"It's difficult to judge where Fane will be at any one time, but I reckon taking out his men would be a good start. The barracks, and then the tower," said Wydrin, tapping the circle to the north of the map. "There is a long tunnel that runs down the centre of the main street, do you see?"

Dreyda nodded. A green line ran from the tavern, turned sharply right, and proceeded up the middle of the street and through the market. There were several tunnels branching off, and two of them led under the barracks building. The main tunnel continued on to the Tower, and passed straight under the walls and out into the forest beyond. Looking at the green lines it was almost as if she recognised the shape, almost... was there something familiar about the way that part *turned*, the way one line crossed another?

"And what do you intend to do in these tunnels?"

In answer Wydrin retrieved a sack from the floor and untied the rope at its neck. The chemical smell increased until Dreyda's eyes began to water.

"This is the accelerant. If we light this it will carry the flame where we wish," said Wydrin. There was a dark powder inside the sack. She closed the neck and opened the second bag, a little more carefully. "And this is the stuff that's going to help us give Fane a very bad day indeed." Inside the sack were a number of pallid, greasy bricks of some semi-solid substance. They smelt powerfully of bad eggs and rotten meat.

"Regnisse, would you care to accompany me on a spot of mayhem?"

Despite herself, Dreyda smiled.

33

Sebastian and Crowleo walked beneath the streets of Pinehold. It was cool and silent, and smelt strongly of damp and green things. Sebastian found his memories turning back to his own boyhood spent training under the mighty god-peaks of Ynnsmouth.

He was reminded of a particular test they all dreaded. The sacred mountains were riddled with caves, and when a boy was considered old enough the Masters would take him to the entrance of the one known as the Demon's Throat. There he would be stripped of all weapons and supplies, and made to change into a thin white shift and linen trousers. Then the boy would be given a full goblet of red wine to hold, and made to walk the length of the Demon's Throat, alone in the dark, without spilling a drop.

It was meant to test the attributes one needed to be a knight of Ynnsmouth, and perhaps it did. You needed bravery and courage to face that pit of blackness alone, and the test encouraged you to use all your senses to find your way, instead of relying purely on sight. There was also a great deal of talk about "listening to the voice of the mountain", which Sebastian had taken very seriously at the time, although during his walk through the Demon's Throat he'd heard only the sound of his own frightened breathing rushing in his ears, and the distant sounds of ice melting. Most of the boys hurt themselves on their first attempt, emerging at the far end with bleeding knees and their white shirts stained with wine, and they would have to walk it all again the following spring. Sebastian's best friend Connor had drunk the entire goblet of wine and emerged the other end unharmed and cheerfully inebriated. That had earned him a beating from the Masters. Sebastian's first walk had been his last;

he'd emerged from the tunnel with a full goblet and not a drop on his clean white shirt. He wondered if they still performed the ritual, but that was a stupid question. *The Order doesn't change*, he thought. *I was the one that changed.*

It had been cold in the Demon's Throat, and frightening, although now he found the stones above his head reassuring. It was good to be out from under the sky, where anything could be watching. He frowned at the memory, and called to Crowleo.

"How much further?"

"We should rejoin the tunnel under the market soon, my friend. Be patient."

Sebastian held up the glass ball of light and watched as Crowleo poured a thin line of black powder onto the floor from the sack in his arms. They had left Frith beneath the Queen's Tower where he'd been arranging the greasy bricks of explosives in a careful pile. The screams from the prisoners above had been loud enough to make them all cringe. Now they were working their way back to the central tunnel where they would meet Wydrin, assuming she found her way down there in time.

"So how did you know about the passage under the temple? It appears no one else in Pinehold knows about the tunnels, or they'd be used as storage rooms and cellars."

"It was a secret, was it not?" Crowleo did not look up from the powder trail. "Holley knew I would have to get in and out of Pinehold without going through the gates, so she shared that one with me. If she knew about the others... I suppose now I shall never be sure."

"I wonder who built them?" Sebastian held the ball of light closer to one of the walls. They were constructed of smooth, flat stones, square and even. In some places moss had obscured great patches and Sebastian could just make out a small pattern in the centre of some of the bricks. He rubbed a portion of the muck away with his free hand and saw a small human face carved into the stone. It was simple and oddly beautiful, depicting a woman with long hair and oval eyes. Her mouth was slightly parted, as if she were about to speak. There was another one a few stones down, a man with a similar serene expression. They appeared to stretch along the entire wall.

"Have you seen these?" said Sebastian. "There are faces carved here."

"Sebastian, the light, please?" Crowleo was standing still with the sack in his arms, a slight smile on his face. Smiles were rare from the young man now, and this one looked uncertain.

"Sorry."

They continued on their way until the passageway turned sharply to the right, and they emerged into a larger space. Wydrin was already waiting for them, with the fire-priestess and an oil lamp.

"You took your time," she said, cheerfully enough.

"It's not a race, Wydrin. And I hope you're being careful with that lamp. An early fire would be most unfortunate, particularly while we're still down here."

"That is why *I* am holding the lamp," said the fire-priestess. She was a tall, bony woman, and the lamplight made her face look sharp and unnatural, but Wydrin had said she was trustworthy, and that was enough for Sebastian.

"Everything is set up," said Wydrin. "Where is our princeling?"

"At the Queen's Tower. There is an exit there, and he'll meet us in the market place."

Wydrin raised an eyebrow.

"So he's not here when the fuse is lit? Typical."

"He is removing the prisoners from the tower, if he can," said Sebastian, although that part of the plan made him uneasy. He'd seen Frith fight and his new blade was wickedly sharp, but he hadn't been happy about leaving him alone. Frith had insisted.

"I shall light the fuse at sundown, when the sun has fully disappeared beneath the treeline," said Crowleo. Sebastian started to protest and the young man shook his head abruptly. "We have discussed this. You must be ready to pick off those guards who survive, and I am no use with a sword. Besides, I want to do this much. For Holley."

Sebastian sighed.

"Fine. You *must* leave as soon as you see it lit. We don't truly know what will happen when the explosives combust. Assuming this works at all."

"Great," said Wydrin. She pulled off the robe she had been wearing to disguise her appearance, and untied the Secret Keeper's goggles from her belt. She held them up to her eyes and buckled the leather strap around the back of her head. The warm glow of the oil lamp sank into the glass eye-pieces and made them glow like pools of sapphires. "I have one last thing to do, then."

"What?"

There was a tone in Wydrin's voice that normally meant a drunken fight outside a tavern, or a merchant pushed off the end of a dock. She unsheathed her daggers and kissed their blades reverentially.

"I'm going to expose the truth. The people of Pinehold could do with a touch of that, I reckon."

34

The Queen's Tower had once been an elegant place.

Frith remembered the visit with his father, sitting in the jarl's study drinking honeyed thistle tea. He'd been bored, kicking his legs against the chair until his father had pointed out the tapestries on the wall, depicting an ancient war between the mages, just the sort of thing to distract him at that age. He vaguely recalled a set of glass doors leading to a balcony and small ceramic lamps dotting the shelves – but the tapestries had stayed with him. Would any of them have survived? And what of the jarl? He'd been an elderly man even then, knuckles thick with arthritis, white hair thinning. No doubt he would have been the first to be put to questioning, if he was even still alive.

Now the tower was cold and draughty, and the stench of blood in the air was overpowering. He'd entered through what had once been the storage room, via a door so ancient the wood had warped within the iron frame and it had taken all his strength to shoulder it open. When he'd managed to squeeze through he'd found himself in a small, dank room, rich with the scent of rotting vegetation and mould. Beyond that were storage rooms, and following the spiral staircase up he'd come to the servants' quarters, now being used as a makeshift dungeon.

He edged around a corner, his sword drawn.

The guard sat with his back to Frith, intent on the bowl of lumpy stew and the chunk of bread he was dipping in it. They were complacent here, Frith noted, certain of their dominion over the town's people. This one wasn't even wearing his helmet, which was propped next to his chair. The rest of the loaf of bread was balanced on top of it.

Walking swiftly and softly in his worn leather boots, Frith came up behind the guard and brought the pommel of his sword down on the back of the man's head. There was a meaty crunch and the guard pitched forward out of the chair. The bowl of stew clattered onto the floor, spilling its brownish contents onto the flagstones.

Frith pushed the guard onto his back with his foot; out cold, possibly dead. He bent, rifled through the man's black tunic and came up with a thick ring of keys. There were muffled sounds coming from the room to his right, the weak, desperate sounds of someone who thought it likely they would never see the light of day again. There had been a time when Frith had made similar noises, when the pain had been too much for him to bear. The memory brought back a hot flush of guilt and shame, so he pushed it firmly from his mind.

The guard now lying on the floor in front of him was the first he'd seen, but no doubt there would be more. For now there was silence, so he fumbled the right key from the ring and opened the door.

He walked into a small room with rushes on the floor. Once, no doubt, it had been a servant's refuge, but all signs of human comfort had been removed. Instead there was a pile of straw in one corner, a bucket in the other, and an emaciated man dressed only in ragged underclothes crouching below the window pane. He had a big frame and large bony hands, but he cowered against the wall and whimpered as Frith approached. The ends of his fingers were raw and bleeding, and there were numerous bruises to his face and neck. His feet were chained together.

"You. What is your name?" Frith glanced behind him into the hallway. It was still clear.

"I've said everything, lord. I've said everything there is to say." The man's voice was little more than a rusted croak.

"I need you to focus, and quickly." Frith frowned; the room smelt of urine. "What is your name? Do you work in the tower?"

The man looked up at him, his eyes almost shut against a half-expected blow.

"Berwick, lord, I was the jarl's footman. Who are you?"

Frith nodded impatiently. His hands were starting to tingle, as they had before the green flames had consumed him in the market square.

"Berwick, you must make your way down to the lower floors."

He came forward and, using the smallest key on the ring, unlocked the manacles that chained Berwick's feet. The nails were missing from his toes, he noticed, and there were livid burn marks on the soft flesh of the man's calf muscles. Frith scowled, and the churning in his chest grew stronger. Berwick just looked at him, his lips loose with spittle.

"Are you listening to me, Berwick? There, you are free. Get up." He helped the man to his feet, and was surprised to find that Berwick was a good head taller than him. Frith took off his cloak and flung it over the man's bare shoulders. "Go down to the storeroom. You know where that is, yes?" The man nodded dumbly. "There is a disused chamber at the very back–"

"Maisie said it was haunted, that's what she said."

Frith bit down his impatience.

"That would be the one. You'll find a door there that leads to a tunnel. Turn left and keep going, it will eventually lead you out into the Blackwood. If you find anyone else, take them with you. If you reveal yourself to a guard or sound the alarm, I will come back and kill you myself."

The man paused in the doorway, and there was a look of growing recognition in his eyes that made Frith uneasy. Was it possible Berwick had been here all those years ago? Would he remember him?

"Just who are you, lord?"

There was a soft *wumph* and Frith's right arm was suddenly bright with emerald fire. Berwick stumbled back into the corridor.

"*What* are you?"

"I am vengeance," said Frith, and immediately felt vaguely foolish. "Now go!"

Berwick went, moving swiftly down the stone steps. Frith looked at his arm in annoyance.

"I have no control," he said to himself bitterly. "The power of the mages has a will of its own." After a few seconds the green light flickered and died, as if to spite him. Frith muttered darkly under his breath and continued his ascent of the staircase.

It took five more rooms, five more released prisoners and three unconscious guards before Frith found him.

He knew, somehow, before he opened the door, what he would

find within. Was it the smell of the man, seeping out from under the slats to greet him? Was it his imagination or did his once shattered leg twinge with remembered agony just before he stepped into the room?

Yellow-Eyed Rin turned at once, an expression of impatience on his greasy, fat face.

"I told you to leave me be with this one, didn' I? I'm to be left alone when I want to be, those are Fane's orders–" His protests died in his throat as he realised the visitor to his make-shift dungeon wasn't a guard. "Who are you? What do you want?"

Frith didn't answer straight away. He was looking at the woman on the bench behind Rin. She had been strapped down over it, her arms pinned behind her head and her rough-spun tunic torn to expose the skin of her belly. Her hair, a wild black bush, framed a face that looked as though it had once smiled often, and now was not likely to smile again. Dark eyes huge with fear stared up at Frith.

Rin was now advancing on Frith, a long scalpel held in one pudgy fist. Frith dragged his eyes back to him and held up his sword.

"You mean you don't remember me, Rin?" he said. There was a fiery pit of rage in his stomach, but his voice was strangely calm. "You wanted to see if my blood was black."

Yellow-Eyed Rin's face went slack, his jowls pouching in an unlovely gathering at his throat.

"You are dead," he said, his voice toneless. The torturer's eyes crawled over Frith, and he could well imagine what he was looking for; the missing ear, the scarred face, the ragged fingertips. Frith watched the confusion on his face and felt a cold joy in his heart. He smiled.

"After what you did I should be dead? But you didn't finish the job, did you? Couldn't resist drawing it out, could you?" Frith glanced at the woman on the bench, who was watching them both with mute terror. Rin took the opportunity to leap forward, slashing the scalpel at his face. Frith knocked his hand aside with the flat of his sword and the small blade fell to the floor, skidding across the flagstones. Rin hissed with pain, grabbing at his wrist with his other hand. Frith held the point of his sword in front of the torturer's face.

"Call for help and I will cut your throat out." Rin looked as though he might shout anyway, so Frith inched the blade closer, resting the tip on the wrinkled skin around the man's Adam's apple. Then he spoke in a softer tone, without looking directly at the girl on the bench. "He will free you in a moment. When he does I want you to run down to the very bottom of this tower, and find a door beyond the storeroom. You won't have seen it open before. Go through it and follow the tunnel north. Do you understand?"

"Yes." The young woman's voice was stronger than he expected. That was good.

"Untie her," he said to Rin. "And know that if you make any sudden move I will take great pleasure in watching your guts defile the floor."

Rin bared rotten teeth at him, but he moved to the bench and undid the straps holding the girl in place. She cringed away from him as soon as she was free, and then darted forward and spat in his face. Rin roared with anger and the girl ran from the room.

"Quiet yourself, Rin," said Frith. He closed the gap between them again, the point of his sword always trained on the torturer's throat. "I have a few questions for you. From what I remember, you were quite fond of questions."

"Why should I tell you anything?" spat Rin. He was frightened; Frith could smell it on him, a rank, insidious smell like stagnant water. The torturer's brow was damp with sweat, and his fingers, fingers that had dealt so much pain to so many innocents, were trembling slightly. Frith tightened the grip on his sword and nursed the hate within him, just as he had once nursed the pain the mages had inflicted on him in the lake.

"Because every second of life you have left is now a gift from me," he said. "You live now only by my sufferance. Where is the Lady Bethan?"

Rin scowled, glancing from the blade at his throat to Frith's steady gaze and back again.

"Not here. I don't know where she is. Off looking for something to line her own pockets with, no doubt."

Frith took hold of Rin by the collar of his greasy tunic and pressed the edge of the blade against the torturer's throat. A thin line of blood oozed across the steel.

"Don't!" Rin's voice was a whine at the back of his throat.

"Tell me where she is," said Frith. "Tell me where she is, you miserable worm, or I swear you will die screaming on these very stones."

"I don't know!" gasped Rin, and there was a genuine frustration in his voice. "After the mess at the castle Fane was angry, he sent her away. Far from Litvania, they said, far from Istria even. Fane knows, not me!"

His revenge, so close it was an appetizing scent on the air, had once again been torn away from him. She had been *there*, she had watched what they did to him, ordered them to shatter his leg...

"NO!"

A great pulse of yellow light swelled from the centre of Frith's chest and filled the room in an instant. Rin was thrown up in the air and then, impossibly, stayed hanging there, unable to move. The knives and pliers and tongs from the bench were similarly suspended, as well as a number of bloody buckets and rags. They hung rigid and immovable, while Frith stood in the centre of it all, amazed.

"What have you done?" cried Rin. The torturer tried to move, his flesh tensing with the effort, but he was as stuck as a fly in amber. Frith, entirely unaffected by the strange pulse of light, slid his sword back into its scabbard and plucked one of the floating knives out of the air.

"It seems, Rin, that you may not die on the floor after all."

35

Roki watched the woman's eyes widen with fear. He smiled at her as he reached over the stall and took the biggest apple from the meagre pile. Keeping his eyes on her, he bit into the slightly wrinkled skin. It would be good to be near her now, to smell the fear as it came over her. Women produced such a delicate scent when they were afraid.

The apple was bitter on his tongue. Roki looked down to see a grub wriggling out of the brownish flesh, half its body missing. He spat the morsel onto the floor.

"This is rotten!"

He threw the apple at the woman's head and it bounced off her shoulder, causing her to shriek and hold her hands up in alarm. Next to him, his brother barked shrill laughter and slapped Roki on the back.

"You think this is funny?"

"I think your aim is terrible." Enri picked up another apple from the pile and threw it with considerable force at the woman, who was now cowering behind her goods. Fane, who liked to witness their daily trawl through the market, boomed laughter at the pair of them.

"That one was rotten too!" said Enri.

"I'm sorry, lords," she stammered, not quite daring to meet their eyes.

"What about this one?" Roki picked up a tomato from another pile and made a show of sniffing it before pitching it at the market vendor. The tomato, long since past its best, exploded in a shower of reddish muck, streaking the woman's face and neck. This time she turned to run, her hands shielding her head, but Enri took his whip from his belt and brandished it at her.

"My good woman! We aren't finished choosing yet."

There was a splash, and suddenly Enri was soaking wet, his long blond hair sticking lankly to his cheeks.

"I think you are," came a voice from behind them.

Roki turned to find the scruffy red-headed woman who had eluded them previously standing behind them. She was holding an empty bucket and grinning. Instead of a helm she was wearing some sort of odd leather hat pushed up onto her forehead, with blue-glass lenses resting just above her eyebrows. Before he could speak, the woman threw the bucket and it struck him in the chest.

"Guards!" bellowed Fane. "Seize this woman!"

Half a dozen guards appeared through the crowd, weapons drawn. The woman drew two long daggers.

"I have a proposition for you, Fane," she said in a strong, clear voice. "I think you'll be interested to hear it."

Fane sighed.

"What is it?"

"I wish to fight your monsters here," she said, jabbing a dagger in the direction of Roki and Enri. "Not these fat, useless guards. Anyone could gut them in a second. I want a fight worthy of the Copper Cat of Crosshaven."

Fane snorted.

"Am I supposed to have heard of you?"

"Not likely. This is my first visit to this delightful place. Next time I am short of ugly men, I shall know where to come."

Enri stepped forward, a grin on his face as sharp as a knife. Roki had seen that look many times, and it always meant a fight. He was pleased. The red-haired woman had a mouth on her, and he looked forward to beating it shut. He loosened his swords in their scabbards.

"Let us play with the little girl," said Enri. He shook his head, showering the ground with droplets of water. "We like to play rough. Would you like that?"

The woman rolled her eyes at him.

"If you must," said Fane, picking idly at the scars on his face. "But keep her alive. This one knows where Lord Frith is, and I've still got a vault to find. Once I have that information we can give her to Bezcavar."

"Wait," she held up one of her blades and pointed at the black-clad guards still hovering behind her. "Send these away. I'm fighting the pretty boys here, and I don't want a sneaky sword in the back from a fat old guard."

"Yes, send them away," agreed Roki. They would play, and then she would die. He wanted to see her eyes widen as he slid the blade home. He wanted to smell her.

Fane nodded to the guards, who melted back into the crowd.

"All the way back!" shouted the red-headed woman.

"An early night, boys," said Fane, smirking slightly, "and tonight we shall drink to this woman's stupidity."

"For Bezcavar," said Roki.

The enchanted gauntlet shivered next to his skin, as it always did, and began to glow. There was that delicious feeling of doubling, and a moment later a copy of himself stood by his side. And then another, and another.

"You wanted to fight a monster," he called to the woman with the daggers. "Let's see you fight a score of them."

So far, so good, thought Wydrin.

She glanced up at the sky. It had been a largely clear day, with a few streaks of cloud dallying on their way to the west, and the sun was making its journey to the horizon now, staining everything crimson and lurid orange. It hung in the sky just above the tree tops, and the shadows were growing long.

They were to light the fuses at sundown. *Not much time left*, thought Wydrin, *but time enough to show these people that Fane and his ilk can be beaten.*

The Children of the Fog advanced, the gauntlets beginning the strange ritual of lights. As she watched they shimmered as though seen through a heat haze, and then there were four of them, then six, then eight. The one she had thrown the bucket of water over shook his head again, shaking droplets of water from his hair, and his fog-brothers all did the same. In the last of the daylight the drops were as ruddy as blood.

Wydrin pulled the Secret Keeper's goggles down over her eyes, and everything turned sea blue, as though she stood on the bottom of the ocean floor. She had a moment to wonder what her father would make of such a thing before Enri's whip snaked towards her out of the air and smacked the air next to her ear. She slid away easily enough, but three of Enri's copies made identical moves, so that the evening breeze was full of the crack of leather. They weaved and shifted amongst each other so that the real Enri and Roki were soon lost in the crowd of identical men, the wicked barbs of their whips glittering in the last of the sun, while the double swords shone like firebrands. And which of them was real?

"Show me," she muttered under her breath, hoping this was the correct way to use the Secret Keeper's creation. "Show me the truth."

And it did.

She could see the Children of the Fog clearly through the lenses, their white-blond hair now a ghostly blue, could see their identical grins as they closed in on her, weapons shining, but now two of them burned with a strange, phosphorescent light. When she had been quite small, her father had taken her and her brother out on one of the fishing boats late at night, and a bloom of jellyfish had swarmed past their boat. They had shone with an eerie white light in the black water, and now Enri and Roki shone with a similar effervescence. The real Children of the Fog were now impossible to miss.

After that, it was fast. Wydrin was not the strongest or the surest blade in Crosshaven, but she was always the quickest. Two of the illusory Rokis stepped up to her, twin swords slashing in a showy attack, and Wydrin slid past them, catching one blade on her dagger and turning it aside. For a brief moment one of the Rokis' sides was exposed and she could have slid her dagger into the soft unprotected leather over his armpit, but to do so would leave her open for an attack from the other Roki, and besides, he was made of mist, so she kept going, letting her momentum carry her past them both. And then she was faced with two Enris, whips curling like sea-snakes in a swift current.

One of the Enris was the true one, burning as bright as the sun amongst the blue. The Enri next to him, who now looked insubstantial in the sapphire light, snaked the whip out at her legs with a deafening crack, and she felt it wrap around her ankle and bite there. The pain was immense.

"I think the Copper Cat has a thorn in her paw!" cried Fane. There was laughter in his voice.

Wydrin feigned an attack at the fake Enri, both daggers brought up to his face, and then she swung to the left, burying Frostling to the hilt in the neck of the grinning blond man. For the barest second it was almost as though he was too surprised to react, and then a spurt of blood poured from the sudden hole in his throat. Wydrin pulled her dagger clear and Enri, the real Enri, pressed a hand to his neck in confusion. He opened his mouth, whether to scream or make some protest Wydrin never knew, and blood flowed from his lips in a dark current.

As he pitched forward to his knees, all the fake Enris, all the men made of mist and fog, winked out of existence. There was a shocked pause from everyone watching, followed by a ragged cheer.

"No!" screamed Roki, and all the other Rokis screamed in unison, their faces twisted with grief and rage. The real Roki, who was still burning like a candle through the crystal goggles, flew at her, swords a blur, but his outrage made him sloppy. Wydrin dropped one knee and avoided the onslaught, then brought her own wickedly sharp blade down on his unprotected hand, putting all her strength into the blow. She felt the blade travel down through his fingers and hit the hilt beneath, saw the crimson droplets leap into the air, and that was when the barracks exploded.

For Sebastian, who watched Wydrin from the edge of the crowd with one hand on his sword, it was as though a huge warm hand came and pushed them all back.

He staggered, almost falling over a smaller man behind him. Shielding his eyes with one hand against the sudden bright light he saw the barracks building on the far side of the market shudder violently, huge waves of orange flame with a greenish glow flashing at every window. There was a second cataclysmic rumble and the evening air was filled with screams from the guards inside. *The floors have collapsed*, thought Sebastian numbly. A second later the thatched roof was ablaze, and then all was chaos.

"You can fight them!" screamed Wydrin. She kicked the wounded Roki, who was staring at his severed hand in shock, and ran to a nearby stall. She climbed on top of it and pointed at the merrily burning building with her bloody dagger. "There are more of you, and *they're* just men. Fight them!"

A handful of guards fled from the barracks, all of them aflame. One dropped to the floor and rolled in the dirt, trying to put the fire out, but whatever chemicals Frith had used ensured it was not so easy.

As Sebastian drew his own sword, a stout middle-aged woman ran to the guard on the ground and put a long-pronged hayfork through his chest. A few seconds later and other townspeople were getting the same idea. Men and women grabbed hoes and scythes and makeshift spears. Sebastian saw one heavy-set man stumble out of the crowd with a meat cleaver his fist, his apron brown with old blood. The guards who had not been in the barracks had joined together at the end of the market, short swords at the ready. They looked nervous.

He brandished his sword at the townspeople.

"I am with you!" he shouted. "For Pinehold!"

There was a bloody slaughter then, fast and terrible. Fane took one look and ran, heading straight for the Queen's Tower. The townspeople howled for his blood, and near rushed after him but a second group of guards headed them off. Sebastian cut through them swiftly, his superior training breaking every defence and sending each attack to its intended mark. His shoulders burned as though he'd been fighting for hours, but when he looked to the Queen's Tower and saw it still standing, he knew it had only been minutes. Wydrin appeared at his shoulder, the goggles pushed back onto her forehead.

"That," she said cheerfully, "is what you get for trusting in enchanted armour."

"The tower," he said. They found themselves in a brief empty space as the battle moved across the market place behind them. "It has yet to fall. Have you seen Frith?"

Wydrin looked around them. The young lord with his shock of white hair should have been easy to spot. She frowned, pulled the leather goggles down over her eyes again and said, "Show me where he is." She looked around the market slowly, and when she finally got to the tower she swore very loudly.

"The stupid bastard's still in there!"

"He can't be."

"I can bloody see him, all lit up like a whore's bedroom!" She tapped the glass for emphasis. Immediately she made to run for the tower. Sebastian grabbed hold of her arm.

"There's no time!"

She shook him off and pelted away, shouting over her shoulder as she went. "I'm faster than you. Win the day out here, or I shall want to know the reason why!"

36

Fane elbowed his way past the guards at the main door of the tower. They were both staring beyond him, jaws slack with surprise, spears held loosely in their hands. No doubt their nostrils were full of the chemical stench too, and the light from the fire now burning out of control in the centre of town had thrown up an eerie glow against the fast-approaching darkness.

It was time to get out. Everything had gone to hell.

Fane could scarcely believe it happened so quickly, but he'd not survived so long without knowing when it was sensible to run, and that was just what he intended to do. There were a few valuables in the tower, some documents he couldn't be without, and then he'd take the last of the guards, and Roki, if he was still alive, and make for some other godforsaken town in this mouldering forest.

One of the guards caught at his arm as he passed.

"My lord, what is happening?"

Fane pushed him away, and then shoved him against the wall for emphasis.

"Gather what you can from the storerooms and make ready to leave. We'll look for the vault elsewhere."

The last Lord Frith, if indeed that's who he was, could rot for all he cared. No doubt he was deep within the Blackwood by now, taken in by some dreadful peasants who thought he was their saviour. Perhaps he would become a local legend, the long-lost lord haunting the forest and waiting for his chance to return. Fane's lips quirked into a smile at the thought; the idea rather entertained him.

Inside the tower he sprinted up the stone steps, moving with a speed that belied his size, and as he did so he passed one of the rooms they'd turned over to the torturer. The door was half open, which was unusual, and a strange red light spilled out on to the flagstones.

"Rin? If you're in there, grab your knives. It's time to leave this piss-pot hole."

Fane pushed open the door fully. The instinct that had been whispering at him to run suddenly screamed in his ear. He shuffled a few steps back, his legs heavy and unresponsive.

The young Lord Frith turned to look at him. There was blood on his cheek, almost black against his dark skin. There was blood on his hands, up to his elbows, in fact, and there was blood in the air, floating like a heavy mist and turning the light from the oil lamps crimson. Beyond him Yellow-Eyed Rin hung suspended above the floor, although yellow was no longer the colour he brought to mind.

"You," said Frith in a flat voice. He dropped the scalpel he'd been holding. "Perhaps you could tell me where the Lady Bethan is? It turns out Rin doesn't like answers nearly as much as he likes questions. I have a friend like that, you know."

Fane's hand hovered over the hilt of his sword, uncertain. He could cut down the slim man in front of him in a few strokes, but the power in the room that was holding Rin and his instruments in the air was a palpable presence, thundering and dangerous.

"YOU WILL ANSWER ME!"

Frith watched Fane's retreating back as he turned and continued his flight up the steps, and all at once the force that had been holding everything up in the air departed. There was a soft pattering as the blood that had so entertainingly flowed from Rin's body to hang in droplets came back down, falling on the flagstones like rain.

Somewhere behind the fog of rage Frith knew there was something he should be doing, a place *he needed to be*, but the sight of Fane's broad shoulders vanishing around the curve of the spiral staircase was more than he could take. No, he would make time for this. Could he let the killer of his father and brothers just *run away*? Unwanted, an image of Tristan rose in his mind, bloodied and broken. Tristan, who had only just started training with a wooden sword, who still needed a lamp by his bedside to get to sleep at night.

There would be time, or else he would go down with the tower.

He ran up after him, following the sound of his rapid footsteps into a wider, more spacious room. For a few seconds Frith was disorientated as memory and sight folded and doubled; this was the old jarl's study, where he had once taken tea and slightly stale bread with his father, an eon ago. The bookcases were empty now and the tapestries were gone, but there were the same tall glass doors looking out onto the small stone balcony, and the same high-backed chair where his father had sat.

Fane was dragging bags of coins from the desk and shoving them into a leather pack. He glanced up at Frith, and his face twitched with a mixture of irritation and apprehension.

"You and I are done, Frith. You want gold? Take it. There's enough here for you to start a new life somewhere else." His lip curled. "Bethan should have made sure you were dead. Never leave a woman to do a man's work."

"We are far from done." Frith drew his sword. So it would be this way then. He might not be able to control the power of the mages, but thanks to the healing properties of the lake he could wield a sword with skill again. "You killed my family, tortured them, destroyed our home."

"I did not."

Frith's grip on his sword tightened until it hurt.

"You ordered it! Why? Why even come here?"

"Why? Because you were rich, and I was not. Or, at least, not as rich as I wished to be, and that's all that matters really." He shoved the last of the coin purses into the pack and slung it over his shoulder. The black rusted helm he'd been carrying in the market was on the desk, and he took it and slipped it over his head so that his brown eyes were narrow and sly. As Frith watched, the rough metal began to glow with the same shapes as those embedded in the gauntlets of the Children of the Fog. Fane grinned.

"You seek to frighten me with your pretty armour?" spat Frith, although in truth he was unnerved. Fighting three or four of this large man would be no easy task.

"Can you guess what it does?" asked Fane. He drew the sword hung at his side and launched into an immediate attack. He didn't split and shimmer to become two or three people, and the move was clumsy and obvious. Frith parried it with ease and swept in with a swift stab at the man's shoulder. To his surprise, Fane spread his arms wide and let him pierce him with the sword; he felt the point of his blade sink into yielding flesh and hit bone beneath. Confused by the ease of his victory Frith withdrew, only to watch the wound close up without spilling a drop of blood. Fane's grin grew even wider.

"It is a fine trick, is it not? My blood can only be spilled in honour of Bezcavar, and the power he grants for that is great."

And then Fane lunged, fighting with the fury and recklessness of a man who knows he cannot be injured. His sword flew through the air, again and again, until it was all that Frith could do to defend himself, let alone cut the outlaw to pieces. He was turned around, forced beyond the desk to the glass doors of the balcony. Fane was grinning, a thin line of saliva leaking from his stretched lips, when there was a meaty thud and his relentless smile faltered. The big man turned slightly to reveal the hilt of a dagger protruding from his shoulder. Wydrin stood in the door to the room, the strange goggles pushed up onto her forehead, making her hair stick up on end. She ignored Fane and glared at Frith.

"What the bloody hell do you think you're playing at?"

"The helm, it makes him–"

"We don't have time for this!"

She ran past Fane without another glance and shoved Frith through the glass doors, which crashed open. Some of the panels fell out and smashed to the floor.

"Unhand me, woman!" cried Frith. "I *must* kill him, don't you see? I must–"

"Even if it means your death? You idiot!"

She pulled Frith up to the balcony ledge, and that was when a tremendous roar filled the air. For a brief second Frith thought of the terrible dragon that had emerged from the ruins of the Citadel, and then the entire tower seemed to lurch under his feet. There was a thunderous, ear-splitting screech as tons of masonry suddenly found that its foundations had turned to powder.

"You owe me one," said Wydrin, before taking his arm and jumping from the tower.

37

Later, much later, when Wydrin tried to recall the leap from the Queen's Tower, she found she could only remember fragments, like the brightly coloured pieces of a broken vase.

And when she faltered over the telling of the tale her audience would normally call loudly for the truth, convinced that not even the notoriously reckless Copper Cat would jump from such a distance, and eventually Wydrin learned to grin and do what she was best at; order another round of drinks, and make the rest up.

In truth, privately she would pore over the details that were left to her and marvel that they survived at all. She remembered a great cloud of dust rising up from the base of the tower as the bottom section crumbled, a plume of grey smoke covering them like a shroud. She remembered holding tight to Frith's arm, his touch warm and solid, and then she lost him, unable to keep a hold as the ground approached. She remembered the scent of fire and the evening sky lit with stars, and a jarring impact that forced the hilt of her own dagger into her stomach, winding her badly, and the sudden lightness of her head as the Secret Keeper's goggles flew off to shatter elsewhere. And then there was, thankfully, the golden smell of hay in her nostrils.

"Of all the luck," said Crowleo for possibly the tenth time. Wydrin had lost count. "You couldn't have known there would be something there to break your fall."

They were seated around a table in the Alynn's Pride, with several plates of fresh meat and vegetables steaming away in front of them and more tankards of ale than even Wydrin could safely drink. Pinehold was free and prosperous once more.

The commotion had taken some time to calm down, with many of the townspeople believing that Fane himself had destroyed the Queen's Tower, and although all the guards had been killed or driven from the town in the ensuing chaos, a number of people had died in the fighting. Initially, there were those who demanded the three adventurers be taken prisoner, for reckless endangerment if nothing else, until Dreyda had stepped forward and quietly explained everything. Wydrin had been impressed with that. The Regnisse had an icy, precise manner that dampened the outrage and turned the townspeople friendly, grateful even. Now Frith wore a fine bear-skin cloak with a silver pin, and at her hip Wydrin had a brand new short sword. It was fine work, the blade as sharp as a winter chill, and the pommel glittered with a piece of the blue crystal they'd salvaged from the Secret Keeper's broken goggles. They had been unable to find Ashes, her beloved dagger, amongst the wreckage of the tower; much like the body of Fane. Equally, there was no sign of Roki, although a few of the townspeople claimed to have seen him running through the southern gate shortly after the explosion, cradling what was left of his hand.

"Luck? Skill and forward thinking, more like," she said, waving a chicken leg for emphasis. "I took note of the hay carts beneath the tower as I ran towards it, of course. It's not my fault you are so unobservant."

Next to her, Dreyda coughed with laughter.

"Born under lucky words," she said. "I knew it as soon as I saw you."

There were a few moments silence then. Wydrin looked at Sebastian. He'd taken a number of small injuries in the fighting, but it had been days since the tower had fallen and he still looked ill and withdrawn. His smiles were brief things, like the sun poking through on an overcast day, and he seemed to have little energy for conversation, instead making the occasional comment and looking away. She was worried about him.

Lord Frith looked as stern as ever, distracted even, and yet they had won a great victory here. It was all quite annoying really. Wydrin threw the gnawed bone down on the plate and wiped her greasy fingers on her shirt sleeves.

"Speaking of words," she said, raising her eyebrows at Dreyda, "I believe you wanted to speak to our princeling about the mages."

Frith looked up sharply.

"What have you said to her?"

Wydrin waved at him dismissively. "Oh, keep your britches on. You've not exactly been hiding it, have you?"

Dreyda leaned forward, her thin face intent.

"It is true, then? You have absorbed the power of the mages?"

Frith glowered at Wydrin.

"It hardly matters. The power is largely useless. It bursts forth without any say so from me, yet when I wish it to do something, the magic remains dormant."

Dreyda raised her eyebrows.

"By all the words – it is true, then. Where did you find such a thing? We thought that the last traces of the mages had all been long discovered."

"Lord Frith gained his powers in the bowels of the Citadel at Creos," said Sebastian. His voice and face were grim. "A place where we also unleashed a terrible creature on the world."

Dreyda looked horrified.

"It is forbidden, strictly forbidden, to explore the Citadel."

"Well, it's all rubble now, so I don't imagine it makes much difference," said Wydrin.

Frith ignored her, leaning over the table to focus his attention on the fire-priestess.

"You know of the mages, then? Can you tell me why the magic is so unreliable?"

Dreyda nodded gravely.

"Our sect reveres the mages as repositories of great wisdom. We aim to use what knowledge they left us to bring peace and better lives for all. I can tell you some of what you need to know." She paused to take a sip of her ale, and Wydrin saw Frith bristle with impatience. "It makes sense that you are unable to use the power as you wish, I'm afraid. The ancient magic was said to be tied to the emotions of the mages. The most terrible were those who could not control their anger."

"I was filled with rage when I first laid eyes on Fane, so the flames came forth. I was frustrated and angry in the tower, so the magic held everything still."

"It works through the medium of your most powerful emotions," agreed Dreyda.

"That can't be entirely right," said Wydrin. "You healed my fractured arm just after we arrived in Litvania. That magic worked."

Frith frowned, but said nothing. Sebastian cleared his throat.

"So how did the mages control it?" he asked.

"By using the correct words." Dreyda rolled up her sleeves, revealing the closely packed blue and black letters etched into her skin. "An ancient language. The fire-priests of Relios have studied it for hundreds of years."

"Words?" asked Wydrin.

"The words are control," said Dreyda. "You write something down, and it becomes fixed in place."

"But without the magic of the mages your words are all useless," said Wydrin.

Dreyda smiled thinly.

"One day, child, you will learn that the written word is powerful precisely because anyone can use it. We learn the words and find great meaning in them, even if we lack the raw power of the mages to work spells."

"How does it work?" asked Frith. His grey eyes were ablaze.

"They would bind their bodies with the words, and the words would act as a conduit for the magic, forcing it along certain paths."

Wydrin's eyes widened.

"Remember the Culoss?" she said. "Their bandages looked like they once had writing on them, and they said they were created by the mages."

"You must tell me all you know immediately," said Frith. "You must teach me every one of these words."

For a moment it looked as though Frith was going to reach across the table and grab Dreyda's tattooed arms. She hurriedly withdrew them.

"These are not the right words. The words *we* took from the mages' teachings were the words for peace, words of wisdom. You require the forbidden texts. We long thought the power of the mages lost for ever, but even so the last words of power were hidden away. To keep them safe. To keep us all safe."

Frith thumped his fist against the wooden slats of the tavern wall, causing a shower of dust that glittered gold in the sunlight from the window.

"By all the gods! And where are those?"

Dreyda sat back in her seat, crossing her arms over her chest. Wydrin thought for a moment that she wasn't going to speak again, but in the end she looked down at the table and gave the smallest shrug.

"It is no secret, not to the children of the Regnisse, anyway, although you would be a fool to go there."

"Where?" said Frith again.

"Whittenfarne," said Dreyda, her voice a whisper now. "Whittenfarne in the Nowhere Isles."

38

Emerald green blood dripped onto the red sands of Relios. Ephemeral, until recently known as the Thirty-Third, found she couldn't look away from it. Her sister knelt on the ground alone, while the rest of the brood army crowded against the walls of the ruins. Y'Ruen loomed above them all, her enormous claws scratching huge furrows in the ancient brickwork, and all around there was silence. A number of words occurred to Ephemeral in the darkness of her own head: threat, danger, alarm, betrayal... death.

And who else has participated in this folly with you?

Mother's voice rang in all their heads at once. Talisman, who had once been the Ninety-Seventh, cringed, her body trembling all over. The initial lash from the dragon's tail had been little more than a tap, but it had easily broken half the bones in Talisman's face, and now blood was oozing from her nose and mouth. She tried to speak, and instead spat a mouthful of blood and teeth into the dust.

That's it, child. Tell me who else has these false names.

The Ninety-Seventh made another strangled noise. *When she gets the words out, I will be up there with her, sharing the punishment,* thought Ephemeral. *Crocus and I will be bleeding into the dust too.* More words came: fear, despair, pain.

Why you ever thought anyone but your mother could name you, I will never know. For a moment Y'Ruen sounded amused. Ephemeral felt her stomach turn over. Their mother contained no real humour, because humour required you to see things from another's perspective. There was no mercy in Y'Ruen, no empathy. And no humanity.

The dragon shifted her huge bulk on the wall, causing a small cascade of stones and dust.

Tell me. Now.

This is it, thought Ephemeral. She sought out the Twelfth in the crowd, now Crocus, and saw her pressed amongst her sisters, her eyes wide with fear. How different she seemed to them now, although Ephemeral wasn't really sure why. *We've never felt this before,* she thought, *this fear of our lives being ended. Not truly.*

"There's no one," said the Ninety-Seventh suddenly. Her voice was thick with blood and slurred, but loud enough for them all to hear it. "There's only ever been me. I was the one with the book, no one else chose their own name."

Ephemeral's breath caught in her throat. More words came: deceit, lies, shock. Hope. *Why is she lying? Why is she protecting us?* The brood army were one, a single unit moving together. To lie to one part of it to save another made no sense. It was unthinkable.

That is what you are saying, is it? All the fake good humour had vanished from Y'Ruen's voice. She lowered her huge scaled head, deepening the shadows around the Ninety-Seventh. *That is what you choose?*

"I choose to be Talisman," said the Ninety-Seventh. "To be me."

There was a low growl of anger from Y'Ruen, so loud that the ground beneath them shook. Her tail lashed out once more, the very end curling around the body of the Ninety-Seventh like a vast snake, covering her up to her neck, and then she flexed, just once. The sound of bones shattering was terribly loud within the walls of the ruins, and Ephemeral watched as her sister vomited a great river of green blood. When it was over, Y'Ruen dropped the body on the floor and took to the skies again. The brood army moved listlessly for a moment, uncertain what to do until the call came from their mother to move on again.

"She was brave."

Ephemeral turned to find Crocus at her side. Her voice was low and she wasn't looking directly at her; instead her brood sister also seemed unable to look away from the crushed body of Talisman.

"Brave," agreed Ephemeral. She tested the word in her mouth, tasting it and all the other words it brought to mind. *Strength, risk, choice.* She took her sister's hand and squeezed it. "Talisman was brave, and we shall be braver."

39

A few days later, Wydrin and Sebastian walked through the forest in the early afternoon's light to visit Crowleo. The apprentice had gone back to the Secret Keeper's house to see if there was anything salvageable left amongst the blackened timbers. Frith had left the tavern they were staying in earlier that day, muttering something about some business he had to wrap up. Wydrin had still been in bed at that time, of course.

"It's a fine day," she said, nodding at the greenery around them. The forest itself seemed a more forgiving place with the disappearance of Fane; sunshine filtered through the leaves, casting a cool green light over everything, and from all around there were the sounds of small animals and birds preparing for another day of virulent life. "When it's like this I can almost see why he wanted to come back here."

Sebastian grunted in response, not looking up from his feet. He was paler this morning, with dark circles under his eyes, and he'd barely touched their breakfast of eggs and cured sausage.

"Just as long as there's a warm fire and a roof over my head at the end of it, mind you." Wydrin paused. As fond as she was of the sound of her own voice, this was starting to become tiresome. She put her hand on Sebastian's arm.

"Sebastian, if you do not tell me what is wrong, I shall christen my new sword by lopping your annoying head off with it."

That earned her the ghost of a smile.

"It is nothing. I am just tired."

Wydrin returned his smile. "I'm fairly bloody knackered myself."

"Do you remember when we first met?"

Wydrin snorted laughter.

"Of course I do. You were so drunk you couldn't get your weapon out of its scabbard and you were still winning a brawl against several of Crosshaven's worst. One of my most treasured memories, that."

"I was so angry." Sebastian kept looking ahead, his face shrouded in dappled shadow. "I wanted to burn the world down, for what they'd done to me."

"Understandable. You're better off without the Order, Seb." Wydrin kicked a stone off the path with more force than was strictly necessary. "They were ignorant fools."

Sebastian shook his head slowly.

"I should have been better. They were wrong, but what we have done…" He paused, and rubbed at his eyes. "I am so tired."

Wydrin nodded.

"We'll have a rest from adventuring for a while, then. Head back to Crosshaven, drop in at the Marrow Markets, perhaps, and see if we can find my brother." She grinned at a sudden upturned memory. "Do you remember last time? I don't know why they call it a festival if they can't take a joke. Might be an idea to ask around before we visit, actually; there might be one or two merchants with long memories…" Her voice trailed off and she looked up at Sebastian, but he was gone again, his blue eyes grave and searching a landscape she couldn't see. They walked in silence the rest of the way, and for Wydrin the forest seemed ominous once more.

When they reached the Secret Keeper's house they found Crowleo standing out on the path, his shirt sleeves rolled up to the elbows and one of Holley's old aprons around his waist. There was a rug beside him covered in various instruments and pieces of old glass, and an old iron bucket filled with broken things. He waved as they approached.

"We've brought you lunch," said Wydrin, placing a basket full of bread and cheese down on the rug. "What are you up to?"

"Sorting through everything that is left," said Crowleo. He gestured at the stone room where the Secret Keeper had worked. "There is not a lot, truth be told, but much of the equipment was too sturdy or heavy for the Children of the Fog to break, and so I have that."

"What will you do now?" asked Sebastian.

"I have decided to stay here and rebuild what I can," said Crowleo, a small smile on his lips. "The priestess woman, Dreyda, has promised to help and she seems to be well versed in getting the people of Pinehold to do as she pleases. There will be people coming with timbers. But listen, I have something for you." He reached into his apron and withdrew a piece of yellowed parchment. He looked apologetic for some reason. "Your friend was here this morning."

"Frith?" Wydrin eyed the parchment uneasily.

"He came up to visit the vault. Walked all the way across there by himself." Crowleo shook his head. "I don't think I shall ever get used to seeing a man walk across thin air. He said he was retrieving some final items, and he asked me to give you this."

Crowleo handed Wydrin the parchment. She unfolded it. In simple, neat handwriting was a brief message: *Your assistance is no longer required – Lord Aaron Frith.*

In spite of herself, Wydrin laughed.

"Not even a thank-you from our princeling," she said. "I don't know why I'm surprised."

"There was also this." Crowleo bent to the rug and retrieved two heavy-looking coin purses, which he passed to the two adventurers. "He said that should be the last of the copper promise. You know what this means, yes?"

"I know what it means," said Wydrin, surprised at the sour note in her own voice. "Did he say what he was doing next?"

Crowleo shook his head.

"He will go to the Nowhere Isles," said Sebastian, tying the coin purse to his belt. "To Whittenfarne, if it exists."

"Then he is a fool," said Wydrin. "The people of Pinehold think he's their saviour. He could take back the Blackwood piece by piece from there, but –" She shrugged suddenly. "What does it matter? Let him go wandering all of Ede, for all the good it will do him."

"There is something else," said Crowleo. "But let us sit. I would rather have food in my belly before I impart this news."

With the afternoon growing warm around them, they sat on the grass and shared out the bread and cheese. There was a bottle of Litvanian wine, light gold in colour, which they drank from chipped clay cups. Eventually Crowleo brushed the crumbs off his fingers and sighed.

"A tinker came by here yesterday. The man dealt with Holley quite regularly, bringing supplies and news from all over. The poor chap was outraged when he saw the house, and devastated at her death, although he was well enough to buy up my scrap. He'd travelled down from the Horns with a barrel of dried fish strapped to his back. Stank to the heavens."

"He brought news?" said Sebastian. His face was tense. He squeezed the bread between his fingers until it broke into pieces.

"The Horns is afire with it, he said. News that a terrible army has come from nowhere to destroy Creos, and now it marches up to Relios. The rumours say that they do not wish to capture territory, for they burn everything and leave no force behind. They kill everyone, take no prisoners. And they say it is a monstrous army, although everyone argues over the details of it. Some say they are all women, that they are hideously ugly or that they are entrancingly beautiful, that they carry weapons that sing and they drink the blood of their enemies. And that is not all. It is said that the one that commands them is a true monster, a great lizard that haunts the land like a plague." Crowleo leaned forward, his eyes wide. "You may laugh at me, my friends, for believing such wild tales, but I beg of you, do not travel back to the West. Whatever it is that has destroyed Creos, it is dangerous."

"It is dangerous," agreed Sebastian, dropping the bread onto the grass. "And I have never felt less like laughing."

Later, Wydrin stood with Sebastian at the cliff's edge as the sun dipped below the horizon. The forest beneath them was deep and black, while the sky overhead raged through its pinks and oranges in a last defiance of the coming night.

"It's not our problem," she said quietly.

"And why is that? Because we're not being paid?"

Wydrin frowned. "What can we do? Against an army? Against a dragon? Sebastian, be realistic."

Sebastian turned to face her. There was an anger in his eyes she hadn't seen before, and she flinched away from it.

"*What can we do*? We let it out, didn't we? It is our fault! All those deaths, all that destruction, all of it is down to us. When those buildings collapsed and the people were screaming, it was like I was there, watching the people burn. I could smell it, Wydrin, the burning flesh. And it's happening right now. Y'Ruen intends to destroy us all."

"Fine. Then tell me how we kill it?" She could feel her anger growing to match his. "I have one dagger left, after all, and it is pretty sharp. Or perhaps if we ask the dragon politely it will just go away."

"You will never understand, will you?" A crowd of birds flew up from the trees below, standing out against the orange sky like black shards of glass before settling elsewhere and vanishing again. "I must try to stop it. If I don't, then I will not be able to live with myself. I must at least try, whatever the cost."

Wydrin sighed and rubbed a hand over her eyes wearily. The Ynnsmouth knights had caused Sebastian so much pain, had shamed him and driven him from the mountains, but in his heart he was still one of them; honourable, stoic, pompous and *stupid*.

"Fine," she said, feeling the anger leave her, only to be replaced with a kind of tired sadness. "But first you must rest. You're not strong enough to go fighting entire armies right now. We both know that, right?" She punched him on the arm lightly, and risked a smile. "Promise?"

"A rest," he said, looking out into the dying light. "I promise."

By morning he was gone.

Wydrin looked at his note and waited to feel surprised, but there was nothing. His words were warmer than Frith's, at least.

There can be no rest for me until this is over, I think you know that. Have a drink on me and go and see your brother – if he can't keep you out of trouble, he can at least lend assistance. Take care of yourself, and don't come after me.

Your friend, Sebastian

He'd left his half of Frith's payment, as if that eased his leaving. She packed all her stuff, paid the tavern keeper for both their rooms, and walked out the gates of Pinehold. She hadn't the will to say goodbye to Dreyda or Crowleo. *More than enough goodbyes for now*, she thought as she gazed at the ruins of the Queen's Tower.

Outside the town walls she paused by the rusted marks where the cages had once hung. The townspeople had taken them down and planted the grass there with wild rose bushes and yellow poppies, and the air was filled with the soft scent of summer. There were a few men and women there now, their arms around each other, talking quietly and crying. Wydrin let them be and walked on into the trees. There was a map in her pocket that would see her to the coast, although for a time she left it there. It was enough just to walk and enjoy the quiet.

After a while she drew the sword the people of Pinehold had given her and turned it over in her hands, watching the morning's pure sunlight filter through the blue crystal in the pommel.

"You are a pretty little thing," she said. Somewhere above her birds called to each other, shrill messages of warning and hope. "I will call you Glassheart, I think."

She looked up, half expecting to hear Sebastian's usual light-hearted mockery – he always found her fondness for naming weapons amusing – but there was no one there.

Wydrin slid the sword back into its scabbard and walked deeper into the forest.

PART THREE

Prince of Wounds

40

The dead man stood and stared at the ruined tower.

He was aware of a number of things at that precise moment. The bustle of the town around him; people going about their lives, shouting greetings, orders, half-joking threats, the harsh sounds of wood being sawn and hammers striking nails, the smell of sawdust and tar. They were rebuilding.

The dead man was aware of the crawl of fresh air against his skin, curling and sticking there like a handful of worms, and the solid presence of his blood, black and unmoving. And there was the twitching, unnatural energy that sparked up and down his limbs, tugging at his eyelids and keeping him moving, always moving, never a moment's peace.

Peace. When Gallo had been alive he'd had no use for peace. Now he could think of nothing else.

"Young man, you are not looking especially well, if you don't mind me saying so."

A woman had appeared next to him. She had the tattoos of a fire-priestess across her cheeks, and her eyes were narrow and shrewd.

"I have travelled a long way, mistress, and I am weary." He tried out his old grin, and watched her grimace in response. "I was looking for some friends of mine, actually. I wonder if you've seen them? They would have been here, oh, around six weeks ago."

The priestess pursed her lips into even thinner lines.

"Six weeks ago Pinehold was a bad place to be," she said.

"You would remember them," continued Gallo. In the street behind them a door opened and the contents of a bucket of offal were strewn across the stones. He was glad; it would cover up some

215

of the smell. "A young woman with short red hair, and a tall man with big shoulders and a broadsword. A knight of Ynnsmouth. You could hardly forget him."

The woman folded her arms over her thin chest. The skin from her wrists to her elbows was crowded with tattoos.

"And what would you want with them?"

Gallo shifted his weight from one foot to the other. His legs were so heavy these days.

"Nothing untoward, my good woman. I understand, of course, that persons such as those might have a number of enemies, made in the course of their work. Sebastian and I were once business partners and I wish to speak to him again."

The use of the knight's name seemed to soften the harsher lines on the woman's face.

"Yes, well. I can't tell you where he went. He left unexpectedly, and without telling Wydrin, as I understand it."

"They do not travel together?"

"No more. She went back home to Crosshaven, or at least that was her plan." For a moment it looked like she would say more, then she frowned. "That's all I know." "Crosshaven, of course." Gallo grinned. "That is so like Wydrin. Thank you."

The priestess sniffed.

"You're welcome. Get yourself some rest, child."

Gallo nodded absently, looking back at the shattered tower, but when the woman turned to go he grabbed hold of her arm. Under his cold fingers her skin felt very warm.

"Relios is burning," he said in a low voice. "Your home is a smoking ruin, can't you smell it? Shouldn't you be there?"

The woman snatched her arm away. Her face drained of colour.

"The rumours are true?"

Gallo smiled mildly. The urgency that moved through him sometimes was gone again, and instead he was left with the steady thickening of his own blood.

"Yes, all the rumours," he said lightly, "and all the nightmares."

41

The Marrow Markets were the pulsing heart of the island of Crosshaven. A diseased, misshapen and congested heart, perhaps, but if you needed something rarer than the fish and spices sold on the docks, or an afternoon's entertainment, this was where you wanted to be. It was also a good place to find an errant half-brother who had a few days off from pirating.

Wydrin stood on the dusty steps of the enormous hexagonal building, watching as people thronged between the tall marble pillars. It was early afternoon, so it was still reasonably quiet. These were people come to buy and sell, or men and women with swords looking for work. As the sun neared the horizon the atmosphere would change, the rabble would grow louder, and a strong scent of beer and cooking meat would waft over these old stones. She loved the Markets at night.

Wydrin raised her arms above her head and stretched, glorying in the warmth of the sun. It was fine to be out and about, exploring again. Even if the Marrow Markets were as familiar as the back of her own hand, it was better than sitting in a tavern nursing a pint that tasted roughly the same going down as coming up. She glanced back at the glittering blue ribbon of sea still visible over the rooftops, and joined the crowds moving into the Markets.

Within the supporting pillars was a small bustling town of tents and shacks and walled pits. Long banners hung from the distant ceiling announcing the various districts and trading areas in a hundred different languages, a thousand different colours, so that to glance above your head was to look into a rainbow of words and symbols. In the centre of the chaos there was a narrow space of peace and quiet like the calm in the centre of a storm: the Temple of the Graces. At this time of day there would be many people making offerings and contemplating the deadly waters, but it was unlikely she would find Jarath there, so she turned away from the light of the Temple and headed deeper into the murk, moving towards the fighting pits.

As she neared the area she heard a ragged cheer go up, followed by the flurry of new odds being offered. There was a crowd around one of the shallow pits, and, judging from the betting slips being passed back and forth, a fight was about to start.

"Thurlos Beaststalker versus Jarath the Crimson Scar!" called one of the men in the high seats. "Place your bets, place your bets now please!"

Wydrin laughed to herself as she pushed her way to the front of the crowd. *The Crimson Scar?*

There were two men in the shallow pit. One was a broad man with thick black hair covering most of his body, culminating in one of the biggest, wildest beards Wydrin had ever seen. It was just about possible to see a ruddy nose and a pair of eyes peeking out from behind all the hair. He wore leather breeches secured with a heavy studded belt and sandals on his huge, dirty feet.

And there he was. Younger, shorter and slimmer, yet Jarath was clearly the crowd's favourite. His body was toned and his skin, the warm brown of dark toffee, was carefully oiled to glisten prettily under the lights. His curly black hair was cropped close to his skull, and he was cheerfully ignoring his opponent, preferring to spend his time grinning and winking at members of the crowd. There were, Wydrin noticed, an inordinate number of young women at today's fight, and they were all gazing lovingly at the Crimson Scar. He also sported a red splash of paint, a long diagonal line from the right-hand side of his chest down to the taut muscles of his lower belly. Otherwise he wore simple cloth shorts that came down to his knees, and his feet were bare.

One of the adjudicators in the tall chairs declared the betting over, and the two men began to circle each other warily. Jarath was still grinning. He held his arms out as if welcoming the larger man into an embrace.

"Come and dance with me, Thurlos!" he called. He had a strikingly deep voice. "I have longed for a dance partner such as you!"

Thurlos Beaststalker growled, loud enough for Wydrin to hear him over the shouts and jeers of the crowd. The hairy man flexed hands the size of hams.

"Tell me," called the Crimson Scar again, "do you get animals trapped in that beard? It looks like you've left half your lunch in there already."

The crowd roared with laughter, and a few of the young women called out the young fighter's name. He raised a hand to them in response, nodding in acknowledgement of his own wit, and that was when Thurlos charged.

Wydrin winced. She had fallen for that trick often enough herself, and always paid for it in bruises and damaged pride.

Jarath stepped to one side as the larger man came, letting him barge past like an enraged bull. Thurlos pulled himself up just in time to avoid colliding with the wall, and the Crimson Scar bowed to the crowd again, just as though he'd won a great victory. The young women screamed with delight.

"Oh dear," said Wydrin, shaking her head slowly.

Thurlos barrelled into the young man again, and this time Jarath let the bigger man knock him to the floor, only his feet somehow managed to find themselves braced against the hairy fighter's midriff, so that rather than being crushed into the dust he straightened his legs and threw Thurlos off easily. The big man collided with the floor heavily enough for Wydrin to feel the impact in her feet, and after that it was all over very quickly. *I should have placed a bet.*

Wydrin tracked Jarath to a nearby drinks tent and found him surrounded by a gaggle of young women. Pushing her way through them, she found him sitting on a stool, sipping a pint of something foamy.

"Really? The Crimson Scar?"

Jarath dropped his drink on the floor, entirely unmindful of the fancy shoes belonging to the young woman standing next to him.

"Wydrin!"

He jumped off the stool and hugged her enthusiastically, lifting her off her feet and covering her clean shirt in oil and red paint. Wydrin could feel a dozen female gazes narrowing at her back. She kissed him on the cheek and gave his neck a squeeze.

"Put me down, you great idiot. Yes, I'm back. What's all this Crimson Scar nonsense?"

Jarath let her go, still grinning. He shrugged and pointed at the remnants of red paint on his chest.

"You remember I got that scar when the Crimson Sea-Witch attacked the Bararian Flotilla? And I just fought on heroically, despite the terrible wound?" He slashed his hand back and forth, mimicking a sword. "People were talking about that for weeks. Well, I thought, why miss the opportunity to get a name people will remember? You taught me that." He poked her lightly in the chest for emphasis. "Copper Cat."

Wydrin laughed and shook her head.

"I see. The Crimson Scar because of the Crimson Sea-Witch, right? I thought you had your own ship these days?"

The women who had been tending Jarath were moving away with sour expressions now as he led Wydrin over to the bar. He waved at the barman, who passed them two cups of hot spiced wine.

"Well, yeah, but Mum's ship is still the more famous, isn't it?" He took a sip from the cup, frowned, and gestured to the barman again. "Is this *wine*?"

"You want a free drink, you get what you're given," said the barman.

"Hey, I brought all these ladies in here, didn't I?" He waved at the rapidly dispersing women. "Anyway," he turned back to Wydrin, "how've you been? What have you been up to? From what I've heard, it was pretty big, whatever it was."

"Hmm." Wydrin looked around the crowded tent. It was hot, and loud, and for some reason it made her uncomfortable. "You could say that."

"And where's Sebastian?"

The wine was slightly sour. As she sipped it she remembered the great feast they'd eaten under the Citadel. How odd, to think of that now.

"Listen," she said, "will you walk with me? I haven't been to the Marrow Markets for the longest time. I want to see what's new."

"Looking for more work?"

"I've got a job coming up. Working with Reilly, a slimy git from the Horns with a faceful of gold teeth. You know him?"

Jarath made a face.

"That nuisance? I know that he's got a reputation, and it's even worse than yours."

Wydrin sighed. "Are you coming for a walk or not?"

"Let's do that." Jarath waved at a member of his crew, who threw him a loose silk shirt. He shrugged it on, unmindful of the oil and paint. "And you can fill me in on your news."

42

They walked away from the fighting pits and into the trade district. Wydrin had done plenty of business here over the years, selling on the more exotic items she and Sebastian had collected on their travels. They paused by a tent selling armour that looked as though it had only recently been recovered from some bloody battlefield. Wydrin bought a new pair of copper wrist-guards, not bothering to haggle the price with the seller, and slipped them on over her arms.

Eventually their wandering brought them to an old bronze statue of a woman, her arms held up as though she was trying to embrace the sky. Everyone had long since forgotten who the statue depicted or what it was for, but the stone steps at its base were often a quiet place in the midst of the markets.

Wydrin sat down, trying to ignore the concerned look on her brother's face.

"Wydrin…"

"What?"

He shrugged extravagantly. "Sure, you don't want to talk to your only brother, I can see that. But I don't know when I've ever seen you buy something and not have a lively discussion with the vendor about price, and normally when you come and see me we're in for a night of drinking until we vomit and fall down some stairs somewhere, yet today you are distracted and you have a face like a flayed bottom."

"Charming."

"And I don't like to see the Copper Cat all serious. That's for my other sisters, the boring ones." He put an arm round her and squeezed her shoulders. She smiled reluctantly. "Tell me what is wrong."

She looked up at the statue. The woman's face was still beatific, after all these years.

"I am fine. How's Mum? You must have some news of her?"

Jarath chuckled.

"I haven't heard from her for two months, maybe three. She struck out for the Bararian coast, said she was going to follow the sun round for a while, see where it took her."

Wydrin looked at her brother sharply.

"She isn't still looking for my father? I hate to say it, but if he were still alive, we'd have heard from him by now. The storms you get beyond the Sea of Bones..." Her voice trailed off.

Jarath rubbed a finger along his jaw line. Wydrin heard the faint rasp of stubble.

"You know how she is. Too long in the same place and she has to go and find somewhere entirely new to make up for it."

"Yes, I know how she is," said Wydrin drily.

"All of which careful dancing round the subject means you have yet to answer my question."

She looked into his dark brown eyes. He knew her too well.

"It was all fine at first," she said softly. "But it got out of control, and I don't even know where Seb is now." She bit her lip, thinking of how he had been in Pinehold. "He just couldn't let it go. Any of it." She shook her head. "I want to go to the Temple." She nodded towards the broad shaft of dusty sunlight that marked the very centre of the Marrow Markets. It hovered in the air like a dream of summer. "You coming?"

Jarath rubbed his chest through the opening of his shirt, frowning. His fingers came away pink and oily.

"You? In the Temple? Now I know you're having some sort of crisis."

"Come on, it's important."

She took his arm and dragged him towards the light and the scent of seawater.

The Temple in the centre of the Marrow Markets was old, some said older than Crosshaven itself. There was a circular pool, cut directly into the rock, and if you stood on the very edge and looked down – if you were brave enough to do so – you would see a deep blue chasm, reaching down into nothing. There were rocks and colonies of coral jutting out from the uneven sides, and plenty of shadows, so you could never be sure where the Graces were hiding. The hole in the roof above allowed the bright afternoon sunshine to play on top of the clear water, and the Temple was a place of shimmering, jumping light.

A few feet away from the central pool were the rings of tanks. Wydrin and Jarath stood by one, considering.

"You want something hefty," said Jarath, tapping the glass. There was a fat fish within, swollen and silver. It wriggled at the disturbance and hid behind a rock. "Something for the Graces to get their teeth into."

Wydrin glanced down the row of tanks. They were made of the finest glass and contained a huge variety of sea creatures; crabs, lobsters, octopi, brightly coloured fish, and, in one huge tank, a gruesome seawater pike. The sunlight that danced constantly off the surface of the water slid along the sides of the tanks, highlighting and then obscuring the animals within. She thought of Holley's house full of enchanted glass.

"A lot of small fish encourage greater movement, though," she said. "And the Graceful Ladies can read more from that, they say."

"There will be no readings today," came a cold voice from behind them. Wydrin and Jarath turned to find one of the Graceful Ladies glaring at them both. She was short and slight, so that the long purple robes seemed to swamp her. The traditional black lines the Ladies drew on the edges of their lips and the creases of their eyes looked very stark against her pallid skin, and her brown hair was slicked back from a slightly bulbous forehead with fish oil; the smell was overpowering. She looked up at them with eyes the colour of sea mud. "No readings, no more offerings," she said again. "We've taken all we will take for today."

The Graceful Lady gestured to the other side of the pool where another of her priesthood stood with a line of nervous-looking attendees. Just by glancing at them Wydrin could tell that these were men and women with money; they had clean faces, fine clothes, and the vaguely worried look of rich folk forced to mix with the people who cleaned their houses or fetched their food.

"You think we don't have the coin?"

The Graceful Lady raised her eyebrows, thick with greasy black make-up. She said nothing.

"I have the coin."

Wydrin untied a coin purse from her belt and dropped it at the priestess's feet. It made a satisfyingly heavy *clink* against the cobbles. The Graceful Lady looked at it as though a gull had shat in her breakfast.

"It is not a case of money alone," she said, her tone suggesting she dealt with exactly this kind of nonsense every day. "It is a question of devotion. Of *faith*. We are not a fortune-telling service for –" she paused to put exactly the right level of disgust into her voice – "sellswords and pirates."

"Devotion?" Suddenly Wydrin was shouting, and she noted with satisfaction the way both the Graceful Lady and Jarath jumped back in surprise. "Faith?" With theatrical poise she held up her left arm and peeled back the sleeve of her shirt, revealing the tattoo of three sharks entwined around her bicep. The tail of the last shark curled under her elbow. "How is this for devotion?" She waved her arm about, taking care to show it to the line of rich patrons waiting on the other side of the pool. "I take the Graces with me wherever I go!"

The Graceful Lady was hissing with annoyance, urging her to keep her voice down. Jarath was laughing softly.

"If just one of those fat merchants has the mark of the Graces on them, I will cut my own arm off and make an offering of that!" She drew out a dagger and waved it about for good measure. "Let them take their clothes off and we shall see!"

The Graceful Lady plucked at her arm fretfully.

"Very well. Truly, you are devoted. We shall move you to the front of the queue."

Still grumbling, the priestess walked away to where a blue silk pillow lay on the floor. On it were three long sticks with chains and balls attached. These were the Bone Whisperers: essential kit for a Graceful Lady. The short woman snatched one up, shaking her head.

"Jarath," said Wydrin in a low voice. "I need you to steal me one of those."

"What?"

"The Bone Whisperer. Grab one for me while I'm making the offering."

"*What?*" Jarath sounded stricken. For all his posturing and extravagance, he made his living off the sea and had no wish to offend the Graces. "Why would you even want one?"

"Just do it. Everyone will be watching me."

At that moment the Graceful Lady returned, her black lips set into a thin line of forbearance.

"Have you chosen your offering?"

"Yes, this one." Wydrin pointed to a random tank. Inside there was a long, silvery eel.

"Would you like to make the offering yourself?"

Some visitors to the Temple were reluctant to get fish bits on their hands and clothes, and would request that someone else perform the messy task of actually getting the creature into the pool. Wydrin turned to address the people at the pool's edge, her arms spread wide. They were all looking at her, pleased with this extra snippet of entertainment.

"I will make the offering to the Graces myself. This is what true devotion is! I am a daughter of the sea!"

The Graceful Lady sighed heavily.

"Then we shall proceed."

The priestess walked primly over to the edge of the pool and held the Bone Whisperer out over the water. The handle was long and made of dark wood, and from the end there dangled a long silver chain, on the very end of which was a delicate silver filigree ball, no bigger than a hen's egg. Inside the ball were a handful of tiny fish bones, milky white and carefully carved with prayer-notes. It was a beautiful thing, and it was said that the Graceful Ladies each constructed their own. Wydrin glanced at Jarath, and he edged closer to the blue pillow.

The priestess walked around the pool, shaking the Bone Whisperer over the waters. There was a tiny, rustling, rattling sound from the silver ball; the sound, they said, of the ocean's prayers. Sunlight streamed down on the water, sending shards and flashes of light out into the Marrow Markets, and for a few seconds the smell of salt was very powerful; the scent of the sea, or of blood.

"Bring the offering," said the Graceful Lady. Her face was intent on the water now, and everyone else was either looking at her, the pool, or Wydrin. *Good*, thought Wydrin. She walked straight-backed over to the tank, reached in and grabbed the eel. It struggled briefly, and she felt the sinewy power of its muscles stretching against her hands, but all day in a tank of warm water had made it sluggish. Holding the creature firmly in both hands, she walked over to the pool.

"For the Graces, from a true daughter of the sea!" she cried. She glimpsed down into the water and – was that movement? A lethal shadow? The priestess called out more words, some prayer or other, but for a few seconds all Wydrin could do was stare at the water. It wasn't a shark she saw; for a moment it was a serpentine shape, a creature of scales and vast, enormous wings. The feeling passed and in a reflexive shudder she threw the eel into the pool.

Immediately, the waters began to churn, and there was a ragged cheer from the watchers on the other side. Wydrin stumbled back, putting one hand up to her eyes – it was the sun in them, that was all – and she missed the violence of the offering. When she looked down again she saw the dappled grey hide of one of the Graces moving with beautiful silence under the water, and a few shreds of silvery gore that had once been the eel.

"An interesting reading," said the priestess. She came over to Wydrin's side with a smug look on her face. She still held the Bone Whisperer, and she shook it at Wydrin as she approached. "The sea brings you dark currents, *devoted one*." She raised her voice a little so the spectators could hear. "The tide has turned and left you behind, and when it comes back in it will bring death with it, so much death. That is your reading, daughter of the sea."

Wydrin nodded politely. Jarath appeared in eyeshot, and she saw that he had one hand behind his back and a determinedly innocent look on his face. Time to leave.

"Thank you, Lady of the Graces. I will adjust my sails accordingly, and so on."

They left swiftly, merging into the crowds beyond the Temple. Jarath had hidden the stolen Bone Whisperer within his shirt.

"I know for a fact that you got that tattoo when you were drunk," he said cheerfully as they weaved their way towards the drinking tents. "It was going to be that or a mermaid with giant barnacles. And what do you want one of these for anyway?"

"I'll tell you later. Come on, there's a cup of wine with your name on it."

43

The small boat moved at a crawling pace though the swirling mists. Every now and then a distant outcrop of jagged black rock would appear and vanish again, announcing the islands that lay hidden there like portents in a nightmare. The captain was taking them slowly, his eyes trawling the fog continually for hidden obstacles. He was a native of the Nowhere Isles, with pale skin and hair so blond it was almost white, but even the people who'd lived in these mysterious islands all their lives mistrusted the waters around Whittenfarne. It was a cursed place, they said.

In fact, they said it somewhat constantly and Frith was getting rather tired of it. His guide, another native of the Nowhere Isles called Jeen, was sitting on the deck filling his pipe. Frith went and stood over him.

"How much further?"

Jeen glanced up at the white, featureless sky, and shrugged. His hair was darker than the captain's, although Frith suspected that was largely due to the lack of soap and water it had seen lately.

"As long as it takes, m'lord," he said, squinting up at Frith. He had a patchy little beard growing in fits and starts along a weak chin. "Can't just go surging up to Whittenfarne. Good way to get scuttled, that."

Frith sighed, and glanced towards the prow, where the captain stood staring out at the water. The boat's figurehead was in the shape of a hideous, tentacled monster – Jeen had told him this was to scare away any restless spirits, which all seemed a little melodramatic for Frith's tastes, but at least the captain looked like he knew what he was doing.

And really, the people of the Nowhere Isles could hardly be blamed for believing in spirits and ghouls. Frith looked out into the shifting whiteness and frowned. He'd arrived on the most populated of the islands a good fortnight back, and even that had been a bleak, unnerving place. The sand was black and the rocks were glassy, refracting the light oddly, while the grey and brown buildings the people had thrown up seemed to cluster together in desperation. Finding a boat and a guide to take him to Whittenfarne had proved extraordinarily difficult. He walked from tavern to tavern, tolerating the terrible smells and vapours of the tobaccos and powders being smoked in every den, and asked with extreme politeness for assistance, but every query got the same responses; frowns, puzzled looks, or outright anger. Eventually though, as was always the case in these matters, the news that a man with a great deal of money was in town found its way to the correct ears, and Jeen had come sidling by. For the price of several fat bricks of tobacco the scruffy man had told Frith everything he knew about Whittenfarne.

And now he was his guide, too.

"And this Jolnir is who I must speak to?"

Jeen nodded happily, clearly glad to be going over a subject he'd already exhausted.

"If you want to know about the old mages that lived on the island, if you want to know about them, then Jolnir is the man. Mystic. He's a mystical man, you see." Jeen took a pinch of the brown tobacco and held it under his nose for a moment. "There are other mystics on the island, of course – not many now, 'cause it's such a nasty place to live, see – but everyone knows Jolnir is the real expert. Everyone knows that."

I didn't, thought Frith, and resisted the temptation to stamp on Jeen's pipe.

"I need to know more than just stories," said Frith severely. "I need to know details. Facts. I need to know about the language they used."

Jeen stuck the stem of the pipe in his mouth. A few puffs later he nodded with satisfaction.

"That's what they study, isn't it? Jolnir is the biggest studier of that stuff. Everyone knows that."

It was a start, at least. Once he had learned the words of power from this Jolnir, he would be able to control the mages' powers and finally take his revenge on Fane and the Lady Bethan. Frith glanced down at his hands, half fearing to see them bright with green fire again. On the long voyage from Litvania to the Nowhere Isles the powers had become even more erratic, bursting into colourful life when it was least appropriate, even dangerous. It was becoming difficult to hide.

"And do you know where this Jolnir...?"

There was a shout from the front of the boat, and an answering murmur from the crew. Frith thought he heard some of them muttering prayers.

"Looks like we're here," said Jeen, pointing. All of the cheer had evaporated from his voice.

Frith looked where he was pointing, and staggered backwards a step. An enormous, monstrous figure loomed out of the mists. It was dark and jagged, its arms held out to either side with fingers reaching as if to grasp at them.

"And what," he said, keeping his voice steady, "is that supposed to be?"

"A mage, m'lord."

It was a man, Frith saw, although it must have been a good two hundred feet tall, so perhaps giant would have been more accurate, and it was carved from the same glassy black rock Frith had seen everywhere in the islands. Its face was a collection of severe lines and deep shadows, and there were long, straight lines coming down from its outstretched hands. Frith couldn't quite decide what they were supposed to be. Ropes? Stylised streams of water? Beyond the enormous statue Frith could make out a suggestion of small, black hills, peppered here and there with stunted trees and shrouds of grey vapour moving across the land like skittish ghosts. He could see no sign of civilisation, or indeed any sign that people lived there at all. Whittenfarne, cursed island of the mystics. To Frith it looked like a great place to maroon someone and steal all their coin.

"Come on then, m'lord," said Jeen. His face had gone milk white, making his beard look like smears of dirt on his chin. "The sooner we find you Jolnir the sooner we'll all be happier, eh?"

The captain left them on the beach with rather more haste than Frith thought was strictly necessary. He watched the little boat move rapidly back out into the steely sea, soon becoming spirit-like in the fog.

"Should he not wait for you?" he asked.

"Nah, he won't hang around the coast here, m'lord," said Jeen. "The weather is too, uh, flighty. I'll signal him when I need to, with a fire."

Frith nodded, and pulled his bearskin cloak a little closer around his shoulders. The beach was a bleak prospect, a place of black sand, jagged rocks, and little else. The statue of the mage loomed away to their right. Frith found he disliked it intensely. When he looked up at the brutal face he remembered the whispered voices in the lake under the Citadel, how they had taunted and tortured him. The man the statue depicted could well have been one of them.

He turned his back on it and faced the rocky hills inland. The sky was still bright and featureless, but he knew the daylight would not last for ever.

"Let us go then."

They walked hurriedly, neither of them happy to have the shadow of the statue lurking behind them. There was the strangest sense, Frith thought, that it was watching their progress. A handful of black birds flew up from beyond the nearest hill, diving this way and that and then disappearing again. Frith noticed Jeen watching them carefully.

"Do you know any more about the statue?"

Jeen jumped, dragging his eyes back from the hills. Just ahead Frith could see a number of shallow impressions in the rocks where water had gathered. There were lots of these pools, and some of them appeared to be gently steaming.

"Not me, m'lord, no. Your Jolnir will know all about them, yes." He seemed to brighten momentarily. "I know there's three more of them, though! At the other sides of the island. North, South, East and West."

Frith looked around, but the island was too shrouded in the mists to see any hint of other statues.

"This was the Western statue," he said, hoping to prompt more information, but Jeen remained silent.

They came to one of the pools. Jeen walked round it, while Frith paused to look down into the water. It was cloudy, and a shiver of steam rolled off the surface in delicate curls. There were small, pale shapes moving in there, he was sure of it. Could fish live in an environment like that? Were the pools deeper than they looked?

There was a harsh cry from ahead; the black birds were back again. A few of them had landed in one of the bent trees that pocked the landscape, and as Frith watched Jeen circled widely around the branches. The birds did not seem especially fearsome – some species of scruffy crow, with wrinkled purple talons and yellow-black eyes – only as insane as your average bird. Frith jogged to catch up with his guide, noticing how the birds turned their heads to follow his progress.

"A strange land," he said.

Jeen nodded without looking at him. He was sweating slightly, sticking his greasy hair to his forehead.

"There are lots of stories about this place, m'lord. Stories about people coming here to find wisdom and not returning. Stories about *things* watching you."

"It also smells abysmal," noted Frith. As well as giving off steam, the shallow pools seemed to produce an oddly chemical stink. It reminded Frith of his father's rooms in Blackwood Keep. "Do you know what causes that?"

"I don't know, m'lord," said Jeen. "But some people say Whittenfarne has paths that lead down beneath the earth, to places where demons sleep. They say that the mages found the paths and made the place evil and–" His voice ended in a squeak as one of the black birds flew overhead. For a second Jeen was frozen in place, and then he moved forward with a lurch. "That's what they say, anyway."

After an hour of walking over the rocky terrain, Frith called a halt by one of the larger pools. A long, white lizard lay on a rock next to the water, its narrow tail dipping down into the pool. It was as bloodless as a toad's underbelly, and its eyes were big black bubbles. It had teeth, too, long and needle-like, and there appeared to be slightly too many to fit in its head.

"And what is that?"

Jeen sat down on the granular black soil and pulled the pack of tobacco from his back pocket.

"Buggered if I know, m'lord," he said. "Place is full of them, ugly creatures. Don't see them on–"

One of the scruffy black birds had alighted just next to Jeen, and as the guide turned to look, it hopped forward and pecked him on the hand. He shot up, screeching and clutching his fingers.

"It's marked me!"

"Calm down." Frith scowled. "It's only a bird."

"It *marked* me!" There was a flurry of black wings and suddenly there were a dozen of the black birds, all perched around the pool and the two men. A few of them hopped towards Jeen, as though they would also like a chance to peck his hand, and with that the guide was up and running, back to the distant shore.

"Hoy!" called Frith, appalled. "Where do you think you're going?"

"Home! Keep your money!" Jeen was a rapidly dwindling shape now, swerving every now and then to avoid the pools and stunted trees. "Cursed bloody place!"

Frith watched him go, uncertain whether to go after him or not. Running on this island seemed a good way to invite a broken leg, and he had no wish to experience that again. Besides, did he really need a superstitious peasant to show him the way?

He looked back down to see the birds all watching him, and then as one they flew up into the mists. For a moment their calls sounded like rasping laughter.

44

Frith walked on into the black hills.

The pools of stinking water became more frequent, so that at times he had to be very careful with his footing just to keep his feet reasonably dry. Every now and then the black birds would pass on overhead, and he saw several more of the fat white lizards lazing on rocks, so still that they looked to be made of bone. A part of him began to wonder if striking out alone had been such a wise choice, but he forced that thought from his mind.

The light in the sky was just starting to dim when he slipped coming down a slope and stumbled straight into a pool. The water was deep enough to come up to his waist and was shockingly cold. Frith cursed it, himself, and the whole island of Whittenfarne as he struggled back towards the edge, and that was when something with long needle-like teeth bit his foot.

Frith bellowed with a mixture of pain, surprise and anger, and as he did so his body was briefly shrouded in bright green flames. Almost immediately the water around him began to bubble, so he climbed out hurriedly, dragging his sodden body out onto the rocky ground. The flames flared once more, then faded.

Frith looked back at the water to see a number of white fish float to the surface with their bellies to the sky. After a few moments they were joined by one of the lizard creatures, also dead.

"Serves you right," he muttered.

There was an answering squawk. One of the black birds was perched on a rock opposite him. It gave him a sideways look, its eye round and yellow, and then it flew off into the darkening sky.

"If this were Litvania, I'd have you in a pie."

Frith examined his boot. The lizard had made a decent job of chomping through the leather and had managed to prick the skin beneath, but there wasn't an awful lot of blood. Just as long as it wasn't poisonous.

The Lord of the Blackwood rubbed the black sand from his fingers and struggled to his feet, wincing slightly as he put his weight on the injured foot. After taking a moment to curse the island once more, he set off again.

Jolnir found him before he'd even got out of sight of the offending pool.

At first, glaring through the fog of his weary bad mood, Frith thought that part of the landscape was shifting and coming towards him. Certainly the figure was dark and oddly jagged like many of the rocks, and it made no more sense the closer it got. It was short and very hunched, and broad at the shoulders, and it wore a scruffy black cloak which came down to its feet. He could see no head; there was, instead, a huge and intricate mask, covering it from shoulder to shoulder – it reminded him of the figurehead on the small boat that had brought him to Whittenfarne, although as it got closer he saw that the effect was rather more avian. An enormous curved beak made up most of the headdress, painted black and silver and yellow, and a pair of large, staring wooden eyes sat either side of it, varnished to shine wetly. The whole thing looked impossibly heavy, and yet the figure moved easily across the rocky ground, waving a pair of long sticks as it came. These rattled and trembled with dozens of small ornaments; tiny rat skulls, seashells, bird's feet, bunches of bright auburn hair… all tied to the sticks with twine.

When the figure eventually reached him it nodded rapidly, causing the mask to fly up and down in an alarming manner. It waved the sticks.

"A traveller comes!" The voice was deep and booming.

Frith shook the last of the water off his boot.

"I have to find a man called Jolnir. Do you know where he is?" "You have found him." The figure nodded again. Frith thought the beak looked vaguely predatory.

"You are Jolnir?"

"Who else?" The figure gestured round at the unforgiving landscape, and Frith had to admit he had a point. There was no one else here. "Why are you here, young traveller? What is it you desire?"

Jolnir came over to Frith, waddling slightly. As he walked, he reached up and put one of his sticks through the back of his cloak, so that it stuck out like a pin in a pincushion. *He must have a bundle under there*, thought Frith. *Likely he is not hunched at all.* Jolnir reached out and took hold of Frith's bearskin cloak, and Frith noted that the man had terribly thin arms and skeletal fingers, covered in tough grey skin so pitted and worn that it looked like leather. *No wonder he wears a mask. How degraded must his face be?*

"I am Lord Aaron Frith of the Blackwood. I have come here to learn from you, Jolnir –" He paused. Talking to the staring wooden eyes was disconcerting. "I have come here to learn from you the lost language of the Mages. It is imperative I know the words of power."

"Of course it is, of course it is." Jolnir nodded. "When is it not?" He smacked Frith on the arm with one of his sticks. "Mages, words, power. Yes, I will tell you what you need to know. It will be diverting."

Frith frowned.

"You will teach me? I had heard that seekers of this knowledge are turned away from the island. That many never return at all."

"But you," Jolnir snatched up Frith's wrist with alarming speed, and squeezed it. He had a very strong grip. After a few seconds it was actually painful. "You are worthy, aren't you, Lord Frith?" He dropped the younger man's arm. "Yes, we have not seen the likes of you for some time. Come." He turned away, head nodding again rapidly.

"That is most kind."

Frith followed on behind, rubbing the feeling back into his wrist. For a moment it had seemed like Jolnir already knew everything about him.

45

Wydrin lay in the bottom of the small boat, propped up on one elbow while she rubbed the pungent fish oil into her hair. She'd already tinted her hair dark brown, and with the thick black lines of make-up over her eyes and mouth she was fairly confident that no one would recognise her. The purple robes had been easy enough to replicate – the uniform of a Graceful Lady was largely unadorned. She just had to hope the guards would be convinced.

With her hair wet and stinking she sat up, eyeing the distant fist of lights that was Sandshield.

I will be far enough from Reilly's boat by now, she thought. *And if I'm not, it's his own bloody lookout.*

She started to row. When she was small, Sandshield had been an islet of some notoriety, part of the archipelago that was also home to Crosshaven, and already well known for its dangerous population of pirates and thieves. Now there was one man in charge on the tiny island. That was Morgul, variously known as Morgul the Biter, Morgul the Cruel, and the Menace of Sandshield. He was a dangerous man, one of the worst, and if it was his flag you saw approaching, your best bet was to turn and run, or hope that you died quickly in the initial fight. He had turned Sandshield into a small fortress, the better to protect the enormous plunder he'd taken, and tonight Morgul the Cruel's eldest son was about to become a man. There was to be a celebration, and that was where Wydrin came in.

She edged closer, until it was possible to see the great hall standing proud on its raised platform, and the small harbour that surrounded it. By torchlight she could see the solid shapes of wooden palisades, and men moving back and forth over the timbers. There were guards in mail hauberks with short swords at their waists, and a number of empty boats tied up at the edge. Many of the guests were already here.

Wydrin lit the oil lamp. After a few moments, one of the small ships circling the island hailed her, and it escorted her into the harbour.

She reached it just as another, larger boat was docking. A flood of men and women poured out, all loud and obnoxious with good humour – few things cheered a pirate, in Wydrin's experience, than the knowledge that you would soon be drinking vast quantities of another man's ale – although they did pause to argue with one of the guards. He was insisting that they leave their weapons in a small tethered boat – it was already heavy in the water with swords and daggers – while they were more of the opinion that he could go gut himself. Wydrin climbed onto the dock, accepting help from the man who had escorted her to the island. She listened to the argument carefully, the Bone Whisperer in one hand.

"It is the rule of Sandshield," said the guard. He had the slightly weary posture of someone who had already spent much of the evening explaining this rule. "No weapons in Morgul's hall."

"What about you?" jeered one of the pirates. "You've still got yours."

"Morgul's men, of course, will still be armed. You want this island to be unprotected? It is our duty, as guards, to protect all of Morgul's allies. You are his allies, aren't you?"

The pirates exchanged glances. None of them wanted to be in any group that wasn't an ally of Morgul. That was generally a dangerous place to be. They grumbled and complained some more, but they untied their sword belts and threw them in the boat. The guard smiled thinly.

"Very good. There's going to be a lot of celebrating later, and we don't want any unhappy accidents, do we?"

"Are you ready, my lady?"

It took Wydrin a moment to realise that the man was addressing her. She turned to the guard who'd helped her onto the dock.

"Yes," she said, hoping she sounded holy enough. "Can you fetch the cask in my boat? It is the wine for the blessing."

The guard gestured to one of his men, who passed up the cask. Wydrin nodded and made for the wooden steps leading up to

Morgul's hall, but the guard laid a hand on her arm.

"Just one moment, lady."

Wydrin bit her lip. So they were going to search her anyway. Damn Reilly and his stupid plans. She tried to think of a reason why a Graceful Lady would have a dagger and a packet of powder strapped to her inner thigh, but couldn't think of one.

"What is it?"

The guard looked apologetic. "I must announce you first."

Wydrin tried not to look too relieved, and let the guard walk up the steps ahead of her. There was a roar of noise coming from the hall, and as he pulled open the wooden doors, Wydrin was hit with a blast of heat, heavily laced with the scent of beer, sweat and roasted meat.

"Lord Morgul, I bring you our Lady of the Graces!"

The guard had to bellow to be heard, but a huge man at the top table stood and held both arms out for quiet. Morgul was in his late middle years now, old for a pirate, but he looked as large and powerful as ever. His long dirty brown moustaches were tied into plaits and braided into his hair, which was tied back with gold rings. He'd lost an eye since Wydrin had seen him last, and now he wore a patch that glittered with rubies. There was a boy sitting next to him, looking tiny and slender next to his father; Morgul had decided to become a father late in life.

"Silence, you dogs!" yelled Morgul. "Show some respect for our Graceful Lady, come to see our Morben into manhood."

Rather than silence the men and women gathered at the tables jeered and shouted rude suggestions, at which Morgul laughed heartily. The boy sitting next to him turned crimson. Wydrin glanced at the tables; they were all heaving with food and drink. Clearly the feast had been going on for some time already. *Time to show them some holiness.*

"Daughters and sons of the sea!" she called, remembering the woman in the Marrow Markets with the mud-brown eyes. "It is time to welcome another into the sea's salty embrace!"

There were some shouts and laughter at the words "salty embrace", but largely the crowd quieted down. Men and women who made their living from the sea were hard folk who lived hard lives, and they clung to their beliefs and superstitions. When a storm could mean being swept overboard or plummeting from the crow's nest, the idea that there were bigger forces at play than the sheer uncaring nature of life was somehow comforting to them. The Graces represented the destructive force of the sea, and showing respect to them was saying that you understood what you were dealing with. The oceans gave you a living, and they could take away your life. You mocked that at your peril.

"Bring the boy to me, and the Graces will see him a man."

Morgul dragged the lad to his feet, and propelled him down the centre of the hall. Up close Morben looked even younger. Wydrin made a show of inspecting him, holding his chin and looking closely at his jaw line. Some of the watchers at the tables shouted encouragement while his father stood to one side, grinning broadly. He was still wearing his sword, she noticed.

"He is ready," she declared to the room in general. "Fetch the sacred wine."

One of the guards brought her the cask, and a single silver goblet. The cask was opened and a dark red wine poured into the vessel. Wydrin held it out in front of her and shook the Bone Whisperer over it.

"Fermented from the tears of the children who returned to the sea at the end of their lives, we will drink the blessed wine." She paused and drank deeply of the goblet; in truth it was a cheap dry red, but the boy wouldn't know any different. "Your blood is the blood of the sea. Your soul is the soul of the sea. Drink!" She refilled the goblet to the very top and gave it carefully to the boy, who looked terrified by the whole business, and while he drank it down she circled him, shaking the Bone Whisperer and muttering under her breath. He had to drink the entire goblet before she'd completed the circle, so she walked slowly, her eyes half closed as if in deep concentration.

Thankfully, the boy managed it, so she took the goblet from him and held it up.

"Morben, son of Morgul, is a boy no longer!"

The hall trembled with the roar of celebration. Men and women threw their drinks at each other, stood up on the tables and kicked plates onto the floor. Morgul demanded that more ale and wine be brought out so that everyone could toast his boy again, and several minor fights broke out over broken tankards.

After that, the party got rowdy.

46

Wydrin collected her cask of "holy" wine and retreated to the back of the room. Now the serious part was over with, it seemed that Morgul's crew were determined to get his son as drunk as possible, although she suspected downing an entire goblet of wine on a nervous stomach was a pretty good start. She cast around for a safe path to the door, but Morgul appeared out of the crowd and laid a meaty hand on her shoulder.

"Good work, my lady, good work. All those words, all proper like, just like when I were a lad." For a moment Wydrin thought his one remaining eye was getting misty. "We've got him a woman up from Crosshaven, to make him a *proper* man, if you know what I mean." He squeezed her shoulder and leered. Wydrin wondered how quickly she could slip the dagger from her leg, but, thankfully, he let her go, his attention caught by a brawl happening in the sawdust. "Good work," he said again over his shoulder as he went off to join the fight. "Proper godly, like."

Wydrin grimaced. It was time to get out of here.

Outside there were only a few guards left on the dock, sitting and supping their ale, or playing cards on upturned crates. She moved silently into the shadows at the side of the raised platform. Above her the rumble of the great hall carried on, but it was the sturdy wooden box it was built on that interested her: Morgul's loot house.

Circling around to the back she found the guards she was looking for. Three of them, all young and all fairly miserable; rather than the exciting duty of frisking the guests or watching the party, they'd been left to keep an eye on the loot-house door.

She paused behind a stack of barrels where the shadows were

darkest, and rolled up her robes to expose her legs. She untied one of the two packets of powder and poured the contents into the cask; combined with the cheap wine the powder made an extremely powerful sedative. Pulling her robes back down she walked round the corner to the three guards. At the sight of her they all stood to attention. Behind them was the door to the loot house, with a heavy bar across it.

"Men, I bring you the blessings of the Graces on this night." She lowered her head solemnly and held out the cask of wine.

They looked unsure for a few seconds, but the severe make-up and purple robes of a Graceful Lady was a reassuring sight. They took the cask with gratitude, and Wydrin retreated to a shadowy corner and watched as one by one they slumped to the floor. Strong stuff.

With that done she frisked their pockets for the keys, slipped the ring into her robes to stop them clinking, and walked swiftly round to the front of the hall once more. Now she had performed her tasks she was eager for this to be over with.

For a few seconds everything was quiet, just as though the world were waiting for her to make a decision. The sky above was clear and studded with stars, while the sea was a moon-kissed carpet of darkness. Sebastian would have said this was a stupid job, too risky, and, let's face it, too morally dubious, but *because* she was here no one would have to lose any blood. She would signal Reilly now and they would come around to the back of the island, empty the loot house and leave. With a bit of luck, Morgul would only know he'd been robbed when he woke up with a hangover in the morning.

Under the cover of night, Wydrin smiled.

Just to be sure, she wandered over to the boat containing the guest's weapons and untied the rope, letting it drift off. The men perched at the front of the harbour were so intent on their card game that they barely noticed she was there. Once that was done she pulled the last packet of powder from within her robe and chucked the whole thing into a nearby fire pit. There was a blast of brilliant white light, and this the guards did notice, but Wydrin stood in front of the pit with her arms raised up and shouted some more things about the sea and waves of adulthood and they went back to their game. *Priests do get away with a lot of nonsense*, she thought.

•••

Reilly appeared round the back of the loot house with several long, graceful ships that would move quickly over the water. She led them silently to the door and passed over the keys before they piled in, sacks at the ready. Wydrin and Reilly stood outside, keeping watch. From above them came the steady roar of the great hall.

"It all went smoothly, then?"

Reilly looked unreasonably pleased with himself, particularly considering he'd barely done anything so far.

"It seems so." Wydrin watched the first of the men coming out with a bulging sack over his shoulder. "It's too easy. Is Morgul really such an idiot?"

Reilly shrugged.

"He's old, getting complacent. He thinks no one can touch him. And he puts a lot of store in this religious nonsense."

Wydrin pursed her lips. Mocking the Graces at this stage made her uneasy.

"You're a pirate too. Don't you believe in it?"

"I'd believe in it more if all the Graceful Ladies looked like you." He grinned at her, his golden tooth catching the light. "Once we're done here I'm planning a little celebration of my own. You, me, a few more casks of that wine. Do you fancy keeping those robes on? There's something about a godly woman..."

"Don't push your luck, Reilly."

One of his men appeared in the doorway, an excited look on his face. They conferred in harsh whispers for a moment. Reilly turned back to her.

"The guests in the hall. Are they armed?"

"Of course not. Morgul isn't stupid enough to let drunken men and women wave their weapons about under his roof, it'd be a bloodbath. Besides," she added smugly, "I got rid of the boat with the weapons in it."

Belatedly she recognised the expression of greed on Reilly's face.

"What is it?"

"There are steps leading up to the hall, and a trap door. We can open it from this side." His eyes were wide. "We can wipe out half the competition in one night. It's risky, but the rewards–"

She caught hold of his arm.

"You can't do that!" she hissed. "We're here to get the gold and get out."

"Think of the opportunity," said Reilly. She could see the shine of ambition in his eyes. "When will I get this chance again?"

"There's a thirteen-year-old boy up there, a stupid kid getting drunk for the first time," she said, hating the desperation in her own voice. "Don't do this."

But he was already turning away from her, giving the order. He ran into the loot house, and after a moment there was a huge crash from above. Wydrin swore as the noise from the hall suddenly increased tenfold.

She untied Frostling from her leg and moved cautiously towards the front steps, pausing as a crowd of guards thundered past, having finally realised that something was wrong. If she could get in the front door there was a chance she could reach Morben and get him out safely.

She had her foot on the first step when a host of desperate people came storming out of the hall doors; these were the sensible ones, the men and women who'd decided not to attempt to use fists against men with steel. They were followed out by Reilly's men, who cut them down mercilessly, and the night rang with screams. Wydrin flew up the steps, avoiding the bloodier fights, when Morgul staggered out, his face thunderous. He caught her eye, taking in the dagger in her hand.

"You!" he bellowed, but there was a gust of flames from behind him and Morgul's hair caught fire.

Reilly's men are burning the whole bloody place down.

Wydrin fled. She took one of Reilly's narrow ships, cursing him as she did so, and headed away from the island as quickly as her rowing arms could take her. Morgul's hall was burning merrily now, and she saw other ships fleeing Sandshield, certain that some of them were Reilly's men escaping with the loot. Or perhaps they would stay, and Sandshield would belong to another pirate in the morning.

As she rowed, she thought about how close she'd got to that door, and the smell of smoke and burning flesh from within. She had had no armour and only one weapon, she'd been encumbered with robes and had not a single ally. She couldn't have saved the boy, not without getting herself killed in the process.

Even so, it felt like running away. Again.

47

The brood army were not difficult to track.

Sebastian sifted through the ashes with the point of his sword. Under the layer of soft black powder there were charred bones, scraps of blackened cloth, and here and there a twisted lump of metal that might have been a sword, or a hoe, or some other household implement.

Judging by the surroundings, Sebastian guessed that the scattered debris had once been farming equipment. And people, of course.

Relios was a fiery red land, thick with clay and fruit trees thriving under the relentless sun. There had been orchards here, before the army came; he could see the occasional blackened remnant of a tree dotting the landscape. There had been a village here too, no doubt full of people making a living from fruit and olives, but nothing remained of that save for smoke and ashes.

He stood, stretching out the tired muscles in his back, and looked to the north. There was a wide, black smear across the lands, leading to a distant heat haze and a smudge of grey smoke. Sometimes, when the day was especially clear and still, he fancied he could see movement there, and the occasional glint of light as the sun shone off their golden armour. He could see them, and when he tried to sleep, he could hear them.

Of Y'Ruen he'd seen little, although he had spotted her once or twice in the last few days. She was a shadow on the clouds, scouting ahead, seeking out fresh lands to destroy.

Sebastian rubbed his fingers over his newly grown beard, remembering the first time he'd seen her, flying over the coast of Relios. The fever that had been slowly growing within him ceased for one terrible moment and his entire body had grown icy cold. *Wydrin was right,* he'd thought, *what can we do against such a creature?*

After weeks of following the army and its monstrous leader, the terror had sunk deep into him, becoming anger instead. Becoming *fury.* If it was hopeless, it was hopeless. He would still die with dragon-blood on his sword.

Today he was more interested in a second group, far to the east of the brood army. He'd spotted some movement in the distance the day before, the tell-tale glinting of sunlight on steel. Initially, he thought it was the final stand of the Relitian army, who had made frequent and increasingly desperate attempts to destroy the dragon's brood, but today he could see it was not them; the Relitian army carried banners of the Regnisse – red silk pennants covered in a language he couldn't read. This group carried a rainbow of different banners, and with a strange mixture of dread and excitement Sebastian realised he recognised them. They were Ynnsmouth knights.

Of course, he thought as he watched their manoeuvres under a distant hill. *How could the Order pass up an opportunity like this? A dragon and an army of monsters, just like a tale from the legends.*

He slung his sword across his back once more and walked away from the remains of the farm.

The novice yawned hugely and picked at the starched cloth of his uniform, trying to peel it away from his sweaty skin. It was too damn hot. He imagined being back under the mountains, slipping his feet into one of the icy lakes, or sleeping on the cool grass. Sleep, in fact, was a fine idea…

"Not much of a lookout, are you?"

The novice jerked awake. There was a man approaching through the low bushes, and he was alarmingly close. How had he got so close? The novice snatched up his spear and scrambled to his feet.

"Halt! Who are you?"

The man paused. He had an unkempt black beard, and long black hair unbound to his waist. His face was streaked with dirt and his clothes were little better; he looked as though he'd been sleeping out in the open for weeks. And there was something about his eyes… The novice gripped the shaft of his spear a little tighter.

"If I were an enemy, do you not think I would have let you sleep? Right up until I cut your throat?" The man paused and shook himself, as though waking up from a dream. "I'm sorry. My name is Sebastian. I am one of your Order. Or at least, I was."

The novice frowned.

"You don't look like a knight."

Sebastian smiled wanly at that. "Here." He pulled something from his cloak and held it up for the boy to see. "I am sworn to the God-Peak Isu, and I carry his sigil."

It certainly looked like one of the badges the elder knights wore. The novice hoped to wear one himself one day.

"I guess you'll come with me, then," he said, and then added, because he felt he should have made a better impression, "and don't try anything!"

Sebastian was marched through the camp with the boy at his back. Everywhere he looked he saw the banners of the god-peaks, men and women with their sigils sewn onto their cloaks, painted on their shields. They were all busy, tending to equipment, brushing down horses or running through drills, but some looked at him curiously as he went past, clearly wondering who this tall scruffy man was. He saw no recognition in their faces, for which he was glad. It was like walking in a dream, or a memory. *How often have I thought about coming back to them?*

The lookout took him to a large tent in the centre of the camp. It was yellow and green silk, the colours of Ynn. There was a brief discussion with the guard at the entrance, who looked at Sebastian with open hostility, and then he was taken inside.

It was hot and close, and it took Sebastian's eyes a few moments to adjust to the gloom. When he saw who was waiting for him, he winced.

There were three men in the tent, standing over a low travel table covered with maps. They looked up as the guard cleared his throat.

"Lord Commander, Novice Cooke found this man skulking at the edges of the camp. He says he is–"

"You!" One of the men at the table straightened up, the look of surprise on his face quickly melting into anger. "Of all the abominations."

"It is good to see you too, Spirron," said Sebastian.

Sir Spirron was a wiry streak of a man, his thin, grey lips always wet with saliva. The boys had called him Sir Spittle behind his back.

"Who is it, Spirron?" The man Sebastian didn't recognise frowned at him over the maps. He had a neat auburn beard and patches of sunburn on the tops of his cheeks.

The last man, a tall, powerfully built knight in his middle years, cleared his throat.

"This is Sir Sebastian, John. He left the Order before you joined us."

"It is good to see *you*, Lord Commander," said Sebastian, and he meant it. Sir Spirron rounded on the older man, his wet lips working.

"May I remind you, Lord Commander, that the title of 'sir' was stripped from this abomination when he was exiled?"

"I am aware of that, thank you, Spirron," said the Lord Commander coldly. There was a moment of silence. Sir John, the man with the auburn beard, shared a glance with Sebastian and raised his eyebrows. Eventually, the Lord Commander rolled up the map in front of him and passed it to Sir Spirron. "Get that to the people on the front, Spirron. Now, Sebastian. What are you doing here?"

Sir Spirron made to leave, but paused at the entrance to the tent.

"Lord Commander, this man was a disgrace to Ynnsmouth." Spirron kept his eyes on the grey-haired knight. "By rights he should be taken prisoner. It is a grave personal insult to me that–"

"I am not *in* Ynnsmouth, Spirron," said Sebastian. "And since I am no longer part of the Order, as you keep pointing out, there is very little you can do. Unless you've started imposing your nonsense on civilians now, too?"

"Enough!" thundered the Lord Commander, and Sebastian felt a chill of recognition on the back of his neck. The Lord Commander was a good man, but you never wanted to be on the receiving end of his anger. "Sir Spirron, I asked you to do something for me, did I not?"

The knight nodded curtly and stalked from the tent. The Lord Commander shook his head slowly.

"There was always an odd, rebellious streak in you, Sebastian." He tugged briefly at his beard, which was white and cropped close to his jaw. "A good knight, one of our best." Sebastian allowed himself a small smile. "But you didn't have the steel. The resolve." The Lord Commander met his eyes briefly, and looked away again. There was disgust in them. Sebastian's smile faded. "Your weakness was your undoing."

"Can you still not speak of it?" Sebastian could feel the old anger rising to the surface.

"That's enough," said Sir John mildly. "You might be exiled from the Order, lad, but you'll keep a civil tongue in your head."

The Lord Commander gestured at the lookout and the guard to leave. Sebastian supposed it would take all of a handful of heartbeats before the entire camp knew who he was and what he'd done.

"What are you here for, Sebastian?" The Lord Commander sounded weary now, and his eyes were back on the maps in front of him. "We have more than enough to worry about without past misdemeanours appearing out of nowhere."

"I imagine I am here for the same reason you are, my Lord Commander. The bloody great dragon flying over Relios."

Sir John chuckled dryly.

"You noticed that, did you?"

"Lord Commander, I can help. I have knowledge of the dragon, and the army that travels with it."

"Knowledge? What can you know that we do not?"

"I know how it moves, my lord. I know how they think."

"And how could you possibly know that, lad?" asked Sir John. He sounded genuinely curious.

Sebastian closed his eyes briefly. Of course they would ask. And what could he say? That his blood had nourished the brood army and birthed them from the ground beneath the Citadel? At best they would cast him out as mad, at worst they would put him to death for allowing such a thing to happen in the first place.

"I would rather not say, sir."

The Lord Commander waved at him dismissively.

"I don't have time for this nonsense. You will leave this camp and if you've any bloody sense you will go far away from here."

"My lord, the brood army leave no prisoners," said Sebastian quickly. "They take no land and keep no resources. They do not leave garrisons behind to defend the lands they have caught." He took a deep breath. "They do not eat and do not appear to sleep, although they sometimes eat the flesh from the men and women they kill. Am I right?"

Sir John frowned. "You are."

"They have few of the weaknesses of a conventional army," Sebastian continued. "They do not need to find food, so they burn everything they come into contact with, and do not need to bring supplies with them. The swords they carry are not made of steel or any other metal, and they very rarely break. They are relentless, tireless, and yet they move slowly through Relios."

"They do," agreed the Lord Commander. "We cannot predict where they are going. They seem to meander."

"It is because their only goal is destruction," said Sebastian. He thought of the smell of ashes and blood in his nose, night after night. "They do not wish to capture kingdoms. They only wish to see them burn."

Sir John picked up a piece of parchment from the table.

"King Mirelle of Relios has sent army after army against them, and the results were bloody, to say the least. Eventually, he sent envoys, asking for terms. These green-skinned women, or the brood army, as you say, sent back the envoy's heads. Or at least, that's what we assumed they were. It was difficult to tell." He frowned, examining the parchment. "Now King Mirelle entreats us to stop them, before his entire country is laid to waste." He put the paper down. "But how to defeat an army when you must always be looking *up*?"

"How is it you know so much of this army, Sebastian?" The Lord Commander crossed his arms over his barrel chest.

"I have been tracking them for weeks," Sebastian replied quickly. "I can assist with any strike you make against them, Lord Commander."

The older man looked at him for a time. He had not changed all that much since Sebastian had last seen him – a few more white hairs at his temples, perhaps, a few more lines around his eyes – and the look of wary consideration was very familiar. He remembered it well from the time of his trial, and suddenly he knew he was about to be denied. He opened his mouth to protest and the Commander spoke over him.

"It is no longer your honour to assist the Order, Sebastian Carverson. You were dismissed and exiled in disgrace, and that was to have been an end to it. The trouble you caused us…" He looked back down at the maps. "Go away from this place. Get out of my sight."

For a moment Sebastian could hardly draw breath.

Over the years he had often contemplated what he would say to the Order, should he ever meet them again. He had composed long arguments, rallies against their injustice and bigotry, their ignorance. In his head he'd said everything he'd ever nursed in his heart and seen shame cross their faces as they realised the mistakes they'd made. The Ynnsmouth knights would regret their actions, and he would triumph.

But in the end, he could say nothing. He nodded once, refusing to bow or salute, and he left the tent.

48

Sir John found him an hour later at the very edge of the camp. Sebastian had managed to scrounge a bucket of water from a squire and was splashing cold water over his face and hands. It wasn't helping. Despite the overcast day the heat was relentless, and his head was pounding.

"What will you do now?"

Sebastian looked up to see the auburn-haired knight standing to his right, staring off across the plains to where they knew the brood army were massing.

"Why do you care?" snapped Sebastian, irritated with the childish petulance in his voice but unable to stop it.

"It's a reasonable enquiry." Sir John lifted himself up on the balls of his feet and let them drop again; an old soldier's trick to keep from getting stiff legs on a long watch. "You seem like a very capable knight, Sebastian Carverson, despite your appearance. Why were you expelled from the Order?"

Sebastian stood up, shaking the water from his hands. He smiled bitterly.

"You mean Spirron hasn't told you?"

The squire who'd given Sebastian the bucket of water had watched him very carefully, as if expecting to be groped at any moment. No doubt his old instructor was spreading his version of the story at every opportunity.

Sir John nodded once.

"I would like to hear it from you."

Sebastian sighed, and threw the damp cloth he'd been using to wipe the mud from his armour into the bucket.

"You are aware of the Order's oath regarding celibacy?"

"Of course." Sir John nodded once more, still staring off at the distant plains. "It is one of my personal favourites."

Despite his exhaustion and anger, Sebastian laughed. "Well, I broke that oath."

Sir John raised an eyebrow.

"I'd heard it was rather more than that."

"That's what it comes down to." Sebastian looked at the older knight. "I was an exemplary novice. You can ask the Lord Commander. I excelled in my training, passed every test they put in front of me. I was made to be a knight, they said, and I agreed. I passed into the Order with flying colours, and for some time I was the man they pointed to as an example for new recruits." He grinned at Sir John. "Can you believe that?"

"What happened?"

"It is not natural, what they ask of us. To live and die with each other, but never to love one another." Sebastian looked down at his feet. He struggled to recall their faces sometimes. "I led a troupe of five men, and over the course of several missions we forged a bond." He looked at Sir John severely. "We were brothers. I'd have died for those men, and they for me."

Sir John said nothing.

"I grew particularly close to a man called Cerjin." It hurt to say his name. "One day we were making our way back across the lower hills, when another group came across our camp. It was the Lord Commander making a surprise inspection. He found Cerjin and I in the same tent together. It was fairly clear we weren't playing cards." He glanced at Sir John. The older man's face gave nothing away. "It was a huge scandal, particularly when it came to light that my men knew about the affair and had protected us. To be aware of a knight breaking his vows and to not report it is – well, you know what it is. And, of course, Cerjin was Sir Spirron's nephew."

"Ah."

"Spirron was mortified. He insisted the matter be taken to trial, although it wasn't long before he twisted everything to sound like it was my fault." Sebastian rubbed the last of the water from his hands. "I was grateful to him for that, at least. Cerjin was a kind, quiet man. Having his business aired like that, in front of the entire Order, was an agony. If they made it look like my fault, then it would save him from some of the shame. Except Spirron wouldn't stop there."

"No wonder the man hates you."

"He shamed the rest of our troupe too, said that we were all 'at it'. Why else, he said, would they cover up for me? The men who served with me were permanently demoted, never to be knights again, and I was exiled."

"What happened to Cerjin?"

"He killed himself. Or someone killed him," said Sebastian. "They found his broken body at the bottom of a crevasse."

"A bad business," said Sir John quietly. "A bad business all round."

"You could say that."

A silence grew between them. Sebastian poured the last of the dirty water from the bucket onto the red soil. It vanished into the thirsty ground almost immediately.

"They must know we are here," Sir John said eventually, gesturing to the west. "Yet they do not seek us out. The army crawls slowly north along the western coast, attacking anything that happens to be in their way. They will sometimes spread out from their path to obliterate the odd village or settlement that is just outside their furrow of destruction, and once everyone is dead the dragon comes and covers everything with fire, a fire which nothing can stand against. I ask you, what is the point?"

"We aren't dealing with a regular army, sir," said Sebastian. Talking about Cerjin again had been exhausting, and all he really wanted to do now was sleep. Proper sleep, with no nightmares, no voices. "You have to think of these creatures as a disease, or a plague of locusts. There is no sense to any of it."

"When I was a boy, there was one summer when our village was beset with hornets. Swarms of the blasted things, some as fat as your knuckle. I must have killed hundreds, and received twice as many stings for my trouble. We only solved that problem when we located the nest, and set it on fire."

Sebastian looked at the older knight.

"They have no nest."

"No, but *she* is their spawning ground and their protector."

Sebastian raised his eyebrows.

"You have a way to kill the dragon?"

Sir John shook his head, and much frustration was evident in that abrupt movement.

"Not as such. The truth is, lad, the men are as nervous as horses for the gelding. They've seen the remains of the Relitian army – hell, they've seen the remains of everything that has come into contact with these creatures."

Sebastian considered telling him that his friend had fought the green-skinned women and survived, but that would mean revealing how he had so much knowledge of the brood army, and he wasn't prepared to do that.

"What we need," continued Sir John, "is something to give the men hope. Something for them to rally behind." He glanced back to the main body of the camp, checking no one was in earshot. "There are ruins south-east of here. They have stood for hundreds of years."

"I saw them in the distance as I worked my way across the plains."

"Good. There is a family that lives in those ruins." Sir John grimaced. "I say family – I don't rightly know what you'd call them – but they have something in their possession. Something that could turn this battle for us."

"What sort of item?"

"A set of armour that grants protection to the wearer." Sir John paused, then laughed at himself. "Of course, that is the point of armour. *This* is demon-touched, enchanted. Our scouts have spoken to what local people are left and they insist there is truth behind it."

Sebastian thought of the Children of the Fog, and Fane, whose body they had never found.

"These things do exist," he said, a touch hesitantly. "Although there is often a cost to their magics, in my experience."

Sir John snorted noisily.

"Against the cost we are paying now? The people of Relios and Creos have already paid more than anyone should. Speaking of cost, though, this family have offered the armour to us, as a loan, but for an enormous amount of money."

"And the Order won't pay?"

"Ah, it's not that, not really. These people, they are – abominations."

"Abominations like me?"

A brief smile passed over Sir John's face.

"Not like you, no. They are demon-worshippers, and if the stories are to be believed, murderers and cannibals. The Order cannot be seen to do business with such creatures. To make common grounds with them would be against everything the

Ynnsmouth knights stand for."

Sebastian shrugged. "I don't know why I'm surprised."

"You should not be," said Sir John. There was a shrewd look in his eye that Sebastian didn't entirely trust. "You, more than anyone, know the strictness of our code."

Suddenly it dawned on Sebastian. He laughed, although there was little humour in it.

"You want me to go. To fetch this armour. Because I am not one of you."

"You are not," agreed Sir John, "and your honour is already in question."

Sebastian rounded on him angrily. "Say what you will, sir, but do not question that. I have more honour–"

"Yes, yes." Sir John waved a hand wearily. "More honour than any of the men in these tents, no doubt, and certainly more honour than the unpleasant Sir Spirron. But you wear the badge of Isu when you have no right to, lad, and if the Lord Commander were less kind, he'd have torn it from your breast himself. You are not one of us, but I am offering you the chance to help us. Help us defeat the dragon and her children."

49

The woman leaned out of the doorway, two flagons clutched to her chest. The lamp above her head made her silvery hair shine like a halo.

"What do you want, gel? I'm busy, as you can well see."

Wydrin glanced back down the alley to make sure they were still alone. The backdoor of The Steaming Pot was usually quiet, save for the occasional drunk making their own steaming deposit, and the intermittent rain was keeping most people off the streets. Still, she was certain someone had been watching her from the shadows on the way here, and there was no harm in being extra cautious.

"I just need to know the lay of things, Nelly. What's the talk tonight?"

Nelly pursed her lips. "You could come in and buy a drink and find out the same way everyone else does."

"Oh, give me a break, Nell." Wydrin reached into her coin purse and gave the old woman a silver bit. "I've done plenty of drinking under your roof, I reckon you can spare me a few words now."

Nelly adjusted her grip on the tankards. "It's a bloody mess is what it is. Morgul's dead, so's half his men, and those that are left are set on revenge. We've already had three fights in the harbour and one boat on fire."

Wydrin cursed under her breath.

"They know who attacked Sandshield, then?"

"Course they do, gel. Reilly's still alive, from what I've heard, but I doubt he'll live long enough to spend that plunder of his." Nelly paused for dramatic effect. "*And* I've heard your name bandied about some."

Shit.

"Oh yes," continued Nelly. "Who else but the Copper Cat? That's what they're saying. Who else would dare to impersonate a Graceful Lady? Who else would be so rash, and stupid, and irresponsible, and–"

"Yes, all right, thank you." Wydrin glanced down the alley again. She thought she'd heard a footstep. "Here, take this." Wydrin passed the old woman the rest of coin purse. "I might not be around to drink in The Steaming Pot for a while. And if my name comes up, do me a favour and mention how I was in here getting drunk at the time, or at least try and convince them I'm not that stupid."

She left Nelly goggling at the coin purse and made to move off up the alley, but the old woman called her back.

"'Ere, there was someone else too. A right rum sort."

"Rummer than Morgul's men?"

Nelly sniffed.

"Skinny, young, pale hair. Looked like he was running a fever, although I expect that was because he was missing half his arm." She made a downward chopping motion halfway up her forearm. "He was very keen to know where you was, but he wasn't a pirate."

Wydrin felt her stomach turn over. *Roki.* But she'd taken off his fingers with her dagger, not his entire hand – although, of course, if the wound had got infected, it could have led to a date with a cleaver and a leather strap to bite on. Given that she'd also killed his twin brother, it was unlikely Roki was tracking her down for an idle chat.

"Thanks, Nelly."

She turned and walked swiftly up the street. *This just gets better and better.* She would have to lie low for a while. Deny all knowledge, wait for the rumours to disperse, or get replaced with better ones, as usually happened.

She paused at the mouth of one alley, peering into the soggy dark. There was a noise, but it was soft, barely audible over the muffling drizzle, and she put it down to a cat or a stray dog.

"Jumping at shadows now," she muttered, and turned round to face three men blocking her way.

Shit, shit, shit.

"Hello, Wydrin," said the man standing at the forefront of the group. She didn't recognise any of them, although they all looked to be men who habitually hung around dark alleys looking unpleasant.

"Or would you prefer our Lady of the Graces?" He grinned, revealing a fine set of cratered teeth.

Wydrin gathered her cloak closer around her, using the movement to pull her dagger from its sheath at the same time. She held it under the fabric, poised. Glassheart was still at her hip.

"You think I'm the Copper Cat? I must say I'm flattered." She shifted her weight, ready to run. "I've heard that she's devastatingly clever and very good at cramped fights in damp alleyways."

The man with the teeth laughed, and pulled a small throwing axe from his belt. His cronies to either side revealed wicked-looking scimitars. Light from the subdued lamps rolled along their edges like liquid gold.

"*I've* heard that Morgul's men are paying a great deal of coin for the Copper Cat's body. Extra if it's cut up into amusing pieces."

"I'm glad they've got a sense of humour about it at least."

The man with the yellow teeth held the throwing axe above his shoulder, still grinning. Wydrin braced herself to jump back into the shadows, hoping she could move fast enough to avoid its bite. If she tried to run past them the other two would take her down. The man's arm tensed.

Suddenly a shadow broke away from the darkness and stood in front of her. The axe, already flying through the air, struck the figure square in the middle of the chest. Wydrin heard the solid, meaty *thunk* it made, and grimaced.

"'Ere," said Yellow Teeth. "What's your bloody game?"

The man from the shadows, still with an axe blade protruding from his chest, pulled a sword from a scabbard at his side and lunged at the three men, slashing the one on the right across his arm. He dropped the scimitar and yelped.

"No one said anything about this. Witchcraft!"

The three men seemed to think better of the entire venture, and as one turned and legged it up the alley. Wydrin raised her eyebrows, impressed.

"That's some serious armour you've got there, mate. I could do with some of that myself."

The man turned to look at her and the words died in her throat.

"Gallo?"

In a heartbeat Wydrin held her dagger to Gallo's throat. She pushed him against the alley wall, pressing the edge of the blade beneath his Adam's apple.

"You!" she hissed. "How are you even alive? How are you *here*?"

"I am not," said Gallo plaintively. "That's to say, I'm not alive. Look." He pointed to the axe in his chest. Without taking the pressure from his throat, Wydrin pulled on the handle of the axe with her free hand. It came out with a bit of tugging, and she saw something black and sluggish in the wound, but no blood. She took the axe and held that to his throat too.

"What," she said, "are you talking about?"

"I'm already dead, Wydrin. Cutting my throat won't do you any good. Stab me, if it makes you feel better."

She took Frostling and sank it into his shoulder. Gallo didn't move.

"See? It's very important that I talk to you–"

She stabbed him again.

"Was that really necessary?"

"I thought so, yes."

"I must talk to you, Wydrin."

"And no matter how much I stab you, you'll keep talking?"

"Yes."

"I don't know. I reckon I could cut out your vocal cords. That would make it difficult."

Gallo sighed. Wydrin felt a puff of air escape from the hole in his chest.

"Your reaction is understandable."

Wydrin stood away. She had just noticed how bad Gallo smelled.

"You nearly killed him, Gallo. You nearly killed Sebastian. I thought you were friends. Hell, I thought you loved him."

Gallo raised a hand and pushed his hair back behind an ear. Even in the gloom Wydrin could see that the ends of his fingers were turning black.

"There is a lot to explain. Can we get out of the rain? It takes me ages to dry off now I have no body heat."

"And you think I'll believe all that?"

Wydrin paused and rubbed her hair with her cloak. They were in the parlour of a pillow house just off Eel Street. Wydrin knew the Madame well, and only had to endure a few questions before securing some time alone in their smallest and least popular room.

It was filled with overstuffed sofas and more cushions than anyone could ever need. Small lamps burnt incense that smelt of spice and citrus fruits: Madame Rosalie did her best to invoke exotic lands far away from the fishy reality of Eel Street, although Gallo's presence was rather spoiling the effect.

He sat on the edge of a sofa, his hands folded carefully on his knees. Inside, under stronger lights, Wydrin could see more clearly how terrible he looked. His skin wasn't just pale, it was *thin*, so she almost fancied she could see the flesh and bones beneath. His blond hair, always his pride and joy, had lost its lustre and even appeared to be falling out in places. The clothes he wore were ragged and torn, but still holding up better than the man wearing them. He looked at her steadily with eyes buried in pits of shadow.

"I remember entering the Citadel with my guide, Chednit, and I remember losing him to something in the ceiling. There was a great force in the dark, rushing towards me –" He paused. "After that it was like being in a nightmare where the world turns around you and you can do nothing to stop it."

"So you claim."

"The entity that existed beneath the Citadel entered my mind and sent me down pitch-black corridors after her own purposes. I was a rider within my own head, being dragged along by a mad steed."

"You know it turned out to be a dragon in the end, right?"

The expression of horror that moved over Gallo's face was terrible to behold.

"I saw the shape of her in my head. It was awful. Can you imagine being so close to a creature that enormous? That dangerous?"

"I can, actually," she replied sourly. "And she made you stab Sebastian?"

"Wydrin." He flexed his fingers. They made dry popping sounds. "You and I may not have always got along, but you know me. Knew me. Would I ever have harmed Sebastian?"

"You hurt him," she said simply. "You went off by yourself. If you hadn't done that, none of this would have happened. Besides, I saw you plunge the dagger into him. I can hardly forget that."

"And I cannot forget the despair of watching that happen."

Wydrin sighed and picked up a glass from the table. Madame Rosalie had filled it with a potent plum brandy.

"Let's pretend I believe you. Why are you here?"

"I watched the Citadel come down around me. I was knocked out by debris. When I woke up, the entity was gone from my head, but it was clear I had not... survived."

"You knew you were dead?"

"Believe me, you know these things."

Wydrin took a sip of the brandy. It was the good stuff, burning away the chill. "How is that possible?"

Gallo shrugged.

"I don't know. I think it is a remnant of *her*, like a fever. It keeps my body moving somehow. I feel it surge through me sometimes in waves."

"All sounds like a steaming pile of dung to me," said Wydrin. "I think I would be best chopping your head off and burying it somewhere, just in case you keep talking."

"Please Wydrin, I must find him and make amends before whatever is moving this body runs out."

"Wherever Sebastian is, I'm sure he's just fine without having to speak to you."

"There is more. I believe he is in danger."

Wydrin paused and took another sip of the brandy.

"What danger?" she asked eventually.

"I will tell him, not you."

"Gallo." Wydrin casually pulled Glassheart from its sheath and held it up to the light as if examining it. "I've no doubt Madame Rosalie would be annoyed with me if I decapitated you in here and ruined her cushions, but I can always buy more."

The dead man on the sofa wrung his blackened fingers together.

"It was his blood that was used to awaken the brood army, yes? You saw them?"

"I saw them. Killed a few."

"They are *her* children, but their blood is his. I fear it has formed a link between them, so that their minds are touching. As mine was with... her. It will drive him mad. I'm sure of it."

Wydrin thought of Sebastian in Pinehold, so ill and distracted. She'd assumed it was the shock of nearly dying under the Citadel. What if it was something else? After all, he'd appeared to get worse over time, not better.

"Please, Wydrin. I must find him and warn him. I have to make amends."

She put the empty glass back down on the table. "Fine. It seems I need to get out of Crosshaven for a while anyway."

Hope briefly animated Gallo's ravaged face.

"You know where he is?"

"Of course I do. He's wherever that bloody dragon is, isn't he?"

Gallo seemed to collapse back into the sofa. The hope on his face was replaced with terror.

"He has gone to find her? By all the gods, why would he do that?"

"Because he's a big stupid brave idiot, of course. You know that." She stood up, and when Gallo didn't move, she reached down and grabbed his sleeve, dragging him to his feet. "Come on, we have a boat to catch."

50

Frith watched them approach across the rocky ground and steaming pools with a sinking feeling in his gut.

Jolnir made his home in the middle of a strange patch of tall blue grass, sprouting incongruously in the natural valley between two black hills. The grass was tough, so much so that the old mystic had constructed a series of conical huts from the material; they made Frith think of strange barnacles, clinging to the dark soil. They were, like his walking sticks, bedecked with all sorts of strange objects – shells, skulls, mummified animals – and inside wasn't much tidier. The black birds, perched on the pointy roofs, squawked and chattered at each other.

"And who are these?" asked Frith, gesturing at the dishevelled figures emerging from the grass.

"Friends, I suppose you would say. Yes, my friends and assistants both. Look lively now, my boy, we'll get this fire roaring."

Jolnir had three "assistants", and they all looked oddly similar. Two were thin and wiry men dressed in dusty black cloth, grey hair held back from their temples with thick white headbands covered in symbols Frith didn't recognise. They both had mild, ageless faces free from lines. The last was a woman, dressed nearly identically to the two men but with wilder hair, sticking out in all directions. She had added a few seashells and ribbons to her headband in an effort to brighten it up. All three of them stared at Frith with unblinking interest.

"Now then! This," Jolnir tapped the woman on the shoulder with his stick, "is Luggin. This is Muggin," a tap to the shoulder of the first man, "and this is Dobs." The last assistant bowed jerkily. "And this is

Lord Frith, come to learn all about the mages."

The assistants said nothing.

"Weren't there other mystics on the island?" asked Frith. Luggin, Muggin and Dobs were warming their hands by the fire.

"Hmmm?" Jolnir twirled his sticks idly, mask nodding. "Oh yes, there were some once. Around here somewhere. Always asking me questions, getting in the way." He paused. "They all appear to have wandered off, though. It's not for everyone, life on Whittenfarne. Still!" He poked one of the sticks into the flames. "I have these three here to keep me company, and they're kind enough to tidy for me, and fetch my documents. Aren't you, Muggin?" Muggin glanced up from the fire, the faintest of smiles at the corner of his lips.

Frith cleared his throat. He was unnerved by the silence of the assistants.

"You will teach me, then?" He despised the hesitancy in his own voice, but he wasn't sure what to make of Jolnir and his friends.

"Teach you, boy?"

The woman called Luggin had removed a packet of powders from her coat and was throwing small handfuls onto the fire, turning it red and green while Jolnir nodded with approval.

"Yes." Frith bit down on the word, making it sharp. "I need information on the mages. It is essential I know their secret words of power, the ones that are no longer generally known. A Regnisse of Relios sent me here. She said you could tell me."

"The secret words, the words of power." Jolnir waved his hands over the fire in what, Frith suspected, he thought was a mystical fashion. "Those of destruction and control." Jolnir nodded rapidly. "Those words are not to be given lightly."

"I must have it. I must have that knowledge."

"My dear friends." Jolnir held up his strange, withered hands, addressing the three assistants. "I have decided to teach this good boy all I know of the mages and the old gods, and indeed, the language they used to talk to each other. It is time the words were passed on to someone worthy, don't you agree?"

Luggin, Muggin and Dobs looked back with polite smiles, just as though he were telling them how he'd decided to take up knitting, or collecting seashells.

"Right, good, excellent!" cried Jolnir. "Get to work, then, my lovelies. Luggin, I wish you to bring me all the relevant books and

papers, and as much linen and ink as you can rustle up. Muggin and
Dobs, we shall have ourselves a feast this eve. Off to the waters with
you, and bring back as many of those tasty little fish as you can find.
Oh, and some clams too. It is a night for clams!"

The three assistants scrambled off on their assigned missions, still
not saying a word. Luggin disappeared into one of the conical huts,
while Muggin and Dobs walked back through the grass towards
the coast. Jolnir and Frith were left alone again, save for the ever-
present black birds.

"And what," said Frith, "was all that about?"

"I like to keep them busy," Jolnir chuckled. It sounded like a
marble rolling around a wooden basin. "I hope you like seafood, lad.
You're going to be here a while."

"Tell me what you know. Of the mages, of the old gods. A man who
comes all the way to Whittenfarne must know much, is that not so?"

They walked in the last of the evening's light, heading out to the
north of the island. Frith doubted the sense of trying to get anywhere
on this godforsaken rock in the dark, but Jolnir had just listened to
all his protests courteously, and then insisted they go anyway. Frith
had attempted to construct a torch from the stiff blue grass but Jolnir
had hit him with his stick until he stopped.

Frith sighed. The mists were drawing in again, while the sun's
last breath of light turned the sky a sickly mauve. He looked down,
watching for holes and hungry lizards.

"I know what anyone knows," he said. "The mages were powerful
men and women who lived thousands of years ago. They were able
to perform amazing feats with the magic they commanded, and
many of them perished in a war with the old gods, which ended
when the last mages trapped them inside the Citadel."

"That's what happened, is it?" Jolnir sounded amused. "I'm sure
you know best. Tell me, Lord Aaron Frith, why do we not perform
these amazing feats any longer?"

Frith's foot slipped on a damp rock and he stumbled.

"I don't know," he snapped. "Because it's gone. The magic went
with the mages."

"But ours is a magical world, is it not?" Jolnir gestured around
at the darkening hills as if this explained everything. "There is a
magic inherent in Ede, a strangeness that leads to mysterious places,

powerful objects, yes?"

Frith remembered Fane's glowing helm, and the unnerving atmosphere under the Citadel.

"Yes," he agreed reluctantly. "But that's different."

Jolnir nodded. The wooden bird mask was rapidly becoming a jagged black shape in the shadows, a sister to the rocks and hills.

"There are two types of magic, Lord Aaron Frith. There is the *Edeian*, a natural force present in the world. It is in the soil, the sky, the air and sea, in the grass and rocks and flesh. And then there is *Edenier*, the magic of the will, a magic that comes of thought and want and personality." He waved his sticks airily. The objects tied to them rattled. "*Edeian* is still with us, of course, but it is largely inert, not generally a power that humans can bend to their will. And *Edenier* has vanished from the world. Isn't that right?"

Frith paused.

"Yes," he said eventually.

Jolnir chuckled. Overhead, Frith could hear the cries of the birds, although the sky was now so dark he could only make out their flittering movements against the clouds.

"Edenier was the magic of the will, the magic of men, a tremendously powerful and dangerous force. We study it, here on Whittenfarne."

The mystic's voice had grown unusually quiet.

"What is so special about Whittenfarne?"

"It was their holy place, where they communed with their gods."

"The mages were priests?"

"You could say that. Jumped-up priests, perhaps. Either way, they spoke to the old gods on these very rocks. Always chattering away about something, demanding this, entreating that." Jolnir cleared his throat, a muffled noise within the headdress. So far Frith had yet to see him take it off. "That was what the words were about, do you see?"

"I don't—"

"Of course you don't!" Jolnir nodded rapidly. "The gods gave them the language so that they could speak to them. That is why the words are so powerful. Once, the mages were on good terms with the old gods, long before that business with the war and the Citadel. The words, with Edenier, could shape and change the world around them."

"Are the words so important?"

"Words are *always* important," said Jolnir. "Even normal, non-magical words, in the right place, can change the world."

Frith took a deep breath. "Can you tell me these words?"

Jolnir waved his spindly hands dismissively. "The mages learned the language of the gods, and much else besides, but eventually things turned sour. Mages were no longer content with learning from the gods, they wanted to be gods themselves."

"You sound as though you thought the mages fools."

Jolnir laughed softly. "The stories tell us that the gods had grown cruel, but I know the truth. These men and women, the mages of Whittenfarne, were greedy."

Frith stumbled on another rock. It was now so dark that the sky still visible through the clouds had only a bare scattering of stars to provide light. In the middle of the island, distant even from the lights of the other islands, full night was likely to be as black as ink.

"This is ridiculous," said Frith. He stopped walking and crossed his arms over his chest. "Where are we going?"

"I am telling you what you wish to know, am I not?" asked Jolnir.

Frith gestured around at the island, not even certain the mystic would be able to see him do that, although he couldn't help noticing that Jolnir hadn't fallen in any pools or stumbled over any rocks.

"It is too dark! We shall break our necks, or become lost. What is the point of this?"

"Sometimes one must stumble, blind, before finding the light."

"Oh yes, very good. I suppose you save that up for every idiot that comes to this godforsaken island looking for enlightenment?"

The birds overhead gave a chorus of raucous cries.

"Not everyone is worthy, Frith, not even a great lord. Perhaps you are not worthy. You have the look of a weak man, after all, one who would fail at the first obstacle and then forever complain that it was unfair."

All at once Frith was back beneath the stones of the Citadel with the whispering voices of the long-dead mages. *You are not strong enough to be what we were, little man.* They had taunted him, and tortured him. Not strong enough, they had said. He remembered the rage that had carried him through, and again it began to warm his belly.

"You do not know me, old man."

There was a soft roar and Frith's hands were suddenly boiling with a violent orange light. The black hills were lit up as bright as midday, and the water of the pools made flame-bright mirrors. There was a crackle, and the light ran up over Frith's arms so that he seemed to be wearing a coat of fire. He held his hands up.

"I have the power already, do you see? I could burn you all, everything on this ridiculous island, because *I have the last of the mages' powers.*"

Jolnir hit him with his stick.

"And now you have your light, yes?"

Frith stopped. "What?"

"Here, tie this around your right hand." Jolnir reached inside his feathery cloak and produced a long, ragged strip of linen. He passed it to Frith, unmindful of the flames. There was a symbol written on the fabric in black ink.

Frith stared at it. "What?"

"Are you deaf as well as stupid? Tie it around your hand, lad."

Frith did so, although the rioting flames made it awkward. Once he'd wrapped the fabric around his hand like a bandage he tied a knot. Instantly the fire covering his arms and chest vanished, to be replaced with a small but fierce ball of light centred around his right hand. He held it up in front of him. It burned steadily like a tiny sun.

"What is this?"

"The words written on that piece of cloth are Guidance and Light. Rather useful, wouldn't you say?"

Frith stared at the light. It was beautiful and, more than that, it was his to control. He wanted it to burn brighter, and it did. It became impossible to look at it directly. He willed it to become dimmer, and it became a soft glowing orb on the ends of his fingers.

"The words force the magic a certain way," he said quietly, awestruck.

"Yes, yes. They are channels siphoning off the raw power, sending it down certain routes. It is a fine thing to see."

"And I do not need to say the word?"

"You have any gods around here you need to speak to? In time, you will learn to see the words in your head, and to write them, and that will direct the Edenier."

Frith looked at the mystic. In the eerie light of the orb the bird headdress was a thing of deep shadows and alarming angles. There was nothing human about it at all.

"You knew. How did you know?"

Jolnir shrugged. "I am the most learned mystic of Whittenfarne, the mysterious and all-knowing Jolnir. How could I not know?"

"Being the most learned of the creatures on this island is hardly something to crow about, old man."

Jolnir barked harsh laughter at that. Frith shook his head in annoyance.

"Such a difficult boy." Jolnir made to hit him with the stick but Frith stepped out of range. "Look at the words, Lord Aaron Frith, the words for Guidance and Light. They are your first."

Frith did look. The words were of no alphabet he recognised. In fact, they barely looked like letters at all to his eye; the shapes were chaotic, swirls bisected with straight lines, circles and dots peppering elegant, curving waves. He thought he could make out where one word ended and the other began, but that was about it.

"There are a great number of words in the mages' language still remaining to us, Lord Aaron Frith, and you will learn to read and write every single one of them. So shut up and listen."

51

Up close the ruins were more intact than Sebastian had initially thought. Once, this had been a temple to a forgotten god, built by someone who'd liked tall, pointed arches and graceful walls that joined one tower to another in odd, sweeping curves. The lower sections of the walls were obscured by the scruffy but virulent thorn bushes that populated so much of Relios, and the huge bricks were the same deep orange as the clay underfoot, so that even on a bright morning such as this the ruins spoke of dried blood and old fires. The shadows that lay on it were black and precise.

Sebastian approached cautiously. From a distance it appeared abandoned, but as he got closer he could see paths through the bushes that led through the last unbroken archway to the courtyard beyond. Someone had trimmed the bushes back to make it easier to move around, and they'd done it fairly recently. *Who worshipped here? What did they worship?* Before he could think on it further something else caught his eye. Movement.

The courtyard was ahead of him. Out of the shadows to his left something round and red rolled towards him rapidly. He stopped it with his boot half a second before he realised it was a human head, all the skin flayed from it until it was a bloody red ball. He snatched his foot away and drew his sword.

"Greetings, sir knight!" came a voice from the shadows. It was high and clear, the voice of a child, and after a moment a slim shape emerged from the dark. It was a girl, no more than ten years old, with long brown hair tied in a braid that fell over one skinny shoulder and large blue eyes, the colour of mountain ice. She wore a strange mixture of rags patched with pieces of leather, while her bare feet left scant markings in the orange dust. She grinned up at Sebastian, and he found he was vaguely unnerved by her teeth; they were all very small and neat and white, while the incisors looked slightly sharper than was necessary.

Sebastian glanced warily around the courtyard. He could see no one else. He took his hand away from his sword.

"You know I am a knight?"

"Of course," said the girl brightly. "You've come from the big group camping down the hill."

He nodded towards the severed head.

"And is this yours?"

Suddenly the girl's face was very serious.

"That belongs to Bezcavar. He is the master of wounds and broken things, big and small."

Bezcavar.

"Who are you?"

"I'm Ip," she said, no longer looking at him. Instead she went over to the head, which was swiftly turning dark and sticky under the hot sun, and placed her bare foot on its bloody cheek. She rocked it back and forth, considering. Sebastian could see blood squelching up between her toes. "When they are done with them, they sometimes give me bits to play with." She looked up and gave him that unsettling grin again. "I like heads best of all."

Sebastian frowned. The smell of the blood was making his headache worse.

"Child... Ip. I think you know why I'm here. Are your people prepared to make a trade?"

Deftly she kicked the head across the courtyard, the top of her small white foot making a very loud smacking noise on the ruined flesh. Then she looked up at him and held out her hand.

She took him across the courtyard and into a large circular room. Part of the ceiling had collapsed, so that dusty sunshine filtered through the shattered bricks down onto the tree growing in the centre. It was a thorn tree, some larger cousin of the bushes, and its unlovely branches twisted out to either side of the room like deadly welcoming arms. Fat orange fruits grew nestled within the clusters of thorns, and on the tree hung the enchanted armour. Sebastian had little time to take that in, however, as Ip's family were watching him with bright interest.

"So they finally sent someone, aye?"

A middle-aged woman stepped forward. Ip ran over to her and the woman enfolded her briefly in her arms.

The family, if that's what they were, were clearly not as friendly as Ip. The woman standing with her had long freckly limbs crossed with livid scars, and a jowly face with a chin hiding in her neck somewhere. She had light grey eyes, so pale that for a moment Sebastian was sure she was blind until she met his gaze and bared a set of yellowed teeth. Beyond her, sitting on the roots of the tree, was a greatly aged man with a long white beard trailing down to his knees. He clasped the roots to either side of him with big knuckled hands, and there was a dirty bandage on his head.

More worrying were the three large men to either side of the tree. They were all uniformly enormous, one at least an inch taller than Sebastian. Two were broad across the shoulders and solid across the gut, while the other, a bald man with bright eyes, was lean and toned. They carried a collection of dirty blades at their belts.

"I have come from the Ynnsmouth knights to make a trade," said Sebastian.

"For our armour." The woman gestured behind her to the tree, and he took a moment to look at it properly. It was an extremely fine set: an exquisitely crafted mail shirt lay under a breastplate constructed from many small pieces of a black metal Sebastian couldn't place. The pauldrons, greaves and rondels at the shoulders were made of a similar material, and the whole thing was covered in runes, shining blackly against the metal. The set was apparently missing its helm and gauntlets.

"What is your name, woman?"

"Mother Maundsley," piped up Ip, "and that's Graffer," she continued, pointing at the elderly man perched on the roots, "and those are her little boys." The three burly men shot her irritated looks, and Mother Maundsley clouted the girl round the ear.

"Enough of your cheek, Ip." The Maundsley woman planted her feet squarely and folded her arms across her chest. They were, Sebastian noticed, all recently wounded. The brothers, the old man – all were covered in scars and fresh cuts. Only Ip was unblemished, her skin clear and white, although her feet were still bloody from the severed head. "Do you even know what yer looking at here, knight?"

Sebastian felt a shiver of irritation move down his back. It was too hot, his head hurt, and the stench of the Maundsley family was scratching at the back of his throat. They smelt of blood and old sweat.

"We are in dire need of the armour, if it can indeed do as claimed. I'm sure you've noticed the dragon and her army currently ravaging the land. With this armour the Ynnsmouth knights can lead an offensive against the creature and have some chance–"

"He don't know, he don't care." The old man on the roots spoke up. His voice was a wheeze squeezed out of diseased lungs. "He knows nothing of Bezcavar."

The three brothers murmured assent and patted their blades. The bald one ran a dry, pink tongue over his blistered lips.

"What does it matter?" Sebastian glanced up at the tree, branches black against the sky. "Are you willing to lend it to them, or not?"

"Are you willing to pay the price?" Mother Maundsley gestured at the roots that boiled up through the broken floor.

Sebastian cautiously edged towards the tree and saw that the roots were intertwined with bones; some of them bleached white, while others still had strips of gristle stuck to them. That explained the smell.

"Bezcavar," intoned Mother Maundsley, "is the king of pain, knight. The prince of wounds and suffering. Agony is his joy, and we live to serve."

"That's what your girl said, yes." Sebastian could feel his patience disappearing behind the fog of his headache.

"The armour is a work of worship, to him, crafted by his greatest pupil." The woman was smiling faintly now, and Sebastian suspected she didn't often get to give this speech. "When gathered together the armour is an unstoppable weapon. When complete, no one can stand against he who wears it."

The old man, Graffer, leaned back and touched one wizened finger to the metal toe cap closest to him, his eyes closed in bliss. *They worship the armour as much as the demon*, thought Sebastian warily. *There is no way they will just lend it to the Order, not for all the coins we can drag over here. They just want to show off.*

"We, the Maundsleys, have been chosen as the keepers of armour. We honour Bezcavar by protecting it, sacrificing to it. There is no greater honour." The woman's eyes flicked over to Ip, then, and Sebastian glanced at the remains amongst the roots. A number of the skulls there were small.

"You haven't been doing a very good job, then, have you?" he said mildly. "There are pieces missing."

Mother and Graffer shared a brief, agitated look. When the woman turned back to Sebastian her teeth were bared in a snarl.

"It is complete! What do you know about it anyway, knight?"

Sebastian gestured to the armour. The sword on his back was feeling very heavy, and his shoulders were starting to ache. The blade would be more comfortable in his hands, no doubt.

"Where is the helm? And the gauntlets are missing." He shifted his weight and rolled his neck until it clicked. "The armour is like a puzzle, and you must have all the pieces."

"You know nothing!" spat Graffer. The old man hoisted himself off the roots and took a few shaky steps forward. He wore a pair of old knives at his belt, thickly crusted with dried blood. "We bleed ourselves and others for Bezcavar, and we guard the armour. It is our honour. We were chosen!"

Sebastian wiped the sweat off his forehead with the back of his hand. It was getting harder to concentrate with the thundering in his head, but at the same time he found he was less concerned. He could feel their words rushing him to a certain path, channelling him to a certain action. There was no avoiding it. He flexed his hands, hoping they weren't too sweaty to grip. Would there be more family members, hiding behind these orange walls somewhere?

"I'll tell you what I know, old man. I know there are pieces missing because I have seen them. Two gauntlets and a helm. Once you had those, sure, then it would be impressive, but now?" He waved a hand dismissively. "This is hardly worth the Order's time."

But a change had come over the family when he mentioned the missing pieces. The three ugly brothers were suddenly alert, and Mother's eyes were wild. Graffer seized hold of her arm and she grabbed him back.

"You know where they are?"

"Of course I do." *Well, most of them*, he thought. Fane's helm was wherever he was, and the same for Roki, if he lived still. Enri's gauntlet was with Dreyda, who had taken it to study the runes.

"Tell us," said the bald brother.

"Why would I do that?" Sebastian smiled. He could smell burnt flesh.

"We will lend you the armour." Mother Maundsley skittered forward, her long arms reaching out to him. "Just tell us where you saw the others and you can take it for your army."

Sebastian laughed.

"You honestly think I will fall for that, do you? Just give you the information and then perhaps meekly lie down so you can stick me with your rusted blades? Then you will have the armour, the whereabouts of its missing pieces, and the money the Order have given me to trade. No, I think I shall go back to the Ynnsmouth knights and return with a small force to take this from you instead."

"The knights are too honourable to steal from common folk," said Graffer. "They will do no such thing."

"I am not a Ynnsmouth knight," said Sebastian. That, he felt, should have been enough warning for them, but the bald man drew his blade and brandished it.

"Then we'll cut it from you," he sneered. His brothers followed suit, and after an anxious glance at his boys, Graffer drew his dirty knife too.

Sebastian smiled and nodded. He drew his own sword, taking care to do it slowly so that they could see how sharp it was, how brilliantly it shone in the light from the broken roof. His head was a bright agony, but the scent of scorched flesh no longer made him feel ill.

"Finally."

52

There were others in the walls, it turned out. Afterwards, Sebastian walked amongst the bodies and counted perhaps ten more, although it was difficult to keep the numbers in his head. The flagstones were slick with blood.

"Bezcavar will be happy enough with this tribute, I think," he muttered. The blood did seem to be flowing towards the roots of the thorn tree, although that may have been a trick of the light. He reached up to pluck one of the strange orange fruits from the tree, and a small voice spoke up behind him.

"You don't wanna eat those."

It was Ip. In all the excitement Sebastian had completely forgotten about her. There was some blood on her arms and face, but it wasn't hers. She was watching him closely, her head tilted slightly to one side as if he were some particularly fascinating insect that had landed on her food.

"Why not?"

"Poison," she said. She stepped carefully over the bodies of her family. "They feed them to the people they catch sometimes. It makes them twitch all over and foam at the mouth."

Sebastian drew his hand away from the tree and rubbed his beard instead.

"This –" he gestured at the bodies on the floor – "this wasn't a good thing for you to see."

The girl shrugged.

"I've seen lots of things."

"*Were* they your family?"

Ip knelt down and pulled a beaded necklace over the head of

Mother Maundsley and slung it around her own neck. For a long moment she didn't say anything, and Sebastian couldn't see her face.

"There was a place with lots of cold white stone," she said eventually. "It had pools of cool water and there were these big birds that walked about everywhere, with long feathers on their backs. They were all different colours. That's the first thing I remember."

Sebastian nodded. That sounded like Onwai to him, a distant country to the east. His father had often talked about how marble had been shipped from there in the past. Either way, it did not sound like anywhere in Relios or Creos, both being lands of red stone and orange clay.

Ip was watching him shrewdly. She seemed to guess what he was thinking.

"They were keeping me to give to the tree," she said, nodding at the bloody roots. "I don't know when, but they didn't ever hurt me much, like they were saving me up." She shrugged. "So when they gave me to Bezcavar it would be special, I suppose."

"You knew all this? And you didn't run away?"

"I'm not stupid. When they started looking at me funny I'd have gone."

Sebastian could well believe that. There was an intelligence to the girl that he hadn't seen in a child so young before.

He turned back to the armour. "What do you know about this?"

Ip walked past him and clambered up onto the roots. She touched her fingers to the fine mail coat.

"It's a puzzle, like you said. You need all the pieces. It was stupid of you to tell them you knew where the others are." She shot him a pitying look over her shoulder. "They were going to kill you anyway, though, so I guess it doesn't matter."

"Good to know." Sebastian grimaced. No doubt Sir John had guessed as much too, but he was only gambling the life of one disgraced ex-knight. "What happens when it's complete?"

Ip shrugged.

"I dunno." She stopped to turn and look directly at him. "Why didn't you kill me too?"

Sebastian's first thought was to lie to the girl, tell her he had no intention of killing children, but somehow he knew that wouldn't be enough. When he'd drawn his blade against the Maundsley family a feverish heat had descended on him, and he hadn't stopped until they were all bleeding on the floor.

"I didn't see you," he said. He felt tired and ill. "In truth, I barely remember any of it. I just had to kill everyone. I didn't think about who they were."

The girl raised her eyebrows. Sebastian had the unpleasant feeling she understood very well what he was trying to say.

"Are you going to kill me now?"

"No, of course not." His tone was terser than he wanted. "What else do you know about the armour?"

"I know that a mage made it a long time ago. He was friends with the demon, but it drove him mad in the end."

"And where did this family get it from?"

"How would I know? They've had it as long as they've had me."

Sebastian sighed. They could split the armour amongst the Order, and hopefully it would give the men enough courage to face the dragon; at this stage, any advantage was worth taking. The armour was fixed to the tree with pins nailed directly into the wood, and it looked very heavy. Getting it back to the Order by himself was going to be difficult.

Again, the girl seemed to know what he was thinking. "They have a mule," she said. "There's a stable round the back."

He looked down at the girl with red feet.

"Would you like to come with me?"

53

Frith shifted his footing and felt his heart skip a beat as a gust of wind pushed him momentarily closer to the edge. Muttering curses, he dipped the end of the brush into the ink once more, and flattened the fabric against the stone. There was a small bundle of strips of cloth next to him. Every now and then Jolnir would poke the bundle with a stick, and nod merrily.

"Tell me about these gods," said Frith. He wanted to take his mind off the deadly drop just in front of him, and as bored as he was of listening to Jolnir's booming, pompous voice, it was a good distraction.

They were perched halfway up the northernmost statue, in a tiny alcove created by the folds of the mage's robe. The island was enclosed in mists once more, although a gusting wind meant that every now and then Frith could see the rocks below through ragged gaps in the cloud, and the occasional glimpse of a slate-grey sea. Other than that, the only thing of interest in sight was a nest of lizard-like creatures clinging to another ledge, just opposite where they crouched. They were like the lizards in the pools, but bat-like wings sprouted from their bony backs and they slunk around on the sheer rock like they'd been born there. Frith supposed they probably had. Their nests were made from a mixture of sand, seashells and seaweed, and they clung like limpets to the stone.

"What do you wish to hear?"

Jolnir, much to Frith's vague annoyance, had experienced no difficulty with the uncomfortable climb up the statue. There was a rough stairway of sorts, carved directly into the stone, although in places it had degenerated into little more than a series of handholds.

Frith had not enjoyed it at all.

"Were they truly gods, for a start?" He slid the brush across the strip of fabric as Jolnir had taught him, but immediately he saw that he'd done it wrong. *That* curve was slightly too thick, *this* line at the wrong angle. He grunted in frustration and pulled a fresh strip from within his sleeve.

"You believe they were not?"

"Gods should be all-powerful, all-knowing, and yet these ones allowed themselves to be trapped in the Citadel. And once they were in there they couldn't get back out again. I will agree that they must have been very strange, and otherworldly –" he paused, thinking of the dragon pushing its head up through the rubble of the Citadel – "and certainly formidable, but gods?"

Jolnir made a clucking noise within his mask. Even up here, he insisted on wearing it, and in all his days on the island Frith had yet to see him take it off.

"You must remember that the gods had shared their knowledge with the mages. A foolish thing to do, in retrospect. The spells on the Citadel were very powerful indeed." He sniffed, and used the end of his stick to push the scraps of used fabric off the ledge. The wind caught them and they spiralled away into the mist. Frith swallowed hard and returned his eyes to his work. "But that is not exactly what happened, anyway. There were five old gods, Lord Frith, did you know that?"

Frith shrugged. This time he almost had the shape of the word right, he could feel it, but a splatter of ink caused the final part to run.

"Five gods," continued Jolnir. "There was Y'gia, a goddess of life and growth, a green creature." Jolnir's headdress waggled back and forth. "Fickle. And there was Y'Ruen, a force of destruction, but I believe you are familiar with her, yes?"

Frith ignored him.

"And there were two more, the Twins, they called them, Res'ni and Res'na, but they were boring, and then there was O'rin, a god of lies and tricks and mischief." Jolnir's voice took on a sudden cheery note. *Someone has a favourite*, thought Frith. "He was the most human of the gods, the one who spent the most time walking in the markets and talking to people. He liked the stories they made up – such imaginations they had – and the extraordinary lengths they would go to deceive each other. He was the most human, and it was both his strength and his weakness. When the war broke out between the gods and the mages, O'rin spent much of his time observing from the sidelines, only interfering when it was interesting to him to do so. When he heard of the Citadel, built to contain all the mages' greatest treasures, he was tempted, oh you can be certain of that. But he was also suspicious. So much time amongst the humans had made him cynical and crafty, and he waited and watched while the other four raced to the Citadel to claim the treasures, and was not all that surprised when the mages sprung their trap."

"What?" Frith paused, the brush poised above the fabric. "You're saying he didn't go in?"

"That is what I am saying."

"But everyone says that all the old gods were trapped inside the Citadel. That it was the end for all of them."

"That was what O'rin wanted everyone to believe. He was the god of lies, remember? And it's not like the mages were going to open their trap to check they had everyone inside, was it, my boy?"

"What happened to this O'rin, then? Where is he now?"

A cold wind blew across the statue. Frith pulled his bearskin cloak closer around his shoulders, while the birds perched above them chattered irritably.

"With the gods gone, the Edeian and Edenier began to fade from the world, and so did O'rin. He hid himself away, not wanting a direct confrontation with the mages. He disappeared."

Frith sat back on his haunches. His legs were aching from crouching in such an uncomfortable position, and he felt damp all over.

"How could you possibly know all this? All the histories say the mages trapped all of the gods, never that one got away..."

"There you go, I think you've got it!" Jolnir scuffled forward and laid one skinny finger on the strip of fabric. "The form is finally correct! You are not blind and stupid after all."

Frith looked down. The word was there, and yes, it did look like the examples in Jolnir's dusty old books.

"What now?"

"You know what. Get on with it, lad!"

Frith picked up the bandage and carefully tied it around his right hand, the inky side facing out. It was awkward with one hand, but he was getting better at it.

"Why do this up here, anyway?" he said. "This could have been demonstrated somewhere more comfortable, or at least at ground level."

Jolnir hit him with his stick.

"You must learn to write the words wherever you are! Do you imagine you will always get to write them in the comfort of your study, Lord Frith? Besides," Jolnir nodded at the nest of white lizards opposite, "I hate those vile creatures."

Frith got to his feet, mindful of the drop inches from his boots. He held his right hand out in front of him, the palm turned towards the lizard's nests.

"Feel the Edenier within you," said Jolnir. "Coax it into being, and then remember the word. See it in your mind, remember the exact shape of it. Let the word and the Edenier connect, let them come together."

Frith took a deep breath, and tried to concentrate only on the word, and the mages' power. It was lying dormant at the moment – he could feel it in his gut, a quiet, restless energy – but the presence of the words seemed to rouse the magic, so that very soon he could feel a tingling in his arms, the strange sense of light building within his chest. He pictured the shape of the word in his mind as clearly as he could, and his fingers began to glow a shimmering orange.

"That's it, that's it…"

There was a sensation of warmth on the palm of his hand, as if he were holding it to a candle, and a globe of fiery light shot from the centre of it, flew across the gap and exploded amongst the nests. Buttery yellow flames crawled over the rock and two of the winged lizards fell smoking into the mist.

"Yes!" cried Jolnir. The black birds above him fluttered in consternation. "Again!"

Fire, thought Frith, *the word is for Fire*, and another fireball shot from his fingers to explode against the nests. There was a faint roar and hiss, but little other noise save for the outraged cries of the lizards. A number of young, pale blue and shiny, crawled rapidly from the beleaguered nest only for the fire to turned their limbs black. He sent three more fireballs just to be sure he'd got them all, and then sent a couple out into the mist, watching with fascination as the eerie orange light made the mist shimmer like sunrise.

"Don't go mad, boy." Jolnir poked him in the back of his leg with his stick. "It is potent, the word for fire."

There was a stinging sensation in his palm, and when he looked down he saw that the bandage where the word had been was now a smear of dark ash.

"It's gone," he said.

"Well, of course. The power is destructive, you see, always destructive. But it is versatile. Next I shall teach you the word for Ever, and you will be able to combine the two and create a continuous stream of fire. Ever-Fire."

Frith looked at the smoking ruin that had once been a thriving nest. As he watched the last winged lizard struggled out of the remains and dropped to its death, its wings now a pair of scorched sticks. He could smell burnt seaweed on the air.

"I will learn them all."

54

The wind escorted Wydrin down the wooden steps to the area her mother had always referred to as the "bellows". To one side was a long cramped cabin filled with the sour stink of lots of people sleeping and working in close proximity to each other, and to the other was a slightly wider room filled with sacks and boxes. Gallo was standing in the doorway to the bunks, a pack of cards clutched in one grey hand. Beyond him she could see a number of grotty hammocks and a few scruffy sailors. There was an upended box in front of them with a bottle of rum on it and a number of tin cups. The men were all desperately ignoring Gallo.

"A quick game of rummy, gents?" he said again. All of the old Gallo cheer and confidence was in his voice, but it did little to hide the poor state of his skin or the vague scent of putrescence wafting off him. The belows were never especially fragrant areas, and Gallo was adding to the problem.

"We don't play with devils," said one of the men in the bunks, glancing from Gallo to Wydrin and back again. He had a pair of dice in one greasy hand. "Playing dice with the devil, won't catch me doing that. That's like something in one of those songs, isn't it?"

Wydrin took hold of Gallo's arm and dragged him out of the doorway. The flesh under his shirt sleeve was cold and hard.

"You're supposed to be staying with the cargo."

"I can't sit in there for the entire voyage! There's barely room to sit, and no one to talk to." Even so, Gallo let Wydrin lead him into the hold. Having established that none of the boxes and sacks contained anything flammable she'd put a small oil lamp in there, along with an old wooden chair. It was pretty cramped, and it smelt of old fish, but she wasn't feeling especially concerned about his comfort.

"My brother didn't want you on his ship at all." She led him over to the chair, and then glared at him until he sat down. "Sea-faring men get anxious if a seagull so much as gives them a funny look, so you can imagine they're beside themselves over a dead man on board. If you don't behave, I'll have you put on the other ship, where I won't be around to stop the men chucking you overboard." Jarath had two ships in his modest fleet: the *Sea King's Terror* and the *Briny Wolf*, the latter of which was carrying a bunch of jobbing adventurers, intent on collecting the bounty on a certain dragon. Wydrin had rolled her eyes when she heard about that. "Very superstitious men, sailors."

Gallo glared down at his hands, his fair eyebrows bunched together in a knot. He was sulking. Wydrin was quite familiar with that look, had seen it many times during his frequent arguments with Sebastian. It was strange; he looked so much like Gallo. Laughed like him, moved like him, sulked like him. The only thing that wasn't familiar was the stink. Gallo had always liked to smell good, even when covered in the dust and dirt of adventuring. Now he smelt like a dog left to vomit itself to death in a barrel of offal. She leaned against one of the boxes and folded her arms, staring down at him.

"Is it really you, Gallo?"

He glanced up at her and said nothing, apparently deciding the question wasn't worth answering. Instead he kicked the heel of one of his boots against the floor.

"Sometimes I can't feel my feet," he said. "Like I've forgotten they're there, and I have to hit them against something to remember."

Wydrin sighed.

"What do you think you'll get out of this? Do you really believe Sebastian will want to talk to you?"

"It doesn't matter if he wants to," he replied. In the dim light it was all too easy to see the shape of the skull beneath his skin. "There are things he needs to know."

Wydrin patted Glassheart where it hung at her hip.

"You know, if Sebastian gives the word, I will quite happily chop you into pieces. Big ones, small ones. I'll be very interested to see if you keep talking when I've separated your head from your neck." Certainly, the axe wound he'd taken in the alleyway didn't appear to have caused him any problems. He'd covered the hole over with a scrap of linen and said no more about it. "I'd do it now, in fact, but

I think that's up to Sebastian to decide. It was him you stabbed after all."

"I told you, that wasn't me! It's like I was trapped inside, unable to stop it."

Wydrin turned and walked to the door, ignoring his excuses.

"Just stay in here and keep quiet," she said. "And stop frightening the pirates."

Moonlight streamed in through the narrow window. Outside the night was still, with only a faint wind bothering their sails. Sighing, Wydrin turned over in the bunk, facing the wall with its stained and warped wood. She could hear the sounds of men working on the deck, performing all those small tasks that keep a ship moving swift and sweet. As bunks went Jarath's was remarkably comfortable – she'd certainly slept in worse places – but she'd been tossing and turning for hours now. Sleep wasn't coming.

She wriggled onto her back and stared at the ceiling. Where was Sebastian now? Closer, hopefully, than he had been. They had been sailing for days, crawling down the coast of Relios. With the mood he'd been in the last time she'd seen him, there was a part of her that wondered if he'd got himself killed already. Her stomach tightened at the thought, but Wydrin forced herself to think on it. He'd travelled back to Creos alone, without giving her any real choice, and sought out a dragon with little other than the sword on his back. And that wasn't to mention those sharp-toothed bitches with their shining swords and golden armour. What chance did he have, really? It was stupid. And he'd lied to her too, risking everything to repair his precious honour.

Slowly the fear in her stomach gave way to anger, and Wydrin relaxed. Anger was better. Anger was easier. Fear caught you rigid and held you in place, helpless, but anger got you moving.

Reluctantly, her mind moved on to Frith. He deserved even less thought, truth be told; a pompous princeling with a dangerous talent for self-preservation that rivalled even Wydrin's own. But there he was, in her head anyway. Those stormy grey eyes, the way his jaw tensed when he was angry, which was pretty much all the time…

Wydrin kicked her legs under the blankets, half annoyed and half amused. Sebastian had always been right about her taste in men, at least.

"Trouble sleeping?"

In an instant Wydrin was out of the bunk, her short sword held steadily in one hand. She hadn't heard the door, so she knew it wasn't Jarath returning or one of his men bringing a message. There was a figure standing in front of the window, blocking out the moonlight. It was tall and slender, and its hair, which came down past its shoulders, shone in the silvery light.

For one confused moment Wydrin thought it was Gallo, but then the figure held out one arm to her, and it ended in a stump.

"Roki?"

Glassheart was comforting in her hand, keeping a good distance between her and the man. She was dressed only in her underclothes and the cabin felt unnaturally cold. Her flesh prickled as every hair tried to stand on end.

"You remember me, then." He took a step forward. "Tell me, do you remember my brother's name?"

The gauntlet was on his left arm, the shapes engraved there glowing softly.

"I don't remember the names of all the idiots I kill," she said. "But his death *was* amusing. Enri, his name was Enri. You're not really here."

Roki came closer. There was no sword in his remaining hand, and she could see no weapons on him. He looked paler than he had before, and there were dark circles under his eyes and a gauntness to his cheeks that suggested he was still recovering from a long illness. He smiled at her faintly.

"Not here," he agreed. "But close."

"What do you want?"

He laughed at that. "You know what I want."

"Then come yourself, and bring a sword." To put her own mind at ease Wydrin struck out with Glassheart, stabbing into Roki's chest. The sword met no resistance. He was indeed a phantom, a creature of fog.

"That would be too easy. Where would the satisfaction be in just killing you? The Copper Cat is a creature of risk. You spend every day under the spectre of death, and you enjoy it. The real pleasure will be in watching you suffer first."

Wydrin shifted her weight. How close was close? What sort of range did the enchanted gauntlet have? Could he be on the *Briny*

Wolf, or even on land somewhere?

"I just wanted you to know," continued Roki, "that I am here, and I will be watching you. Don't forget."

And with that he was gone. Moonlight streamed into the room once more. Wydrin looked down at her feet, bare and white against the floorboards. She pushed Glassheart back into its scabbard.

"Not much chance of that."

"Take me to the *Briny Wolf*."

Jarath looked up from the map he was studying.

"I thought you were asleep. If you're not, I'll go and reclaim my bed."

"No time for that, come on. I want to visit the other ship."

"Why?"

"Because I'm older than you and I said so."

For some reason Wydrin found she didn't want to tell Jarath about the visit from Roki, at least not yet. She had told him something of her recent adventures, emphasizing the parts that made her look daring and heroic and skipping over some of the more troubling details. Even so, speaking of Roki under the clear night's sky felt too much like summoning him. There would be time to talk later, when she was sure that both ships were safe.

But Jarath was giving her a sour look.

"I'm the captain here, Wyd."

Wydrin took a deep breath. "Please?"

Jarath sighed and rolled up the map. "Bill? Signal the *Wolf* to tell her we're coming aboard."

"Don't," said Wydrin, putting a hand on her brother's arm. "Let's just go now. No need to tell them we're coming."

"Wydrin, what is all this about?"

"Just trust your older sister for once."

In the end they went across in a small boat, approaching the *Briny Wolf* under a canopy of stars. Jarath, who knew his sister well enough to listen to her more serious requests, gave her a full tour of the ship, taking her into each cargo hold without needing to be asked. They found nothing.

When eventually they returned to the deck the sky was turning from deep indigo to that frail, impossible blue that comes just before dawn. Wydrin rubbed her arms, trying to draw off some of the chill.

Where was the little bastard?

"So, are you going to tell me now, Wyd?"

Jarath was giving her a look of unimpressed and weary patience.

"It's nothing. I've just been jumpy lately. The stuff with the Citadel, with bloody Sebastian doing a runner. I guess I'm looking for monsters in shadows these days." *Which isn't all that ludicrous*, she added silently.

"You know, I remember you being a better liar than this." Jarath sighed. "Look, maybe you just need more sleep. I don't mind–"

There was a burst of laughter from behind them, and Wydrin turned to see two figures approaching. There was a tall, solid-looking man with a carefully combed red beard, and a slim woman with black hair and sharp cheekbones. Wydrin recognised them from around Crosshaven: Draken the Dragon's Ire and Errine Hoarsfrost.

"Ho," called Draken when he spotted them. "The Copper Cat, as I live and breathe! What rare company this is."

Errine Hoarsfrost frowned slightly, then inclined her head in greeting.

"Hello, Draken, Errine," said Wydrin. "How goes it?"

"Good, good." Draken took hold of Wydrin's hand and shook it brusquely, squeezing just a shade too hard. "Couldn't be better really. Have you heard how much the King of Relios is paying to get rid of this creature? A king's ransom, literally! But of course you know, otherwise, why would you be here?" Draken might look like a fool, reflected Wydrin, but he was actually quite a suspicious little shit. "Although rumour has it you might have more than one reason to be getting out of Crosshaven at the moment, aside from chasing after coin."

Wydrin extracted her hand.

"That's what they're saying, is it?" She turned to Errine. "And how are you, Hoarsfrost?"

"You are going after the dragon?" said the black-haired woman. Her voice was soft, but Wydrin sensed a fair amount of threat in it all the same.

"Straight to the point, as ever." Wydrin smiled brightly at the pair of adventurers. "It's none of your business."

"It is if you're planning on taking our bounty," said Errine. "Draken and I have communicated with the king's envoy directly and terms have been agreed."

"You and Draken can take a quick dip in the sea with your heaviest armour on for all I care."

"Now then..." started Jarath as Errine stepped up to Wydrin, a long slim blade sliding from her silk sleeve.

"The dragon is ours."

Wydrin bunched her hands into fists. *Idiots.* As if the creature that crawled out the ruins of the Citadel was something they could barter for. As if actually killing it was no more than an afterthought, a problem to be considered later.

"Yours?" She saw the sliver of steel in Errine's palm and it only made her angrier. "You won't get within a mile of it before it cooks you in your own bloody armour, you stupid, arrogant, embarrassing excuses for–"

There was a shout from the rigging then, breaking into Wydrin's rant and causing a flurry of activity on deck. Suddenly everyone was looking beyond her shoulder.

"What is it?"

Jarath pointed. Wydrin turned to see the coast of Relios, the first blush of dawn highlighting the waves in soft violet and pink. And far in land, lighting up the sky like an impossible sunset, the bright orange glow of dragon-fire.

55

Travelling with the armour, the mule and Ip, it took Sebastian another full day to hike back to the Order's camp. By the next morning, he already knew he was too late.

"By all the gods."

They stood at the top of a low hill, looking across the plain to the north. The sky was dark with cloud, promising rain, but it was still easy enough to see the battle raging in the distance. The brood army had clashed with the Order and their troops just beyond the camp, although it looked as though the Ynnsmouth knights were being pushed back. He could feel the brood's joy in the fight like the aftertaste of something sweet on his tongue, and he even felt an itch to join them, to be down there in the writhing chaos. He shook his head briskly, trying to brush those thoughts away. He forced himself to think of the knights down there, young recruits who were likely new to the Order and lacking in any battle experience, particularly against beautiful dragon-women with blood on their teeth. They must be terrified. At least there was no sign of Y'Ruen. Yet.

Ip, who was leading the mule on a rope, raised an eyebrow at him.

"Looks like they're in trouble."

Sebastian ran a hand through his hair. It was thick with dust now, and tangled. His fingers, he noticed, were trembling ever so slightly.

Sebastian took a deep breath.

"It's my fault. I have to do something."

"Then may I make a suggestion?"

Sebastian turned at the sound of that voice – it was soft and cultured and *old*, not the voice of a child at all. Ip still stood next to the mule, but her icy blue eyes were filled with blood from lid to lid. Seeing his surprise, she grinned, revealing her unnervingly white teeth. When she opened her mouth it wasn't Ip that spoke.

"I have been watching you, Sir Sebastian. I must say I very much enjoyed your efforts at my shrine. You can't pay money for a desecration that good these days."

"What are you?" Sebastian drew his sword and pointed it at the girl. "You're not Ip."

"Well spotted. Ip is one of my children, a life dedicated to me. Once she would have been a sacrifice, but I rather prefer her as a disguise. She will, I think, be a priestess one day. I am Bezcavar."

"Demon," said Sebastian. "You will get out of that child. Now."

Bezcavar laughed.

"Or you will do what? Kill the girl? You might have done it in your blood-rage, but a thinking, calculated act? I very much doubt it. Besides which, you don't have time for this." Ip turned her blank, red gaze up to Sebastian. "Your men and women are dying, Sir Sebastian. It's such a waste. All that pain and suffering, and none of it in my name."

"What are you talking about?"

Sebastian still held the sword at arm's length, the point levelled at Ip's throat.

"I am offering you a deal, good sir knight. Dedicate your sword to me, and all those you kill with it. All the pain you cause will be mine."

Sebastian felt bile rising in his throat.

"Never! My sword is sworn to Isu. I could never be in thrall to a demon."

"So you would abandon those men and women, Sir Sebastian? It is the only way to save them now, we both know that."

Slowly, the sword dropped towards the ground.

"In return for my sword?"

"I will ensure that you have the strength to reach the fight before it's over."

"That's not enough."

Ip inclined her head once.

"And at least some of your army shall survive the battle. I will keep their wounds from being fatal as long as I'm able."

"You can do that?"

"I am the Prince of Wounds, am I not?" Ip tipped her head and smiled.

"I swore an oath to the mountain," said Sebastian. He could hear the wavering in his own voice and hated it. "To be pure of heart, to do only good."

Bezcavar snorted.

"And how much good is that doing you, exactly? Swear your sword to me, Sir Sebastian, wear my armour, and let me show you what you're really capable of."

A gust of wind blew the smell of smoke and blood across the plain to them. There were voices in pain, although he could no longer tell if he were hearing them in his head or on the air. Sebastian ran a hand over his face. He needed strength to fight again, and he had none.

"Tell me what I must do."

Sebastian pulled on the armour, Ip's small fingers deftly untying and tying straps, helping him position the plate and mail in all its intricate pieces. He thought it would be much too large, but as each section was slotted into place the metal would shift and contract, until it fitted him perfectly. Eventually he stood, moving his arms around, feeling how the armour settled against him. It wasn't even as heavy as he'd expected. Ip regarded him critically with her red eyes.

"Yes, it looks fine on. I would even say you were born to wear it."

Sebastian rubbed at a speck of rust.

"I was not born to do a demon's bidding."

Bezcavar laughed.

"You'd be surprised how often I hear that. Now, kneel, sir knight. And present your sword."

Kneeling in the dust, Sebastian held out the blade lengthwise. Ip stood in front of him, small and slender and solemn.

"Do you swear to wield your sword in the name of Bezcavar, Lord of Pain and Prince of Wounds? Do you swear to offer up every drop of blood spilled to me?"

Sebastian thought of the mountains in Ynnsmouth. The Shrine of Isu, with its ice and moss and rocks. It would be cold there, and the snow washed everything away. He felt very far from home.

"I swear."

Ip laid one tiny hand on the blade and the metal shimmered until the dull, practical steel turned a brittle grey, the colour of ash.

"It is done." She smiled. "Now seal it in blood."

With almost every part of him covered in leather or mail or plate, Sebastian hesitated. In the end he pressed the edge of his blade against his cheek and felt a sharp sting as the skin parted. Ip grinned, delighted.

"Perfect!" cried Bezcavar. The girl reached over to him, and for a strange moment Sebastian thought she was going to give him a hug. Instead he felt the dry rasp of her tongue against his cheek as she licked the blood away.

She stood back.

"Now, run," she said. "You must run."

When Sebastian stood again, strength rushed into his arms and legs like a summer's river overflowing. The armour wasn't heavy; it was light. He was no longer tired; he was more awake than he'd ever been. And he was ready to run.

He turned and flew down the hill, feeling like a youth again, while Ip cheered and whooped behind him. Perhaps all was not lost, after all.

56

Sir John stumbled back behind the shield wall, one hand clasped to his side. He was very deliberately not looking at the wound, as he was sure it would only put him in a bad mood, but he could feel the heat of his life's blood passing out of him.

"Shore up the ends!" he shouted to a gaggle of men within his line of sight. They were as ragged and bloody as him, yet they brightened at the sound of his shout. He could see the relief on their faces that someone was still in charge. Sir John didn't know where the Lord Commander was – suspected, in fact, that he was face down under the foot of one of these monstrosities. What had the lad Sebastian called them? The brood army, aye, that fit well enough. He watched as the men joined the end of the shield wall and for a few moments their retreat was stilled.

"Sir, they are flanking us." A young man, his face white with shock under the dirt, appeared at his elbow. Sir John forced his legs to hold him a little straighter. "Do you have orders?"

"Reinforce the shield wall, keep pushing them back. Do we have any of the mounted division left?"

The boy seemed to turn a shade paler. "No, I mean, I don't know. Sir, shouldn't we retreat?"

"Yes, why not? Let's retreat all the way back to Onwai and spend the afternoon eating cheese and drinking iced wine." Sir John grunted as the pain in his gut grew sharper. "If we retreat, lad, they'll just chase us down and stab us in the back. We'll be rabbits running from a pack of dogs. Wounded rabbits. Our only hope is to hold the shield wall."

He could see from the look on the boy's face that this wasn't the answer he'd been hoping for.

"Go. See if you can round up any of the mounted section."

The boy, glad at least to be sent elsewhere, fled. A man in the shield wall fell, a red mess where his face should be, and the dragon's soldiers surged towards the gap in the line. Sir John redoubled the grip on his sword and forced his feet forward. They must hold, they must. If nothing else, they could never say that he ran from the battle...

There was a shout from his left, followed by a chorus of shrieking from the brood army. The green-skinned woman that stood in front of him was suddenly knocked to the ground. Sir John recovered his composure quickly enough to thrust his blade through her throat, barely registering the green blood that soaked him to the elbow. When he looked up, there was a giant on the field, a demon in human form, carving his way through the ranks of the brood.

The men beside him closed up the gap, touching shield edge to shield edge, but Sir John couldn't take his eyes from the knight in the centre of the fight. His sword moved as a blur, carving limbs and heads from bodies with abandon, while the brood army's shining blue swords slid off his armour. The armour!

"Who is that?" bellowed Sir John, but he already knew. The knight wore no helm, and his black hair fell down his back in a tangled wave. Sebastian's face was a mask of concentration, streaked here and there with the blood of his enemies.

"Rally!" Sir John urged the men forward. "To me! To me!"

Spotting the confusion in the ranks of the brood army, the men pressed forward as one, shields held tight together and short swords ready. The brood army, never truly regimented, scattered. They were caught now between Sebastian, who had become a whirling instrument of death, and the surging line of knights coming towards them. Sir John caught the eye of one of them and although there was no fear there, he could see uncertainty. For the first time Sir John dared to hope they might survive the day.

In minutes, the brood army broke, heading away from the camp. Where there had been chaos there was a sudden stillness. The cries of wounded and dying men were everywhere.

"Do what you can for them," he snapped at the nearest able knight. "Get them back to the tents, and call the surgeons. I'll need as many of you up on your feet as soon as possible." He strode past the men towards the figure standing next to a pile of bodies.

"Sebastian!" He slapped the big man on the shoulder, then backed away when he turned to face him. For a moment the ex-knight's face had been entirely blank, and Sir John feared for his life. Then Sebastian blinked, and looked down at the mess around him with an expression of faint surprise on his face. Reassured, Sir John gestured to the bodies at their feet. "I don't mind telling you I think you saved us there." The brood army were still retreating. Sir John rather suspected they weren't entirely sure what had happened either, but that was often the way it went in battle; it only took one brave act, or even a foolish one, to rally the men and turn the tide. He'd seen it happen before.

"I retrieved the armour."

"I can see that, yes." Sir John glanced at the gleaming mail, now covered in green blood. "What does it do exactly?"

"I've not had much time to find out," Sebastian said quietly. The big man still looked distracted, even uncertain as to where he was. "You sent me up there knowing there would be no trade."

"Yes, well." Sir John cleared his throat. "It was a risk, I'll give you that. But this appears to be a time for desperate risks, wouldn't you say? How did you get it, in the end?"

"I killed them all," replied Sebastian in that same quiet voice, and despite the heat of battle in his blood Sir John felt cold. He was a man who'd seen a lot of killing, but here was a detachment that worried him.

"I think you're in need of a rest, Sir Sebastian." He tried to take the knight's arm. It was like moving stone. "We've lost many, and we need you at your peak. I'd also like to take a look at that armour before the brood army comes back."

There was a rumble that started in the ground beneath their feet, and at first Sir John thought Relios was experiencing one of the earthquakes it was famous for, but the sound grew louder, and louder, until it was a force pushing against his ears. The grey clouds above them parted and a nightmare tore through, all shining blue scales and the smell of destruction.

"I think she might have something to say about that," said Sebastian mildly.

The dragon fell out of the sky faster than Sebastian could believe possible. He had a brief moment to really take in how enormous the creature was – *she could swallow us in one bite* – and then she unfurled her wings, covering everything in shadow. There was a pause, a stillness broken only by the screams of men – how tiny they sounded after that roar – and she opened her mouth and spewed flame down on them all.

There was light, and heat, unbelievable heat. Sebastian staggered away, grabbing a shield from a fallen knight and holding it up to the onslaught, while around him everything burned. Sheltering beneath the shield he looked at the red clay of the ground, scuffed and strewn with the marks of battle. There was a tiny plant there, somehow not squashed into the mud, but as he watched it burst into flame. He closed his eyes tight. The roar of her flames deafened him, the stench of burned flesh filled his nostrils, sweat rolled down his face and back. *I'll cook in this armour*, he thought, and that struck him as funny, so he laughed.

And then just as suddenly, it was over.

Sebastian peered out from beneath the shield. Everything was black, scorched into unrecognisable lumps. There were bodies of men everywhere, although it was now impossible to tell who had died in the fighting and who had died under Y'Ruen's flames; all the bodies were charred and twisted. Thick swathes of smoke rolled across the ruined landscape. What was left of the camp was now on fire, and he could see no one moving to put it out. No one was moving at all.

Daring at last to look up into the sky, he caught sight of Y'Ruen's tail as she flew back up into the clouds. Her job here was done, after all.

"*Bezcavar!*" His voice was hoarse, torn by the fierce heat. "You lied to me!" He threw his sword down. "I couldn't save them. I couldn't save any of them!"

57

The stick turned slowly in mid-air, the shells and bones and other items shaking with some unseen force. Frith tipped his hand and the stick began to turn the other way, gradually gathering speed.

"Good, good." Jolnir stood by the fire, pushing balls of clay into the embers. It was a clear day on the island for once, and the sky was as blue as the grasses around Jolnir's hut. "You've done this one before, I think."

Frith nodded. In his head he held an image of the word for Hold. He could see it clearly now. Wrapped around his hands were a number of long strips of fabric, all covered in swirls of ink. The Edenier was a constant warmth in his chest, ever present. It was like a loyal dog, eager to obey and to please.

"I did it to a man once. Held him in the air like this, along with a number of other objects."

"Interesting. Is that what you wanted to happen? Did the Edenier do as you commanded?"

For a moment Frith was quiet, thinking back to the tower in Pinehold. It was difficult to remember, as though it was a dream he'd had years ago.

"I was angry and the man wasn't cooperating. He was thinking of fleeing, and I wanted him held in place. So I suppose it did obey me, in a fashion."

"And what happened to this man?"

"None of your business."

Frith changed the word in his head from *hold* to *fly*. In an instant the stick flew up into the air as if thrown with incredible force, twirled briefly against the blue sky, and then fell to earth somewhere roughly on the other side of the island. Jolnir made a disapproving noise.

"Now you are showing off."

"It comes so easily now." Frith held his hands out in front of him. The strips of fabric that bound his palms were covered in the words for Hold, Fly, Light, Guidance, Control and Fire. They all disintegrated after sustained use, but that didn't matter. He had the words in his head now, and fabric and ink were easy enough to come by. He had finally mastered the power of the mages. How sweet it would be, he thought, to return to the Citadel and show their ghosts what he'd achieved. The bastards.

"There were times when I did other spells too. I brought a man back to life once."

Jolnir looked up from the fire sharply.

"You did?"

"Dead, or as close to it as makes no difference." Frith held his hand out to the fire and conjured the word for Hold. One of the clay balls rose shakily out of the flames. "I healed his wound and brought him back. Is there a word for that?"

Jolnir pulled another stick from his hump and poked at the fire. There was an odd, dry rattle coming from within his headdress. It took Frith a moment to realise the mystic was laughing.

"What is it?"

"You have no idea – what you did was very dangerous, young Lord Frith. Very dangerous. To give life with the Edenier is to lose something of yourself too. It also greatly depletes the amount of Edenier within you. All the other words are essentially about force." He waved his spindly hands in the air. "Move *this* over there, hold *that* in the air. Encourage these molecules to move faster, to become hot. The word for life, for healing, is about giving."

Frith scowled.

"What are you talking about?"

"Tell me, how did you feel after you had brought this man back from the dead?"

"I... well, I passed out."

Jolnir nodded as though this were to be expected.

"You are lucky the Edenier was so powerful within you. You could have done yourself serious harm, or expended all the Edenier in one go."

"I did it twice," Frith admitted. He let the clay ball drop to the ground where it split in two, revealing the freshly cooked shellfish within. "There was an injured woman…"

Jolnir chortled.

"Really? You do not strike me as the chivalrous type, Lord Frith."

Frith bent down and retrieved the seashell. The meat inside was both salty and sweet, and by far the tastiest thing he'd found so far on Whittenfarne. He chewed for a moment, remembering the night in the Blackwood when he'd healed Wydrin's fractured arm. They'd both been cold and angry, but the magic had formed a warmth between them. It had been pleasant.

"So you're saying it would be dangerous to do it again?"

The birds perched on the conical huts let out a series of squawks. Jolnir waved a stick at them irritably.

"Many of the mages elected not to learn that word, lest they were called upon to use it." He cleared his throat. "They were a selfish lot, really. I will teach you the word for Heal, and give you this advice: remember that it will deplete the Edenier, and you, to use it too often."

"Fine." Frith picked another ball of clay out of the fire and dropped it on the rocks, revealing more cooked shellfish. Jolnir picked the meat out with his long grey fingers and then his hand disappeared under the bird mask. After a few moments there came the sound of noisy chewing, as though the mystic had no teeth and had to gum his food to death. Frith watched him.

"Do you never take it off?"

Jolnir chuckled and shook his head carefully from side to side. Frith was about to ask why when the old man stood up again, waving his remaining stick.

"There is another secret to show you, young Lord Frith. Come!" He ran off into the tall grass.

Once more they walked across the island, Jolnir skittering over the rocks with apparently boundless energy, Frith following on behind. Now that he could use the mages' powers with some control he was using them a lot more, and that seemed to bring on a particular sort of tiredness. His fingers would tingle after long periods of the magic flowing through them, and he often felt lightheaded. It was a warm day too, and although he'd left his bearskin cloak at Jolnir's hut he was still much too hot. They walked up and down hills, skirted around pools and jumped across the occasional crack in the ground, until Jolnir stopped so suddenly that Frith walked right into the back of him. Above their heads, the ever-present birds screamed with apparent amusement.

"What is it?" snapped Frith. "Why have we stopped?"

"We're here," said Jolnir. "At the final secret of Whittenfarne."

They were standing at the edge of a wide pool filled with steaming water. It looked just like all the others to Frith, although he supposed it was rather more circular than usual. In fact, the more he looked at it the more he suspected it was not a natural formation; the edges were too regular, too uniform. A handful of lizards clustered at the far rim, eyeing them warily.

"I have had more than enough of these," he said. He raised his right hand, contemplating a fireball at the creatures.

"*Pft*. Just wait one moment."

Jolnir reached down and pushed one of the black rocks at his feet. It sunk into the ground as though there were nothing but soft sand beneath it. There was a loud, rasping gurgle, and the water in the pool began to drain away. Frith raised his eyebrows.

"Do they all do that?"

"Of course not. Come on."

Jolnir walked into the depression left by the retreating water. Frith followed slightly more cautiously, remembering how he'd almost broken an ankle when he'd first arrived on the island. Sunk into the very centre of the circle there was, of all things, a door. It was round, made of white rock with silver veins running through it, and there was a face carved in the middle. It was a serene face, sexless. The eyes and mouth were closed. Just beneath its chin was a wide silver handle.

"Lift that," said Jolnir.

Frith wrapped both hands around the handle and tugged. It was just as heavy as it looked, and it took a fair amount of straining before he got the door fully open. It swung upward on hinges that barely squeaked, revealing a set of stone steps leading down into pitch-blackness. Jolnir whacked Frith across the back of the legs with his stick.

"Light, remember," he said. "Guidance."

Frith brought the words to mind, and a soft globe of pearlescent light appeared in front of his hand.

"You go first," said Jolnir.

Frith descended the stone steps. Inevitably he was reminded of the endless walk under the Citadel, where the sense of threat had been heavy on all sides, but these stairs appeared peaceful. They walked for a short time, heading deeper into the island, while the light revealed smooth black walls carved directly into the rock. Eventually the steps ended and they came to a long corridor.

"What is this place?"

Jolnir said nothing, so they kept on walking. Faces appeared on the walls, just like the face on the door. They all had their eyes closed, and they all gave the impression that they were about to speak. Soon they came to openings in the rock, leading off into identical-looking corridors. Frith followed one of these and found more of the same; more corridors, more faces. Eventually he stopped and turned to face Jolnir.

"There are tunnels like this under Pinehold," he said. "Tunnels like it under several places in the Blackwood, according to my father's maps. But you already know that, don't you?"

Jolnir nodded.

Frith took a step, intending to grab hold of Jolnir's ragged cloak, wanting to shake the knowledge out of him, but something stilled his hand.

"What does it mean? You must tell me. My father studied those maps. He obviously thought it was important."

Jolnir reached up to one of the stone faces and ran his wizened fingers across it lightly.

"The mages were not the only people to find the power of the old gods disturbing. There were others who thought that one day it would be necessary to stop them. Permanently."

"Who were these people?"

Jolnir waved his hand dismissively.

"Ancients. Under the instruction of a single master they built these tunnels all over Ede. Such an undertaking was extraordinary. A masterwork. They excavated and built, all in secret, for hundreds of years. All that time and all that effort, and they were never used. Such a shame."

"Never used? What do you mean, the tunnels were never used?"

"They were a weapon, my dear Lord Frith. A weapon to be used against the old gods."

●●●

By the time they emerged back into the daylight, Frith's mood had worsened considerably. Jolnir had, after imparting one impossible piece of information, retreated back to his usual tactic of answering questions with questions. Frith stomped to the edge of the pool, still shouting queries over his shoulder.

"But who were they? Who ordered it? How does it work?"

Jolnir emerged from the hidden door. Immediately three of the black birds fluttered down to land on his hunched shoulders.

"There, my lovelies, I wasn't gone long, was I? Never far from the sky, never far."

"Jolnir, it is very important you tell me..."

"Always full of questions. Come along, I need to give you the word for healing, do I not?"

They made their way back to the mystic's home in silence, and as Jolnir pottered about inside his hut Frith stood by the fire. One of Jolnir's assistants, the woman Luggin, was sitting by the embers trying to warm a kettle over the meagre flames.

"I can help you with that."

Frith formed a small ball of fire and let it settle gently into the coals. After a moment the fire grew in size, licking the bottom of the battered kettle.

"There you go..."

To his surprise, Luggin took hold of his wrist, bony fingers gripping like a vice. She stared at him with wide eyes.

"What is it?"

She pointed to the fire, then back to his hand. The headband around her forehead was slipping and she pushed it back up in one distracted movement.

"You want to see it again?"

When she nodded, he summoned another ball of fire in his free hand, and she made a shrill noise of delight. There was a rustling from the grasses and, as though called there by some signal Frith couldn't hear, Muggin and Dobs came shuffling through the grass, their eyes as bright as the female assistant's.

"Here." Jolnir emerged from the hut with a piece of parchment in his hand. When he saw the three assistants crowded round Frith he chuckled. "It appears you have an adoring audience, Lord Frith! Go ahead, show them what you can do."

Smiling a little, Frith pictured the word for Hold, and there was a collective gasp as a ring of black stones rose from the ground to hover above the fire. Luggin ran her fingers over the strips of fabric hanging from his wrist, murmuring under her breath.

"It's almost as if they remember!" Jolnir came over to the fire and handed Frith the parchment. There was a new word on it, inscribed in black ink. "Your healing spell, as promised." He drew one of the sticks from his hump and poked Luggin in the midriff. "Is this echoing in that empty mind of yours? Does it remind you of something?"

Frith dropped his hand, letting the rocks fall.

"What do you mean, remember?"

"You'd think such knowledge would be long gone, but it seems they do recognise Edenier when it's right in front of them. I always said they wouldn't know real magic if it bit them on their arses, but it seems I was wrong about that."

Frith found his eyes were drawn to the headbands worn by Luggin, Muggin and Dobs, and the symbols drawn there. They were familiar, weren't they? And what sort of names were Luggin, Muggin and Dobs, anyway?

"Who are they, Jolnir?"

"Nonsense theories, they used to say. Looking down their noses at me, the only one who knew the truth. Ha!" There was an edge to Jolnir's voice now. "They're more use doing my fetching and carrying."

Frith cleared his throat.

"The mystics of Whittenfarne, the *other* ones. That's who they are, isn't it? What did you do to them?"

Jolnir waved a stick.

"Made them more useful, is what I did." He poked at Dobs, pushing the bewildered man back a few inches. "Just the tiniest touch, is all it took. Such weak minds. I have more knowledge in my fingertip than the lot of you combined!" His voice was steadily rising, echoing within the bird-mask. "I have seen things you idiots wouldn't be able to comprehend! Ridiculous creatures, crawling around in the mud. Trying to make sense of the words of gods!" Suddenly, he was bellowing. "Show them, Frith! Show them what my nonsense has wrought!"

There was an odd frequency to his voice, and for a moment Frith found his hands rising of their own accord.

"No, I will not. I am no mummer's dog, jumping through hoops."

The bird mask swung towards him rapidly, and Frith took a step back.

"Then I will show the fools myself!"

Jolnir reached under his mask and jerked it up over his head. He threw it down onto the rocky ground, revealing a huge, monstrous bird's head, nearly identical to the mask he'd discarded, except the eyes were yellow and wet and real, and his razor sharp beak opened to reveal a wrinkled black tongue. With the mask removed he seemed to unfold somchow, his cloak falling away to reveal a pair of enormous black wings. He unfolded further, becoming taller, while his spindly grey arms flexed and stretched. The thing that was Jolnir rolled its head on its shoulders and snapped its beak, apparently relieved to be free of its confinement. He was a good eight feet tall now, and although it was difficult to see his body through the remnants of rags and swathes of feathers, Frith thought he was partly human. Or human shaped, at least.

"I am O'rin, you idiots!" cried Jolnir. He bellowed with laughter again, and his birds rose up in attendance around him. Frith edged away.

A god? How could a god be here?

Muggin and Dobs were cowering in the dirt, while Luggin was already running, heading for the distant black hills.

"The god of lies," muttered Frith in amazement.

"Well done, my lad," said O'rin. It was unnerving to hear that voice coming from a face with no lips. The eyes rolled toward him in approval. "You see? This one listens. I am the last old god, the only one not stupid enough to fall for the mages' trap, although what use is that, I ask you? The magic all gone, my brothers and sisters trapped, and the world all full of foolish little people like you." He pointed at the mystics with one grey finger. "I hid away, and over the years I became smaller, less powerful. I watched as the Edenier drained from this world, and there was nothing I could do about it. Although that's not quite the case any more."

Frith was already moving, already trying to remember the swiftest direction back to the shore, but O'rin was faster. His hand shot down and grasped Frith by the shoulder, squeezing tight.

"One last taste, my young student. I don't think that's too much to ask."

The strength dropped from Frith's legs in one sickening wave. He fell to the ground, trying to pull away from O'rin's grip even as his vision faded and started to turn dark at the edges. The last thing he saw as the rocks came up to meet him was the swirling of soot-black feathers.

58

The attack came just after lunch.

The *Sea King's Terror* and the *Briny Wolf* were skirting the coast of Relios, looking for a place to make landfall. Jarath, who had sailed this section of the Creos Sea many times, claimed that the cliffs softened the further south you went, and that there was a small fishing village called Lockey's Rock where they could stop and take on supplies.

Wydrin wondered if Lockey's Rock was still standing. From the patches of thick black smoke they'd seen inland it was likely to be a smouldering ruin by now.

"How're you going to find him, Wyd?"

She sat with her brother on the deck, chairs either side of an upturned barrel. They had some hard black bread, half a wheel of strong cheese and a chunk of salted pork between them. The food made her think of her mother, who had provided similar fare on her infrequent visits. She sipped weak mead from a battered tin cup.

"He'll be there, somewhere. I'll just look for the biggest source of trouble." She paused, smiling slightly. That was what Sebastian had always said about her, of course. Jarath did not look amused; his normally cheerful face was pinched with worry.

"Sure, and the biggest source of trouble is a bloody great dragon. I don't like it, Wydrin. I know you and Sebastian are friends..."

"He is like a brother to me. A brother that doesn't whine as much as my real brother."

Jarath sighed.

"He wouldn't have wanted you to go and put yourself in danger like this."

"You're talking about him like he's dead already." She said it lightly, but once the words were out she realised she couldn't take them back. Jarath just looked at her, and she knew well what that look said. She turned away from him and cut a thick slice from the pork.

"You worry too much," she said eventually. She held up her hands around three feet apart. "I was *this* close to the dragon before and I survived. The Copper Cat is a hard creature to kill."

"Yes, when you had your lordling there to whisk you away."

"That is nonsense and you know it." Wydrin shifted in her chair, more annoyed than she wanted to admit. She should never have told Jarath about any of it. Of course he would see it that way, the idiot. "Frith caused more trouble than he solved."

"I always thought that was your sort of thing."

Wydrin shot her brother a poisonous look, and drank down the rest of her mead.

"We're here now, Jarath. I'm going to find Sebastian, and you're not going to talk me out of it."

He raised both hands, admitting defeat, but she could see from the lines on his face that he was still annoyed with her.

"And what about your stinky friend? You'd better be taking him with you when you go."

Wydrin stood up, wiping greasy fingers on her trousers.

"I will. Don't worry, we'll be out of your hair soon."

With that she turned and left, heading for the belows. It was a cold, bright day, the sky streaked with thin white clouds all pointing to the east. A chill wind was blowing, pushing them ever closer to the coast. *It's always the same with family*, Wydrin reflected. *You spend your life consumed with guilt that you're letting them down somehow, and then when you meet up with them you can't wait to get away again.*

Down in the belows, Gallo was seated in the dark. The oil lamp had gone out some time ago and he hadn't bothered to relight it. In the light from the doorway he looked like a dishevelled corpse propped upright in a chair, until he wearily lifted his head in greeting and bared his teeth in what Wydrin assumed was supposed to be a smile.

"Come to check on your stowaway?"

"We're nearly there." Wydrin paused in the doorway. She wasn't sure why she'd come down here at all. Perhaps she wanted to see a friendly face, although she doubted Gallo counted as that any more; his face was more likely to cause nightmares. "Do you eat? I mean, do you still eat?"

Gallo shrugged.

"I can put food in my mouth and swallow, if that's what you mean. Can't really taste it any more – or at least, the tastes don't appear to matter. Does that make sense?"

"Not really."

"When I first crawled my way out of the Citadel and realised I was free of Y'Ruen, I went straight to a tavern. It was being looted at the time, so I found a crate of wine and started drinking. Good, Istrian wine it was, rich and dark." He coughed, a dry rattle in his chest. "I drank the entire crate, one bottle after another. I wanted to get to that stage of drunk where you can't remember your own name. I wanted to erase the memory of everything that had happened inside that damned place, but no matter how much I drank, I stayed sober. I started to feel bloated and strange, yet even my stomach wouldn't heave it up. I was inert." Gallo shrugged. "I can't get drunk, and I derive no pleasure from food."

Wydrin frowned.

"That sounds awful."

"It is," agreed Gallo. "I hope there will be an end to it soon. You say we are close?"

"There's a fishing village not far from here. We'll put in there, then you and me and no doubt the two sell-sword idiots from the *Briny Wolf* will see what the situation is in Relios. That's assuming–"

A series of shouts from above caught the words in her throat. A ship was always ringing with shouted commands, but these were tinged with panic. She lifted her head, listening for them to come again.

"Dragon!" came the call. "'Tis a bloody dragon!"

Wydrin shot back up the stairs, with Gallo close on her heels. When she reached the deck she saw men and women running for the port side. She joined them, her heart in her throat. At first she could see nothing, just the same rugged cliffs they'd been sailing along for days, and then a huge, graceful shape appeared above the rocks. It was the dragon, sleek and fast and impossibly big. The wings alone would dwarf the *Sea King's Terror*, and the long tail tapered to a wicked point. Her dark blue scales glittered under the sun like a wall of sapphires. She banked, throwing up one fibrous wing and turning back inland. Wydrin felt a puff of wind brush against her face, and was certain it was from the dragon's passing. They saw her for perhaps five or six seconds, and then she was out of sight.

The crew stood, stunned, on the decks. Wydrin spotted Jarath to her right, and grabbed hold of his arm. Now they were here and they had seen the beast, it felt like they were sitting targets.

"I think we should move," she said quietly. When he didn't respond she tugged sharply on his sleeve. "Get the ships out further into the water and keep our heads down."

He looked at her then, his eyes very white and wide.

"Let's do that," he said. He began shouting orders to his crew, and signals were passed to the *Briny Wolf*. Wydrin felt the ship turning under her feet, and she allowed herself some small measure of relief. Gallo was standing next to her, his eyes riveted to the horizon.

"Do you think it'll come back?"

Gallo didn't answer. When she touched his elbow she found he was trembling slightly all over; it made her think of a mouse caught under the gaze of a hungry cat, too terrified to run. Wydrin glanced over to the *Briny Wolf* and caught sight of Draken and Errine on the deck, pointing excitedly at the horizon. *They're pleased, at least*, she thought, although she had no idea what they hoped to achieve against such a creature.

She grabbed one of the men bustling past her.

"Hoy, Bill! Do you have bows? Any weapons like that?" She already knew the *Sea King* had no cannons; such weaponry slowed down a raider.

Bill had gone very pale under his bristling beard.

"Aye, we keep a few in the armoury. Don't get used much, 'cause the damp tends to warp the wood."

"Get them," said Wydrin. "Bring them all up here. We don't know–"

There was an ear-splitting roar. Wydrin felt every hair stand on end, and for a moment she was the mouse too terrified to move. The dragon appeared once more over the edge of the cliffs, her giant maw open to reveal row upon row of jagged, yellow teeth. Wydrin thought she could have counted every one, if she'd had a mind to.

"Don't come over here," she whispered. "Just carry on with your business, no need to take any notice of us."

But the dragon turned again and with a few flaps of her enormous wings she was heading straight for them.

"Arrows!" screamed Wydrin. "Whatever you've got, fire it up there!"

The dragon swooped down across the water, dragging the end of its tail across the tips of the waves. The enormous head lowered for a moment, and for one absurd second Wydrin thought Y'Ruen was just having a drink, and then the terrible jaws opened and a gout of blood-coloured flame exploded forth.

"Take cover!" came several cries from around the deck. The initial fireball passed harmlessly between the two ships, rousing a hot wave of steam in its wake. Y'Ruen flew back up into the air until she was poised directly above them. Somehow Wydrin found Jarath amongst the chaos.

"How fast can you move this ship?"

"I've men on every oar."

They both tensed as the dragon roared again. There was a hollow clatter as a handful of arrows struck the creature's scales and bounced harmlessly away, and then Y'Ruen opened her mouth and another boiling column of flame shot down, right into the centre of the *Briny Wolf*.

Wydrin heard her brother shouting, heard the screams of the men and women on the other ship. She elbowed her way to the side rail and watched as the smaller ship was engulfed in flames. The sails went up first, like a ragged set of orange flags, and soon the deck was alight too. Men and women ran from the fire, some of them with their hair and clothes already catching, while others were blackened figures, lost to the inferno. She saw that Draken and Errine were still there, and she thought Errine had produced a cross-bow. Others were already abandoning ship.

"We have to get out of here," she cried to no one in particular.

The dragon circled once more, a sinuous shape in the heavens, and dived at the smaller ship. The bulk of the monster obscured her view, but when Y'Ruen rose again Draken was nowhere to be seen, and the dragon's teeth were working busily. Its jaws snapped and its neck pulsed, just like a heron eating a particularly large fish. There was a moment's pause as the creature finished its meal before unleashing another blast of flame at the *Briny Wolf*. This time there was no space untouched by fire, and within seconds the ship was reduced to a fiercely burning bonfire. The dragon circled above them, triumphant.

"Fetch the ropes," said Jarath. "Get those people out of the water." Wydrin ran to his side.

"You have to go! Leave them!"

"Wydrin–"

"Now!" She pointedly wildly to the dragon above them. It seemed fascinated by the burning ship. "They will have to fend for themselves, Jarath. I'm sorry, but if we don't get moving now we're as good as dead."

There was sorrow in her brother's dark eyes, and it broke her heart. Reluctantly he gave the order to pull out, with all speed, and every man and woman leapt to action. Many of them would have had friends, even relatives, on board the *Wolf*, and now they were fleeing to save their own lives. Wydrin rubbed a hand over her face, suddenly very tired.

With every hand on deck they gained speed rapidly, turning and heading out away from the coast of Relios. Wydrin kept her eyes on Y'Ruen, hoping that the dragon would want to stay close to the land where her brood army were camped. The dragon roared again, and turned her enormous head towards their swiftly escaping ship.

No, no, no.

It was too late.

The mouth opened, a yawning furnace ringed with teeth, and this time Wydrin saw the ball of fire coming directly towards them. She threw herself to the deck, wincing as all the wind was knocked out of her lungs, and the fireball passed directly overhead. There was a pause filled with the screams of men and women unable to get out of its path, and then everything was light and heat.

Wydrin was thrown back against the rail, her head colliding painfully with the wooden beams, her throat full of black smoke. When she opened her eyes again there was chaos. The fireball had just missed the main sail and licked along the deck, leaving a trail of flames and debris. The crew who hadn't simply been blown to bits in the initial explosion were now screaming as the ruby flames consumed their clothes, their hair, and their bodies. Wydrin scrambled to her feet, stumbling as her head span.

"Water! Get some buckets and get that bloody fire out!"

She risked a glance upwards and saw the dragon circling again.

"And keep on those oars, I want to see every oar moving!"

The crew who were still able ran to fetch buckets, and soon there was a soothing slosh and hiss as they worked to put out the rapidly spreading fire, while clouds of black smoke rolled across the deck, obscuring some of the mayhem. *Our only hope is to get away and pray that she doesn't follow.*

And then an extraordinary thing happened. The dragon banked away from the swiftly moving *Sea King's Terror*, and flew back to the remains of the *Briny Wolf*. As Wydrin watched, the creature circled the water around the merrily burning wreck, occasionally darting its head down to pick something out of the water. Its jaws snapped, crunching and swallowing.

She's eating the dead, thought Wydrin. *Or picking off the survivors.* Her stomach turned over. Perhaps the small shower of arrows they'd provided had been enough to dissuade her, or the tasty meal now floating in the ocean was too tempting; either way, it was their chance to flee.

"Out to sea!" she hollered behind her. "Keep her moving!" The ship sped on and out into the deeper waters, and still the dragon didn't pursue. Perhaps they would make it. Perhaps they would be safe.

"You bitch," muttered Wydrin, watching the dragon as it retreated. "I swear by the Graces I will have your blood."

"She will not leave her brood for long," said Gallo. He was by her side again. His face was almost a pasty green in the daylight, and smudged with smoke. The eyes he turned on her were full of despair. "Your brother–"

Wydrin spun round. She hadn't heard his voice since the explosion.

"Jarath?"

They took her to him.

Bill and another man she knew vaguely as Edvard had pulled him clear of the fires, and now he lay on a blanket in his cabin. The blast had hit him on his left, and the skin on that side of his body had been crisped away, leaving raw flesh beneath. He stared up at the ceiling, his eyes blank with pain. His hair was gone entirely, leaving a blistered and bloody scalp.

"He's lucky to be alive." Bettany was the ship's medic, a sour-faced man with an ugly scar twisting across his right cheek. "Most would be dead from the pain already. I've given him some poppy milk for it."

"Lucky?" said Wydrin. Her voice sounded distant and odd in her own ears. She wondered if her hearing was damaged from the explosion, or if part of her simply didn't want to connect with what was happening.

"Aye. What good it'll do him, though, I don't know. It would be kinder to–"

"No," said Wydrin. "No." She sunk to her knees and took hold of her brother's good hand. The other was little more than a blackened claw. "Not that."

"It hurts me to say it, miss, it does." Bill spoke up from the back of the small room. His voice was muffled, as though he were holding back tears. "But it'd be the best thing for him. He won't live long enough to reach land, and we can't go back to Relios."

"Even if we reached land safe enough there's nowt anyone can do for him. I'll give him some more of the milk," said Bettany gruffly. "He'll know nothing about it."

"I said *no*." Wydrin squeezed her brother's hand in her own. She entwined her fingers through his, marvelling at their warm brown tones against her own pale skin. "I know someone who can help him. Someone who can heal him." Bending her head she pressed her lips to Jarath's hand and kissed it. Then she placed it carefully back on the blanket and stood up. "We need to sail for the Nowhere Isles. To Whittenfarne."

PART FOUR

Upon the Ashen Blade

59

Y'Ruen spread wings the colour of twilight and flew up through the cloud cover, revelling in the cold wisps of vapour as they curled against her scales. Her wings tore through the cloud, scattering and tearing, until she raised her head into a clear blue sky. The air was thin here, and cold, although she barely registered that; it was nothing compared to the boiling furnace she carried within her.

What is in the mind of a dragon? What does a god think about?

They were moving beyond the red lands of Relios now, and the clay-ridden earth had given way to plains full of hardy grass. Beyond those, Y'Ruen could make out lush green fields and the distant blue mountains that rimmed the northern edge of this continent. A flood of simple pleasure moved through her body at the thought of all that green space, all those fresh hills. Relios contained plenty of humans to consume, that was true, and the destruction of Creos, so long the site of her prison, had been a source of fierce joy, but these southern lands were already dry and sun baked. How pleasant it would be to see the water-fed lands of the north curling and turning black under her flames, while her children bloodied their swords.

Still, there was no rush.

The bone horns on either side of her long head were gathering ice crystals, and she could see the sky above darkening as she ran out of atmosphere. Turning gracefully, she dipped her head below the clouds once more and dived, seeking her children on the ground. The brood army marched below, a glistening tapestry of green and gold. There was almost too much to do. After thousands of years trapped within the Citadel she wanted to see everything turned to ash, and now there was no one to hold her back.

Long ago, when the world was young and Y'Ruen was already so old, there had been other gods. Brothers and sisters, creatures like her but not like her. There was the green woman, she remembered, who was forever telling her not to do this and not to do that. The green woman liked to see things grow and had encouraged the humans in their efforts, and so she and Y'Ruen had fought constantly. When the mages trapped them all within the Citadel – all save for one, although Y'Ruen barely remembered *him* – the green woman had seemed a lot smaller, and a lot less powerful. They all had.

It had taken a number of years – gods are not so easily consumed – but after centuries of being shredded between Y'Ruen's teeth her siblings were finally nothing more than memories and ghosts in the rock.

Below the clouds the air was warmer, balmy almost. She flew down slowly, letting the heated air push comfortably against her membranous wings. She kept her eyes on her children, watching them as they marched. They had left the remains of the last village behind, and she could feel the eagerness of some of them for a new fight and fresh blood, matching her own hunger for destruction.

And some of them were talking again.

There wasn't an awful lot that could make Y'Ruen uneasy. In fact, she had rarely experienced the sensation, save for the terrible moment when the doors of the Citadel had closed behind her and she'd felt the net of spells descend over them all. She didn't expect her daughters to produce such worrying emotions. She had birthed them all in the dark of the Citadel, had she not? Clawed a nest in the raw rock and formed them from her own flesh and will? They were hers, and hers alone, and yet…

There was the other one. The man whose blood had woken them to life. And now some of her children were thinking in ways that were alien to her, keeping secrets from their mother and their sisters, treasuring words and names like they actually meant something. Like there was anything beyond the purity of fire and the joy of destruction.

Y'Ruen was displeased.

She put it from her mind. The green hills were coming and the blue mountains beyond, and soon it would all burn. Little else mattered.

60

The *Sea King's Terror* limped past the islands like a wounded animal, still stinking of smoke and ashes. Wydrin paced the deck, peering out into the mists. In one hand she held a damp cloth, which she squeezed reflexively between her fingers; she'd been using it to moisten her brother's brow, for all the good that had done him.

"How close are we, Bill?"

The squat sailor pursed his lips, causing his beard to bristle up like a particularly ugly hedgehog. He shrugged at the fog enveloping the ship.

"Not far now, uh, lady. It's the weather, see, we have to go careful to avoid tearing out our arse on these rocks. The Nowhere Isles is always like this. Nasty, cursed place, if you ask me." He paused, as if considering the wisdom of saying more. "Waste of bloody time, if you ask *me*."

Wydrin reached over and grabbed him by the front of his filthy tunic. She pushed her face close to his, ignoring the meaty stink of his breath.

"So we should just let him die, is that what you are saying?" She gave him a shake. "Because I would suggest you think very carefully before you say that to *me*."

The small patch of Bill's face that wasn't bearded turned pink.

"What good will it do? We're chasing wisps and mermaids out 'ere! I'm mightily fond of the captain but it's plain no one can help."

Wydrin shook him again.

"I know someone," she said. She looked down and noticed the bloody rag still clasped in her fingers; it smelt of fever-sweat and desperation. She let go of Bill and dropped the rag onto the floor, feeling faintly ill. "We just have to get to Whittenfarne."

Of course, it was possible that Frith hadn't gone there at all, or had been and left already. Knowing her luck, the awkward sod had been killed on his way to the islands, waylaid by thieves with an eye for his fancy sword and fat coin purse. But there was a chance, and as long as there was a chance she wasn't letting go. She stalked away from Bill, tired of the weary sympathy in his eyes, and looked back into the mists.

An hour later, when eventually she saw the island, she thought her eyes were playing tricks on her. There was a faint blue glow coming from the blanket of white mist to the north-east of the ship, a soft light that seemed to shift and flicker. As they drew closer the patch of light grew larger, its movements more violent. There were shouts from the lookouts.

She grabbed the nearest crewman.

"That's where Whittenfarne is, isn't it?"

The crewman nodded.

"Does it usually look like that?"

He raised his eyebrows.

"No, ma'am, islands don't normally glow all blue like."

Another shout from the rigging turned her back to the eerie sight. Whittenfarne finally came into view, and like most of the islands in this strange little archipelago it was all black rock and jagged hills, with patches of stunted trees and hardy vegetation. It was an unappealing place, but it wasn't the geographical make-up that drew the eye. It was the storm.

Wydrin could think of no other name for it. The faint blue glow they'd seen through the mist had given no indication of the violence of light that now doused Whittenfarne. It was a shifting caul of indigo brilliance, riddled with crackling veins of lightning. There were dark clouds within the storm, swirling in a tight circle over the island, while everything beyond it was as still and calm as ever.

"So this is Whittenfarne," she sighed. "Of course it bloody is."

They sailed on, passing two gigantic black statues, the tops of both lost in the swirling clouds, before they finally came to a small, ramshackle dock built of greenish wood. There was a single bedraggled figure sitting there, and Wydrin recognised him instantly; it was difficult to mistake that white hair. Hope seized her heart, and something else too. With a start she realised she was glad to see the stupid princeling, despite everything.

"I must really be desperate," she murmured.

Frith watched the small boat approach from where he sat on the rotting dock. Distantly he was aware he should be glad, that this was probably his only way back to civilisation, but it was difficult to muster the energy to care. *Let them come*, he thought. *Let them go. It is all the same to me.* There were two figures in the boat, a man and a woman, both rowing steadily. The woman turned and shouted something back to the ship, her voice flat against the fog. Frith blinked.

"It cannot be," he said aloud.

He watched the small figure in the boat as it edged closer to the dock, taking in the mess of red hair, the way she sat slightly forward, tightly focussed on their destination, the ill-matched collection of leather armour... Yes, it *was*. Closer still and he could see the tattoo on her arm, the dagger at her waist. He struggled to his feet, ignoring the wave of light-headedness that passed through him. He walked to the end of the dock, and now he was waving too, and as the boat came alongside and she clambered onto the steps, he realised an odd thing: he was smiling. It felt strange on his face, after everything that had happened.

She glanced up at him, green eyes flashing, and he was struck by how serious she looked.

"The Copper Cat of Crosshaven," he called down to her. "I'm fairly certain your contract was at an end." He reached down an arm to help her up, and she took it. There was an awkward moment as they stood together on the dock, hands entwined, and then she pulled away, looking at the island beyond.

"Oh, I thought you'd have some sort of trouble you'd need me to deal with." She waved at the silent storm, stopped as if she was going to say something, then waved her arms about some more. "What," she said eventually, "is all this?"

Frith sighed.

"This," he said, "is the wrath of the gods."

It took some time to explain, from all sides.

There was some initial confusion when finally Frith recognised the other occupant of the boat. He looked from Gallo to Wydrin, his hand hovering over the hilt of his sword.

"A dead man walking around? You expect me to believe that?"

Wydrin shrugged.

"You can come over here and smell him if you like. I may not believe him about a lot of things, but he's definitely rotten. Listen, we need to talk."

"And where's Sebastian?"

"That is who I seek," said Gallo. Frith frowned. The man certainly looked dead; his skin was as white as parchment, save for those parts that were turning black and green. "We believe he's in Relios, tracking the dragon you set free."

"I did nothing of the sort."

"What is all this, Frith?" Wydrin nodded at the storm of lights.

They were perched on the small part of the beach untouched by the light. It was unnerving to be standing so close to it; the raw power seemed to push at Frith's back, and he could feel his hair trying to stand on end.

"I came here to learn how to control the mages' powers. I met with a mystic called Jolnir." Frith cleared his throat. "He wore a mask, and underneath it he wasn't human. And now he's whipped up this magical storm. I believe that his assistants were once the other mystics of Whittenfarne, now under O'rin's spell. The storm is impenetrable, and–"

"What?"

"Jolnir was a creature called O'rin, one of the old gods."

Wydrin ran a hand over her face, squeezing her eyes shut.

"I don't have time for this." She took Frith by the arm. "Come on, I need you to come back to the ship with me."

"What?"

"My brother is injured. We ran into the dragon while we were looking for Sebastian and apparently pirate ship versus dragon isn't a well-matched fight. He's dying, Frith, and I need your help."

She began to drag him back to the dock, so he shook her off.

"No, I can't."

"Yes, you can." She took hold of him again, with both hands this time. Gallo stood off to one side, silent. "I need you to do what you did with me, remember? When you healed my arm? With the pink light?"

"I said I can't."

"I'll pay you! I'll do anything you want. Just come with me and help him. I'll do anything." She looked up at him with desperation in her eyes and Frith felt a stab of annoyance.

"I mean that I am incapable." He shrugged her off again, wincing at how much those words stung.

"What do you mean?"

"Jolnir took it from me." Frith took a deep breath. To be weak again. *Again.* It was almost more than he could take. "He took the magic from me. That's what he's using to generate this storm."

There was silence. Wydrin stared at him, swaying slightly on her feet. Her face was ashen.

"Took it from you?"

"I didn't know you had a brother," Frith said quietly, then wondered why he'd said it. "Yes, after he revealed what he was he drained the Edenier from me somehow. I passed out. I don't remember much of what happened afterwards..."

"And the blue light is a barrier?" asked Wydrin. She sounded very tired.

"Yes," said Frith. "Look." He picked up a piece of wood from the beach, washed smooth with seawater, and threw it at the storm-light. When it hit the light, it seemed to stop, held in place for a moment, and then it was consumed in writhing, searing light. It flew back at them with an audible pop, landing at Frith's feet. It was smoking slightly. "He's in there still, him and his birds." He pointed up at the dark, swirling cloud. Wydrin came a few steps closer, almost too close, so that Frith had to hold her back with one hand.

"They're black birds," she said after a moment. "The cloud is made up of thousands of birds. And there's something larger flying with them?"

"That's O'rin himself," said Frith. "He isn't exactly human."

"And he has your powers."

"I did try to go back in, but the barrier is dangerous." He held up his left hand, one side of which was red with blisters. "There is nothing we can do."

They stood and looked up at the flickering blue barrier. The storm of birds flowed and surged and crackled silently above them.

"I beg your pardon," said Gallo into the silence. "But I might have an idea."

61

"If you lie there like that all day you'll get sunburnt."

Sebastian opened his eyes. Ip was staring down at him, one bare foot resting on his arm. When she saw that he was awake she gave him another small kick. Her eyes, he noticed, were no longer blood red; they were back to their icy blue. Beyond her the sky was almost too bright to look at.

"I've been asleep long?"

"All morning you've been dead to the world." Ip gestured behind her. "Just like everyone else, really."

Sebastian struggled to his feet. He'd been lying in ashes and his hands were grey. Even the finely wrought armour, which he had yet to gather the energy to remove, was smeared thickly with ash and blood. The skin on his face felt tight and hot, although he wasn't sure if that was a result of the dragon's fire or the sun on his face while he was sleeping.

"We should go somewhere else," said Ip. "I've eaten all the food in your pack and I'm starving."

Sebastian peered at her through the thumping of his head.

"Where is the other one?"

The small girl sighed extravagantly, as though Sebastian were possibly the most boring person in the world.

"He's not here." She tapped her head. "He's not always here."

"But you know about him? It?"

She shrugged.

"Can't hardly miss a demon in my head, can I? He used to be a picture in my mind. Then a little while ago the picture started talking." She sighed and turned a slow circle with her arms held out to either side. "I'm *hungry*."

Sebastian looked around. They were still in the middle of the scrubby patch of land where the Ynnsmouth knights' final stand had taken place; it was now a warped and twisted field of ash and blackened corpses. Most had been burnt right down to the bone, and jagged skeletons seemed to sprout all around. *We've sown the seeds,* thought Sebastian, *and now we have a field of the freshly harvested dead.* He was dimly aware that some time had passed since Y'Ruen's attack, and that he'd been sleeping in this cursed place for – how many nights? He wasn't sure. A charred body lay just next to where he'd been sleeping, the skull twisted into the dirt, as though the hapless soldier had pressed his face into the ground at the last minute in a desperate attempt to escape the flames.

I lay here all night in the arms of the dead. What would Wydrin make of it all?

Thinking of his friend brought a tremor of feeling, at least. He rubbed a filthy hand across his eyes.

A gust of wind swirled the ashes up into a fine cloud that danced briefly around his ankles and settled again. Sebastian began to walk towards what had been the camp, now the smoking remains of the army's supplies, tents and cooking apparatus. Ip ran alongside, occasionally hopping and skipping over twisted bones.

"Why did I survive?" he asked suddenly. It was the question that had been threatening to surface ever since he'd opened his eyes. "Everyone else here perished under the dragon fire. Bezcavar's doing?"

"You swore your sword to him," replied Ip. "That does come with some benefits, you know."

Not enough to save anyone else.

They came to a pile of soot-covered rubble with a twisted confusion of melted metal at its centre. Next to what might have been the Commander's folding table there was a blackened corpse; the heat had caused it to bend in on itself, like a child curled within a womb.

Sebastian squatted next to the body, trying to recognise something about it. He felt that if he knew for sure this corpse was the Lord Commander he would be able to understand what had happened, process it somehow. The skull grinned up at him, jaws agape. There was something wet and meaty at the back of the eye sockets, and part of the ribcage had shattered with the heat. He had no way of telling who this unfortunate soul had been.

"This isn't half bad," said Ip from behind him. "They didn't always cook it back at the temple."

Sebastian stood up.

"What are you doing?"

Ip was crouched over another body, her deft fingers picking away at a charred section of flesh still clinging to the skeleton's thigh bone. As Sebastian watched, she peeled away the black to reveal something red and raw underneath. She took a piece of that and stuck it in her mouth, chewing with relish.

"Stop that." Before he knew he was moving Sebastian was next to her, pulling her up by her arm with more force than was necessary. "Stop it!" He gave her a shake, and she flopped at the end of his arm like a fish on a line. "What do you think you are doing?"

"Eating! I'm hungry." She glared up at him, an obscene smear of blood on her lips. "I've been all over this place while you were asleep and there's nothing left to eat but what's on the bones."

He dropped the girl, shaking his head. He didn't know if he was more repulsed by her behaviour or his own rage.

"These are brave men and women who died a terrible death. They deserve more respect than to be picked at by little vultures."

"The birds do it," Ip pointed out sulkily. "Although there's hardly enough left here for ravens."

Sebastian scratched at his beard, trying to ignore the ash that floated up from it as he did so. They would have to move or they would starve, that much was clear. The brood army had been marching steadily north, and now he had lost sight of them on the plains.

"Have you searched the other end of the battlefield?" he asked Ip. The girl shrugged.

They set off back across the field of ash, until the scorch marks ended and the dead mainly consisted of green-skinned women in golden armour. There were pitifully few. When he'd been filled with the battle-rage he could have sworn he'd felled hundreds, but in reality he hadn't made much of a dent in their numbers. Just enough, he'd thought, to turn the tide of the battle. What a joke that had been.

He spotted something sitting on the dirt. Amongst the devastation it looked strangely whole and untouched. It was a water skin, although not one he'd ever seen a soldier or a sell-sword wear. It appeared to be made of some sort of golden scaled material, like the carapace of a huge beetle. It sloshed as he picked it up.

"Here." He passed it down to Ip, who snatched at it greedily. "Have a sip of that. Just a sip, mind, we'll need to be careful."

Ip took a few rapid gulps before he could get it back off her. Once he had it back in his hands he noticed there was a tightly rolled piece of parchment wedged in the strap that would normally attach the water skin to a belt. It was as if someone had deliberately removed the skin, pushed the parchment into a gap that would hold it and then left it out in plain sight.

"What's that?" asked Ip, wiping her mouth and smearing the blood there onto her chin.

"I don't know." Sebastian removed the piece of parchment and unravelled it carefully. It was, he realised, a page from a book – there were lines about crop rotation and irrigation on one side, and on the other someone had written a message in large, slightly wobbly letters. It looked as though it had been scrawled by someone very young, or very unused to writing. "Greetings Father," he read out loud. "We feel that you are here. We do not seek you in the fight. We go now to Ynnsmouth." He paused as a cold hand gripped his heart. The dragon was taking the army to his home. "We hope to see you, Father." He stopped and turned the page over in case there was more. "Then there's just a list of odd words underneath that," he told Ip. "Ephemeral, Crocus, Ennui, Toast, Glorify, Belonging, Maelstrom... it doesn't make any sense."

"Some of it does," said Ip, bending down to examine the body of a green-skinned warrior who had spilled her guts into the dust. She slipped a finger into the ropey purple innards, but didn't appear to find it to her taste. "Sounds like someone likes you. *Father.*"

Sebastian sighed.

"See what else you can find," he told the girl. Ip leapt up again and began to skip from corpse to corpse, as cheerily as a child looking for blackberries in spring. Sebastian pushed the page into his belt, trying to ignore the dread now weighing on his shoulders. He should have known. Ynnsmouth, where his mother still tended his father's grave, where no doubt she still thought of her son and contemplated the shame he'd brought on the family. Where the last of the Order of Ynnsmouth Knights would even now be wondering what had happened to their army. Y'Ruen was taking her brood there, where even the might of the god-peaks would offer no mercy from the dragon fire.

And there was nothing he could about it.

62

The wall of storm-light stretched away in either direction, curving as the island curved to shroud it in a dome of lightning. Gallo stood at its very edge, his fingertips hovering above the surface.

"It's the silence that's truly strange. To see so much violence and movement without noise is unsettling."

"Are you sure about this?" asked Wydrin. She had her hands on her hips, and if there was no real concern for him on her face, there was at least an echo of doubt. "We can't know what this will do to you."

"You will not go to Sebastian until your brother is healed. Am I right?"

"Yes."

"Then I will take the risk." His features twitched into a grin. "What have I got to lose, after all?"

"O'rin might not be easy to reason with," said Frith. "He is unpredictable."

"I have some experience of talking to gods," Gallo replied. "I'll do what I can. It's worth a try."

He watched as Wydrin and Frith exchanged a look, and then the red-haired woman shrugged.

"Get on with it, then."

Gallo nodded, and stepped into the barrier.

At first it was like pushing through a sheet of stiff fabric; it pushed back at him, holding him out. There was a series of tiny shocks like a thousand snakes biting with needle-thin teeth, and after a few moments of this, a great heat began to envelope him all over.

He looked down at his hand, calmly observing the twists of smoke beginning to emerge from his skin.

"I imagine that if I were alive, this would be very uncomfortable."

Putting all his weight behind it, he thrust forward, and fell through to the other side. The eerie silence was replaced with a high-pitched wailing punctuated with the cries of birds. Everything within the storm-light was stained a sickly blue – the rocks, the trees, the pools of water – and there were shifting shadows everywhere. At first Gallo thought this was an effect of the flickering light, until he started to see impossible shadows, huge, hulking inhuman things with too many arms, or immense shapes that seemed to resemble buildings. The strangest thing about it was that it wasn't strange. It was familiar.

It had been much the same within Y'Ruen's mind.

Gallo took a few cautious steps, and when the flesh didn't immediately fly from his bones, took a few more. Perhaps this wouldn't be so hard.

"What are you, little dead thing?" came a booming voice from above. Gallo looked up to see a huge winged shape hovering some distance above him. He cupped both hands around his mouth to shout over the din of birds.

"I think you've answered your own question there!"

"How curious!" Gallo could just make out the suggestion of a huge beak and a pair of shining, wet eyes. "What do you want?"

"To talk to you!" Gallo paused. "My lungs aren't what they were. How about you come down here to talk?"

"Down?" The creature called O'rin laughed merrily. "Oh no, my little dead friend, I've spent far too many years down there. If you want to talk to me, you will have to come up." O'rin flew out of the swirl of birds and banked towards the east of the island. For a few moments Gallo thought the god was just showing off, but then he grimaced as he settled on the enormous statue on the eastern point of the island.

He set off at a pace, feeling the queer energy that drove him surging into life in his chest. Once, his blood would have stirred at the anticipation of a new adventure, his skin would have prickled with sweat and his mouth might have been dry. Now his mouth was always dry, his blood was a black sludge beneath his skin and he couldn't even remember what it felt like to sweat.

"One last adventure anyway," he muttered as he climbed small jagged hills and stepped carefully around pools of water. The fish inside them were all dead, floating belly-up on the surface.

When eventually he stood at the foot of the statue he saw there was a rough series of steps cut into the side of it, just next to one gigantic foot. The further up they went the more perfunctory they became, and even in the height of his adventuring days Gallo would have thought twice about it.

"Only one thing for it, then," he said aloud. "One hand after the other, that's what I always told Sebastian. Keep moving and don't look down."

He began to climb the rough steps. It was only a few minutes before he found himself crawling up the vertical rock face, fingers wedged painfully into ledges that seemed to be growing too narrow too quickly. Still he did not sweat, although the skin on his hands and forearms was soon stiff and raw, and more than once his boots slipped and skidded across the surface. The worst of it, in Gallo's opinion, was the bloody birds. The higher he got, the louder their noise.

"It reminds me of the Chattering Men in Relios." Gallo blew air out through his lips. "You remember that, Seb?" The handholds were further apart now, so that he had to stretch to reach the next one. He had no real idea how high up he was. "Figures of clay, all waiting in the dark, pottery mouths full of stolen teeth. A heavy footstep was all it took, and you were never good at being quiet, were you, Seb?" He paused to risk a look down, and immediately wished he hadn't. He'd been climbing swiftly and now the ground looked very far away. "Of course, by the time we had what we were after and were legging it out of the temple doors, there were hundreds of the buggers. Never known a noise like it. Save for this one, of course."

The wind whipped up around him, blowing strands of lank hair across his face.

"Who are you talking to?"

The voice was coming from directly above him. Gallo looked up to see a huge man-shaped creature with a great pair of black wings and a bird's head. The eyes were large and intelligent, the feathers glossy and black. O'rin was perched on a wide ledge just above him, apparently part of the statue's ornate belt.

"A friend I haven't seen for a while," said Gallo, trying to keep his voice as casual as possible, just as though he chatted to giant bird-men all the time. "Would you mind terribly giving me a hand up?"

A long thin hand descended and dragged Gallo up onto the narrow platform. For a moment he was certain O'rin would just throw him off, as he would sweep a beetle from his shirt, but instead he stood there, peering at him with open curiosity.

"You've certainly made an effort to come and talk to me. What do you want, human? If I can even call you that any more."

"I want you to return the mages' powers to the man called Frith," he replied. There was no point in dancing around the subject. "I'd also like you to quieten these birds, but that's rather secondary."

O'rin tipped his head to one side, looking eerily like a pigeon considering its next worm.

"And why should I do that?"

"Because they were his. Believe me, I saw some of what he went through to get them. And my friend needs the magic to save her brother."

O'rin looked away, out into the storm-light.

"I've been hiding on this putrid island for centuries, do you know that? Once my brothers and sisters were trapped in the Citadel, and the mages eventually disappeared too, the Edenier just began to leak out of the world. And I grew smaller, and smaller, and smaller, until I was little more than a wizened creature, too tired to be a god any longer. If I'd know there was still Edenier in the world, perhaps I would have ventured to the Citadel myself – or perhaps not."

"Perhaps not," agreed Gallo. "Not if you suspected who might be waiting there for you."

O'rin turned sharply, enormous beak opening and closing slightly.

"What do you know of it?"

"I know your sister." Gallo grimaced. "I knew her very well at one point."

O'rin leaned closer, wet eyes swivelling in their sockets.

"I can smell her on you," he said after a moment. "She was in your head."

"She was indeed," agreed Gallo. His voice was sour. "And when she left I was dead."

O'rin jerked his head away. A handful of the black birds had separated themselves from the rest of the flock and settled on the rock near them. They watched silently.

"It doesn't matter," said O'rin. "I reckon I'll just throw you off this statue and carry on with what I'm doing. It's been years since I've had the freedom of the sky. I don't have time to listen to the witterings of mortals."

"I think you do, actually." Gallo stepped up to the huge bird creature, squaring his shoulders. His shoulders were never as broad as Sebastian's but he was always good at squaring them heroically. "Because if you don't come with me now, I shall call Y'Ruen." O'rin flinched slightly at the sound of her name. "I will call her to come here now and see you. How would that be?"

O'rin hissed softly.

"Why should that worry me?" But Gallo thought he was worried, for all that.

"A dragon against... whatever you are? I'd be worried."

"You can't do it. You're lying."

Gallo shrugged.

"I can still feel her, in my head. It would only take a small effort for me to reach out to her, touch her mind as she touched mine. And even if you pushed me from this ledge," he added quickly as O'rin shifted his weight, "I wouldn't die when I hit the ground. There would be enough of me left to send for her. And I'm sure Y'Ruen would be very interested to know her brother is alive and... uneaten."

There was a long silence then, broken only by the screaming of the birds and the high-pitched whine of the storm-light. Blue and black shadows crawled across the stone like expectant ghosts, while O'rin's wings twitched and shivered on his back. Gallo felt a moment of true fear.

But when the god spoke again, it was with weary resignation.

"Frith's not a bad lad. Well, he's a shit, but I think that's why I liked him." O'rin tipped his head, and in that instant the storm-light vanished, revealing an overcast sky. Gallo blinked rapidly in the change of light. "And I suspect you'll be needing my help more than you realise."

63

Wydrin watched uneasily as a god walked across the sands of Whittenfarne towards them. Even with the huge wings folded neatly behind O'rin's back, Gallo looked like a sickly child next to him, and she noticed a handful of black birds circled above their heads. She also noticed they were walking too bloody slowly. She cupped her hands around her mouth.

"I haven't got all day, you know!"

She saw the creature called O'rin tip his head to one side – what was that? Anger? Amusement? It was impossible to tell and Wydrin was a long way from caring; inside the cabin of the *Sea King* her brother was teetering on the edge of death. Not for the first time she glanced back to the ship, half expecting to see a signal from Bill, telling her that she was too late. Time, it was all about time. Jarath had so little left.

"That might not be wise," said Frith in her ear. "Jolnir isn't human, remember, and he was able–"

"If he wants to kill me he can bloody well try," she snapped. "I need you back up in working order."

"Wydrin–"

"Hello again, young Lord Frith," said the creature calling itself O'rin. Wydrin shifted her weight from foot to foot. "I probably owe you some sort of apology." He didn't sound apologetic at all to Wydrin.

"I imagine you do," said Frith. His voice dripped with caution.

O'rin shrugged, shifting the black wings.

"I won't give you one, of course – gods don't apologise, I'm sure you're aware – but at least you know you're owed one."

"I'm still not entirely sure that's what you are," said Frith. "Remember I asked you about that? Whether the old gods really were what they said?"

"Of course." The strange bird head dipped, yellow eyes flashing, and Wydrin decided that look was amusement after all. "I can't tell you how much I've enjoyed our little conversations. That's one of the things I've always loved about humans, all the tiny questions and thoughts and imaginings. God's minds are like mountains, huge, immovable and solid, while humans have minds like mountain streams, splitting off every which way. When the world was young–"

"Can we save the lectures for later?" Wydrin stepped between O'rin and Frith, walking on the balls of her feet. She could smell the stink of Jarath's cabin on her skin. "Give him back whatever it is you took. He needs the magic now. I need it now."

O'rin turned those shrewd eyes on her. He didn't speak immediately.

"This is the woman you healed," he said.

The corners of Frith's mouth turned down ever so slightly.

"How do you know that?"

"I can see the connection between the two of you. Part of you is in her."

To Wydrin's surprise Frith's cheeks turned slightly pink. She shook her head at the pair of them.

"Yes, and I need him to do that again. The healing thing." She waved a hand back at the ship. "My brother is close to death and that pink light business is the only chance he's got."

O'rin nodded graciously.

"Ah, your reasons for urgency become clear." He looked at Frith again, and there was a hint of slyness there now. "You will do that, will you? Heal this woman's brother?"

"It's Wydrin, actually," she added.

Frith looked pained for a moment, then he met her eyes and grimaced.

"I will."

"Interesting," said O'rin, and he reached out a withered grey hand, tapped Frith once on the shoulder, and there was a blinding flash of green light. When Wydrin's eyes had recovered she looked up to see Frith staring at his hands in wonder.

"It's back," he said softly. "The Edenier is back with me."

"I'm over the moon for you." Wydrin grabbed him by the arm. "Now, princeling, you and I have a date."

It was unbearably hot inside the cabin despite the miasma of fog outside, almost as if Jarath's burns were somehow leaking heat into the small room. He lay on the narrow bunk with a thin blanket covering his legs. They had pressed wet rags to him where they could, and the ship's surgeon had, under Wydrin's withering eye, applied as many ointments as possible, although he had made it clear that any number of balms were unlikely to help. The blisters were red and seeping, and it hurt Wydrin to look at them.

Jarath was unconscious. She supposed that was for the best, although she kept one eye on his chest as it rose and fell rapidly.

"Are you done?"

Frith stood by the bed, carefully wrapping ink-covered bandages around his hands. He had explained, in a voice tight with some emotion she couldn't place, that this was how the magic was channelled, so it was more likely to work. So she let him get on with it.

Up to a point.

"I am just about ready, I believe."

And yet still he paused. They were alone in the cabin. O'rin and Gallo were out on the deck, no doubt putting the wind up the crew. Wydrin nibbled at the edge of a fingernail, already bitten until it was rough and unpleasant against her tongue.

"You waiting for something?"

"I… no." His grey eyes looked black in the dim light of the cabin. "I have the words," he held up his hands briefly, "so I'll see what I can do. If I can't–"

"Never mind that," she said, brushing over the outcome that was too terrible to mention. "Just try. Please."

He nodded once, and knelt by Jarath's bed. Holding out his hands over her brother's ruined chest, his face was rigid with concentration. After a few seconds a soft pink light spread from his fingers in a sudden cloud, like bright paint spilled in water. It looked a lot stronger than the light that had healed her arm, and Wydrin allowed herself to feel hopeful. It grew in brilliance until the entire room was lit with the rosy glow and the light swept over Jarath in a tide.

"Is that supposed to happen?"

But Frith still had his head down. The ends of his fingers were trembling, and now his shoulders were shaking too. Despite her concern for her brother Wydrin took a few steps towards Frith, wondering if she should steady him somehow.

"Stay back!" he spat. "I *must* concentrate. I must..."

The light doubled in strength, so that Wydrin had to avert her eyes, and then just as suddenly it was gone. Frith slumped to the floor as though all his muscles had turned to water, while Wydrin blinked rapidly, trying to clear her eyes of the after-image left by the magic.

"What happened? Is it over?"

"Wyd?" It was Jarath. His skin was smooth and brown and beautiful again. He was looking up at her with an expression of deep confusion. She grinned and grabbed his face, kissing him firmly on the forehead. There was sweat on his brow from the fever and he was smeared here and there with soot, but otherwise he looked exactly as he always had. Even the long diagonal scar on his chest had been smoothed away by Frith's magic.

Frith...

"Princeling?"

The young lord was wedged between the bed and the cabin wall, his head bowed on his chest as though in a very deep sleep. Wydrin's stomach turned over.

"Frith?"

She scrambled up and went to his side of the bed. Jarath was saying something, but she wasn't listening.

"Frith, don't you bloody dare."

She dragged him into an upright position, his body limp and clammy, but when she pressed her fingers to his chest there was a faint heartbeat there, as soft and frantic as a trapped bird.

"By all the gods..." She let out a breath she wasn't aware she'd been holding and gave him a little shake. His eyelids fluttered, and he mumbled something unintelligible.

"Who's that?" asked Jarath. He was sitting up in bed now, frowning at his stinking bandages.

"Frith? Frith, are you with me?"

"Oh, *Frith*," said Jarath. "Why do I smell so bad?"

Wydrin took hold of Frith's jaw, forcing him to look at her, and noticed something that made her stomach turn over; there was a long winding scar on the left-hand side of his face, just where it had been before the mages' lake had healed all his wounds. It was fainter than before, but unmistakably there. Carefully she pushed his hair back from his face, and was relieved to see he had both his ears still.

"What are you doing?" His voice was little more than a croak, but the grey eyes that met her own were steady.

"You!" She threw her arms around his neck and briefly buried her nose in his hair. He smelt of salt and winter. "You're a bloody fool and I hate you," she told his neck.

Frith made a noise that might have been a laugh, and for the briefest moment he hugged her back.

"Hold on," said Jarath. "There are some things no brother should watch his sister doing. And I really need a drink."

64

Jarath was not pleased about the state of his ship, and he was even less happy to be reminded of the fate of the *Briny Wolf*.

He ran a hand over his face, a gesture Frith was sure he'd seen Wydrin do many times. They did not look very much alike, even for siblings who only shared one parent, but they had a certain way of standing, a posture of confidence that was very similar.

"There were no survivors?" he asked again.

"Not that we know of," said Wydrin. "There might have been those that made it to the water, but I doubt many lived through that. I'm sorry, Jarath. We had to get away or it would have been us next."

"My sister shows no mercy," said O'rin. "That was always her nature."

They stood, a small group crowded around a god, in the stern of the ship. Evening was coming on and they were heading away from Whittenfarne at a goodly pace. The crew, obviously spooked by the sight of a giant man with a bird's head on their deck, were concentrating on getting the wounded ship moving and keeping their distance. Outside of the mists of the islands the sky was largely clear, with only a few scattered clouds dipped in the fading orange of sunset.

Frith shifted his weight, trying to ignore how his leg ached. It wasn't the white-hot agony it had been before the Citadel, not at all, but the ghost of that pain was more than enough. Jolnir had been right about the dangers of the healing magic, that much was obvious.

"Your *sister* needs to be destroyed," said Wydrin. "I wasn't certain before. I thought – I don't know, that we could ignore it and the problem would go away." She pursed her lips. "But it turns out there's no ignoring a dragon."

"I have always thought so," said O'rin. His deep voice was calm, as though they discussed the weather or the best way to cook a lizard. "I built a weapon to that end once, a long, long time ago."

Gallo raised his eyebrows.

"You planned to kill your own sister?"

"I planned to kill all of them. Not in a blood-thirsty way, you must understand, but as a fail-safe. I saw them becoming more and more powerful, just as the mages did, and I knew better than anyone how dangerous that could be. The mages got there before I did, as it happened."

"And does this weapon still exist?" asked Frith.

"In a sense, yes," said O'rin. He turned his yellow eyes towards him, nodding his head rapidly just as he had inside the mask. "You've seen it, in fact."

"I've what?"

"It's here? In the Nowhere Isles?" said Wydrin.

"Lord Frith, fetch your father's maps, and all will become clear."

Frith scowled, unhappy about being ordered about, but he went to his bags and removed the scrolls, now sealed in rough parchment tubes. He opened one, the map of Pinehold, and spread it on a nearby crate.

"Now, Lord Frith, with your human head full of new knowledge, look at the maps and tell me what you see."

"I've looked at these a hundred times since we got them from the vault," he said. "They are just maps. Ancient, yes, but–"

And then he saw it. It was like looking up to the sky and seeing a castle formed of clouds, or one of those paintings where the artist has cleverly hidden a skull in an accident of shadows and cloth. There was Pinehold, depicted in steady black lines, and there were the green lines that indicated the existence of the tunnels hidden beneath the town. Except he recognised them now.

"How is that possible?"

He grabbed the tube and shook out another map, one of Levenstan, a small city in Pathania. Again, there were the familiar lines of streets and lanes, neatly rowed squares indicating houses and hovels and even one big castle, and then laid over the top of that, stranger lines in red ink. The tunnels. But if you forgot that's what they were, you could see that they were also words.

"What is it?" asked Wydrin.

"Those tunnels we lined with explosives in Pinehold? If you look at them from above – I never saw it before because I didn't know – they depict the words of power." He looked up at O'rin, narrowing his eyes. "There was a Regnisse in Pinehold. She saw the maps. Why didn't she recognise it?"

"The words of *Power* are forbidden, remember? Only the mystics of Whittenfarne are permitted to know them. The knowledge never leaves the island." O'rin reached out one hand to smooth down the map. "Your father, though. I wonder if he knew something? A clever man for sure."

"We'll never know now."

"So, the tunnels spell out magic words," said Wydrin. She took a sip from a flask at her waist and shrugged. "What good does that do, exactly?"

"Words, my dear girl, channel the Edenier, or the magic, as you would put it. Lord Frith, I believe we require a demonstration for the young lady, please."

"Now?"

"Yes, now."

Frith took a length of linen from his belt, and an ink pot and brush from inside a small bag at his hip; he'd taken to having both on him at all times while O'rin was teaching him. He crouched at the crate and began to paint the words for Fire and Control onto the white strip.

"Edenier is the magic that comes from pure will," said O'rin, his voice taking on a slightly pompous quality. "It is powerful but erratic. With the words we gave the mages, humans can control it."

Frith tied the bandage around the palm of his left hand. The ink was cool against his skin.

"Thousands of years ago, I excavated tunnels beneath the skin of Ede. I wrote secret words beneath the earth, just in case I should ever need to subdue my siblings. Words written in the fabric of Edeian, the natural magical force of the world, to be activated by Edenier, the magic of will."

On cue, Frith held his arm up, facing out to sea, and a ball of bright fire appeared at his fingertips. A smile twitched at his lips. It was good to be powerful again.

"Would you mind putting that out?" said Jarath. "Enough of my ship has burned down already."

Frith closed his hand and the fireball vanished. *Peasants.*

"So the princeling here now has the power to activate your weapon? That's what you're saying?"

"He does, but it is a complicated spell of many parts. Many words, I should say. You will need to travel to each and activate each in a certain order."

"We don't have time for that!" Wydrin gestured at the ship, still blackened in places with dragon fire. "And why can't you do it, anyway? It's your bloody weapon."

"I gave the Edenier back, did I not? Besides which, I have no wish to alert my sister to my continued existence. I haven't survived all these years just to wave at her and ask to be destroyed."

"You have to help us," said Wydrin, lifting her chin slightly. *She really has no fear of him,* thought Frith, *or she is very good at hiding it.* "You're a god, it's practically your job."

O'rin laughed long and deep at that.

"If you truly believe such things, girl, then you know nothing of gods at all." He glanced up into the rigging, where his ever-present black birds waited. "Although… it was always my biggest weakness, you know, my affection for your people. I will give you two more gifts, Lord Frith. Use them wisely." O'rin pulled one of the long sticks from his back, tapped it to the floor once, and suddenly it was a long roll of parchment. He shook it by a corner until it unrolled, revealing what appeared to be an ancient map of the Eastern continents. The parchment was slightly yellow, and the landmasses had been coloured here and there with faded inks.

"You will travel here," said O'rin, pointing with one grey finger at a green shape in the top right-hand corner. "It is a place called the Rookery. It was once my home, when this world was young. I kept many of my secrets there, and it is there that you will find more of the maps your father was collecting, along with the details of the spell capable of destroying the god of destruction." He paused, nodding. "Not a bad piece of work, if I do say so myself."

Jarath was peering closely at the map.

"That's practically on the other side of the world." He rubbed his chin. "We'd have to go down past Old God's Cape and on through the Sea of Bones, and north through the Demon's Straight." He straightened up. "Even if we survived that, it would take six weeks to get there, at the very least."

"And that brings me to my second gift." O'rin turned to Frith once more. "I give you my honour guard, Lord Frith."

There was a dry whirring of feathers and three black birds landed on the deck in the space between them.

"You will forgive me, Jolnir, but I will personally be very glad to see the back of your flying vermin."

"Here." The god bowed shortly. "I believe they will be of more use to you in this form."

There was the briefest pause followed by a great rush of air that threatened to blow them all off their feet. The black birds ruffled their feathers, indignant at this sudden change of weather, but as Frith watched they began to grow. They swelled and bulged, suddenly the size of cats, then dogs, and now they had four legs and their heads were thickening, wet eyes bulging.

"Hell's teeth," cried Wydrin.

Beaks that were small and sharp became huge and curved, more suited to a giant bird of prey, and their wings became long and smooth, sharp as blades. The feet that had been wrinkled and tipped with talons were now flat, powerful paws, like those of a huge cat.

When the wind stopped, Frith found himself pressed up against the guardrail with Wydrin, Gallo and Jarath, all instinctively trying to put as much space between them and the monsters as possible.

"My griffins," said O'rin fondly. He patted one on the head and it opened its beak, revealing a dark pink throat. It made an odd keening warble. Now fully grown, they were roughly the size of large horses; animals with the bodies of giant, lithe cats and the heads and wings of eagles. They were still black, but the feathers on their wings shone with a soft, oily rainbow of blues, greens and yellows. "Yours to command now, Lord Frith. They will do as you say – and, believe me, they can fly like the wind."

Wydrin slowly shook her head. "Ye gods and little fishes. What are you supposed to feed those things?"

65

When the shadow passed over them, Sebastian shoved Ip down into the dirt and covered her body with his own. The shield he'd picked up from the battlefield was still strapped to the mule, but there was no time to wrestle it free. He would have to hope that Y'Ruen would miss them on this first pass, and there would be time to protect themselves sufficiently before she came back...

"What are you doing?" Ip's voice was slightly muffled.

"Trying to stop you from getting burnt to cinders." Sebastian tensed, waiting for the roar that would precede their grisly deaths. But it didn't come. Instead, he very much thought he could hear laughter on the wind. Familiar laughter.

He risked a glance upwards. There in the sky were three of the biggest birds Sebastian had ever seen. They circled above, casting gigantic shadows onto the scrubby grass below, and it was only when they swept in to land that he realised they weren't birds at all. They had the heads and wings of eagles, certainly, but their bodies were those of huge, four-legged animals, thickly muscled and powerful. As they came closer, a pale face with a shock of red hair leaned over the side of one, partially obscured by a giant black wing. A slim arm covered in tattoos waved. Sebastian stumbled backwards, nearly knocking Ip off her feet.

"Wydrin?"

"You should see the look on your face!"

The griffins – the word came to Sebastian then – landed one by one, powerful wings sending up clouds of dust and pushing waves through the short grass. Wydrin was perched on the back of one, her hands curled around the straps of a makeshift leather harness. She dismounted on slightly wobbly legs, laughing wildly.

"I tell you what, you have to be bloody careful about holding on. I'm not sure if I want to throw up or not."

There were two other passengers. Lord Frith climbed down from the back of another griffin, looking rather paler than when Sebastian had seen him last, and another man he didn't recognise who looked absolutely dreadful. Sebastian started to turn to Wydrin, but something drew his eye back to the stranger, with his grey skin and deeply sunken eyes. His hair had been blond once, but now it hung in darkened, greasy clumps. The shape of him, the way he held himself...

Sebastian looked down at the ground, blinking rapidly. *I've been under this sun too long,* he thought. *The dragon attack, the demon child – it's all been too much.*

Wydrin threw her arms around him, solid and strong and most definitely there. She squeezed him tight, unmindful of the armour he wore.

"I've missed you, you idiot," she said. Her voice was tight, somehow on edge, but her hair smelt as it always did, of smoke and ale and a lack of soap. She pulled away to peer up into his face. "You look like a sack of dog's testicles, you know that? And I don't mean that in a nice way."

"Thank you. Where did you find the griffins?"

"They are my honour guard." Frith stepped forward. He appeared to be adjusting a thick bandage around the palm of his hand, although Sebastian could see no wound. "A gift from a god, now mine to command." He paused, looking pleased with himself, and nodded at Sebastian. "It is good to see you are in one piece, Sir Sebastian."

"Likewise."

The other man took a few steps nearer. He was hesitant, unsure, as well he might be. Sebastian swallowed hard. There was bile in his mouth and his head was throbbing again.

"And who is this?"

Wydrin's sunny expression disappeared, and she bit her lower lip. It was her face more than anything that told him it was true.

"I think you know me, Sebastian," said Gallo.

Sebastian pulled his sword from its sheath. Its newly silvered surface glittered under the sun like frost on a lake.

"Last time I saw you, Gallo, you were running away, clutching a dagger covered in my blood. I assume Wydrin must have brought you here so I can return the favour."

The man claiming to be Gallo held up his hands in a gesture of submission. The fingers were bruise-black, the skin on the palms thin and torn.

It can't be him. I'd rather think of him dead under the stones of the Citadel than this walking ruin, Sebastian thought.

"I came here to help, if I can," said Gallo. It was his voice all right. A little ragged perhaps, but there was an echo of his old charm there. "If anyone can help you deal with Y'Ruen, it's me. She was in my mind, Sebastian, controlling my actions while all I could do is watch. And now, if her mind is touching yours, then I know what you're going through."

Sebastian felt his hands tighten around the pommel of his sword, his lips pulling back from his teeth in a grimace. Unbidden, memories of the slaughter at the ruins rose up, rich with blood and *freedom*. So much easier just to silence the voices than listen. The pain in his head would ease, and he would be stronger...

Wydrin stepped between them. "We've obviously got a lot to talk about, and I for one could do with sitting down for a time. You wouldn't believe what riding one of those things does to your rear end." She walked over to one of the griffins and unbuckled a heavy pack from its back. "Jarath packed us some food and ale, and I propose we sit and eat it before anyone starts cutting anyone else to pieces."

Sebastian lowered his sword and took a long steadying breath.

"Food, then."

"Food!" cried Ip. She skipped up to Wydrin and tried to snatch the pack from her arms. Wydrin frowned and held it up out of the child's reach.

"All right," she glared at Sebastian, "who's the brat?"

"What do you remember of it?"

Gallo didn't answer immediately, looking up at the moon instead. Off to their right Wydrin, Frith and Ip sat round the fire, sharing the last of Jarath's cured pork and black bread. Sebastian dragged his eyes away from his old lover to watch them for a moment, trying to find some peace in the normalcy of the scene. Just people breaking bread together, no dragons, no demons, no dead men. Wydrin and

Ip were squabbling over a cup of wine while Frith ignored them both.

"It was like being underwater," Gallo said eventually. A cloud passed over the moon and his ravaged face, turned away from the fire, was hidden. "That's the best way I can describe it. I could see what was going on, and hear it, but everything was muffled, and any attempt to free myself..." He took a slow breath. "The pressure of her mind, Seb. It crushed me like an ox crushing a beetle under its hoof. I saw my hand with the dagger, saw it pierce you. How do you imagine that felt?"

"How do you imagine it felt to be stabbed?" replied Sebastian, although there was no heat behind his words. "I nearly died. I would certainly be dead if Frith hadn't healed me."

"Yes, he's a strange one." Gallo glanced over to the small group. "What does he want, I wonder?"

"What do *you* want, Gallo? What are you even doing here?"

"To help you, of course." Gallo took a step towards him. Sebastian looked away. "What else can I do to make up for what happened?" He lowered his voice. "She was in my head. I know what that is like. You have a connection to her, don't you?"

"Sometimes, when I dream, I think I can sense her." Despite the chill of the night, Sebastian found he was sweating. "And her army. I think I hear their voices."

"You must be cautious, Seb. Men were not made to know the minds of gods. It nearly broke me." He shrugged and gestured at his rotting skin. "Hell, it did break me. But it may be useful too. The connection goes both ways, I'm almost sure of it."

"What good will that do?" He was thinking of the strange note found on the battlefield, now folded within his belt.

"I don't know, my old friend, I don't know. But I believe you are in great danger, all the same."

"You are not my friend," said Sebastian. "Whatever you are, you are not my friend."

66

The world spread out below them like the richest tapestry ever woven.

Frith clung to the griffin as best he could, one hand gripping the odd mixture of fur and feathers, the other gingerly wrapped around Wydrin's waist. Just beyond his feet he could see green valleys veined with silver rivers, fields of crops like squares of precious metal, and flurries of forest so deep in their greenness they were almost black. They were flying over the lands of Litvania, now so far enough north that the sprawling forest was broken up with wide stretches of open land.

Wydrin said something, but the words were snatched away in the wind and the thundering of the griffin's wings. Frith lowered his head so that his ear was closer to her face.

"What?"

"The birds can't keep up with us!"

Frith saw that she was right. White and grey gulls passed below, lost in their wake. Just in front of them Sebastian and Ip shared a griffin, and to the left Gallo flew on alone, his eyes on the distant horizon. He alone seemed unconcerned by their mode of travel.

"This is strong magic," he murmured. It almost seemed to him that the air itself parted to make way for them.

Wydrin leaned forward, pointing to a series of hills in the distance. They were the faint blue of dusk, and carved into one of them was a tall, humanoid shape. The sun broke through the clouds above and the raw chalk was briefly illuminated, glowing white against the blue.

"What's that?" she yelled.

"It's the King of the Under," he said. "Will you please stop moving about?"

"King of the what?" Wydrin half twisted round to look at him, pressing her shoulder blade into his chest. Her hair whipped around her head, blown in every direction by the wind.

"The Under." When she still frowned at him he sighed and leaned forward to talk directly into her ear. "There are legends of a kingdom beneath the hills, full of a long-lived folk who sometimes snatch the unwary to go and live with them." He sucked in another breath. "The people of this land carved the image into the chalk in the hopes that the King would stop stealing their children away."

"Did it work?"

Frith frowned. Wydrin shifted about, pushing back against him to get a better grip on the griffin's neck. Sitting with her so close while they both clung on for dear life was very uncomfortable. He could feel the warmth of her, could smell the leather she wore.

"I have no idea. Can you keep still? You'll have us both off in a minute."

"I love stories like that," said Wydrin. "Kings hidden under hills, magic in the ground." She went quiet for a moment. "Although it's less entertaining when it's actually happening to you."

They flew on for hours, through clouds that soaked them to the bone, through blazing sunshine that baked the moisture right off them. The land moved under them like a fast-flowing river, and Frith had to admit it was extraordinary to see Litvania laid out below him in such vast detail. There were places he had never seen, passing beneath them in shadow and sunlight, all the secrets of the lands spread out before him. His father would have been entranced by such a view.

The sun began to set in the west, softening the edges of the sky into a subdued rainbow of violets, pinks and indigos. Stars appeared, a handful at first, and then thicker bands of starlight that shone like dew on a web. Frith was so caught up with watching the heavens come to life just above their heads that it was quite dark before Wydrin elbowed him again.

"I don't know about you, but I don't fancy flying much further in this light." The wind had died down considerably but she still had to raise her voice. "It makes the drop look worse, for one thing." Before he could stop himself Frith glanced beyond the tip of the griffin's wing; the blanket of trees directly below them was now a featureless black mass. It was like looking into a deep cave. "Not only that, but my arse is killing me," she continued. "Shall we stop for the night?"

Frith didn't much like the thought of trying to land the griffins amongst the high trees.

"Where? There's no space."

"Look." Wydrin pointed to the north-east, where it was still possible to make out a plain beyond the trees that bordered a huge lake. The water was silver and black, and on the shores were a number of bright white lights clustered together. For a confused moment Frith took them to be stars reflected in the lake, but they were much too bright and close. "There are people down there."

"Yes," said Frith. "They will be Cherolia, travelling people. They move their tents up and down Litvania, Pathania and Istria, moving on when the weather grows worse."

"Do they take in travellers?"

Frith started to shrug, and then thought better of it.

"They sell everything thing they can, including floor space. I'm sure we will find shelter there."

Wydrin turned round and began to wave at the griffins behind, sliding dangerously to one side. Frith grimaced and put one hand on her hip to hold her steady.

"We're landing!" she yelled. "Follow us!"

They landed in the cover of the trees and the three griffins returned to normal bird size, much to Sebastian's horror. They approached the settlement slowly, cautious of what they'd find, but the gathering of tents and people was busy and welcoming. The Cherolia were a tall people with burnished copper-coloured skin and tightly curled auburn hair, but there were plenty of locals there too, shopping at stalls filled with a range of produce collected from all over the continent. It was a mobile town of brightly coloured tents, and they soon found someone willing to rent them shelter for the evening.

"Be ready to move again at dawn," said Frith, pulling open the entrance flap of his tent. The three black birds fluttered down to perch on the top of it. "I won't be waiting around."

Gallo and Ip were already climbing into their own separate quarters, the girl yawning so widely her head threatened to topple off. Sebastian was looking at the narrow entrance to his own tent with his lips turned down at the corners.

"I will have a devil of a time sleeping in there."

"Just remember to take your armour off first," said Wydrin, "that might help." She paused. In the pearly light of the lamps Sebastian's armour looked very fine indeed, the delicate gold chasing on the mail glittering like the scales of an exotic fish. It was the first time she'd really looked at it closely, and there was something familiar about it. "Where did you get that from?"

Sebastian rubbed at his beard, his eyes not quite meeting hers.

"It belonged to the Ynnsmouth knights." He cleared his throat. "I was given it before – well, before the attack."

"They gave you that?" Wydrin leaned against a tent pole, crossing her arms over her chest. One of the advantages of being a champion level liar was being able to spot those less skilled in the art. "From what I remember, you weren't on the best of terms with the Order."

"Perhaps they were desperate enough to feel they needed me on their side." Sebastian began to unbuckle the straps that held his breastplate. "For all the good that did them."

"Do you need a hand getting out of that?"

"I'll manage."

And with that he crouched and went into his own tent.

Wydrin sighed. She glanced up at the birds, who were watching her with black liquid eyes.

"And you can take that look off your beaky faces."

Inside, the tent was narrow and cosy, with a thick carpet of blankets that smelt only slightly of horse, and long strings of prayer beads hung from the ceiling. A small spherical lamp sat in one corner on top of a block of wood, the only piece of furniture in the tiny room. Wydrin unbuckled her own leathers, noticing as she did so that the light from the neighbouring tents cast soft shadows onto the fabric walls. She could see the outline of Frith, sitting up with what was probably a map spread across his knees, and on the other side was Sebastian's huge bulk, already lying down and preparing for sleep. It was a strange inn, she thought, where the only privacy was a sheet of crimson silk.

Wriggling beneath the blankets, she stared up at the prayer beads. They were carved to represent animals – a fox, a cow, a bear, a bird. One of them, she noticed, was a shark, so she leaned up out of the blankets to touch it with her fingertips. After all, she'd done little to earn the love of the Graces lately and they needed all the luck they could get.

67

Wydrin woke a few hours later to a cold blade pressed to her throat. It was dark, the little lamp having burned out a long time ago, and there was only a faint red glow from a distant tent to show the face leering above her. Roki's skin was waxy and slick with sweat, and strands of his golden hair were stuck to his forehead.

"Good evening." His voice was quiet, less than a whisper, as though it were coming from very far away. "You are almost pretty when you're asleep, did you know that?"

Wydrin cringed at the wave of revulsion that passed through her. How long had he been here in the dark, just watching?

"Whereas you look half dead."

Roki bared his teeth in something that might have been a grin.

"I feel more alive than I ever have."

"You can't be anywhere near us now. We flew across seas, across Litvania. Nothing could follow us. How are you here?"

The metal was cold at her throat, and all too real.

"Last time I saw you, you told me to bring a blade," he said, ignoring her question. "So here I am. Tell me, do you like it?"

He increased the pressure, the edge just beginning to bite into her skin. Wydrin suddenly found it very hard to swallow.

"It's a pretty sword," she said, trying to keep her voice steady. "Almost as pretty as you and your brother. Although I reckon Enri has lost some of his looks to the worms by now."

Roki snorted, spraying saliva through his teeth. Wydrin saw the drops of moisture but didn't feel them land on her face. He was little more than a ghost – if only she could say the same for his blade. The enchanted gauntlet glowed softly in the darkness, touching the walls of the tent with a sickly orange light. Slowly she inched her hand through the blankets towards her sword belt.

"I will enjoy killing you," said Roki. "I will do it slowly, and by the end of it you will be begging to join my brother in the ground."

"You do everything slowly, Roki. It's very boring. How are you here? Where are you really?"

"I have made certain... sacrifices." Roki's grin widened, and for a moment Wydrin felt real fear make a grasp for her heart. There wasn't a scrap of sanity in that smile. "You made it easy, really." He held up the stump in front of her face. "Bezcavar rewards those willing to shed blood in his name, even when it's your own blood. I can find you, wherever you are. I can come to you when you are resting, sleeping, when you think you are safe."

Wydrin's questing fingers closed around the hilt of Glassheart.

"Making a deal with a demon doesn't sound like a very clever idea to me. Not the move of an intelligent man. Why am I not surprised? *Sebastian!*"

Roki jumped at her sudden shout, and glanced towards the tent wall as Sebastian sat up, his shape shadowed against the fabric. It was enough for Wydrin to get her free hand under the blade and push it firmly away from her throat. There was a sting as the sword cut into her fingers but then she was standing with Glassheart held out in front of her, keeping Roki's weapon at bay.

"What's going on?" Sebastian was rising and already she could hear Frith complaining in the tent on the other side. Roki scrambled back towards the entrance to the tent.

"I'll come back for you, little girl," he said. Wydrin flew forward, Glassheart flashing like steely death in the dark and she met his blade with tremendous force, hoping to break it and render him harmless, but the sword held. There was a loud ripping noise from just behind her as Sebastian tore a long slash in the tent wall with his own sword.

"Wydrin? What's happening?"

Lights were flickering on in adjacent tents, and in the soft red glow she could see a smear of her own blood along the edge of Roki's blade. Suddenly furious, she surged forward with a flurry of blows, pushing the last of the Children of the Fog to the front of the tent, where he staggered out into the night. She followed, bellowing threats, even as somewhere in the cooler part of her head she knew very well she could no more harm him in this form than she could mould the clouds with her hands.

"That's the way, little kitten," he called softly as he blocked one shattering blow after another. "Show me everything you have."

Wydrin became aware that the others had come out of their tents and were standing behind her, so she paused in her onslaught and took a few swift steps backwards, trying to get her breath back, to regain some control. Sebastian appeared at her elbow dressed only in a vest and a long pair of under trousers that came down to his knees. As he stepped into the light Roki's grin only widened.

"You as well? This is quite the reunion!"

"Do you know where Fane is?" Frith was pulling his bearskin cloak over his shoulders. Despite her anger, Wydrin took a moment to notice the taut muscles on his narrow waist. "Or the Lady Bethan? What of her whereabouts?"

Roki laughed, his voice as shrill as the wind. He waved his sword at them as though it were a tankard of ale and Frith had just made a particularly good joke.

"Fane? The man who left me for dead in that piss-soaked little town? I would sooner cut off my other arm than—"

All at once his ravings dried up. Ip, ghostly and slight under the white lamps, stepped in front of Sebastian. Roki's mouth dropped open in surprise.

"You!" He looked from the little girl to Sebastian and back again. "But how can you...? I don't understand..."

Ip tipped her head to one side, the gesture of a child contemplating which leg to pull off the spider next. Roki stumbled backwards, appeared to be about to say something else, and then vanished.

For a few heartbeats there was silence, before everyone started talking at once.

"Who the hell was that?"

"I thought we killed him in Pinehold!"

"Is he close? The power of the armour—"

Wydrin held up her hands for silence. A stiff breeze blew in off the lake, and quite suddenly she was very aware that most of her clothes were still in the tent.

"Yes, that was Roki, and no, I do not believe that he is nearby. He has traded with the demon that made his gauntlet to increase its powers, somehow, to enhance its range." She waved her hands impatiently as this only provoked more questions. "What I want to know is, why was he so scared of this little shrimp?" She pointed at Ip, who twirled on the spot and yawned hugely. "Well?"

"I don't know, do I?" she replied. "Can I go back to bed now?"

"It's time you left our company, I think."

Sebastian knelt so that he was face to face with Ip. The owner of the tents hadn't been best pleased with the hole they'd left in his silks so they'd been encouraged to leave. At knife point. Now the others were trawling the markets for provisions, and he and Ip stood at the back of a small audience watching a mummer's show. Periodically children would come round with hats, begging for coins.

"You can't leave me here," said Ip. Her voice was utterly flat. "I'm just a child."

"Really? Is that why Roki, a hardened assassin, near wet his britches at the sight of you? We both know what you are."

The girl blinked, and her eyes were blood red once more.

"Can you really do that, good sir knight? Ip is my priestess, true, but when I am not here she is still a child. One that has had a hard life. And you, the only person to show her a modicum of kindness, is to abandon her?"

Sebastian stood up.

"I've spoken to the mummer's company already. They're always looking for new blood to train up. They'll feed you, and get you some proper shoes. It'll be safer than travelling with a bunch of adventurers."

Ip reached out and took hold of his hand. For a moment Sebastian felt his resolve waver. She was so young, under it all – but then the tiny hand gripped his fingers hard, digging in sharp nails. Ip bared her teeth at him.

"You can't escape me, Sir Sebastian, as much as you'd like to. You wear my armour, and your sword is sworn to me." She tightened her grip until Sebastian was sure she'd broken the skin. "You think that by leaving me here your friends won't find out what you've done, *but your soul is mine*." She hissed the last, her face so contorted that she barely looked human, let alone a child. Suddenly it was quite easy to leave her behind.

Sebastian shook her off.

"I'm sorry, Ip, if you're still in there. Truly, I am."

He called to a short fat man with ginger whiskers, who was watching the show from the sidelines. The man waddled over at a pace.

"This is the girl, no?"

"This is her, Zevranna," said Sebastian. "She has no family. If you could find a place for her I'd be eternally grateful."

"Oh, but she has spirit, this one, I can see it!" Zevranna beamed at the child, while Sebastian cleared his throat.

"You could say that."

"I see a great future for you, girl. You will be a star! Ip, wasn't it?"

"Yes," said Ip. Her eyes were back to their icy blue. "It was."

"Worry not, my friend." Zevranna patted Sebastian's arm with a clammy hand. "I can see you are concerned for the child, because you have a good heart, but she will have a life few children can even dream off! Fame, fortune, the open road. It will be an adventure, no?" He addressed this last to Ip, who was unmoved. "Come." He held out his plump hand, and after a moment she took it. "I will introduce you to our other children. It will be grand!"

Sebastian watched them walk away. He expected Ip, or Bezcavar, to give him one last baleful look over the shoulder, but she never looked back. They disappeared into the crowd, who were roaring with laughter at the antics of the two men on stage. She would be better off, he told himself again. If they were to face Y'Ruen at the end of all this, then they didn't need a child to look after too.

Even so, he wasn't sure who he felt most sorry for – Ip, or her new carers.

They walked some distance from the settlement in the morning light, looking to put a reasonable amount of space between them and the tents before the griffins made their transformation. Wydrin stalked off in front, her shoulders hunched against the chill and her eyes on the ground. The cut on her right hand was sore but shallow, and she couldn't bring herself to ask Frith for assistance with it. Instead she concentrated on the mild throb in her fingers and tried not to think about Roki's face hanging over her in the dark, the cold bite of his blade... to be caught unawares, helpless... She kicked at a lump of dirt, sending it skittering across the grass.

"How could you not tell me?"

She glanced up to see that Sebastian had caught up with her.

"We'd only just found you again." The plaintive tone of her own voice only served to make her angrier. "And how am I supposed to tell you anything when you piss off in the middle of the night and leave me stranded in a town with one stinking tavern?"

"You told no one," Sebastian said. He was keeping his voice level, a tactic he always used in arguments and one that never failed to annoy the living piss out of her. "Roki could have attacked at any moment and you didn't think that was worth mentioning?"

Wydrin rounded on him, clenching her fists at her sides. The sharp pain of the cut was glorious, somehow. She welcomed it.

"Roki is my problem. And what are you keeping from us, exactly?" She nodded at Frith and Gallo following on behind. "Who was the kid? Or should I say, *what* is the kid? And where did you get that armour from? For years you only had bitterness for the Order but then you go running back to them, and they give you this armour." She took a step towards him and raised her chin. "I'm not buying it. And I'm no fan of brats but even I would question leaving a kid with a bunch of strangers."

"She's better off with them. Our path is too dangerous…"

She shook her head angrily, cutting him off.

"What happened in Relios, Sebastian? Why were you the only one to survive?"

Sebastian's eyes were very wide; he looked lost, and it frightened her. A moment ago she'd been ready to land one on his jaw but now she reached out and touched his arm.

"You can tell me, Seb," she said. "You're my sworn brother, aren't you? You can tell me anything."

For the briefest second she could see the shadow of the old Sebastian on his weathered face – kindness, weary patience, strength – and then it was gone. He shook her arm off brusquely.

"Y'Ruen killed them all, and I was lucky. I found the girl wandering, half-starved." He pulled at his beard and looked away from her. "Just as I told you. Frith, get these griffins ready, we've come far enough."

Frith caught up with them, the trio of birds circling overhead. He seemed about to say something, then apparently thought the better of it. He gestured at the birds and the wind roared into life about their feet. They twisted and grew until the griffins once more stood on the grass, their regal heads like carved statues in the sunlight.

Wydrin turned away from Sebastian and went to one of the animals. She patted the great creature's powerful neck, taking in the exotic scent of the beast, seashells and orange blossom and sweat.

"Let's go," she said, not looking at any of them. "Let's go to this blasted Rookery."

68

When Frith had been a boy, his older brother Leon had passed on to him a set of wooden toys. Pieces of the Blackwood skilfully carved to look like castles, horses, knights and people to rescue – everything he could need to create his own kingdom to rule over. When he was older Leon showed him how to carve the wood himself, so that he could add to the collection, just as Leon had done. Aaron Frith had carved all the great heroes – Alynn the Wise, Roland of Phen, The Steadfast Seven – and added them to his kingdom, making it, in his opinion, the greatest in all of Ede. On quiet days he would take all the pieces and build his city on the rug beside the Great Stairs, and when it was done he would go to the top of the landing and look down, pretending he was a god watching his loyal subjects from the sky.

Flying over the City of Verneh reminded him of this so strongly that for a moment he was dizzy; did he fly far above the world, or was he a child again, lost in that giant castle? He dragged his eyes back up to the mountains that loomed before them. He had been planning to pass the toys on to Tristan soon, he remembered. Well, he'd been thinking about it, at least. Tristan already had so many toys… Unbidden, a memory of his little brother came back to him; Tristan just learning to walk, patiently climbing his way up the great stairs.

I should have given them to him a long time ago, he thought. *Should have done so many things.*

In truth, aside from that trick of perspective, Verneh looked little like his wooden city. It was a sprawling place of white and yellow brick, lying between a wide river dotted with boats and a confusion of jagged mountains. Domes of green tile sprouted everywhere like elegant mushrooms. They called it, Frith remembered, the Silken City, because the surrounding forests contained giant silk worms, and it was said that even the poorest beggar in Verneh wore the finest clothes. Indeed, silk flags and banners of all colours flew from every roof, window and corner, bright and alive under the hot sun.

"Nice place," said Wydrin. "You'd think O'rin would live here rather than the mountains."

"Just like him to be difficult."

Frith pressed his heels to the griffin's sides and they took on a new burst of speed. He turned around to check that the other griffins were following. He saw Gallo leaning out to one side to watch where they were going, his skin grey under the sunlight, and Sebastian, his wild hair once more tamed in a braid. The griffins bowed their powerful heads and up they all went, leaving the city behind and climbing into thinner, colder air. Below them the lower reaches of the mountains were still covered in the thick foliage of the forest, but as they climbed higher the trees were fewer and fewer, until rocky fingers pushed through the ground, and they saw deep chasms and hidden caves. The air grew frigid, and soon Frith could see his breath in front of him in puffs of white vapour.

"Look," said Wydrin, pointing. There was snow here too, stubborn white highlights left over from some winter storm, preserved by the chilly air. "This is a strange place, hot on one side and freezing on the other. What do you suppose the Rookery looks like?"

"I suspect we'll know it when we see it."

In the end, that was partially correct. They flew back and forth over the mountains, looking for a gabled palace or a golden longhall, but saw nothing save for rocks, ice, and forbidding caverns. The griffins flitted back and forth, until eventually Wydrin nodded to the highest, most perilous peak. The central mountain rose from the others like the end of a broad sword, sheer sides tapering to a lethal point.

"I bet that's where it bloody is," she said. "If you can fly, and you don't want anyone popping over making a nuisance of themselves, that's where you'd stick your palace."

Even with the griffins Frith did not relish the idea of climbing to the top of that. It would be like touching the sky. Still, the map was somewhat vague on the precise location, with the letters R-O-O-K-

E-R-Y delicately scrawled across half the mountain range, and he had a terrible suspicion that Wydrin was right. Trust a sell-sword to sniff out the hidden temple.

They turned to approach the central mountain, and the griffins began to gain speed, as though they were starting to recognise where they were. Frith heard Sebastian shout with surprise as they all held on for dear life, and in moments they passed the peak and were above it, spinning in the thin cloud cover. Cold water droplets covered their skin and hair, tingling like a kiss in the dark.

"Can you see anything?" said Wydrin. She was leaning over, peering past the griffin's wings. "We must be directly over the top, I reckon."

Fog swirled beneath them, but there was a suggestion of solid ground somewhere down there.

"I can't see beyond this blasted mist." Holding the words for Fire and Control in his mind, he held out his bandaged fist and a small, almost delicate fireball the size of a duck's egg swam forth into the fog. The heat of it dissipated the mist into a fine rain, and the view became clearer. Gallo and Sebastian joined them, their griffins hovering like hawks pinpointing a kill.

"Well, gents, there it is," said Wydrin. Her voice was full of wonder. "We've found the Rookery."

69

It nestled atop the mountain like an improbable castle. And nestled was, Wydrin realised, exactly the right word for it. The Rookery was a complex confection of wood; not straight pieces cut from the flesh of the tree as a carpenter might build, with planks and arches and pillars, but an almost organic collection of vegetation, twisted together to form a tower, woven into shape like a bird's nest. It was difficult to be sure from their vantage point, but she was certain she could see branches, twigs, even whole trees, sculpted into one giant formation.

"By all the gods," Frith muttered from behind her. "Who could have made such a thing?"

"I think you've answered your own question there," replied Wydrin.

They circled the structure in a downward spiral. The outer wall was shaped like a crown, dipping down into troughs and then rising to peaks, where Wydrin imagined lamps had once been posted. In the middle of this was the tower, although it was unlike any she'd seen before. It rose out of the twisted wood to form a shape more like a tree than a structure built by a man. At the top there was a deep indent, like a bowl, and from there a series of ledges that could have been steps leading down to a hole in the middle of the tower. Wisps of cloud moved restlessly around the whole thing, as though the very sky sought to conceal it.

"We should land on the top," she said. "It looks to be the only way to get into the tower."

The griffins spread their wings and landed in the centre of the bowl with a flurry of squawking and black feathers.

There were nests here, hidden from the outside by the raised lip of the wall, like oversized pigeon lofts. As the adventurers dismounted, one by one the griffins retreated to the alcoves, making soft cooing noises at each other.

"Someone's glad to be home." Wydrin nodded to Frith. "What are you doing?"

Frith was removing strips of linen from his belt and tying them around the palms of his hands. Every time they'd paused on their long journey he'd painted new words on fresh pieces, hunched over the fabric with his ink pot and brush.

"Preparing for whatever might be down there. Can you give me a hand with this?"

Wydrin went to him and pulled his sleeves up. She took a strip and tied it around his forearm.

"What do you expect to find?" asked Sebastian. His face was wet from the clouds, and the cut on his cheek looked livid.

"I do not know," said Frith. "But if I've learned anything in the last month or so, it's that it is foolish to trust a god. Here, tie this last one to my left arm."

Wydrin frowned at him and gave the knot a swift jerk.

"I concur with you on that one, old man," said Gallo. He was looking away from them, up into the sky, almost as if he expected a giant flying lizard to swoop down from the clouds.

"What do they all do?" Seeing Frith with his arms and hands covered in the inky bandages made her think of the Culoss, the strange little men with blades for hands that had guarded the Citadel. To make that connection here, now, made her uneasy.

"A great deal," he replied, shortly. "I have the words for Fire, Force, Ice, Control, Hold, Constrict–"

"What about the healing spell?"

He glanced up at her, his lips pressed into a thin line.

"No."

Wydrin nodded. Ever since Jarath's cabin she'd suspected that the pink light had some sort of debilitating effect on the young lord. He'd limped for days afterwards, and there was the reappearance of the scar. If it had been anyone else she would have thanked him again, offered drinks, favours, anything, in recompense for what he'd done. But he was who he was, so she said nothing.

"The steps start from over here," called Gallo. He'd walked the circumference of the platform and come to a slim gap in the wall. Wydrin joined him, peering over the edge. The lower part of the Rookery spread out below them, leading to the crown-like outer keep. It was a very long drop.

"Are they supposed to be steps?" said Wydrin, entirely failing to hide the horror in her voice. "They're like ledges. Afterthoughts!"

"Who needs steps when you can fly?" said Frith from behind her. "I doubt O'rin had much use for them."

"Well, that's great," said Wydrin. "If I make it down those without throwing up, I'll buy everyone a pint."

She did make it, in the end, although by the time they got to the dark entrance way she felt as though her bones had been replaced with fish guts. The hole in the side of the tower was a lot larger than it had appeared from the backs of the griffins; the ceiling disappeared into darkness overhead. Egg-shaped globes sunk into the floor glowed with a ghostly white light, leading the way deep into the Rookery, and now that they were out of the wind, Wydrin paused to examine the walls more closely. They were, as she had suspected, made of a vast collection of scavenged bits of wood. She saw branches as thick as her arm in there, alongside pieces of driftwood worn smooth by the sea, and old barrels broken up and sunk into the walls like structural supports. There were other objects too; old nets, rotten feathers, seashells, even old bones sitting flush with bark and wood. They walked on down the tunnel until they came to a staircase spiralling down.

"Looks like this is the way," said Gallo, unnecessarily. Wydrin looked up at their faces, ghoulish in the light from the globes. She knew they were all thinking the same thing.

"I'm sure it won't be as bad as the last time we explored a weird old building," she said. "I mean, there's almost certainly no dragons in this one."

Sebastian ran a hand through his wild hair. His eyes looked haunted. "It certainly couldn't be any worse," he said.

"There is no point in discussing it," said Frith. He flexed his fingers, almost entirely hidden under bandages and ink. "We've flown halfway across Ede to get here."

"In that case, princeling, given you're the one with fireballs at your disposal, you can go first." Wydrin bowed low and swept a hand towards the stairs.

"Very well." Frith frowned at her and moved to the staircase.

"For what it's worth," said Gallo, following on behind, "I'm not entirely certain that using fire in here would be such a top plan. These walls are practically made of kindling, after all."

"I have many spells," said Frith shortly.

Wydrin touched the hilt of her sword. "Let's hope they're enough."

They descended into the Rookery.

The air was close, and somehow old, as though it had been trapped inside this ancient place for hundreds of years, even though logic suggested that a tower made of bits of wood should be draughty as hell. The wind was a distant memory, with only the occasional creak to remind them that they stood at the top of a mountain.

They walked winding tunnels lit by the strange, egg-shaped lights, following a gradual spiral down into the heart of O'rin's strange home. Frith and Wydrin moved slightly ahead, while Sebastian found himself walking next to Gallo. He stole a glance at his old comrade and was once again taken aback by how much he looked like a corpse. In the stark light of the lamps his face was a mask made of old paper, and he was starting to walk with a shuffling limp, as though the muscles in his legs had grown leathery and stiff.

"Does it hurt?"

Gallo looked up at Sebastian, and then away again. "Not as such, no," he said eventually. "It feels strange, unfamiliar. I can feel myself drifting apart, and that is unnerving. It is a terrible thing to know that your body no longer works as it should."

Sebastian didn't know what to say to that. He found himself looking at the walls instead.

"When Y'Ruen was finished with me, I felt like a ghost haunting my own body," continued Gallo in a low voice. "It is true that her presence probably saturates my soul by now. Being possessed or beholden to a being such as her... it leaves a mark."

Sebastian kept his silence.

"So," said Gallo, "do you want to tell me what happened to you?"

He shook his head irritably.

"You know full well what happened to me. It was your hand on the other end of the dagger!"

Gallo winced. A portion of the skin below his left eye tore with the pressure, revealing blackened flesh beneath. "That is not what

I'm talking about, as well you know."

"Why are you here, Gallo?" Sebastian's head was aching again. The sword on his back felt heavier than it should, to say nothing of the demon's armour. "So you're still walking and talking somehow. Why seek me out?"

"What else should I do?" There was anger in Gallo's voice now, or the beginnings of it. "Wander the world as a leper? I would rather go out fighting." He sighed, the anger seeping out of his words as quickly as it had appeared. "I thought I could help you in some way, Sebastian. That it might make up for some of what happened."

"For trying to kill me?"

"That *wasn't* me. I wanted to make up for leaving you in Creos, Seb. For not waiting like you said we should." The dead man took a deep breath, the air whistling through his rotting lungs. "I am truly sorry. You were right. We should have gone in there prepared. We should have gone in there together."

Sebastian scratched his cheek. The wound there, the one he'd cut in Bezcavar's name, seemed reluctant to heal properly. He didn't have room in his head for all this. There was no time, no space for apologies. "It hardly matters now," he said.

Up ahead Wydrin and Frith had stopped in front of a dark opening in the wall of the tunnel.

"This is it," said Wydrin. "There's nowhere else to go."

Sebastian leaned through the parting in the wood and looked down into a spherical chamber. There were more lights, revealing more of the twisted branches and warped tree trunks, and very little else. He could see no sign of any way out save for the one they stood in front of.

"There's nothing down there," said Frith. "Perhaps the god of lies was lying after all."

"We shall have to go down and look," said Sebastian, already shifting to climb down through the opening. It was only just big enough to take his frame. "I haven't come all this way for nothing."

"How would we get back out?" said Gallo. "It's a reasonable drop to the floor."

"We'll climb!" said Wydrin cheerfully, slapping him on the back. "Don't tell me you've never climbed a tree, Gallo?"

One by one they stepped through the hole and scrambled down the curved walls onto the floor of the chamber. Once they were inside Wydrin realised it was unnervingly like being closed inside a nest. One made for a truly monstrous bird.

"Look around," said Sebastian. "I want to be absolutely sure we're not missing anything."

They searched for some time, but aside from the soft, egg-shaped lights the chamber was largely featureless, and they found nothing.

"Perhaps what O'rin was keeping here was stolen," said Wydrin. She put her hands flat on the wall and leaned close, trying to see if anything lay beyond the branches. "Some enterprising sell-sword with a head for heights…"

Something in the darkness beyond the wall caught her eye. Something white. She hooked her fingers around the twisted section of wall, and suddenly the branches and roots shrank away from her, constricting and shifting like a living thing. The wall creaked alarmingly, and the others turned back, just as a white face loomed out at her.

In seconds Glassheart was unsheathed and in her hands.

"We've got company down here, Sebastian."

The man in the wall was almost impossibly tall, a full head and a half taller than Sebastian. He was bone white, as though he'd been carved from chalk, and, although he was entirely naked, he was oddly featureless – or at least, he was missing the usual features Wydrin looked for first in a naked man. He did have tattoos, or what Wydrin assumed were tattoos. Black swirls and shapes colonised his arms and his broad chest, and there were similar patterns on the smooth flanks of his thighs. His hair was as white as his skin, and pushed back from his forehead in strange, downy clumps. He stepped out of the chamber wall and regarded them with polite curiosity.

"You are not O'rin," he said.

His eyes were round, yellow and slightly too far apart to be comfortable.

"We're not, no," said Wydrin. "But we're, uh, friends of his. Who are you?" She was still gripping the sword tightly.

"We are his doves," said the chalk-white man. As he spoke, more sections of the chamber wall split open to reveal four men identical to him. Sebastian gave a low cry and drew his sword, while Gallo slipped the bow from his back and nocked an arrow. The men didn't appear to be carrying any weapons.

"We've been sent here by O'rin," said Wydrin. She glanced at the others. "He gave us a map."

"You will take us to where O'rin keeps his secrets," said Frith. He held up his hands in what he probably thought was a threatening gesture. The chalk-white man tipped his head slightly to one side in an uncannily bird-like motion.

"The Edenier," he said, and there was a low murmur from the other "doves".

"That's right," Wydrin nodded. "Our friend here is a mage. Sebastian and I have very sharp swords, and Gallo here will, I don't know, breathe on you. It's not pleasant, believe me."

The doves gathered round, peering curiously at Frith, who looked alarmed by the attention.

"You are not O'rin," repeated the first chalk-white man, "but you carry the Edenier with you."

"That's correct," said Sebastian. He moved out of the way slightly to let one of the tall men past him. Three of them now stood looking at Frith with an eerie kind of flat curiosity, like a bird watching something pink and worm-like in the grass. "We're here on O'rin's behalf. How long has it been since he was here?"

"The Rookery has been empty for longer than we know how to say," answered the first man. The others were touching Frith's cloak, examining the rough bear hide, while the young lord grimaced.

"Not completely empty though, right?" said Wydrin. She lowered her sword. The doves were unnerving, and they looked powerful, muscles taught across their shoulders and chests, but they were also softly spoken, with slow, precise movements. "I mean, you're all here."

"We sleep," said the first dove. "And we wait, and we guard."

"We haven't felt the touch of the Edenier for the longest time," said one of the others. "It is almost like having O'rin home."

"Well, old man," laughed Gallo, "it looks like you've finally found some friends."

The atmosphere changed instantly. The five doves turned to look at Gallo as one, and there was nothing slow or soft about the movement. The chalk-white man who had been talking to Wydrin was suddenly rigid with tension.

"You speak with her voice," he said.

"What? I…" Gallo backed away, looking hurriedly from one to the other.

"It is an echo, but it is there."

Wydrin raised her sword again. "Now, hold on a minute—"

The dove nearest to Gallo reached out one arm and grabbed him, quick as a snake. He picked the adventurer up like he was a doll, and shook him. Gallo's fine bow clattered to the floor.

"Her smell is all over him," the dove said, as if confirming something. "Y'Ruen has her finger on this one's heart."

"No," protested Gallo, "it's gone now, she's gone! For the love of the gods, man, set me down!"

But the doves were already changing. A dark purple bruising broke out over their foreheads and cheeks, and as Wydrin watched, stiff, jagged feathers burst through the skin, sprouting like crocuses in spring. The dove who'd spoken to her first turned to glare at her, and she saw that his yellow eyes had turned black.

"You brought an agent of our master's sister into his home?"

"We're here to find something that will *kill* Y'Ruen!"

The one holding Gallo threw him heavily into the wall. Wydrin clearly heard a number of bones snap.

"For thousands of years we have kept the Rookery safe, untainted. It was written onto our skins. It is our purpose, to keep the Rookery safe, for ever." The first dove, his face now twisted and distorted with the feathers, held his arms out to either side as if to embrace her but, instead, long, silvery barbs worked their way out of the skin on his forearms. They looked wickedly sharp. "We will kill you all for this."

70

Frith threw up his arms and a wave of pure force flew across the chamber. Wydrin felt the edge of it push past her and she stumbled, but it seemed to be little more than a summer's breeze to the doves, who stood where they were, unmoved. The one who'd been speaking to her tensed his arms and a shower of the silvery barbs flew towards them. Wydrin jumped back, but, as large as the chamber was, there was no cover, and she yelped as one of the barbs caught in the tough leather of her leggings.

"There is no need for this." Sebastian was advancing on them, his hands held in front of him, empty. "We are not here to harm you or O'rin."

"The Rookery must be cleansed," said the dove, and Wydrin realised with a start that the creatures were still changing. It was like watching a cake cooked for too long suddenly expanding beyond the pan – they swelled up, white arms becoming thick with muscle, shoulders widening, the definition of their faces melting like candle wax. Their heads became elongated and their mouths fell open like wet wounds, revealing rows of long, peg-like teeth, and the dark blue feathers sprouted all over, with silver barbs hidden in their depths. When the dove spoke again, its voice was a wet croak. "It is our purpose."

Sebastian shouted for calm again, but Frith had his arms outstretched and a stream of icy shards flew across the chamber, pelting harmlessly against the doves' feathery hides. The two at the front opened their huge, frog-like mouths and spat, long yellowish cords leaping from the backs of their throats. Wydrin cried out in disgust as one of the sticky ropes slapped against her leg and clung there. Instinctively, she grabbed at it to pull it away from her leathers but it was fearsomely sticky, and the slimy substance it was coated in burnt the unprotected skin of her fingers.

"Bastard stuff burns!"

And then all was chaos. Sebastian drew his broadsword and charged the doves, and the air was suddenly full of stinging rope and flying barbs. Wydrin hurriedly used Frostling to peel the cord away from her leg, only for another to wrap, whip-tight, around her wrist, pinning her arm to the wall. The same dove who had spat at her released a flurry of silver barbs, and only the vanbraces on her forearm saved her from a sudden blinding.

Frith appeared in front of her, covering her with the Edenier so she had time to cut the cord away, but Sebastian was not faring so well. He caught one of the doves across the chest with what should have been a killing blow from his sword, yet the strange, bruised flesh of the doves only peeled away, revealing more of the same below. Identifying Sebastian as the more immediate threat, they directed the full brunt of their attack towards him, and soon there was so much of the acidic cord attached to his legs and feet he could move no further, and his armour bristled with silver barbs.

Wydrin scrambled up and dived at the doves, dancing around their attacks, but her dagger found no more purchase on them than Sebastian's blade did. She came too close to one and it struck her, sending her flying back onto the curved chamber wall and winding her badly.

"Sebastian!"

Gallo was there, one broken arm held awkwardly to his chest, a sharp knife clutched in his other hand. He stood in front of Sebastian and began cutting away at the restricting cords, as fast as he could. The doves refocussed their attack on his unprotected back, sending a suffocating barrage of the burning ropes, but he ignored them, concentrating on his task.

Wydrin climbed to her feet again, pulling a needle-sharp barb from where it had lodged in her shoulder. She saw Sebastian say something to Gallo, but she couldn't make out the words. The blond man was now almost lost under a covering of the slimy threads; Wydrin could smell his dead flesh reacting to the acidic coating.

"The Edenier is useless against them," spat Frith, next to her. He looked furious. "There is one spell left to try…"

"Wait!" As Wydrin watched, Sebastian finally broke free of his bonds and charged towards the doves, his enormous broadsword held above his shoulders. The doves spat more of the cord but his momentum was too great, and this blow took the head from the nearest guardian, flinging it halfway across the chamber. There was no blood. "We might have a chance–"

But Frith already had his hands up and a curtain of fire swept across the chamber, so bright that Wydrin could barely look at it. The flames crashed over the doves and they went up like tapers, their dark feathers burning strange, oily colours. They screamed as one and Wydrin, her head already ringing from her collision with the wall, staggered back from the force of it.

Sebastian jumped back from the blaze, but the strings of cord they had spat in a sticky web across the chamber flared up, clearly as flammable as the unfortunate doves. In seconds the space was filled with bright lines of fire, and at the centre of it, the form of Gallo, wreathed in flame. Through the confusion of smoke and fire Wydrin saw Sebastian's eyes widen in horror at the sight of his friend.

"Gallo, get down!" Wydrin ran to him, meaning to push him to the floor, roll him in Sebastian's cloak, *something*, but he was already too hot to draw close to, everything that was recognisably Gallo lost in the churning light. The chamber itself was merrily ablaze too, and although the doves were no longer a threat, the hole in the wall above their heads that was their only exit was now ringed with fire.

"Frith," screamed Wydrin, "what have you done?"

She saw his face, half shrouded in smoke, and he looked stricken.

"Wait," he said, "I can fix this, I can…" Some of the strips of linen dangling from his hands and arms were starting to smoulder.

Wydrin stumbled against the wall, gasping for breath. The stench of burning hair and flesh and wood was coating the back of her throat.

"Hurry!"

Frith threw up his arms again, and an orb of blue light appeared at his chest. It grew, encompassing him, and then expanded to cover the entire chamber. When it hit Wydrin she cried out in shock – it was freezing, a cold so deep and complete it was like being hit with a wall of ice. She saw Sebastian's hair suddenly fringed with white where the sweat had frozen. There was a pause as the cold grew so sharp she could hardly breathe, and then the room was filled with a whirling cloud of thick ice particles.

Frith had conjured a blizzard.

He stood at the centre of it all, his arms outspread and an expression of fierce concentration on his face, and then he was lost in the white. Wydrin stumbled, trying to see what had happened to Gallo, but there was nothing but the snow. A strong hand caught hold of her arm and Sebastian was there next to her, his face white and his eyes closed against the cold. His lips were starting to turn blue.

"The fires!" she shouted in his ear. "Have they gone?"

"I don't – I can't see!"

There was a roar, although whether it was from Frith or the blizzard Wydrin couldn't tell, and for a few moments the cold grew to such an intensity that she was sure they would all die here, hearts stopped, frozen in their chests...

And then it was gone. The snow vanished abruptly, leaving drifts of ice on the floor and crusting the wooden walls. The doves were strange, twisted shapes, their enormous limbs curled in on themselves like the legs of dead spiders. They were dotted here and there with silvery smears, the only remnants of the metal barbs.

"By all the gods," said Wydrin. She pulled a lump of ice out of her hair and glared at Frith. "That's how magic works, is it? It's a bloody blunt instrument, that's what it is! Try to do anything with it and you're likely to get yourself killed!"

Frith was looking around the chamber. Parts of it were still smouldering, while other parts were covered in a layer of frost. He shook himself, as though trying to wake up from a dream.

"It saved us, didn't it?" he said. His voice trembled slightly. "We're still alive."

"Not all of us," said Sebastian. He was looking at a pile of blackened bones and ash. A skull, Gallo's skull, peeked out of the mess.

"I'm so sorry, Sebastian," said Wydrin. She went to his side. Whatever had been moving Gallo, whatever strange energy had been keeping him alive, it was gone now. "He went up so quickly, I couldn't get to him."

Sebastian looked away from her. "As far as we knew he was already dead, wasn't he? Dead since he walked into the Citadel."

Wydrin swallowed hard. Somehow Sebastian's cold manner was harder to take than Gallo's grisly death.

"What did he say to you?" she said, not truly sure she wanted to know. "Just before the end?"

He looked at her, his blue eyes icy in a face smudged with soot.

"It doesn't matter. Let's get out of this death-trap."

The Rookery gave up its final secret as they tried to leave the chamber.

Frith walked towards the wall, eager to get out of the stinking place, only to see the floor of twisted branches shrink away from his foot, revealing a smooth wooden door. There was a serene face carved into its surface, its mouth and eyes closed, and a slim handle that looked to be made of bone.

"Just like the door in Whittenfarne," he remarked uneasily.

"Is this it, then?" said Wydrin, peering over his shoulder. "We just had to burn down half his home to find the hidden entrance?"

"Who can guess at the minds of gods?" said Sebastian. He bent down and grasped the bone handle, wrenching the door open with rather more force than was necessary. Beneath there was a second chamber, much smaller than the one they stood in, with softer lights… and nestled at its bottom were four enormous eggs. Immediately Wydrin sat and dangled her legs through the opening, bracing her arms on either side.

"What are you doing?" snapped Frith. "There could be anything down there."

"Those have to be the spells, don't they?" she said, grunting as she lowered herself down. "There's nothing else here."

She made quick work of it, climbing down as easily as an alley cat, and then, with rather more difficulty, passing the four eggs back up, each big enough to fit a healthy lamb inside, let alone a baby bird. They were pale blue and speckled with brown spots, and there were symbols in a darker blue on top of each: a woman, arms held out as if to embrace the world, a pair of wolves, identical, and on the final egg, the sinuous shape of the dragon.

"One for each of his siblings, with the spells hidden inside," said Sebastian, his hand resting on the dragon-marked egg.

Wydrin pulled a face.

"Do you think O'rin *produced* these himself? Is it wise to go around breaking a god's eggs?"

"If O'rin cannot bring himself to warn us that his guards are less than friendly, then I don't think we should worry too much about his property. Let's smash it and get out of here." Sebastian ignored the surprised look Wydrin threw him and drew his sword.

Frith nodded.

"Do it, then."

Sebastian gave the egg with the dragon symbol a firm tap with the edge of his sword. There was a satisfying crack, and the egg fell to pieces. Inside there were a number of rolled-up maps, yellow with age. Wydrin was just pulling them out of the shards of eggshell when Frith took hold of her hand to still it.

"Look at the inside of the egg," he said, his voice low.

"The tricksy bastard!" cried Wydrin.

The words of the mages were written on the inside of the eggshell, curling jagged shapes that were all too familiar to Frith, all carefully printed on the delicate inner surface. Except that now, of course, they were a confusion of shards and pieces. A puzzle.

"How much do you bet that's the spell?" said Wydrin.

"Curse him," snapped Frith. "Here, we'll put the pieces into a sack and figure it out later."

They gathered everything together, trying not to break any more of the pieces, and Wydrin tied the sack securely to her belt.

"We are done here, I think." Frith cleared his throat, and glanced at the remains of Gallo. "Do you wish to...?"

Sebastian shook his head curtly and said nothing.

"Very well."

Frith marched over to the far wall and kicked at a large section of blackened wood until it started to break up. Chinks of blue and white began to show through the gaps, and a large section fell away into nothing, revealing the sky beyond. It looked impossibly clean and clear.

Frith cupped his hands around his mouth and began to whistle for the griffins.

71

Wydrin watched as Frith placed a piece of shattered eggshell next to another piece. Both were covered in the curling black shapes of the mages' words, although they meant nothing to her. Feeling that she should be doing something with her hands too, she pulled the game board towards her and began to arrange the tokens. Frith glanced up, a flicker of annoyance passing over his face.

"What is that?"

"It's a Chik-Choks set. You've never played?"

The lurid pink curtains of their booth twitched and a slim bejewelled man slid between them. He carried two tall glasses filled with liquid the colour of a violent sunset, and he was, in Wydrin's opinion, as beautiful as any woman she'd ever seen. He had eyes like pools of black ink and skin dusted with gold, while tiny red gems dotted his eyebrows. His cheekbones were sharp enough to put an edge on your sword. He smiled at them demurely and set the drinks down on the table, careful to avoid the wreckage of the eggshell.

"Are you certain I cannot fetch you anything else?" He eyed the contents of their table with more disappointment than curiosity. Somewhere, in another booth, Wydrin could hear soft laughter. "We have concoctions here that can ease all worries, and sooth all – rages." He looked pointedly at Frith as he said this. "Alternatively, this table can be upturned to provide a comfortable and sturdy bed." Now he was winking at Wydrin, who snorted into her drink. "All the booths at The Music of the Gods can be swiftly converted–"

"Thank you, we're fine," said Frith without looking up. The server raised one perfect eyebrow and retreated beyond the curtains once more.

"You know what sort of place this is, right?" said Wydrin.

"We needed somewhere quiet to do this." Frith was turning a shard of shell over and over in his hands. Some of it had been turned to powder in their flight from the Rookery, but he was confident there was enough left to make sense of O'rin's spell. "Somewhere private."

"It's certainly *private* enough," said Wydrin.

"What is this game, then?" he said, ignoring the look she was shooting him over the rim of her glass. "Is it, by any chance, a game you can play by yourself without bothering me?"

"All the best games involve two players, as well you know," said Wydrin. She picked up one of the tokens and placed it carefully on the board. It was carved from yellow crystal and shaped like a monkey. All the pieces were monkeys of differing colours. "Chik-Chok can be played with two or more players, and the aim of the game is to wipe your opponent's pieces from the board. It's called Chik-Chok because of the noise it makes when you put a piece down." She demonstrated by dropping the token onto the marble board, where it made a flat clacking sound, but Frith didn't look up from his work. "My dad taught me to play, a long, long time ago. He kept a set in his cabin, and when there was a storm he'd lose all the pieces. Never a set as pretty as this one though. How much do you suppose these crystals are worth?"

"Your father owns a ship?"

"Owned. He was a merchant sailor. With a touch of piracy on the side, when my mother was about."

Frith looked up.

"Your father is dead? I am sorry."

Wydrin chuckled.

"You don't pay too much attention to anything outside that handsome head of yours, do you, princeling? He's dead. He sailed off to investigate some wild tales and never came back." She shifted in her seat. Like so many things in Verneh, it was covered in silk and her bottom kept threatening to slip off. "The sea is unforgiving." She shrugged. "He's swimming with the Graces now."

"Which wild tales were these?"

"Oh, the usual stuff." She waved a hand airily, nearly knocking her drink over. "It's said that there is a beach where every grain of sand is a tiny jewel, and the natives carve their homes from giant pearls." She burped. "It's all bilge, really, but if there was a chance of a new trade route then my father would have been the first one up there."

"He sounds like an interesting man," said Frith, his eyes drifting back to the eggshell pieces. "If the maps are anything to go by, then it seems my father was more interested in wild tales than I ever–" His words stumbled to a halt. He pushed two shards together, and then a third piece, as big as the palm of his hand. He frowned.

"What is it?"

"There's a new word here," he said. "Jolnir didn't teach me everything, it seems."

"Can you read it?"

"Of course I can. It is the word for Seeing." He reached into his belt and pulled out the ink and brush. "From what I can make out, this part of the spell allows you to find your quarry wherever they might be."

Wydrin thought of Roki, leering over her in the night. Frith was unwinding a length of fabric from his belt.

"You're not going to do it here, are you?" she said, surprised at the sudden clench of alarm in her stomach. "What if the dragon senses you, or something? It could be dangerous."

"I won't try it with Y'Ruen, no. Where is Sebastian now?"

"He's mooching around the city." Wydrin hadn't been happy about it, but Sebastian seemed singularly uninterested in her opinion these days. "Said he wanted some fresh air." Why you'd need fresh air after flying around a bloody mountain on a bloody griffin, she did not know.

"Then I shall try with him." Frith deftly copied the word onto a long strip of the linen, and tied the bandage to his left hand. Wydrin watched his face become utterly still as he concentrated. After a few moments he muttered, "Sebastian."

"You should get some silk while you're here. More fetching than those bandages…"

There was a flicker of dusty light in the air above the table and her words died in her throat. The light hung in the air like a ball of bright cloud, and there were pictures moving on it. She could see a tiny version of Sebastian, as though she was looking down at him from some great distance. He was standing outside a temple, watching as a crowd filed through the door. Wydrin couldn't tell whose temple it was – Ede was rifewith gods and demons and nymphs – but it wasn't for want of detail. She could see tiny brown clay lanterns in the dirt either side of the door, and fish carved into the stone of the roof. After a few seconds the light flickered out and was gone.

"Now that is a useful trick." She was grinning with the wonder of it. "Imagine the trouble you could cause with this spell! The blackmail opportunities alone…"

But Frith wasn't listening. She knew what he was about to do before his lips began to form the name.

"Are you sure that's wise?"

"Fane."

And there he was. The man who had ordered the murder of the Frith family, who had tried to kill them all in Pinehold, the man who had worn a demon-enchanted helm to cheat death…

He was a little thinner than Wydrin remembered, his chin shadowed with stubble, but he was smiling and laughing. He sat in a tall throne carved of some dark wood, and there were grey stones rising behind him, partially covered by a ragged standard showing a black tree against a pale blue background. There were small white shapes in the branches that could have been fruits or stars.

"He is in my home!" Frith stood, sending the Chik-Chok board and its pieces flying. The vision of Fane stuttered and vanished.

"Hold on a minute, princeling."

"He is in my castle." Frith's face was contorted with rage. "I would know that throne anywhere."

He threw the curtains back and stormed out.

"You can't just go!"

Swearing loudly, Wydrin hurriedly gathered the pieces of the eggshell together and threw them back into their sack. She stumbled out of the booth in time to see Frith leaving through the front doors, his back rigid.

"You are leaving so soon?" The man with the jewelled face appeared at her side.

"It looks that way, doesn't it?" Wydrin pressed a handful of coins into his perfumed hand and ran out the door.

72

Outside it was early evening and the streets were full of Verneh's citizens just starting their night of revelry. She saw Frith some distance away, spotted the flutter of black wings descending towards him.

"Oh, great."

There was a rush of wind and several startled screams from onlookers, and the griffin rose out of the frightened crowd at an alarming speed. Frith didn't look back as he rose into the sky like an errant shooting star, and then he was lost in the gathering clouds.

Wydrin, the sack still clenched in one fist, raised her arms and then dropped them. "Oh, *great*," she said again. She had a moment to note that only one griffin had left with Frith when something sharp jabbed her in the lower back. She spun, Frostling drawn in her free hand, to find herself face to face with Roki once more.

"Oh no. Was that your pretty lord leaving you all behind?" he said. His face was oddly yellow, and she wondered if he was ill until she realised it was simply the light from an oil lamp. Wherever he was truly, he was standing near one. "Maybe you'll be mine to play with now."

The crowd were still gathering where the griffin had appeared, none of them taking any notice of the two people with their weapons drawn. Sebastian was out there somewhere, but he was too far away to help.

"I don't have time for this. Why don't you just piss off, Roki?"

"And why should I do that?" The sleeve of his shirt on his wounded arm was pulled right up, so she could see the red ruin of the stump. It didn't look like it had healed properly at all. "I can find you wherever you are. You can use those weird feathered creatures to go to the furthest corners of Ede, and I'll still be able to find you. I can haunt you forever." He raised the stump, and Wydrin grimaced.

"It's true I wouldn't relish having to look at your ugly face every day," she said, keeping her dagger pointed towards him. "It must have been doubly annoying for your brother, having to look at your face and his face in the mirror every day, poor sod. At least he doesn't have to put up with that any more."

Roki nodded. Not in agreement, but in acknowledgement that he expected nothing better from her.

"As annoying as that would no doubt be," continued Wydrin, "I still don't see why you don't just kill me. I know you can do plenty of damage, even in that form." She nodded towards the sword in his left hand. "So why not just kill me?"

Roki shifted his weight, his lips twisting as though he chewed a tough piece of gristle.

"It is better to haunt you, to slowly pick at your mind, and experience the pleasure of watching you fall apart. You'll never know a moment's peace, and I will enjoy every–"

"Hold on." Wydrin gestured with the dagger. "I don't buy it. You wish to irritate me to death from a distance, when you could just run me through with that sword? No, I don't believe it." She took a couple of steps forward, putting herself in range of his weapon. It was dangerous, but it would confirm what she suspected. "Is it because you can't smell me, Roki? Because if you kill me now, in this fog form of yours, you'd never get to taste my blood, or feel my heart slow under your fingers?"

She saw from the way his eyes widened that this was the truth. *This could be useful*, thought Wydrin. *I need to draw him out into a real fight, one where he's solid and I can run him through.*

"Wouldn't that be best, Roki?" She leaned in as though about to kiss a lover, close enough for him to see the pulse in her neck, and stopped. He could strike her down, but if she was right, he wouldn't. He would miss too much. "You like to taste the fear, don't you?"

"You know nothing about me!" There was sweat on his forehead now, yellow under the lamplight.

Wydrin stepped back. "I don't think you're anywhere near us now, not with the effort it's taking you to reach me. Am I right?"

Roki said nothing.

"Come and meet me in the Blackwood, Roki," she said, her voice soft. "I will be there, waiting. Come and find me there, and bring more than this ghost version of you. Then we'll have a *real* fight."

His lips twisted, as though he wanted to say more, and then he vanished. Wydrin let out a breath she didn't know she'd been holding, and pushed Frostling back into its scabbard.

"Just one disaster at a time," she muttered. "That's all I'm asking."

73

The Blackwood passed below him like a storm-darkened sea. There was a roaring in his ears, although whether it was the wind or the churning of the Edenier, Frith couldn't tell.

He is in my home.

The vision seemed to hang in front of his eyes, immovable. The man who had ordered the invasion of the Blackwood and the murder of his family was now sitting on the Blackwood throne. *My father's chair.* Lord Frith had sat there, listening to the concerns of his people, or reading documents, or doing any of a hundred tasks that demanded his attention. And Leon should have sat there next, and then his sons, if he had them, or Frith, if he did not. Instead, his brother had bled to death in his own dungeon. In the vision provided by the Edenier, Fane had been lounging in the chair, grinning at his guards and whoever else he'd assembled there. *Grinning,* thought Frith, *because he got away from me. Because he escaped before I could have my vengeance. I could have killed him in the tower at Pinehold, I could have, but the opportunity was snatched away from me.*

He dug his fingers into the thick black feathers around the griffin's neck, urging the great animal onwards, until he saw it; Blackwood Keep rising out of the ocean of trees, grey as the skies above it, a solid formation of smoke-stone and glass, flags and lead.

"Home," said Frith. The word was torn from his lips and scattered to the wind, but it remained on his heart.

They flew over the smattering of buildings that nestled outside the castle, beyond the first set of tall grey walls and landed lightly in the outer keep. There were shouts from the guards on lookout, and one or two arrows shot past Frith to clatter against the flagstones, but they seemed oddly distant. The griffin became a bird again and flew up to the higher reaches of the main tower, and Frith absently threw a wall of flickering white force up to the men with the arrows. There were screams, followed by a handful of thumps and crunches as they landed in the forest beyond.

Frith flexed his fingers, and remembered.

They had been taken entirely unawares. Lady Bethan's men were experienced woodsmen, travelling through the trees in silence, their faces smeared with mud and hidden easily under a cloudy night sky. There was a fierce fight at the southern gate, waking him from a deep sleep – Frith had been out late that night, and had fallen asleep still clothed – and he'd gone running to the window. He'd seen the carnage in the courtyard below and stared, unbelieving. It had seemed unreal, like a waking nightmare.

Now, as he stood in the courtyard of a home he hadn't seen for months, a guard came straight at him, a spear gripped tightly in both hands. Frith looked at the man's face, oddly constricted under the leather cap he wore jammed down over his ears. Had he been here, that night? Had he charged the inner keep's doors? Had he been the one to drag Tristan from his bed?

Frith saw the word for Fire in his mind and that seemed right, so he held up his hand and the guard was a churning mass of light. Frith heard the screaming, could even smell the flesh boiling off the man's bones, but distantly, distantly.

He moved on. The gate to the inner keep had already lost its small contingent of guards – they'd seen what was coming and had quite wisely decided to relocate to another part of the castle – but it was a thick, heavy door, and barred from behind. Frith stopped to consider it.

On that night he'd run down the great stairs and found his father and his brother Leon in the main hall, both hurriedly strapping on armour. Lord Frith was shouting instructions to the castle's men, and the huge door was shuddering as something enormous pounded on it from the outside. Frith had seen swords shining under the lamplight and felt instantly foolish. Where was his sword? His armour?

"Aaron," his brother had called. "Go and find Tristan, he'll be frightened."

But Frith hadn't done that, had he? He had wanted to fight, wanted to stand with his father and the men from the castle. When the door had shattered into a hundred splintered pieces he'd watched his father's face become rigid with anger, turning his scholar's eyes cold.

Now, Frith brought forth the words for Force and Control and punched through the thick wooden panels. The metal hinges twisted and buckled, and he was through into the inner keep, the towers where his family had lived and died rising above him like a monument. Here there were more guards.

"Stay right where you are!" shouted one. Frith felt his eyes settle on the man, taking in his ruddy face, the scuff marks on his leather armour. They were all brandishing swords and shields, although as yet they seemed reluctant to rush him.

"I am one man. And I've not drawn a sword," he pointed out in a mild tone of voice. The guard who'd spoken gave a strangled laugh.

"Such as you don't need swords. You'll put those hands of yours down or we'll cut your bleedin' throat."

"These hands?" asked Frith, holding them up, and the Edenier rushed out of him like a tidal wave. Ribbons of green light slammed into the assembled men and sent them flying against the stonework behind. There were cries as bones shattered, and when the moaning continued Frith sent a shower of ice shards at them, each with a point as deadly as Wydrin's daggers. The moaning stopped.

And finally, he was here. He pushed open the doors to the great hall and was greeted with a thick, metallic smell. It was so familiar that for a moment he couldn't tell if it was a memory leaching into the here and now, but no, the stench was here too, the stink of...

... blood, flying in a bright shout from his brother's temple as a huge man, bristling with plate armour, threw a gauntleted fist at his head. Leon stumbled backwards, still raising his sword, his eyes unfocussed. There were strangers in the hall now, so many that Frith had already lost sight of his father, and the castle guard with their pale blue surcoats were like flecks of snow on a black field. He could hear a woman's voice, shouting orders from beyond the door, and in the back of his mind was the knowledge that the castle was surely taken, but still Frith snatched a sword from a fallen body and cut the throat of the man in front of him. It was the first time he'd killed a man, the first time he'd ever wielded his sword in anything but a lesson or a competition, and then more men surged forward, red faces painted on their shields like an army of demons. Frith gritted his teeth as a fierce rage filled his chest. *They will all die,* he'd thought, *they will all die under my sword!*

He'd never seen the man who struck him.

Now, looking down at the flagstones where, no doubt, he'd fallen, Frith could only remember a sudden thunder-clap of pain and a burst of light behind his eyes. After that, nothing. Darkness and then the dungeon, and the cunning fingers of Yellow-Eyed Rin.

A rising tide of whispers brought him back to the present. Frith raised his head and looked at the ruin of the hall.

Always a wide, empty place, with windows too close to the ceiling to give much light and four great fireplaces lining the walls, the hall was now filled with suffering; an abattoir with marble pillars. Fane sat on the throne, just as Frith had seen him, although now he was rising from his seat. To all sides were frightened men and women and children, bound at the ankle and wrist with steel cuffs, while the guards stood at their sides, swords ready. In the centre of the room was a huge iron cauldron Frith recognised from the kitchens – it was the one the cook only ever used at festivals and celebrations, when huge numbers of people needed feeding. As he drew closer he saw it was filled almost to the top with blood. Other shapes floated in the crimson soup, shapes Frith didn't care to dwell on. Instead he looked at the prisoners. Did he recognise some of their faces? He thought he did. He saw the open wounds on their arms and legs, the bloody stumps where limbs had been removed. He saw the blank, exhausted terror on their faces, written in bruises and scars.

"The prodigal son has returned!"

Fane was stepping down from the dais, an eagerness to his steps as though he longed to greet a cherished friend. The half-helm was already wedged over his ears. Frith said nothing.

"I'm sure your people are glad to see you." Fane gestured at the prisoners chained to either side of the hall. Frith doubted they even knew who he was; all sense looked to have been beaten out of them a long time ago. "How does it feel to be home?"

"You have not taken very good care of my castle." As well as the cauldron of blood the floor was smeared with gore, and all four of the fires were alight, so that the smoke and heat were oppressive, even in such a large room. Fane approached the cauldron and tapped the edge of it with one fat knuckle.

"Offerings to Bezcavar. Your good people here have been helping to feed the cauldron." The guards by the prisoners were restless now, watching the two men closely. Their leader had given them no orders to seize the man who'd walked into the hall, but no doubt they'd listened to the sounds of his approach and were nervous. Fane, however, looked unconcerned. "Your offering will be gratefully received, no doubt. The suffering of those with power is prized by Bezcavar, Prince of Wounds. Oh, that reminds me, we have a friend of yours here."

Frith watched as Fane went to the line of prisoners and dragged a body out from behind them. It was a woman whose chestnut hair was now caked with blood and filth, and her eyes were wide and sightless. It took Frith a few moments to recognise her, and then it slotted into place. The last time he'd seen her he'd been tied to a rack, and she had been looking down at him with a mixture of contempt and exasperation. The Lady Bethan.

"You killed her?"

"A trusted ally is a fine sacrifice to Bezcavar," said Fane. He pushed the hair from her face almost fondly, and then dropped her to the floor. "Although I think I can tell you, Lord Frith, that she'd long since outlived her usefulness. Istria was always her cause, not mine, and when we couldn't find that vault of yours –" he shook his head and smiled, as though at a poor joke – "well, she started making demands of me."

The strange veil of distance that had been hanging over Frith since he stepped off the griffin disappeared, and all at once he was furious. Frith felt the Edenier rise up inside him, and he had to clench his fists to keep it from pouring out in a tide of rage. *She was mine to kill!*

"You had no right to do that," he spat, before taking a deep, steadying breath. "I've come to put an end to this, Fane. You'll die here, now, under my roof and by my hand."

There was a stirring from the guards then, but Fane waved them down. Instead he drew a sword from the scabbard at his waist. The blade was still smeared with blood from some earlier kill. *He does not even keep his weapons clean.*

"You forget." Fane tapped the helm lightly with his free hand. "You cannot harm me while I wear this. I only bleed for Bezcavar."

"And you forget what I am capable of!"

A guard made a run at him, short sword in his hand, and Frith supposed he must look an inviting victim; he carried no obvious weapons and wore traveller's clothes, not armour. He tossed a hand towards the man, not quite looking at him, and pictured the word for Cold in his mind. The guard gave a strangled scream as his hands twisted in on themselves, blue with ice. More came at him, abandoning their posts at the sides of the prisoners, and Frith knocked them aside as though they were pine cones. Here it was, finally, the control he'd needed the last time he'd faced Fane, when his body had burned with a fire he could not direct.

"You have learned a few tricks," said Fane. There was a false note in his voice now, an attempt at jollity that wasn't quite succeeding. "I'll give you that."

The men he'd scattered were trying to rise. Frith held up his right hand, covered in bandages, and slowly closed his fingers into a fist. Force. Control. Crush.

Their bones shattered, making a noise not unlike a knot of wood popping on a fire. There were screams. Fane came forward now, his sword out in front of him. The skin around his scars was paler than it had been before.

"There's no point to any of this, Lord Frith, when you know you can't kill me."

"Oh yes," said Frith. "The helmet."

He sent a wave of force at Fane, but it passed over him like a summer breeze. A ball of flame crisped the leather of his jerkin, but did little else. And then Fane was on him, the sword flying through the air with terrible weight. Frith jumped away, the tip of the weapon missing him by inches.

"I don't know where the rest of you Friths are," Fane was saying through gritted teeth. "So I'll chuck you out in the forest somewhere. Could be that the same bears who ate your family's leavings will have you too."

The sword came again and again, a silvery arc pushing Frith back and back. He would have to be fast now, and precise, more precise than he'd ever been with the Edenier. Because Fane was right. If now, after all this, he still couldn't kill him, then what was the point of anything?

He pictured the word for Fire, the word for heat, and kept it still in his mind even as he danced nimbly out the way of Fane's strikes. Next to it he pictured the word for Control, and narrowed that control down to a fine point. And then he aimed the spell at the top of Fane's head.

The effect was immediate. The dusty iron of the helm went from black to a rosy red in the space of seconds, growing brighter and brighter until Fane gave a strangled shriek and yanked it off. The hair underneath was smouldering, and his cheeks and forehead were raw with burns. It was as Frith had hoped: Fane could only bleed for Bezcavar, and as the helm was an extension of the demon it could harm him.

It clattered to the floor, and Fane took a few hurried steps backwards. Smoke was rising from his head and there was a sweet scent of cooked flesh in the air.

"It doesn't matter!" His eyes were very white against his scorched skin. "Bezcavar will protect me! I am his faithful servant!"

"Only a fool puts his faith in demons."

Frith reached out with the control, still focussed down to a fine point, and aimed towards the big man's chest. There was an explosive tearing, and the leather jerkin was suddenly a ragged ruin pierced with shattered ribs. Fane fell backwards, stumbling into the cauldron and upsetting its contents all over the floor. He wriggled in the mess, making an odd mewling sound as he tried to scream through lungs that were no longer there. Frith looked down into his face, noting with pleasure the panic in his eyes as the life seeped out of his body.

"Your blood will feed the trees of the Blackwood." He placed his boot against the dying man's cheek and leaned on it, pushing his face towards the flagstones. "Now and forever."

74

"Well, I suppose we can guess what happened to Fane, then."

Wydrin and Sebastian stood at the gates to Blackwood Keep in the warm afternoon sunshine. They were both dishevelled from their somewhat frantic flight across Ede, and in the trees at the edge of the forest a pair of black birds were having a well-deserved rest. From where they stood the castle looked empty – no sign of any guards on the walls – but a single body was slung over the battlements, hanging from a rope like a bag of offal. The man's chest was a red ruin, punctured here and there with fragments of what Sebastian assumed were bone. It was unnerving to see a body like that, turned almost inside out. His head looked like it had been boiled at some point, but they could see enough of his face, and its scars, to recognise him. It seemed Fane had met an eventful end.

"Do you think Frith will still be here?"

Wydrin shrugged. "Where else would he be?"

At that moment the heavy gates jerked open and a waxen face fringed with soft grey hair peered out at them. The man wore ragged, homespun clothes with a slightly stained surcoat over the top. He kept trying to smooth it down as he talked.

"Y-You are the sell-swords?" One of his eyes was swollen down to a crack.

"We are," said Wydrin, a note of surprise in her voice.

"He said you would probably turn up." The grey-haired man beckoned them towards the gate. "You'd better come in."

As they followed him into the castle, the man told them that his name was Eric and he was the new groundskeeper, appointed by Lord Frith himself.

"You know he's not dead, then?"

"Oh yes, miss. We could hardly miss him, really, what with him turning up at the castle and being a mage now and everything."

Once they were inside the keep Sebastian saw that the place wasn't deserted after all. There were people here, moving slowly through the grounds, most carrying sacks and crates, others tools and weapons. Almost all of them appeared to have been injured in some way, and Sebastian saw plenty of bloodstained bandages.

"We're trying to put the place back to rights," said Eric. He didn't look at them as he spoke, but nodded firmly to himself. "Been too long under that monster's rule."

"What happened to Fane's men?" asked Sebastian.

Eric frowned at the use of the man's name.

"Our lord dealt with them, so he did. May the gods bless him."

They followed Eric through a set of double doors into a great throne room. There were people in here too, mostly mopping the floors – Sebastian couldn't help noticing that the water in their buckets was pink – and there was a huge cauldron turned on its side, empty. The scent of soap was overpowering.

"Were these people at the castle before – before Frith came?" asked Wydrin.

"Aye," said Eric. "They was all here, in chains, before our lord freed them. Now we're restoring the castle to how it should be."

Frith was sitting on the throne at the far end of the room. Long blue banners embroidered with black trees hung from the walls, and his white hair looked bright against them. His hands were curled over the ends of the armrests, but his shoulders were still tense and he did not look up as they approached.

"My lord," said Eric. He bowed once then decided he hadn't done it properly the first time, so he bobbed up and down for a bit. "The guests you were expecting?"

Frith raised his head. His grey eyes were as cool as distant clouds. "I suspected you would follow me."

Wydrin laughed, although there was an uneasy note to her voice.

"We don't have a lot of choice, do we, princeling? You're the key to getting rid of this dragon." Frith didn't answer. "Thanks, by the way, for leaving us in Verneh with a big sack of mystical eggshells, and, by the way, the bar bill."

"You knew where I was going," said Frith. His words were short, clipped at the ends.

"Well, yeah, but that's not really the point." Wydrin crossed her arms over her chest.

"We still need you to figure out the spell," Sebastian broke in. "Y'Ruen will be in Ynnsmouth by now, and I dread to think of the damage she will be causing. We must stop her."

Frith looked away from them, as though they talked of nothing more than a spot of bad weather, or the year's harvests.

"There is much to be done," he said eventually, gesturing at the hall with its freshly scrubbed flagstones. "Although word of his death is spreading, some of Fane's men are still in the Blackwood. They are melting into the night, making their way to Istria or elsewhere. I've sent messengers to all the settlements, letting them know there is a Frith on the Blackwood throne once more." His right hand gripped the armrest so tightly for a moment that his knuckles turned white. "There is still much to do."

"Are you even listening?" Wydrin took a few angry steps forward.

Frith stood, not meeting her gaze.

"I've had rooms prepared for you both," he said. "I'm sure you will want to rest." He stepped down from the dais and left the room through a curtained doorway to the right of the throne.

Wydrin turned to Sebastian, her eyebrows disappearing into the thatch of her fringe. "What do you suppose that was all about?"

"I'm not certain," said Sebastian. "But I think we might be in trouble."

When Wydrin woke the next day it took her some time to remember where she was. She looked up at the billowing white sheets covering the top of the four-poster bed and felt silks under her skin.

What have I been up to, to end up in such a fancy bed?

It did not take long for it to all come back. Fane's shredded body hanging from the castle walls, Frith's head bowed, not looking at them. As Sebastian had said: trouble.

Picking up her clothes from where she'd dropped them the night before, Wydrin looked out the window to the courtyard below. It was a bright day, with great chunks of cloud like torn bread dotting the sky, and, judging by where the sun was, she'd been asleep for longer than she'd intended. Swearing under her breath and hopping to get into her trousers, she left the room and found herself at the top of a set of spiral stairs, which she followed down and down until she found a small yard, lazy with captured heat.

From there she wandered, padding quietly through the castle and the grounds, taking note of the people running back and forth with supplies and tools. It was an empty place, sombre grey walls rising on all sides, and they were rushing to fill it. She supposed that was a good thing, but what of Frith? What would fill him now that his vengeance was satisfied?

Eventually she found him at the top of the tallest tower.

"I don't know how you can live in a place like this," she said, leaning on the doorframe. "Don't you get lost all the time?"

Frith looked up. He was sitting in a room full of empty bookcases, at a table that looked as though it had been borrowed from somewhere less regal. The small desk was covered in papers, and there was a pile of sacks and boxes stacked under the window.

"You get used to it," he said, turning back to the pages in front of him.

Wydrin came into the room cautiously, keeping her eyes on the young lord. "I like it though," she said, running a hand over the wall. "All this space, great views. I bet you've had some wild times here." As soon as the words were out she regretted them, but Frith didn't appear to notice.

"This was my father's study," he said. "He would sit in here at all hours, with just a couple of lamps lit..." His voice trailed off.

There was a cough, and Sebastian appeared at the door. Wydrin found she was almost glad to see him, although he'd certainly looked better; his eyes were shadowed, and the scab on his cheek was livid.

"You found your way here, then," she said, injecting as much cheer into her voice as was humanly possible. "As I was just telling the princeling, I practically had to interrogate a girl with cabbages to find my way–"

"Have you looked at O'rin's spell again yet?" said Sebastian. He came over and stood in front of Frith's desk, casting a shadow over the papers. "We don't have much time."

Frith looked up at him. There was some of the old anger in his eyes. "You are standing in my light."

"What is it you're doing, anyway?" asked Wydrin. She poked hopefully at the bags by the wall, looking for anything bottle-shaped. "What is all this stuff?"

"I am taking stock of what little Fane left behind."

Wydrin spotted something black and blood-stained in the corner of one of the crates, so she fished it out. Fane's helm was even heavier than she had imagined, and it still smelled slightly of burnt flesh.

"This has got to be valuable," she said, holding it up to the light so that she could see the delicate runes engraved into the surface. She glanced at Sebastian, and noticed two things at once: first, that Sebastian looked afraid, and second, that the exotic shapes engraved in the helm matched those of the armour Sebastian wore.

"Where did you say you got that breastplate again, Seb?"

Sebastian said nothing.

"Because it looks an awful lot like this helm. Like it might be part of a matching set."

"It is the same," agreed Frith, looking from the helm to the breastplate. "And the same as the gauntlets the Children of the Fog wore."

"Sebastian," said Wydrin, trying to keep her voice level. "What have you done?"

"It was the only way I could survive," he said hurriedly. There was sweat on his brow. "The attack from Y'Ruen, you didn't see it. How else could I live through that? I was trying to save them."

"The armour protects you?"

"Bezcavar protects me," he said, too quickly. "My sword is sworn to him, and in return I was unstoppable. They were dying in their hundreds. You weren't there!"

"You have become like Fane," said Frith, an expression of enormous distaste on his face. "The lackey of a demon."

"I have not!" Suddenly Sebastian was shouting. There were dots of colour high on his cheeks, very red against his pale skin. "I did what needed to be done!"

"And what of your gods, Sebastian?" Wydrin threw the helm back into the crate with a crash. "Wasn't your sword sworn to Isu? Does that mean nothing?"

"What do you care?" spat Sebastian, his face twisted into an expression of such bitterness Wydrin found herself taking a step away from him. "You've never given the slightest thought to the gods."

"*You* cared, that was the point!" she cried. "All those years following the code of your stupid knights despite what they did to you, praying to your stupid mountain gods. You are better than this! Better than a demon that demands pain and blood for his favours."

Words ran out, and there was silence between them all. Wydrin found that she was breathing hard, as though she'd just run up the stairs.

"Maybe I'm tired of being the good one," said Sebastian eventually.

All at once, she couldn't bear to be in the same room as him. She stormed out, taking care to kick the door on the way, and she fled down the stairs, and out of the gates.

Wydrin marched until she reached the treeline and there she paused to catch her breath. The air under the trees was still and cool, and full of the rich green smell of the forest. She breathed in deeply, closing her eyes. It would all right, she told herself. Seb might have made a stupid decision, but it was nothing that couldn't be undone. She would find this demon herself if she had too, and force it to take the oath back. It might be a demon, but she was bloody annoyed and–

There was a snapping of twigs behind her, which was all the warning she got before something heavy connected with the back of her head and the forest exploded in a sea of black stars.

75

Frith moved restlessly from room to room, peering into corners, running his hands over the bare stones of poorly lit passages. He tried to remember how they'd looked before, when the place had been full of people and life; the library heavy with books, his mother's room quiet with memories and the ghost of perfume. Now and then he caught himself looking for things that were no longer there, like the painting of a ship that had hung in Leon's room, or the rows of steel pans that hung from the kitchen ceiling. None of these items were worth very much – from what he remembered, his brother's painting had been a cheap thing picked up in a local market – but they were all gone, just the same. Everything his family had ever chosen, or made, or touched, had been carted off and sold, or thrown outside to be burnt like leaves in the autumn. Fane had kept a few of their things to make the castle habitable, but those items that made the place feel like a home were long gone.

He paused in his brother Tristan's room. It was as bare as all the others, with just the wooden bed frame remaining. He bent to look at the back of one of the struts where he and Leon and Tristan had carved their names once. It had been a fancy of Leon's that they should mark every room in the castle with a secret sign that only they would know. At the time it had seemed faintly ridiculous to Frith. After all, wasn't the entire castle a tribute to the Frith family name? Every stone, every room, every tower was indelibly marked with their being. Like most of Leon's enthusiasms the idea hadn't lasted more than a few hours, and Frith found himself regretting that. With everything so empty, was this still their home?

"I have taken the castle back," he said aloud to the empty room.

"I killed him, Father, the man who did this to us."

There was only the answering silence. Dead, they were all dead. All of his enemies, and all of his family. What now, then?

Eric appeared at the door, his feet not quite daring to step over the threshold.

"My Lord, the new smith has arrived from Barkhome. He asks if you have any specific instructions."

"Instructions?"

"Well, my lord, there's a lot to repair, a great many things to replace, and he wondered if there was anything you wanted done first?"

A great many things to replace. For a moment Frith felt dizzy, as though he stood on the precipice of a cliff with only a looming darkness below him. The darkness, so long ignored, was calling to him to jump. He staggered back a step, his leg throbbing with remembered pain.

"I don't care," he said, his voice harsher than he'd intended. "Do whatever you think best. And do not disturb me."

Later, he found himself back in the Great Hall. The floors had been scrubbed, the fireplaces cleaned, and someone had even thought to replace the ragged banner behind the throne. It was a little makeshift, and Frith suspected someone had put it together in a hurry in the last couple of days, but it was bright and clean and full of hope. He turned away from it to see Sebastian striding across the hall towards him. The knight didn't look any better for his brief stay at the castle. His long black hair was unkempt, despite his attempts to tie it back, and although he'd trimmed his beard it did little to distract from his gaunt face.

"Wydrin is missing," he said shortly.

Frith sat in his father's chair, glad to get the weight off his leg for a moment.

"I suspect it's more likely that she is simply not speaking to you. Bezcavar was responsible for a lot of suffering in Pinehold. A lot of suffering in this very hall." He remembered the cauldron of blood. "I'm surprised you have forgotten this so soon."

Sebastian shook his head. He still wore the breastplate and the greaves, and the demon-sworn sword was still slung across his back.

"Wydrin would have cooled off enough to come and start another fight with me by now. No one's seen her since she stormed out."

"Have you checked the kitchens? I expect she's already drinking me out of wine."

"She's not there." The big knight's eyes were wide and bloodshot. "I have looked everywhere. I spoke to the guards on your gate and they saw her walk to the edge of the forest, and she hasn't returned."

"That's your answer, then," said Frith. He shifted in the chair, uncomfortable. He'd hoped to talk to her before she left, he'd wanted – well, he wasn't sure exactly what he'd wanted, but it wasn't this. "She's had enough of the pair of us, no doubt."

"There was blood." Sebastian stepped up to the throne, lowering his voice. "I went out to where they said she went, and... since I swore my sword, it's almost like I can smell it. As a dog does." He took a slow, steadying breath. "There was fresh blood on the grass. If it was hers, then she may have been badly injured."

Frith flexed his fingers. There was a tightening in his chest, although whether it was the Edenier or something else he wasn't sure. "Are you certain?"

Sebastian's face was grim. "I need you to find her as you found Fane. Can you do that?"

Frith stood. Since he'd returned to the castle he'd removed all the linen strips from his hands, and placed the ink and the brushes in his father's study. It had felt like lifting a great weight from his shoulders.

"Come with me."

The first thing Wydrin was aware of was the smell. Sour and rich and slightly sickly, it was the stench of old meat and strange chemicals left in jars too long. It coated her throat and made her cough, which in turn forced her to open her eyes. There was a skeleton hanging just above her, its bones yellow with age and its arms stretched out to either side as if to embrace her.

She jerked up, but there were cords digging into her arms and legs, and a thunderous pain in the back of her head that made everything go dim for a moment. She slumped back, taking deep breaths and trying not to choke on the smell.

"What...?"

Craning her head up as best she could, she looked around the cramped room. There was indeed a skeleton in the ceiling, directly above the long table she was tied to, but there were lots of other bones too, all set into the walls, and where there weren't bones there were uneven shelves filled with jars and bottles of all sizes. A fire burned in a fireplace in the corner of the room, and that was where she discovered the main source of the smell; a corpse was curled there behind the grate, its head and shoulders now a blackened mess in the centre of the fire. It was naked, and she could see that it had once been an elderly woman with sallow skin and a deep scar down one arm. Wydrin swallowed hard. The old woman's feet were thick with dirt, as though she went around constantly barefoot. *Not any more you won't*, thought Wydrin.

There was a crash from behind her, a door being thrown open that she couldn't see, and Roki strode into the room. The smell was on him too, a feverish hot stink, and he looked very little like the handsome boy with the cruel eyes she remembered from Pinehold. His silvery hair was lank and matted to his head with sweat and dirt, and the bones of his face were too evident through skin that looked grey. His eyes at least were filled with energy. They glittered with hate as he caught sight of her.

"You're awake at last!" He came over to the table. Wydrin tried pulling her arms free again, longing to wrap her fingers around his throat but there was no give in the cord. "Don't wear yourself out, it's quite pointless."

Wydrin lay still. Wriggling was making her head ache anyway.

"Who are you cooking?"

Roki glanced at the fire as though he'd completely forgotten about the corpse lying there.

"Oh her! That's Irilda, the old woman who found me after Pinehold. I was wandering the forest, blood pouring from the mess where my hand used to be, half mad with pain, and she found me and brought me here." He spoke fondly, as though these were some of his most treasured memories. Wydrin suspected Roki had lost his sanity along with his hand in Pinehold. "She cleaned it, healed me as best she could. The dreadful old hag fed me with a spoon when I was delirious, can you believe that? Fed me and cleaned me and gave me these stinking medicines until I was better."

"So why is she now roasting on her own fire?"

"I needed to get Bezcavar's attention." He leaned back again, and drew his sword from where it rested at his hip. "A death in his name, and then a pound of flesh in sacrifice." He held up the stump again. His sleeve was rolled up past the elbow and Wydrin could see twisted red scar tissue where an old wound had been opened again and again, never given enough time to heal properly. "It was worth it, to watch you running, and to visit you in your sleep. You talk about the strangest things in your sleep. Does he – ?"

"What else did Bezcavar give you?" she said hurriedly. The copper cuffs at her wrists were digging into the thin cord, so she began to twist her arm back and forth, ever so slightly. "Don't tell me that's all you got for cutting the end of your own arm off? Fane really didn't employ you for your brains."

"Shut up." He touched the end of the sword to her throat, resting the point in the soft hollow at the base of her neck. Wydrin stopped moving. "I never thought you'd be stupid enough to come back to the Blackwood, but here you are, and now we're going to have some fun." He leaned over her again, his sweating face a few inches above hers. "You were right, it's so much better when I can smell you." He bent his head, and for a terrible moment Wydrin thought he was going to kiss her but instead he licked her cheek. His tongue was dry and his breath smelled of dung. Wydrin wrenched her head away, grimacing.

"So, are you going to kill me then, or what?" She was angry now, even more so because there was fear underneath it. Luring his physical presence to the Blackwood was one thing, but she hadn't expected to get hit from behind.

"Kill you?" Roki grinned, showing nearly all his teeth. "Irilda might have been a hideous old baggage, but she was very good at medicine. All these jars and ointments, they did the job on me, I promise you that. Oh no, my little copper kitty." He ran the edge of the sword up to her chin, not quite breaking the skin. "I'm going to keep you alive for a very, very long time."

76

"You are sure of it?"

Frith paused. They were standing in the midst of the Blackwood, with four guards at their backs. Sebastian watched as the young lord fought to keep his temper under control.

"No, I am not *sure*. I can't feasibly know every inch of the forest."

Even so, he did the spell again, conjuring a flickering image of the miserable hut where Wydrin lay tied to a table. She was moving now, which was good – when they'd seen her earlier she had been unconscious, and it hadn't been clear whether she was breathing or not. The small version of Wydrin in the vision strained against her bonds, the cords in her neck standing rigid with the effort. Then Frith muttered another name, and the view changed to outside the hut. Roki was there now, standing in a small clearing with the hut behind him. He was wrestling with a pile of firewood, obviously having trouble manoeuvring it with one good arm, but they were more interested in the other end of the grassy patch. It sloped up towards a small bare hill, and there, at the top, were a number of tall stones aligned in a circle.

"Standing stones are quite common in the Blackwood," said Frith, before he dropped his hand and the vision blinked out of existence. "But if those are the ones I am thinking of, then Roki and Wydrin aren't far from here."

"I think you're right, m'lord," stuttered one of the guards. He was young, little more than a boy to Sebastian's eyes, and his ears protruded like jug handles from his leather helm. "I know of them too, I'm sure. You have the way of it."

Frith glanced at the guard, but said nothing.

They idolise him already, thought Sebastian. *I wouldn't be surprised if they declare him a god on his next birthday.* He scratched at the wound on his face. *Of course, they don't know yet what a complete and utter shit he is.*

"I hope you're right. My lord."

Roki threw another log on the fire. The heat in the hovel was already stifling, and the flames flared up hungrily. The charred woman's body began to blister, and once the fire was hot and bright he leaned an iron poker into the heart of it.

"We'll let it get hot a while," he said. "And then Bezcavar will have all the offerings he could possibly need."

Wydrin held her head up, watching his back. There were a few frayed fibres on the cords holding her now, but progress was very slow. *I should have gone for the cheaper bracelets. They'd have had sharper edges.* As it was, Roki would have his poker glowing and ready long before she'd cut her way free of the table. She'd have to try something else.

"Can this demon bring your brother back from the dead, then?" She watched his shoulders stiffen and he turned back to her, eyes narrowed. "That's got to be worth a hand or two, I'd have thought. I don't suppose it occurred to you to ask for that, did it? Instead you waste your own flesh and blood on, well, someone who isn't your own flesh and blood."

Roki swept over to the table, his sword brandished once more at her throat. "Stop talking about him!"

"Who? The demon? Or your brother?"

"I will cut you." He leaned down over her, the sword against her breastbone and his other arm, the one that ended in a ragged mess, resting next to her cheek. His face filled her vision, waxy and speckled with sweat. *Closer, a little closer.* "I will cut off pieces of you – your fingers, your eyelids, your pretty lips – and I will feed them to Bezcavar, Prince of Wounds."

This close the stench of him was overpowering. Wydrin could feel bile rising in the back of her throat, but she met his eyes steadily.

"And then what? You get to live the rest of your life in this hovel with only Mr Bones up there for company? Great deal, that, well done."

Now he was leaning on her, his chest crushing her breasts. His wounded arm scraped against her ear.

"You can't shut up, can you?"

"It's true, my mouth is always getting me into trouble." She wrenched her head to one side and bit into the end of Roki's stump with all her strength. The flesh there was rotten and soft and tore open easily, so a hot stream of blood filled her mouth and splattered over the table.

Roki shrieked and dropped his sword, clamping his remaining hand over the suddenly reopened wound, while Wydrin twisted her hand round to grab the blade. It was awkward and she damn near cut her own fingers off, but she managed to force the edge against the taut cord and it snapped. Immediately, her bonds loosened and she struggled upright, but then Roki was on her, screaming incoherently and they both went crashing down onto the floor.

Wydrin, finding herself briefly on top, crashed an elbow down onto his nose and felt a satisfying crack as the delicate bones there shattered, but he bucked her off and slammed her head into the wooden floor. The lump on the back of her head exploded with pain, and for a frightening handful of seconds the edges of her vision went dark. When everything came back into focus he had his hand round her throat, squeezing, squeezing. He may have only had the one hand but he still had the strength of a man not entirely in touch with his sanity, and Wydrin could feel her windpipe constricting.

Gasping for air, she brought her fist flying round to connect with his ear. It was enough to knock him off her and onto the floor, and for a brief moment they both lay there, dazed and covered in blood from Roki's arm.

It was a shout from outside that got her moving. It sounded like Frith, and he was angry.

She scrambled up, racing for the door. Roki grabbed at her legs, and almost, almost she went flat back on her face but then she was falling through the rickety door and out into the blessedly cool evening air.

"Wydrin!" Sebastian was there, along with Frith and four men in patchwork armour. They were at the edge of the small clearing, their weapons drawn. "Are you all right?"

"I..."

Before she could answer Roki burst through the door behind her. And then another came out. And another. He'd retrieved Bezcavar's gauntlet and it was glowing softly, while the other arm left a trail of blood behind it. Wydrin backed off, watching with her lips pressed together as the gauntlet shivered with light and three, four, six, eight Rokis sprang into being, all with swords, all with ragged, bloody arms.

"Stand aside!" bellowed Frith, and she just managed to leap out the way before he threw a wave of freezing cold at the group. The air crackled with it, and each sword in its path was frosted white, but where it hit the men who looked like Roki it did nothing at all. They surged forward, multiplying as they came until the little clearing was filled with the last Child of the Fog. The real Roki was lost.

Wydrin ran to Frith and reached for his belt.

"Do excuse me, princeling."

She pulled his dagger from the sheath and turned in time to deflect a blade, while the guards, expressions of total confusion on their faces, took blow after blow on their shields. Sebastian joined the fray, sword against sword, and Frith was sending fireballs now, lighting the evening with bright orange flames. All was chaos.

She caught Frith's eye and briefly squeezed his arm. "Try not to hit me with those things." And she threw herself into the crowd.

She heard Frith shout something at her, a warning to stay back, perhaps, but this had all gone on long enough. It was time to trust to her instincts, or accept a life spent continually looking over her shoulder.

Ducking and spinning and diving, her newly acquired dagger a blur, Wydrin watched the tangle of bodies, listened to the ringing song of blade against blade, and, yes – there it was.

A stench.

Neatly avoiding a lunge from one of the ghostly Rokis, she turned her spin into a thrust and pushed her dagger into the heart of the man standing right behind her. The blade found solid flesh and she sunk it into the hilt, twisting as much as her sore hand would allow. She kept her eyes on Roki's as she did so. His eyebrows were raised, an expression of dim surprise on his sweating face.

"I could *smell* you a mile away, you idiot."

He gasped, a tiny noise that became a thick gurgle, and black blood flowed over his lips. He tried to speak – an appeal to Bezcavar or a curse, perhaps – but the words caught in his throat. The duplicate Rokis vanished and he dropped to the ground in a boneless heap.

Wydrin gave him a kick while he was down there.

"Wydrin." Sebastian appeared at her elbow. Her eyes were drawn to the breastplate, scrawled with Bezcavar's markings. "Are you all right?"

"Of course I'm bloody all right. My weapons are still in that hut. Grab them for me, and let's get out of here." He began to walk away, but she held up a hand. "Actually, wait." She bent down to Roki's corpse and untied the straps on the gauntlet. It wasn't glowing any more. "You should take this." She threw it at Sebastian, and he caught it awkwardly against his chest. "May as well have the full set."

77

With the threat of torture and death removed, Pinehold seemed a much brighter place to Sebastian. The ruins of the barrack and the tower had been swept away, and new structures had been built in their place. The outer walls, which had once been dotted with gore-streaked cages, were now bright with trailing vines and flowers. More than that, though, the mark of fear had left the faces of the people, so that as he walked through the busy marketplace Sebastian exchanged greetings with men and women who looked happy enough to be getting on with their working day. It seemed like a simple thing, but it gave him a small sense of hope that he hadn't felt in quite a while.

Dreyda had moved her premises from the disused warehouse to the stone temple he, Wydrin and Frith had once used to flee the town. It had been abandoned before, its dull facade filled with broken windows, but Dreyda had been busy. The temple was now as fine as any in Relios, with merrily burning lamps and banners covered in sacred words. As he approached a woman carrying a wriggling child in her arms came out of the temple doors, exchanging a few last words with the fire-priestess.

"She's a fine size for her age, Annie, stop fretting so. If you're still worried, bring her back next week."

The young woman nodded, her eyes settling briefly on Sebastian. He smiled, but she turned away and hurried up the street.

"Sir Sebastian," Dreyda regarded him with sharp curiosity. "It is… good to see you." She looked him up and down, her lips pressed into a thin line. "Come inside."

There were more lamps burning within the temple, and three

large fonts on the altar at the front gave off a soft, spicy smoke. A handful of men and women sat in the pews, their heads bent in quiet thought. Dreyda led him to an alcove off to one side, hidden from the congregation by a curtain. There were piles and piles of books inside. When she saw Sebastian looking she shrugged.

"I've decided to make this place my home. For a while, at least. I wrote to the Head Regnisse in Relios and asked him to send my things to me." She sighed. "The letter that came back was full of alarming news, I'm afraid. Relios burns. I don't know if he even..." Her words ran out and she held up her hands in a gesture of defeat. In the dim light of the room the tattoos on her arms and face ran together like wet ink. "Instead of sending my own possessions, he sent me the library. He wanted to get it to safety, you see."

"I am sorry, Regnisse."

"Sorry? What have you got to be sorry for?" She peered up at him shrewdly. Sebastian suspected she knew very well what he was sorry for. "You know, it's funny. The buildings we blew up have been cleared away, and yet the tunnels beneath the town are all still standing. Whoever made them certainly knew what they were doing."

Sebastian nodded, unsure how much to say. "That is remarkable."

She pursed her lips at that. "Your friend. Did he find you?"

"My friend?"

"There was a man here asking after you and the girl. He had blond hair, and he looked ill."

"Ah." Sebastian ran his fingers over the leather cover of one of the books. "Yes, he found us. Thank you."

"I hope that boy got some rest. He was the sickest man I've seen still walking and talking."

Sebastian cleared his throat. "Yes, he did. Dreyda, the gauntlet that was recovered after we blew up the tower, the one that belonged to Enri..."

"You want it, do you?" She pulled a wooden box out from beneath a table and dragged out a handful of oil rags. Underneath it was the gauntlet, the twin to the one they'd taken from Roki. The final piece of Bezcavar's armour. It was very warm inside the little room. "Take it then, I'm not touching it."

Sebastian picked it up, turning it over in his hands. "Thank you."

"And what are you planning to do with it, exactly?" Dreyda

sniffed. "It's the work of a demon, you know that. No good came of it. Men and women have died—"

"We need it." Sebastian cut across her, the words tight in his throat. "We're going to kill the dragon that's terrorising your home, Dreyda. We need every advantage we can get." Sebastian wondered who he was trying to convince. "Frith has figured out the spell and it's time to – it's time to make things right."

"Ah, the lordling." Some of the hostility left the Regnisse's face to be replaced with pointed interest. "He went to Whittenfarne, then? Did he learn the forbidden words?"

"He did." For some reason Sebastian found he no longer wanted to be in this little alcove, or in the temple at all. Not with this woman who looked at him like she could see every dubious decision he'd ever made. "He did, and now we think we have a way to kill the monster, so I must go."

She laid a hand on his arm as he turned away.

"The armour is cursed, Sir Sebastian. You know that well enough. It was dedicated to a demon in the name of suffering, and suffering is all it will bring you."

Sebastian pulled his arm away, faster than he'd meant to. "If it helps us to undo what we've done, then I will wear it."

He swept aside the curtain and walked out of the temple without looking back.

Outside the cool air was like a balm on his face, and he felt a surge of annoyance for the temple and the tattooed woman within it. What did she know of suffering?

He was out of the gates and pounding the road back to the castle when a soft voice called to him from the trees.

"Sebastian?"

A slim figure slipped from the shadows, and for a strange moment Sebastian almost didn't recognise him. *I knew this man*, he thought, *in another life, perhaps*. And then Crowleo laughed gently at the confusion on his face and it came back to him. Too much wine in a dishevelled room, a young man with warm brown eyes, and the grass glittering with broken glass.

"Your face, Sebastian, is filled with thunder," said Crowleo. They stood on the path together, and for the second time that day Sebastian felt himself under the close scrutiny of a pair of clever eyes. "How are you? It looks as though your road was a rough one, yes?"

"You could say that. What are you doing, skulking about in the trees?"

Crowleo laughed again. Sebastian remembered the boy they had left, his face creased with grief. *At least some of us are getting better.*

"I was on my way to visit Dreyda," he said. "She's partial to the strawberries I've been growing in the backyard." He held up the small covered basket he was carrying. "There's so much space, and Holley never used it for anything and I – well." He cleared his throat and looked vaguely embarrassed. "I might have seen you in one of the glasses, walking through Pinehold. Thought perhaps I could catch you, yes?"

To his own surprise Sebastian found he was smiling. "And you did."

They found a patch of grass beyond the trees and sat for a while. Crowleo had brought more than strawberries; his wicker basket also contained bread, cheese and a bottle of sweet red wine. Sebastian opened his mouth to make some small words about the weather or the state of the town, and instead found himself telling Crowleo everything. All of it. The monsters in the Citadel, the dragon and her children, the voices that seemed to crowd the edge of every night's sleep, and the demon who'd come to him as a small girl. And the armour, of course, the armour worn by the man who'd killed Holley.

Once it was all out, they sat together in silence. The forest seemed to rush to fill it with soft forest sounds. Sebastian found himself hoping that no one would ever speak again, so he could sit here for ever in the gentle music of the trees.

Eventually Crowleo reached into his pocket and pulled out a small glass globe. It was a deep indigo, like the sky on the very edge of night.

"I made you this."

Sebastian stared at him.

"That is all you have to say?"

Crowleo held the bauble out to him until he was forced to take it. "I believe it is important, yes. Keep it with you, please."

"But everything I have told you – are you not shocked? Angry? I have sworn my sword to the very demon who killed your mistress! I have killed in his name."

Crowleo regarded him steadily. The easy humour had disappeared from his face, but there was no hate there either.

"You do not need me to tell you what is right, Sebastian. You know what you must do. You know what is right."

"I do, do I?" There was no keeping the bitterness from his voice.

"I know it."

"Fine." Sebastian got to his feet, knocking over the last of the wine in his hurry. "I am glad that you are so certain."

"Sebastian –"

"Thank you for the gift."

He turned and left Crowleo where he was sitting and headed back to the road. It was a long walk to the castle and it wasn't wise to be in the forest after dark.

78

The long table was covered in strips of linen, all of them inscribed with the looping black patterns of ink. Wydrin picked up another, wondering what it meant. The one part of the table not taken up by the strips was covered in the shattered eggshell pieces, which were now, finally, arranged in their original shape, or at least as close as they could decipher. Next to that were the maps. Frith had spent all night poring over them, arranging the order of the spell.

"Bind that one to my right arm," said Frith.

He was standing stripped to the waist with his arms held out in front of him. She had already tied several of the strips to his left arm, and several around his chest. *He thinks that if he takes all of the words, we cannot fail*, thought Wydrin. She hoped it was that simple.

"Here you go." She looped the fabric around his bicep until it was tied into place.

"Your hands are cold," he complained again.

"Do you think the ancient mages had servants to do this for them?" She picked up another bandage, running it between her fingers. "Or scantily clad ladies, perhaps, all perfumed and oiled?"

Frith coughed. "You'll do."

"Oh, thanks very much."

More strips, more spells. More ways to channel the Edenier. He was leaving nothing to chance.

"Why did you change your mind?" When he frowned at her she shrugged. "I mean, before you didn't seem particularly keen on facing the dragon. You'd got your home back, and the revenge you've been after all this time. I thought you'd decided to let someone else deal with it. But now you've got me doing this."

Frith cleared his throat. "It has become clear to me that some things are too important to ignore. Certain events have made me see things from a new angle. And yes, I have my castle back and the Blackwood will be cleared of Istrian scum, but what will that matter when Y'Ruen crosses the Yellow Sea? The Blackwood will be nothing but ash, my castle a pile of rubble. I must act."

"Well, I'm glad to hear that. I don't think we'd get very far without your magic."

She tied the next piece of fabric around his narrow waist, letting her fingers brush against the taut muscles of his stomach. He jumped a little, and Wydrin bit down a smirk. The bandages looked very white against his skin, a contrast that pleased her for reasons she couldn't quite put her finger on. She found herself wondering how that warm brown skin would look against clean white sheets, for example.

"We thought you were dead."

Wydrin blinked rapidly, trying to drag her mind back to the task at hand. "What?"

"When you were missing, and I used the Edenier to find you, we saw you lying prone on the table. We couldn't tell if you were alive or dead. Not then."

Wydrin chuckled, slipping the end of one piece of linen under another. Pulling it tight, making a knot.

"Aw, don't tell me you were worried?"

Frith didn't reply. The silence drew out until she had to look up into his face to see what was wrong. His grey eyes were dark, the colour of an oncoming storm.

"What if I was?" he said.

He took hold of her hand, snatching it up from where it was still tying knots, and he rubbed the pad of his thumb over the delicate skin on the underside of her wrist. "What if that's exactly what I'm trying to tell you?"

There was not a scrap of humour in his eyes. Wydrin thought she'd never seen a face so far from smiling. "Frith–"

"I find it difficult to – care for other people. Dangerous. And yet you are an impossible woman."

"And you are an impossible princeling. I'm sure I've said that before."

He drew her closer. To her own surprise she found her heart was beating faster, like a frightened bird, and there was a warmth coming from his body, a warmth her own body was returning. When his other hand pressed at the small of her back and she reached up to touch his face, a single thought flew across her mind like a comet – *this is new* – and then he was bending his head to her own and–

The doors to the hall crashed open and they jumped apart like they'd been pinched. Sebastian was striding into the hall, the gauntlet gripped in one hand. There was a look like black fury on his face.

"By all the graces," cried Wydrin, "don't you ever bloody *knock*?"

He glared at her. "Since when were you one to stand on ceremony? I have the last piece of the armour now."

Wydrin let out a shaky breath and rubbed a bead of sweat from her forehead. She found she couldn't quite bring herself to look at Frith, who was standing up very straight.

"Do you even know what the armour does when you have all the pieces together?"

Sebastian looked down at the gauntlet in his hands. "I suppose we shall see. What of the spell?"

"I have rearranged it," said Frith. He walked over to the table and smoothed down a piece of parchment. "And copied it again here. There are essentially four parts to the spell. Once we have located Y'Ruen, we must lure the dragon to the location of O'rin's first trap." He picked up a map. "They form a square. The first word is written underneath the ruins of Gostarae in Relios, the second under Pinehold itself, the third–"

"Do we know what the spell does when it goes off?" said Wydrin. "I mean, is it going to affect the places above the tunnels?"

"O'rin gave us no information on that," replied Frith, picking up another map. "As Sebastian says, I suppose we shall find out. The third sits under the Horns, and the final piece of the trap is to be activated in Ynnsmouth."

"Oh good, so we *are* going around in a circle," said Wydrin.

"Ynnsmouth?" Sebastian scratched at the scar under his eye. "Whereabouts in Ynnsmouth?"

Frith consulted the map once again.

"The God-Peak Grove. Do you know it?"

Sebastian looked down at his feet. "I do. It is one of our most sacred places, in the centre of a city called Baneswatch. It is very ancient, so it is entirely possible that a god had some say in its construction."

Frith nodded. "We must move Y'Ruen from location to location, and once she is over the traps I will summon the words and use the Edenier to activate the tunnels. Assuming they are still all in place, assuming we get the dragon to where we need her to be, assuming that we survive being in close proximity to a dragon, and assuming that O'rin, a trickster god, didn't just lie to us –" Frith cleared his throat – "then it should work."

"Well," Wydrin slapped him on the shoulder, "when you put it like that, princeling, I don't see how it could go wrong! I tell you what, I'd hate to be a dragon right now, not with us on the job. Is there any wine in your kitchens yet, by any chance? Maybe some rum? Something with a bit of kick might be handy."

Silence bloomed between them then, as they stood by the table filled with maps and spells. Wydrin thought back to the first time they'd met Frith in Creos, how he'd limped into the Hands of Fate tavern like a man who lived under the constant shadow of death. It had seemed like a simple job, a quick job, sure to lead to riches and stories and *danger*, yes, but nothing they couldn't handle. A copper promise, sealed in ale and dipped in bravado, and here they were now. Really, it was a gift of the Graces that they weren't dead already.

"This is really it, isn't it?" she said. "This is the end of it."

Frith caught her eye again for the first time since he'd taken her into his arms. "Yes," he said. "Whatever happens next, this is the end."

79

The mountains of Ynnsmouth rose against the horizon like a line of broken teeth tearing at the sky. *The god-peaks*, thought Sebastian, although he looked away before the names of the gods could come back to him. Instead he looked down, where silvered lakes and valleys were passing below them, and the city of Baneswatch belched smoke from a hundred fires.

"There she is," called Wydrin from the back of her own griffin. She was bent low over its neck, and she was pointing to the marshland beyond the city. At first Sebastian couldn't make out anything thanks to the thick clouds of black smoke, but a shard of sunlight caught a shivering of blue scales, and there was Y'Ruen, rising out of the fog like a gaudy snake. The western wall of the city was obscured with flames.

"This is the place?" called Frith. The young lord's arms were wrapped in spells, the ends of which were flapping in the wind like banners. Those over his chest were covered in a black velvet doublet. He'd decided against armour in the end, reasoning that the weight would slow the griffin down, and if he were caught in Y'Ruen's fire it was unlikely to save him anyway. Sebastian had made no such compromise: Bezcavar's armour was all he could bring to the fight so he wore it despite the heat and the weight. The helm was wedged between his legs.

"Baneswatch," answered Sebastian. "Ynnsmouth's greatest city. God-Peak Grove is at its heart."

"Damn." Wydrin craned her neck to look. "Jolnir's tunnels are sturdy, but, you know, I wouldn't be surprised if the fire power of another god could destroy them."

"We'd best get moving," said Frith.

They flew on, and soon the southern gates of Baneswatch were in sight. There were hundreds of people there, swarming in a mass of panic and fear. Some of them appeared to be trying to flee the city, while others were fighting the brood army.

"I see Y'Ruen brought her children to the party," shouted Wydrin against the wind. They were a green storm, locusts moving over a field of wheat, and where they touched the army of Baneswatch it fell back in pieces. Sebastian scanned the crowds, pushing the griffin lower and lower, until he could see the standards. Bright squares of material amongst the churning chaos, most of them the blue and red of Baneswatch, but there were others. Light blue and silver, orange and white – the colours of the Order.

"There are knights down there. They must be the remnants of the Order!" His throat was suddenly tight.

"Let's hope they can hold the gates," called Wydrin. "Perhaps if they do that–"

"I have to go to them," Sebastian cut over her, already urging his griffin to land.

"What?"

"We stick to the plan," bellowed Frith. His griffin swept in to Sebastian's left as though to shove him back into line. "You and Wydrin must lead the dragon away, while I–"

"Your spell will come to nothing if God-Peak Grove is destroyed by dragon fire," Sebastian shouted back. "If I can help them hold the city, we might have a chance. It's where I need to be."

"I don't–"

"Frith, let him go." Wydrin's voice was resigned. "I can get the dragon where we need it."

Sebastian looked at them both. Frith was scowling as ever, while Wydrin just looked sad. Her red hair fell across her face and was whipped back by the wind, again and again.

"Good luck," he said, and meant it. "I will see you again."

He turned the griffin and dropped from the sky, the freezing wind roaring in his ears. The city wall came up to meet him, and he caught a few shouts from below as some of the army within the city caught sight of what was falling towards them. There were even a few arrows flying up past him, and then he was down and dismounting. He was immediately surrounded by bristling swords and spears.

"I'm on your side!" He looked round at the faces under the helmets. Every one looked tired, frightened, close to panic. "I'm here to help."

There was a gasp as the griffin turned bird-sized once more and flew off into the roofs behind them.

"Who are you? What is that?" A man stepped forward out of the crowd. He'd had a red beard once but parts of it had recently been singed off. "I don't know if you've noticed but we've had rather enough of flying bloody monsters!"

As if to support his words there was a roar from the marshes beyond the walls, and an answering shout from the brood army. Sebastian swallowed hard.

"My name is Sebastian, and I am a Ynnsmouth knight. I bring you a good sword arm," he drew his sword and held it up. "And I come to hold this city."

The crowd began to lower their swords, looking at each other uncertainly.

"A Ynnsmouth knight, aye? Your lot are beyond the gate, getting sliced to pieces. You want to go out there and help them, that's fine, but we ain't going nowhere."

"Will no one join me?" Sebastian cast around the crowd. Those eyes that met his were terrified. Most looked away. "I will need some men just to get out of the gate."

"Well you ain't getting no help from us!"

"He won't need it."

Sebastian looked down to see a slim white shape standing barefoot in the mud. Ip grinned up at him.

"How are you here?"

"Mysterious ways, my friend." She blinked, and for a second her eyes were filled with blood. Another blink and they were clear again. "I see that you have collected all the pieces of my armour. Do you know what happens when you wear them all together?"

"No," replied Sebastian, a sour note in his voice. "You wouldn't tell me."

Her grin widened until it was a rictus, too wide and sharp for a human face.

"Put the helm on, Sir Sebastian. Open the gate."

The armed men were watching this exchange with increasing incredulity when there came a flurry of howls from beyond the wall, and the dragon passed directly overhead. A ball of flame as big as a loaded cart shot past them and exploded in the row of houses behind. All at once, everything was fire and chaos.

Ignoring the girl Sebastian pulled the helm down over his head and headed for the gate. Whatever it did, he needed to get where the fighting was.

"Remember, you kill in my name!" called Ip. "The suffering you cause today is mine. And the Cursed Company are yours to command."

It seemed to Sebastian that the sky grew dark, and he looked up, expecting to see the dragon, expecting to be boiled to pieces within the suit of armour, but there was a thick fog around him, growing darker by the moment. The crowd shouted in confusion, and the smoky fog drew in on itself, growing solid. As he watched, men began to form out of the swirling mists, grey men bristling with vicious-looking barbed armour. Every one of them was as tall as him, and every one as broad. They held huge battered broadswords and jagged metal shields like broken ice, and they lined up behind Sebastian in neat, precise lines. There had to be a hundred of them.

"What are you?"

"This is the Cursed Company," said Ip brightly. She walked up to one of the men and rapped her knuckles against his dusty breastplate. "They obey whoever wears my armour, and they will not stop until you tell them to. Many battles have been turned by the Cursed Company. More than history credits them for, that's for certain."

Sebastian peered at the nearest warrior; he wore a close-fitting helm and inside it there was a face. Of sorts.

"These are... these aren't men."

"Oh, but they were once," said Ip. "These are those left behind for the ravens. Whatever wasn't nipped up by their clever little beaks was chucked into a pile by the victors and burnt. You've seen that, haven't you, Sebastian? Piles of the dead burning on the battlefield. I've claimed them. All through time I've claimed the ashes of the fallen and built them anew. No need to thank me."

The face inside the helm was a crushed mixture of soot and bone, with the occasional ragged piece of charred flesh or pinkish sinew holding it all together. The warriors had no eyes – such tasty morsels were the first choice of any self-respecting raven – but Sebastian thought he could feel the man watching him anyway.

He turned away, and shouted at the men on the gate.

"Open up and let us out! We fight for Baneswatch!"

The gatekeeper gestured them forward.

"Keep close! I'll be shutting this gate as soon as you're through, so move quickly. I don't want none of those green creatures getting past." He glanced at the army of smoke-wraiths, obviously unsure if they could hear or understand him. He caught Sebastian's eye instead. "You hear me?"

"Yes." Sebastian held his sword at the ready, and he couldn't help noticing that it was the same ashen grey as those of the Cursed Company. "We heard you."

The gates rumbled open, revealing the cold scrubland of the road beyond. The ground was thick with blood, and smoke rolled in ponderous clouds of black and grey, while here and there he could see the shadows of people running, fighting, dying. The shadows of people and monsters.

"For Baneswatch!" he called as he charged out onto the battlefield, hoping that perhaps one or two of the city's guards would be inspired to join him, but there was no answering rally; only the eerie silence of the Cursed Company, pounding the ground next to him.

"For me, you mean," whispered Ip in his ear.

"You will get your blood, demon."

Just before he met the throng of exhausted, ragged fighters, he glanced up. Y'Ruen was there, twisting and turning against the blue, and two black specks danced around her, looking impossibly small.

"We'll all be killed," he grunted as his blade sunk home into the shoulder of the first brood warrior.

We'll all be killed. But at least that will be an end to it.

80

Frith dug his fingers deep into the griffin's feathers and urged the creature on. He and Wydrin were flying at a terrible speed now, racing to keep up with the constant movement of the dragon. The ground sped by in a blur, too fast to make out more than vague impressions of men and women fighting.

Wydrin was in front, her narrow back bent over the griffin, sword in one hand. The dragon was still circling the western gate and as yet it hadn't noticed them. Its snout was pointing downwards, huge yellow eyes fixed on the fighting below. This close, Frith could see the glinting perfection of each scale, the wet precision of its teeth, the sheer physical weight of the creature. His stomach was clenching with a deep primal fear – *I am small and hunted* – but there was also a dizzying sense of dislocation. A creature that big, flying with such easy grace – it shouldn't exist. He'd experienced a shadow of that feeling before when Jolnir had thrown off his mask and revealed the face of a god beneath it. The world he'd known had tipped crazily, like a boat in a storm, and shown him an underside crawling with things he didn't understand.

The dragon snapped its jaws and flame crawled across the crowds below. The stink of sulphur and cooked flesh assaulted his nose.

"This is it," cried Wydrin from just ahead of him. "Get ready to fly your arse off, princeling!"

He had a moment to think that they should have changed their weapons – Wydrin still brandished Glassheart, and a spear would have made more sense, of course it would – before Wydrin pressed her knees to the sides of her griffin and dived, dropping like a stone.

He could hear her shouting but couldn't make out the words. For a terrible few seconds he thought she'd misjudged everything and was going to crash headlong into the giant beast, but she pulled up at the last minute, just behind the tangled cluster of horns that sprouted from Y'Ruen's head. Leaning down, one hand holding fast to the griffin's black feathers, she swiped Glassheart across the back of the dragon's neck. The blade scraped harmlessly across the scales, but Y'Ruen gave an odd bark of surprise and whipped her head round.

It was almost all over in that instant. The great head whirled like a cobra striking and Frith heard Wydrin shout a very loud and very clear curse word, but the dragon just missed, teeth closing on empty air.

This was it, then. Frith summoned the words for Ice and Control and the Edenier leapt from his hands, crackling with energy. Two, three spheres of freezing ice crashed against the corner of Y'Ruen's jaw, and Frith suspected that at least gave her a toothache, because she turned, baleful yellow eyes fixed on him. The enormous bat-like wings gave one huge lazy flap and she was up in the air with them. Frith clung to the griffin's back as the wind from her flight threatened to unseat him; just being caught in the monster's updraft was dangerous.

"We've got her attention! Let's move!" Wydrin was flying at him and, madly, impossibly, she was laughing.

And she was right.

Y'Ruen had turned away from the burning city below and was coming after them.

Frith put his heels to the griffin and turned south. As the one who'd memorised the maps he had to lead them to Relios and beyond, which meant keeping his eyes ahead much of the time. Immediately, the skin on his back began to crawl as he imagined death eyeing his unprotected flesh.

Glancing over his shoulder he saw Wydrin circling the dragon like a bee around a hive. The dragon would dart her head forward every now and then, teeth long and yellow against a black tongue, but Wydrin was dodging like she'd been flying griffins all her life. Intermittently she would swoop in, now a bee with its stinger, and drive her sword at the dragon's enormous bulk. And always she was moving forward, drawing the creature on. The city of Baneswatch was falling behind them.

But all it would take was one mistake and Wydrin would be torn to pieces, her guts scattered to the sky.

Frith leaned back on the griffin, ignoring the eye-watering drop below, and threw a wave of force behind him, a cracking curtain of violet light. It hit the dragon square in the face, and there was another of those ear-splitting roars.

Wydrin laughed again, delighting in Y'Ruen's rage. But he could feel the dragon looking at him now, a huge pressure on the back of his head. He could feel her mind pushing at his; questing, curious.

I have her attention, he thought, his mouth dry as dust. *She sees a mage. And the last mages she saw were the ones who sealed her in the Citadel.*

Damn.

It was a frantic flight to Relios.

The sky was filled with the fury of the dragon, the griffins soaring and dipping and sometimes just plain scrambling out of the way. More than once Frith felt the heat of the fire so close that the ends of his hair started to crisp and every now and then he would have to pat down the griffin as the occasional feather caught fire. He did his best to keep Wydrin in the corner of his eye, throwing back sheets of ice and lightning when he could so that the dragon was always torn between two targets.

Perhaps it was the god's curiosity that saved them, or perhaps she was bored of chasing distant targets on the ground. Eventually the landscape beneath them changed from the cool grasses of Ynnsmouth to the reddish clay soil of Relios, and they began to pass over signs that the dragon had already been this way; streaks of soot that had once been villages, and fields of mud churned under the feet of the brood army.

When he saw the ruins of Gostarae in the distance, Frith felt a small tremor of relief in his stomach. Under the mess of old grey stones there was a network of tunnels that, if you were looking down on them from above, would spell the word for Stillness. According to the information O'rin had left them, anyway.

"This is it," he shouted across to Wydrin. She waved in acknowledgement before diving to one side to avoid a lunge from the dragon.

The ruins were underneath them. The Edenier churned within Frith's chest, as though sensing what was about to happen. Y'Ruen flew on, almost passing completely over the stones below, but Wydrin spiralled back and up, flying up towards the clouds in a complicated corkscrew, and the dragon followed. *Now or never, then.*

Frith summoned the word for Stillness in his mind, picturing it as clearly as he could. The corresponding binding on his right hand grew cold, and then colder, so cold it was painful. A ribbon of light shot from the end of his fingers, bright as lightning, and rippled down to the ground, faster than his eyes could follow. There was a tugging in his stomach, and his arms and legs grew numb as though the spell were draining all his strength. *It could be, for all I know,* thought Frith, staring down at the jumbled ruins. Above him Wydrin and the dragon hung suspended in the air, and...

"Nothing's happening!" he yelled, knowing full well Wydrin couldn't hear him. "Nothing..."

...Deep within the red earth, the faces carved into the walls of the tunnels were licked with a pale and ghostly light, silvery and god-touched. One by one their eyes and mouths opened, and a shout issued forth...

Frith saw the word briefly, inscribed in light below him as clearly as it had been in his mind, and then shards of light so bright that they were almost solid leapt up into sky, shooting past them like pillars of impossible marble. The griffin screamed, high and panicked, and Frith had to hold on tight to avoid being pitched from its back. He wrenched his head up, half blind but needing to see, and saw the shards of light pass up and through the dragon, appearing to illuminate the monster from within. For the barest second he thought he could see its bones, twinned with violet lightning, and there was a roar so loud it was like the world crying out in furious pain.

And then the light was gone.

Wydrin sped towards him as, above them, the dragon writhed like a nest of snakes.

"Better get ready to fly, Frith," she said, blinking furiously. "I think we've really pissed it off now."

81

The air was thick with misted blood. The brood army, the Order, the Cursed Company; all were little more than churning shadows amongst the chaos.

Under the helm Sebastian blinked sweat away from his eyes. He could taste salt on his lips, and it seemed that every muscle sang with energy. The battle lust he'd felt in the demon's ruins was with him again. How much of it was Bezcavar's influence he couldn't tell, but it hardly mattered. He moved through the crowd of soldiers with relentless efficiency, and his sword left a trail of green blood in its wake.

He saw the battle in shattered moments, fire-vivid and fever-bright. One of Y'Ruen's children rose up before him with a golden sword in each hand, her teeth bared. He traced where his blade would go in his mind – up and across the chest, where part of her armour had come away – and then his sword seemed to move of its own accord. Blood splattered his face and there was more salt on his lips.

The Cursed Company were an eerie patch of silence amongst the screaming and shouting. Sebastian caught glimpses of them, never far from him, moving with a precision and a relentlessness he thought oddly familiar until he recognised it as his own. They were wraiths of ash and bone, built in his image. Their ashen swords hacked and crushed and disembowelled relentlessly, cutting a great swath through the brood army by themselves.

Soon Sebastian found he was wading through a soup of green and red blood, thick with entrails and other body parts, and yet still he was not tired.

I could kill for ever.

"Glorious, isn't it?"

Ip appeared next to him, or something that looked like Ip, at least. She wore a simple white shift that came down to her ankles, impossibly clean against the carnage.

Sebastian paused, suddenly in the midst of a quiet spot in the battlefield. He suspected that was Bezcavar's doing.

"What do you want?" He did not want quiet, or to stop.

"Just surveying my glory." Ip raised her hands and spun in a slow circle. "All of this pain, death, fear. All in my name. I haven't had a day this good in centuries."

Sebastian lowered his sword slowly. How long had he been fighting? The smoke from the fires made everything dark and unknowable. How many had he killed? Now that he'd stopped he could feel the ache in his head again.

"Did they lead the dragon away? Is she gone?"

Ip shrugged as though this were the least interesting question she'd ever heard.

"Is that important? The joy is here, after all."

"Of course it's important." Sebastian forced his fingers up under the helm, trying to wipe the sweat away from his eyes. It was important. He was just finding it difficult to remember why. "Wydrin's up there, she's in danger–"

"And you're down here. This is where your job is."

Ip grinned and vanished as the battle roared back into life around him. Sebastian raised his sword and stepped back into the fray.

It was a relief.

The worst of the pain, Wydrin noted, was in her fingers. She was well used to gripping a sword for long periods of time, but gripping it and swinging it and taking care not to drop it at any point or you would never bloody see it again – that took rather more effort. Second to that pain was the dull ache in her knees and thighs, strained with holding on to the griffin. Let go of that at any point, and you'd never see anything a-bloody-gain.

The Yellow Sea glittered below them and she could almost make out their reflections in the water; her griffin, ducking and swerving and swooping, Frith on his, occasionally lit with magical explosions, and the dragon, coming on behind them with its neck stretched out like a dog with a scent. It was, she suspected, the sort of image you couldn't look at for too long without going a little mad, so she ripped her eyes away from it and pulled the griffin up and up just in time to avoid another lance of fire. The heat from it licked at the bottom of her boots, making her feet uncomfortably hot.

"That was an admirable try!" she shouted into the wind. "But you have to get up earlier than that to catch the Copper Cat."

Frith glanced up at her, his white hair flapping like a flag in a storm.

"Litvania coming up!"

It was true. A great dark mass was speeding towards them now, and already she could see the trees crowded on the coast.

"Let's get this bitch where she needs to be."

The dragon roared again, and without Wydrin having to tell it to, the griffin banked sharply to the right, so fast her stomach surged up under her throat. She looked out along the sharp point of its tapered wing and saw that they had fallen back alongside Y'Ruen, the great vast bulk of her stomach so close that she could have reached out and touched it if she wanted. She grinned. This griffin was her kind of animal.

"Under we go!"

Holding her sword directly above her head, she nudged the griffin and they swept under the dragon's belly, scoring a fine line across the creature's shining scales. An answering roar and Y'Ruen twisted in the air, jaws snapping, but they were already speeding ahead once more. She caught up with Frith, who was throwing orange balls of fire over his shoulder towards the beast.

"Do you have to do that?" he shouted. "It's annoyed enough as it is."

"We want to keep her interested don't we?"

"I suspect we've done that." Frith kept looking back. "I think it's the Edenier that's drawing her on now – she wants to know where it's coming from."

"Either way, we're here." Wydrin pointed. The sea had given away to the forests of the Blackwood, and in the distance there was a walled town. Frith had the maps memorised, but she recognised Pinehold well enough. She'd helped to blow half of it up, after all. "Get ready."

•••

Dreyda left the temple at a run, her arms still full of the ceremonial incense papers she intended to burn that evening. The roar had shaken the very stones of the building, causing a fine layer of dust to drift down from the ceiling onto the pews and the townspeople sitting there.

Sometimes in Relios the earth itself would shake, causing huge cracks in the ground and a flurry of newly devoted worshippers to the temples, but she had never heard of such a thing happening in Litvania. Besides which, this roar sounded as though it were coming from the *sky*.

She looked up, squinting into the sunshine, dimly aware of other people doing the same. At first all she saw were birds, lots and lots of them flying madly in all directions as though they didn't know where to get to first, and then something huge flew into view, casting an enormous shadow over the town.

Dreyda dropped the papers, and they danced around her feet in the sudden wind caused by the dragon's wings. She felt very small, very small indeed, and she remembered the man who had been looking for Sebastian. The man with blond hair and grey skin, and what had he said to her? Relios is burning, and all the tales are true.

"What is it?" Alice was clutching at her elbow. "What is it?"

"You can see what it bloody well is," she snapped, wrenching her arm out of the younger woman's grasp. "Get everyone back inside before we're all—"

The ground shook again, and this time it was so violent that Dreyda struggled to stay upright.

"Get inside! Everyone, go back inside your houses!"

Light leapt up from the cobbles beneath her feet, light so bright that it was like suddenly being struck blind. Dreyda felt her arms rising towards the sky of their own accord, as though she were being dragged up with the beams. *Time*, she thought, *time passing and moving us forever onward, like a river you can never swim against or a tide that will always crush you against the shore...*

The light vanished. Dreyda fell to the ground, scraping her knees painfully against the cobbles. The incense papers were all burning, sending up slim swirls of smoke that smelt of cinnamon and scorpion oil.

"By all the gods..."

The dragon flew off to the North, its long tail flicking. Dreyda watched it go with the smell of smoke in her nostrils, muttering the words for Peace and Protection, over and over.

82

Frith slumped forward on the griffin, pitching dangerously over to one side.

"Woah! Stay with me now, princeling!"

Urging her own mount as close as she dared, Wydrin reached across and gave Frith's arm a shake. The dragon was reeling too, curling in on itself like a snake poked with a stick, and she estimated that they had no more than a few seconds of safety before it was back on their heels. She shook Frith again, and he groaned, his eyelids flickering.

"Get offa me…"

"Frith, wake up! We have to get to the Horns."

He sat up straighter. Wydrin was relieved to see some sense starting to return to his face.

"It worked?"

"It's definitely doing something." There was a pressure in the air that wasn't there before, some sort of gathering force pushing down on her eardrums and making it difficult to focus. The sky was full of magic.

"Just twice more," said Frith. It sounded as though he were trying to convince himself as much as her. "Two more words to go and then I can rest."

She squeezed his shoulder, fixing his grey eyes with her own.

"We can do it."

They flew on, and with a roar and a blast of flame, the dragon followed.

Things started to go wrong when he realised he recognised their faces.

Sebastian knocked another blade out of his path and buried his sword in the belly of the brood soldier in front of him. She vomited blood over his arm and looked up, her forehead creased into an expression of confusion and pain, and her eyes widened slightly. She started to say something, but Sebastian dragged his sword free again and blood gushed from the wound in a flood that soaked his boots. Sebastian frowned. What could she have been trying to say? And more importantly, why did he feel like he knew her?

The battle raged on around him. There were piles of bodies from both sides now, and half the fight was getting to the enemy to kill them. The knights that were left were starting to tire, and wherever he looked he saw faces strained with exhaustion and fear. How much longer could this go on for? Would he be left to defeat the brood army alone?

"You could fight on for ever, if I let you," Bezcavar whispered in his ear.

"For ever?"

"You will be a god of war." Sebastian could see Ip from the corner of his eye now, a slip of whiteness against the carnage. "Forget the armour, I can make *you* the vessel of pain. I will craft you as the armour was crafted, and all the suffering you bring will make me more powerful."

"To fight for ever…"

Another face loomed in front of him, and for a second he thought he knew her – how could they have met before? And then the feeling was gone. Sebastian's sword crashed against the brood soldier's blade almost lazily, and as he forced it away he noticed that she was different to her sisters. The golden scaled armour was patched over here and there with pieces of different fabric; a strip of grey wool, a swatch of crimson cotton slung over her shoulder. Hanging from her belt were other incongruous objects; a seashell, a tiny wooden doll with a painted face, a hairbrush with half its needles missing. There was something strapped to her back too. Sebastian thought it might be a book.

"Father?" she said.

For the first time on that endless day Sebastian stumbled, his sword flying wide of its target. He was open on his left side and it would have been the easiest thing in the world to take him down, but the brood soldier didn't move. She was lowering her sword.

"Father?"

"What?" Sebastian knew her voice too. Over her shoulder other brood soldiers were pausing, glancing over to them. "What are you talking about?"

"You are the man who gave us our blood!" The tip of the soldier's sword touched the ground. "And the words in our heads."

"I – you are creatures of the dragon, not –" The Cursed Company were fighting their way towards him, sensing the pause in the fight. And Bezcavar couldn't have that, of course. "Who are you?"

"I am Ephemeral." The brood soldier smiled, as though glad she had been asked. "It is my own name, I chose it. And this," she gestured over her shoulder, "is Crocus, and Falling, and Anemone. There are more of us."

"What do you mean, more of you? What are you?"

"We are the sisters who have chosen our names. We are your daughters, Father."

"I don't understand."

The Cursed Company were closer now. All around them the fight churned on.

"You can stop this, Father. You just have to ask them."

"Stop this? What about the dragon? All the people you've killed?"

A member of the Cursed Company charged out of the blood-soaked mist and skewered the soldier to the right of Ephemeral, spilling fresh green blood down the rusted sword. There was a chorus of shouts from the last of the Order forming a shield wall to Sebastian's left as the formation broke down again, and he was back in the midst of the fight, the soldier calling herself Ephemeral lost from sight.

Sebastian took a few breaths, trying to understand what she'd said, to fit it together with what he knew to be true. He'd nearly died under the Citadel and his blood had roused the brood army. He'd dreamed of them, marching and killing and burning, had even heard their voices on the edge of sleep. Had they also heard his?

New strength flowed into his arms and legs, and all those thoughts were forced from his mind. Time to fight, and to kill.

They came upon the Horns as the setting sun began to light the waves with flares of orange and red. Wydrin had visited the islands more than once, a smaller, paler shadow of Crosshaven, with worse food and less competent pirates. According to Frith and his maps, this was where O'rin had carved the word for Change.

"I think she's falling back," called Frith. Wydrin looked and saw he was right. Instead of following them across the central island, she was circling around them, keeping just out of range of where they needed her.

"Do you think she's figured out what we're doing?"

Frith didn't answer. Wydrin glanced down. She could make out a small port town below, and people had come out to see what was going on. There was no way to see their faces, but from their movements she could guess that they weren't very happy about what they saw. She couldn't blame them.

The dragon moved so fast that the first Wydrin knew about it she was already falling, the warm solidity of the griffin ripped from under her and a roaring in her ears. She tried to shout but the wind ripped the noise from her throat, where her stomach was now trying to take up residence. She saw the sky, vividly pink like an infected wound, and the ground, grey and spinning, and now and then a part of the dragon, filling her vision like a tumour.

You still have to, she thought, *you still have to do it, Frith, you have to do it and at least it will be quick I–*

She crashed into something but it was soft and covered with feathers. She flung her arms around the griffin and for a few seconds they span together as the bird-beast tried to right itself.

"By all the Graces!" Wydrin gasped air into her lungs, trying not to pass out with relief. "You great big beautiful animal you, thank all the gods for griffins, even the stupid bird-headed one. If we get out of this alive I'm building you a temple."

The griffin squawked and a split second later they were consumed in light as the Horns below them released the third part of O'rin's spell.

"Frith!"

She saw him briefly with his arms held out to either side, his knees clamped to the griffin and the Edenier crawling over his body like summer lightning. The dragon was *screaming* now, long tail lashing through the air, and then the spell was over and Frith began to tip backwards, eyes rolled up to the whites.

"Quickly now!"

The griffin shot up like a rocket, wings folded back, straight as an arrow. As they passed Frith, Wydrin reached down as far as she could and slapped him hard across the face. Instantly he sat bolt upright.

"How dare you…" He faltered, touching one hand to the red mark on his cheek. "I saw you fall."

"I got caught. Come on," Wydrin nodded to Y'Ruen, who was shaking her snout back and forth like a dog with a bee in its mouth.

They flew again, faster now, as fast as they could. Over the Yellow Sea until the coast of Ynnsmouth grew on the horizon, a thin shadow and then a fat line. The mountains sprang up, a solid blue fracture across the sky. They were coming in from the North and would have to fly over the god-peaks, as Sebastian called them. It was the quickest way to reach Baneswatch. If Baneswatch was still standing.

"One more spell to go, princeling. You reckon you've got it in you?"

To her surprise, Frith smiled. "Just as long as you're around to slap me awake."

"Oh, any time. In fact–"

A wall of sound hit them from behind. Y'Ruen was roaring again, but this time there was a strange, sonorous quality to it, like someone shouting from the bottom of a well. The air around them seemed to vibrate with it, and when Wydrin pressed her hands over her ears it made no difference at all.

83

The noise rolled like thunder over the battlefield, and Sebastian felt rather than saw everyone pause, fearful faces turned up to the sky. No dragon appeared, but from the back of the brood army there was a flurry of movement. A brood soldier in front of him shuddered violently, the carapace of armour across her back shifting, cracking. A long pair of wet membranous wings slid from the gaps. She flapped them once, twice, and Sebastian was reminded of dragonflies on the lakes emerging from the water. All over the battlefield brood soldiers were releasing wings.

"What are they?" screamed a man next to him. "We can't fight flying demons!"

Newly sprouted wings began to vibrate, throwing a thin mist of golden droplets into the air, and then, as one, they rose up, moving with an inhuman grace. Not all of them went; there were still more than enough regular troops on the ground. One of them lurched towards Sebastian again and his sword was up and moving before he realised it was Ephemeral.

"They're going to Mother," she said. There was red blood on her face now, pooling at the corner of one eye. "And they will kill your friends. Please, Father, you have to speak to them while she is not here. You can get them to stop!"

"Stopping is not what I made you for." Ip laid one cool hand on his arm. Somehow he could feel it, small and icy through the leather. "Your sword is mine, your life is mine. Kill this creature and be done with it."

"No, Father." Ephemeral was holding out her hands now. Each of her fingers was tipped with a sharp claw. "No."

Sebastian shook his head at the both of them, taking a step backwards. All around him men and women were dying. There was a fire burning in his head again, the same fire that had been burning since he'd woken up on the dark soil of Litvania. Could there ever be an end to it?

He lifted his eyes to the mountains, to the air that was now thick with the flying brood army. They were swarming towards a larger shape. Looking at it his mouth filled with the taste of blood.

The dragon was coming back.

At first Frith thought it was a trick of the setting sun. The sky in front of them was filled with a thousand flecks of gold, dancing and shifting like motes in a sunbeam. Then the dragon roared again, and the brood army added their shrill voices to the call.

"We have to get through them to reach Baneswatch." Wydrin bent low over her griffin. "I'll try to clear a path for you."

"Wait!"

But she was already gone, shooting forward with Glassheart held above her head. As he watched she flew past the nearest flying brood soldier and slashed open her belly, before turning to meet the next. The second, third and fourth fell in a similar manner, but there were always more, and always the dragon was at their backs. Frith threw a wall of ice at the brood army, and this proved to be especially effective; their delicate wings crumpled under the extreme cold, and those that were not knocked out of the sky by the initial blast fell when their wings failed to work.

The dragon roared again, spewing a ball of fire that Frith just managed to dodge. It exploded into the centre of her army, sending charred bodies down to the mountains below. It seemed she was not above sacrificing her own children.

A group of the soldiers were converging on Wydrin now. The griffin turned its beak on them, tearing through green flesh and piercing the golden armour. There were screams, shouts of rage. In the distance Frith could see Baneswatch, still burning in places, but they were making progress. They might even make it.

One of the brood army pulled a bow from her back, and as if it were a signal all the others did too. Wydrin shouted a warning, and suddenly the air was full of golden arrows.

"Move!"

Frith urged the griffin on, trying to fly as low as possible without being torn apart by the jagged rocks. Wydrin was just in front of him, sword whirling from one side to the other, cutting down any brood soldier that got too close.

It's not far now.

He was throwing another wall of ice ahead to clear their path when one of the golden arrows hit Wydrin's griffin in the flank. The animal gave an anguished screech and lurched awkwardly, obviously in some pain. Wydrin turned to look, and Frith saw the expression of horror on her face.

"Keep going!"

She nodded to him, but another arrow hit a hand's breadth from the first, and then another, just below the creature's breastbone. Now the griffin was falling, and Wydrin with it.

No.

Frith conjured the word for Stillness and threw it at them, and their descent slowed long enough for him to catch up. He leaned down as far as he could, holding out his arm.

"Take my hand!"

"You will fight for me, Sebastian. You will be a god of war. A prince of suffering."

Sebastian looked up. The shapes coming over the mountain were close enough now for him to make out the two griffins, the two figures atop them fighting desperately. Close enough for him to see one of them fall.

He was fighting, yes. That *was* what he was made for. But there was something else too. Why was it so hard to remember?

"Are you listening to me?"

The demon in the shape of a girl was shouting at him, bony arms crossed over a bony chest. He didn't look at her. He was remembering the green-skinned woman who called him "Father", and a young man with eyes like amber. He'd told him to remember something, hadn't he? He'd told him to keep something with him.

Almost of their own accord Sebastian's fingers reached into one of his belt pockets and closed over a solid glass globe. He held it up to his eyes and looked into its blue shadows. He saw…

…a tall boy with black hair walking in a dream, listening to the mountain as it talked. The snow in spring when it was still light, glowing like nothing

else on Ede. A walk through the heart of the rock in pitch-blackness, and he
remembered.

He remembered the voice of Isu.

"Enough," he said.

Ip glared up at him, eyes full of blood. "What?"

"Enough, little demon. My sword is no longer yours."

He reached up and unbuckled the breastplate, and then the gauntlets, letting them drop to the gore-streaked ground. The greaves went next, and finally the helm. He took a deep breath, glorying in it. How long since he'd breathed free air?

"You will die!" Bezcavar roared through Ip's throat. "How will you fight without my sword, my armour? They will tear you apart. You are my creature now, knight, and you were made to kill."

Sebastian ignored her.

"Daughters!" He held his arms out to either side, feeling the eyes of the brood army settle on him as one. "Daughters, listen to me! It's time to stop."

"We won't make it." Frith's voice was a gruff croak in her ear.

"We have to."

Wydrin clung to the last remaining griffin, one arm circling Frith's waist and the other still brandishing Glassheart. There was an arrow sticking through one of the animal's wings and they were losing height rapidly. Baneswatch wasn't far now, but from the angle of their descent it looked like they would have a reunion with the ground sooner than they wanted.

A brood soldier flew towards them and Frith threw an ice ball at her, crisping her wings into icicles. And then, for no reason that Wydrin could see, half of them dropped away, and began to fly back down to the ground. She caught the look on a few of their faces and they seemed confused. Some of them were shaking their heads as though trying to dislodge something.

"What's going on now?"

Y'Ruen roared, and fire was everywhere. Wydrin, Frith, the griffin, all screamed as one, and for a moment Wydrin thought they were all going to fall. Frith dragged them onwards but the griffin's wing was on fire now. Wydrin tried to beat it out with her hands, only succeeding in burning her fingers.

"Shit! We'll have to land, Frith, and do the rest on foot."

Frith glanced behind them.

"Then we definitely won't make it. Hold on, I have an idea."

He shuddered in her grasp and a soft pink light spread out along the griffin's wing. The fire went out with a puff of smoke and the griffin gave a grateful squawk.

"You can't do that." Wydrin shook him, remembering the scar that had reappeared after he'd healed Jarath. "You know what that'll do."

"Shut. Up. Concentrating."

After a few more seconds the pink light vanished, and the griffin picked up speed once more. Now there were buildings below them, and here and there the startled faces of people looking up. Frith was leaning forward over the griffin's neck, breathing heavily.

"Are you all right?"

"I'm fine," he gasped, although his voice was faint. "We're here."

Wydrin just had time to make out a great stone circle like the arenas in the Marrow Markets and then they were crashing into it. She was flung from the griffin's back and landed in a heap on the stones, the wind forced from her lungs.

She opened her eyes to see Frith face down on the ground. Y'Ruen hovered above them, enormous wings beating the air into a hurricane. The dragon finally had them trapped. There was nowhere else to go, nothing left to do.

But the final spell.

"Frith!"

Gathering what strength she had left Wydrin scrambled to her feet and sprinted to the prone shape, horribly aware of the fiery death waiting above. Turning him over she saw that Frith's scar was even more vivid now, and part of his ear was gone. His eyes were shut.

"Wake up! Princeling, we need the final word!"

He murmured something, so she shook him again.

"The word, Frith. Don't leave me now!"

The dragon still wasn't attacking. If anything, the huge scaly head was turned away from them now, back towards the battlefield. Whatever Sebastian was doing, it was getting her attention.

"You have to, we're so close." She slapped him across the cheek, but it didn't rouse him as it had before. She glanced up and saw Y'Ruen's brilliant yellow eyes settle on them once more. The dragon opened its mouth, and Wydrin could see the beginnings of their doom glowing in the back of its throat. "Oh shit."

She pulled him up and hugged him to her, burying her face in his neck. At least it would be quick...

"Open."

She felt him speak the word more than heard it; a tremor that moved through his chest into hers, the quickening of the Edenier. The ground beneath buckled and shook. His arms tightened around her and everything was light, light...

Sebastian saw it. The sky over the distant ocean tore itself open, and there was a howling darkness beyond. The dragon, now so tiny in comparison to that terrible hole, screamed and twisted in the air, belching fire and smoke in all directions, but the tear in the sky seemed to exert a relentless pull on the creature, and she was dragged, roaring, into the blackness behind the universe. He saw her beautiful blue scales, so bright and shining, turn black and dull as she entered that place with no light and no hope. For the briefest second he almost felt sorry for her, and then the tear vanished, healing over in an instant as though it were never there in the first place.

Y'Ruen was gone.

And now her daughters turned to him, weapons limp in their hands.

84

"So where have they gone?"

Sebastian stretched his legs out under the table, wincing as every muscle there twinged painfully. The sounds of Baneswatch putting itself back together drifted in from outside.

"They've gone into the mountains." He paused to sip at his ale. "I've told them where they need to go, and I will meet them there later. I didn't think it was wise to keep them near the city."

After all, not all of the brood army had wanted to listen to him. Once Y'Ruen was gone, sucked into the abyss created by O'rin's spell, there had been a brief fight between those daughters of the dragon who recognised Sebastian as their father, and those who did not. It had been bloody. There were around two hundred of them left now; two hundred people who had not existed a year ago, two hundred people with no experience save for murder and war. It would take some sorting out.

Frith nodded. "I am not at all certain *we* are welcome here, let alone the dragon's daughters. I doubt the people of this city understand what we did at all."

"Welcome to the life of a sell-sword, princeling." Wydrin tipped her tankard to him. "You do all the bloody work and not a word of genuine thanks from anyone."

"I am not a sell-sword," said Frith, smudging a bit of dirt from his wine glass with his thumb. "I am a lord." In Sebastian's opinion the Lord of the Blackwood looked exhausted. There were dark circles under his eyes and his limp was back in a big way, but Sebastian also thought he looked as happy as he'd ever seen him. Some of the anger had faded from his face, making him look younger, and now there was a shrewd thoughtfulness there instead. Sebastian noticed that his gaze went to Wydrin often, and when it did the faintest hint of a smile blossomed at the corner of his mouth.

"You're a lord?" Wydrin widened her eyes in mock wonder. "Well, I wish you'd mentioned it before."

They all laughed at that.

"So what now?" she said eventually. "Are you really going to train Y'Ruen's daughters, Sebastian?"

Sebastian shrugged and reached into his pocket for the glass globe Crowleo had given him. He set it down on the tavern table and spun it lazily between his fingers.

"The Order is all but decimated, and there are training grounds up in the god-peaks that will rot away to nothing if no one uses them. The daughters of the brood need guidance, help, and time to come to terms with everything." There was a sadness in his chest, and he smiled on through it. "Maybe I do too."

Wydrin frowned at that, but didn't question him.

"What about you, Lord Frith?"

"I will go back to the Blackwood, I expect," he said, looking down into his wine. "There is still much to repair, to rebuild."

"The Blackwood, princeling?" Wydrin rolled her eyes at the both of them. "Why, by all the ugly fire-breathing gods, would you want to go back there?"

"Come back with me and perhaps I'll make you a princess."

Wydrin laughed until mead came out of her nose and the innkeeper started to give them strange looks.

"Oh, honestly," she spluttered, swallowing down the last of her giggles and trying to soak up some of what she'd spilt with the back of her arm. "Is this really it? The end of our agreement?"

Frith cleared his throat.

"I'm pretty sure I've paid you both. More than once, in fact."

"No, I mean... is this really the end of it?" Wydrin leaned on the table, looking up at them through the unruly mop of her hair. Her green eyes glittered with mischief. "We have the world's only mage, the world's only brood army, and the world's only Copper Cat. Think of all the trouble we can cause now."

Sebastian laughed, noting the contemplative look on Frith's face. There was a lord who wasn't going home any time soon.

"Oh no, I think this was just the start of the trouble we can cause," he said, spinning the glass between his fingers so that shards of blue light scattered across the tabletop. "Another round?"

Acknowledgements

Getting this book out into the world has been a long and strange journey, with many unexpected diversions and the occasional wrong turn. A number of people kindly leant their time to stop me wandering off cliff edges or into haunted forests, and I'd like to do my best to say thank you to some of them here.

Thank you, first of all, to the readers who took a chance on *The Copper Promise* in its original form – a sword and sorcery novella with a bitch of a cliff-hanger. Because you read it, and because you said lovely things, I had the confidence to write the rest of that story. Keep taking those chances, because you rock.

Enormous thanks to the beta readers who took on *The Copper Promise* in its Ultimate-Mega-Form, and gave general story advice at all stages of writing: Roy Butlin, Andrew Reid, Kate Sherrod, and Stuart Turner. I greatly valued your fresh eyeballs and endless enthusiasm.

Gigantic thanks to the Non-Aligned League of Super Awesome Writers, who have been on hand at all times to offer advice, sarcastic emails and the occasional alcoholic beverage. Particular gratitude to Adam Christopher, who was there at the beginning of this craziness and has been ridiculously supportive, from giving me a kick up the arse when I needed it to making sure I actually turn up to these convention things – I still owe you a ginger beer, mister.

Thanks also to Den Patrick, who once bought me a hot chocolate as big as my head, and the unflappable Liz de Jager, who taught me to strut and had burritos with me when I was feeling rubbish.

I have been enormously fortunate with this publishing lark, I really have, and a large part of that is down to my agent, the tremendous

Juliet Mushens. Not only did she make a dream of mine come true, she made the book better, gave me a huge shot of confidence when I needed it most, and did it all with endless style and humour. Bravo, lady!

If you need more evidence that I was born under a lucky publishing-star, John Wordsworth is my editor. Enormous thanks to John for turning a potentially scary thing into a fantastically fun experience, and for being infinitely wiser than me. Thanks also to Christina Demosthenous and the rest of the team at Headline, who have been marvellous.

Huge thanks to Angry Robot (as well as a promise to be on their side when the mechanical uprising comes). Marc Gascoigne, Penny Reeve and Mike Underwood have been a delight to work with, and their dedication to spreading the legend of the Copper Cat has earned them many pints down the tavern of their choice.

My covers really are very special indeed – thanks to Patrick Insole and the team at Headline, and to Gene Mollica. Sword and sorcery has never looked so awesome.

I have much to thank my mum for, who always encouraged my book obsession and (most of the time) let me read up the dinner table, and my dear friend Jenni, who has been a voice of reason since we were knee high to grasshoppers.

Finally, the biggest, sauciest thanks of all must go to my partner, Marty Perrett. Thank you for making me laugh when I needed it, for putting up with my nonsense and my kick-the-oven tantrums, and for believing, with no room for doubt, that I could do it.